To Friend,

May you enjoy reading this as much as I enjoyed writing it.

Sincerely,
Jim Hickman
Aug. 2017

Numbers 6: 24-26

ALSO BY JIM L. HICKMAN

"You Smell Like A Grandpa" and other Campfire Stories

MULE SHOES
TO
SANTA FE

A novel based on circumstances
of travel, trade, and international
intrigue in the mountains, on the
rivers and on the Santa Fe Trail.
1840

JIM L. HICKMAN

LifeRich Publishing is a registered trademark of The Reader's Digest Association, Inc.

LifeRich Publishing books may be ordered through booksellers or by contacting:

LifeRich Publishing
1663 Liberty Drive
Bloomington, IN 47403
www.liferichpublishing.com
1 (888) 238-8637

Because of the dynamic nature of the Internet, any web addresses or links contained in this book may have changed since publication and may no longer be valid. The views expressed in this work are solely those of the author and do not necessarily reflect the views of the publisher, and the publisher hereby disclaims any responsibility for them.

Scripture quotations marked HCSB are from the Holman Christian Standard Bible®. HCSB®. Copyright ©1999, 2000, 2002, 2003 by Holman Bible Publishers. Used by permission. Holman Christian Standard Bible®, Holman CSB®, and HCSB® are federally registered trademarks of Holman Bible Publishers

Any people depicted in stock imagery provided by Thinkstock are models, and such images are being used for illustrative purposes only. Certain stock imagery © Thinkstock.

ISBN: 978-1-4897-1270-7 (sc)
ISBN: 978-1-4897-1269-1 (hc)
ISBN: 978-1-4897-1268-4 (e)

Library of Congress Control Number: 2017910729

Print information available on the last page.

LifeRich Publishing rev. date: 07/27/2017

DEDICATION AND ACKNOWLEDGEMENTS

Dedicated To My Family and Friends

In Memory Of My Mother, Ellen Irene, and Grandparents, William and Mary Bunch, who introduced me to the Love of God, and to the Wonders of God's Creation.

My heartfelt thanks to:

Jimmie (Gemma) Hickman, my wife, encourager and excellent critic;

Anne Nall Stallworth, Author, and writing instructor;

Marie McKay, my cousin, Author, encourager and critic;

and others who assisted in many ways, including;

Ross and Paige Hickman;

Gale Crain;

Robert Hicks.

TENNESSEE TO SANTA FE 1840

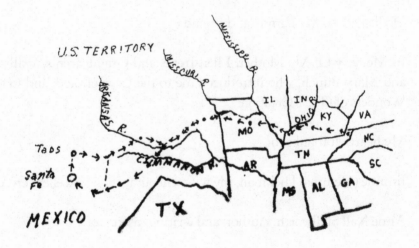

PREFACE

The modern domestic horse and mule were introduced into what is now the United States sometime in the early 1500's. It occurred on the Florida peninsula, and was followed in the late 1500's and early 1600's, by horses and mules introduced in the southwest by Spanish conquest and colonization from Mexico. Horses then appeared in the colonies on the east coast and among the Plains Indian tribes, and by 1750 all the Plains Indians had horses.

The horse and mule became major factors in the development of the new Republic. Consider the mountain men who rode horses and mules as they first moved across the plains and deserts, and into the immense mountains of the west. They were followed by trading caravans, and then the vast migration west, south and north of pioneers, with horses, mules, oxen, and some donkeys and burros. A report from Fort Laramie in 1850 stated more than 60,000 working animals had passed that year, by the end of July.

The mounted troops of the US Army required hundreds of saddle horses and working mules. The Civil War took tens of thousands of horses and mules, many of which were destroyed in battle. When the railroads started building across the young nation, they were constructed by use of the horse, mule and ox.

There are books about all these activities, and the constant demand for the animals. Seldom do the books, either fact or fiction, address who supplied the animals, or where they came from. They generally just appear in a story when needed. This historical novel explains and describes how it happened for some and the vision of the future in 1840. First, traveling across the known United States, with the hazards of the times, including travel on and around the large rivers. Then, leaving its boundaries to enter unsettled, untamed land of the frontier on the Santa Fe Trail, and into another country, while dealing with constant threats from agents of the other country.

CHAPTER 1

Nobody can say the Greenup's are slow to take action. Sometimes we exercise caution more than others might, but it has given us exciting lives and lots of stories through several generations. Right now I'm moving fast.

The trail I'm on is a footpath winding about three miles from our cove up over a high ridge where it joins a well-used wagon road, which connects several villages in the main valley of the Clinch River. The wagon road from our little cove joins the same main road but where I'm headed it's a couple of miles farther. I prefer traveling the trail anyway. The wet leaves and bark have a strong earthy smell and a few minutes ago an owl hooted.

I've been climbing steadily for an hour and the storm is not letting up. It's about a stone's throw to the main road and I slow up and start moving cautiously. Now it's just light enough in the woods that the wagon road can be seen through the trees and rain, so I stop to look and listen. Once again Pa's training reminded me to be extra careful if I was excited or nervous. It's too easy to miss signs of trouble.

There is a small opening and wide place where the trail comes out and often teams of mules or horses and occasional oxen will be pulled off the road to rest or let others go by. At first there is nothing but the rain and wind in the trees, than I hear the sounds of a horse and buggy splashing along the road. A single horse pulling a buggy appears and I instantly recognize the horse as belonging to Uncle Richard, my Pa's brother.

It's driven by the very person I'm on my way to see, my cousin, Tim. Beside him in the buggy is his step-sister, Rachel, a skinny, freckle faced girl with long rusty colored hair and green eyes. I start to call them as they come along the track, when suddenly out of the trees just opposite where I'm standing step two tough looking men I've never seen before. They are bearded, dark looking, with big slouch hats and dirty, heavy coats. One is carrying a long barreled rifle.

"Howdy Bub, pull up your horse." One of them yells at Tim.

Tim immediately snaps the reins and yells at the horse but one of the men jumps and grabs the horses bridle, pulling horse and buggy to a stop. Rachel has grabbed a long barreled pistol from a holster in front of her on the buggy dash, but before she can level it the second man has grabbed her arm and is trying to jerk her from the buggy. Tim has dropped the reins and is trying to get his rifle in action when the man holding the horse's bridle draws a pistol and levels it at Tim.

"Drop it sonny, or I'll blow you right in two" he growls. "Get out of the buggy and leave your gun in it."

Rachel screams as she is jerked from the buggy and thrown into the brush at the edge of the road. Her long skirt gets tangled in the brush and reveals she is wearing moccasins and leggings like Tim and me. This has all taken place mighty fast, but it's long enough for me to have the long barreled rifle up and sighted right at the chest of the man holding the pistol on Tim. One thing Pa and Grandpa always told us:

'There are some men who you can be reasonable and discuss things with and work out a problem. Others you have to instantly be more violent than they are. I hope you are always able to make the right choice."

I yell at the man holding the pistol leveled at Tim:

"Drop that gun, right now!"

Quick as a flash he turns and fires right at me. The tree limbs save my life. The big slug tears into a limb right in front of me and screams up and over my head. It is sure clear this man had been in tight places before. He jumped the instant his pistol fired but he was too late. My long rifle booms and the bullet hit him right in the chest, knocking him over backward into the mud. The other robber was raising his rifle to shoot at me but he is too slow and Tim's bullet hit his rifle, knocking it away. The horse reared and lunged and jerked the buggy around but I run past it, drawing my Bowie knife as I run. The robber is bent over picking up his rifle when I smash down on his back as hard as I can and grab his hair. He is big and heavy but turned like a cat under me. I jerk his head back and slip the wicked edge of that big Bowie right against his windpipe.

"Tim, look after Rachel!" I yell.

About then that redhead came clawing out of the brush at the edge of the road. You don't need to look after me!" she screeched. "Give me that knife, Ross, and I'll cut that brute's throat myself."

I probably should give it to her to see if she would actually do it.

"Rachel, get your pistol and make sure it's working, and then hold it on this cuss while we get gathered up".

She got the pistol and stood about six feet from the robber while he cursed and snarled.

"Mister, she'll shoot your guts out if you make a wrong move." I tell him.

I get a lead rope from the buggy box, tie his hands behind him and then tie a rope around his neck and to the rear axle of the buggy.

Meantime, Tim has taken a look at the other man lying on his back in the mud. Tim's eyes are big and his face white when he turns toward me.

"Hey Ross, I think he's dead" he says in a low voice. I consider this a moment, then walk over behind the man tied up. I grab his long black hair, stick my leg behind him and throw him heavily to the ground. It put a strain on his neck and he groaned and cursed.

"Now Rachel, you just keep that pistol on him, and if he tries to get up or even roll over shoot him through the body." Rachel just nods.

When I look down at the dead man's face I know instantly what Pa was talking about, when he said killing a man left you with a terrible feeling which you never quite forget. This had been a living human being just like me a few minutes ago. He may have a family some where waiting for him, and now it is all over. He made a choice, and so did I. Except our choices left him dead and me alive. I get weak in the knees and turn away toward the trees. I close my eyes and wait for my head to clear. Tim stands right beside me but does not say a word. I know he is feeling the same upheaval inside. Standing there in the muddy road with the rain dripping off my hat brim, I can smell the wet leaves and hear the patter of rain on the bare tree branches. I take a deep breath and thank God for my own life.

My head begins to clear and after a minute I go back to the body and with Tim watching and helping go through his coat pockets and pants pockets. There is a wicked knife in an arm band which I toss in the buggy. Turning him over we find a large puddle of blood in the mud of the road. That big old slug sure done a lot of damage going through him. Knowing where my own weapons are makes it easy to search him. There is a long slim bladed knife hanging down his back from a cord around his neck. This feller was sure loaded for bear. Pulling the blade out of its scabbard I cut the cord, put the knife back in the scabbard and toss it in the buggy.

"Tim, get that rifle and unload it."

Tim is now recovered and gathers up the rifle, unloads it by firing it and puts it and the shot pouch into the buggy. I feel the man's back to see if he has another weapon when I feel some kind of belt under his shirt. Rolling him over again I open his shirt and find a thick canvas belt with a pocket sewn into it.

"Tim!" I said, then shut up and motion to him.

I open the pocket and find a lot of gold coins, and some kind of foreign paper money. I've never seen any money like this before. I quickly close the pocket, pull the belt off and throw it into the buggy.

"Ross, will you hurry. I'm soaked to the skin and cold." yells Rachel. "Tim, grab hold!"

I grab one of the dead man's arms and Tim the other and we pull him off the muddy track and into the brush. Then we go back to Rachel. Tim takes the pistol from her.

"Rachel, get in the buggy and cover up." I said. "Load Tim's rifle and keep it ready to shoot."

I slowly and carefully approach the bound man on the ground, staying away from his feet. Searching him I find another pistol and knife which go into the front of the buggy. There is no money belt. He has a leather wallet with a few coins inside, none of them gold. I put it back in his pocket and then walk over to stand by Tim.

"I was on my way over to your place and I'll tell you why later, but where were you and Rachel going?" I ask.

"Lena's sister, Carrie, is down with a fever over in Chalk Level and Rachel is going over to help with the kids till she's up agin and feelin better," Tim said. "Then I'm going to pick up some salt, powder and lead. Might even have some sarsaparilla."

He grinned, then sobered and looked at the other robber lying at the edge of the road in the brush.

"Sure glad you came along. What are we going to do with this skunk?" and he indicated the bound man. I think a minute.

"Isn't there a new Marshall there in McCloud?" I say. "Let's take him there, but first lets take a look around. You keep this guy on the ground and I'll be right back."

I grab my rifle and start into the woods, but about then Rachel climbs out of the buggy.

"I'm going too," she announces as she takes the big pistol out of the buggy. About fifty yards back in the trees we find their camp under the huge trunk of a fallen tree. An old tarp is tied to some limbs for shelter and a couple of dirty rolled up bedrolls are on the ground. There is also a poor, skinny mule tied to a tree with an old saddle of some kind on its back. It looked like they were getting ready to leave when they heard the horse and buggy and decided to do their dirty work. There are a few beat up old pots and pans and a blackened coffee pot is sitting next to a cold fire. It is a miserable looking camp and looks like they have been there for a couple of days. I look at their stuff and then untie the mule and lead it out to the trace.

"OK Mister, you can ride the mule or walk behind the buggy." I tell him.

He looked at the muddy trace and then the mule and growled.

"I'll ride the mule."

Tim untied the lead rope from the axle, with the other end still around the man's neck. He holds the loose end and Rachel stands with her pistol in hand while I help him on the mule with his hands still tied. Then I tie his feet together under the mule's belly. I take the lead rope off his neck, put it on the mule and tie it to the back of the buggy. The rain has slacked off but we are all sure wet and muddy when we crawl into the buggy and crowd together in the seat. I keep an eye open to the back as Tim starts the horse.

"We need to talk about this some." I say quietly.

Rachel does not know about the money and I do not say anything about it, but pick up the canvas belt and silently show it to her. She lets out a little gasp as she sees the gold pieces.

"We can keep it and not say anything about it." I say quietly.

At the same time I know we cannot do any such thing. We have been raised to hate liars and thieves, and keeping the money would be doing both. Tim mentioned we do not know the Marshall. So can we trust him?

"I've an idea." Say's Rachel. "Let's go to the blacksmith shop and tell Uncle Jeremy about the whole thing. Then maybe he will go with us to the sheriff and be a witness so everything is done right. He will know exactly what to do."

Much as I hate to admit it, she has a good idea. Not only that but probably Tim and I will have to come back with the Marshall to where we left the body in the brush. I still haven't said anything to Tim about why I've come to see him. That can wait till we start back to his place.

We drive into the village of McCloud and immediately get the attention of the few folks who are up and about. When they see the man tied on the mule and being led behind the buggy they sure get interested. The streets are muddy but there is a boardwalk in front of the stores. Chimney smoke is rising slowly in the light rain and mist, and a smoky haze is hanging over town. There is noise and smoke coming from one barn-like building on the right. There is a wagon and a buggy in front of the building and the big door is open. There are two mules tied to a hitch rail and a horse is standing in the door. There is the sound of steel on steel as Tim reins in the horse to a stop beside the wagon.

"Uncle Jeremy!" called Rachel, as we climb out of the buggy.

A man with big shoulders and bulging muscles appears by the horse standing in the open door. He limps toward us and it is obvious he has one wooden leg.

When the war with Mexico started Jeremy Bliss had gone away as a cavalryman with his good friend, Colonel Jackson. He would probably not have gone to Texas except Colonel Jackson paid him a special visit one day and convinced Jeremy to join him. So Jeremy rode off on a fine big black Morgan stallion that was his pride and joy. Six months later a thin, limping black stallion pulling a battered buckboard came slowly into McCloud. The horse was driven by an equally thin and worn woman. Lying on a corn shuck bed in the buckboard was a feverish and suffering Jeremy Bliss. Eliza Greenup Jenkins, driving the buckboard, is my Pa's sister. Bert Jenkins, her late husband, had been killed by Indians several years before in Kentucky territory. Eliza was trying to feed herself and a fifteen year old boy when the trouble started in Texas. The boy had gone with the Union troops when the wounded Jeremy was left to die at the farmhouse. Eliza had cared for him, and finding out he was from McCloud had loaded him in the buckboard and driven him home to be with kin when he died. Her good care had saved his life and eventually they had married and now are pillars in the community. Jeremy is known as one of the best blacksmiths in the hills.

Jeremy smiled his big smile when he saw Rachel.

"Where you youngins goin?" he said as he limped toward us.

Then his eyes grew questioning when he saw the man on the mule.

"Uncle Jeremy, this is what happened."

Briefly I explain, including the finding of the money.

"We thought we'd best report this all to the Marshall", I say, "but I'm worried about the money.

Jeremy thought a minute.

"You leave it with me. We have a new Marshall and I'm just not sure yet what he's like. After we see him we can decide what to do about the money. He is probably having a mug of coffee at Megan's Inn."

The Inn is just two doors down, past the livery stable. I look at Tim, who has not had a chance to say anything.

"Tim, will you watch this feller while Rachel and me go with Uncle Jeremy to see the Marshall!"

Rachel reaches in the front of the buggy and gets the money belt, keeping it out of sight of the man on the mule. She walks into the shop with Jeremy, then they both come out and we walk down the boardwalk in the misting rain.

When I open the door to the Inn, I look around real careful as Pa has taught me. The room is dim, with one lamp and the fire in the big fireplace furnishing most of the light. The Marshall is the only person in the room. He has a platter in front of him and is just finishing breakfast with a big mug of hot coffee. He watches us with little expression as we walk toward him.

"Marshall Dunn," says Jeremy. "This is my niece and nephew, Rachel and Ross Greenup, and they have a story you need to hear."

The Marshall didn't stand, but I stick out my hand.

"Good Morning, Marshall."

His grip is hard and strong and I think he is a bit surprised at the strength of my hand. His eyes are wary as he looks at me.

"Well, get on with it." he growls.

Suddenly I have a feeling of caution about this man.

"Marshall, we've got a man tied up outside, and he and another feller tried to rob my cousins out on the trace this morning just after daylight. They were about a mile from here and I happened along just in time. But I had to shoot one of them. He's lying out by the side of the road and we can show you where it happened."

The Marshall's eyes sharpen with interest as I tell him this.

"So you left a dead man lying out on the trace, huh. Did he have any papers to tell who he was?"

"No Sir, at least we didn't find any."

This is the truth, since there were no papers in the money belt to identify him and we had not asked the other man any questions. The Marshall took one last swig of coffee and stood up. He is not as tall as I am, but is sure stocky built. Saying no more he leads the way out of the Inn and back to the buggy. He walks around the buggy and stops at the sight of the bound prisoner on the mule. After a moment of silence Marshall Dunn says,

"Howdy, Jenk!"

CHAPTER 2

It hadn't entered my mind that the scoundrel who had just recently threatened our lives, and Marshall Dunn, might be acquainted.

"Howdy Dunn." said the man Jenk. There was no great pleasure in his face as he spoke.

"Marshal, is this man a friend of yours?" spoke up Uncle Jeremy.

"Well, Jeremy. Let's say we have met before." said Dunn.

Dunn looked at me.

"Ross, you untie him and get him off the mule."

I looked at Tim, still holding the rifle carefully pointed at Jenk. About then Rachel said:

"Ross, be careful. I've seen copperheads I'd trust more than that man."

"Marshall, I'll untie his feet and help him off the mule, but I'll let you or someone else untie his hands. Tim, keep that rifle ready. Remember, just a little while ago he tried to rob and kill you."

My temper was showing. Dunn grinned as I walked over to the mule, untied Jenk's feet, then reached up and grabbed his arm, pulling him sideways off the mule. He staggered as he hit the ground and I steadied him till he was standing, then stepped back as he snarled a curse at me. Marshall Dunn motioned at him to come over. Dunn took a folding knife out of his pocket.

"Marshall, that's a good rope. Don't cut it. I'll untie it." Uncle Jeremy said as he stepped toward Jenk.

Dunn stopped him. "On second thought, leave him tied." Then Dunn turned to me.

"Ross, I'm going to put this feller in jail while we go out to the trace and look for the other one you claim to have shot."

Then he looked at Jenk.

"You care to tell me who you were traveling with?"

Jenks only reply was a curse directed at the Marshall.

"Well now, I kinda figured that would be your answer." Dunn growled.

"Marshall, I'm going with you." said Uncle Jeremy as he limped back to the blacksmith shop to gather up a rain slicker.

Marshall Dunn motioned at Jenk, and led the way down the boardwalk. I noticed he did not untie Jenk before they stepped into the small jail and office. The rain started to come down hard again, and when Dunn came out of the office he had on a blue Army saddle slicker. Uncle Jeremy untied the horse harnessed to the buggy in front of the blacksmith shop. The Marshall gets in with him, and after tying the mule to the hitch-rail, Tim, Rachel and I crowd into Tim's buggy again and lead the way out of town. No one else has been along the trace since we came in and our tracks are still visible. It is a much faster trip without the mule tied in back and in a few minutes we are back at the turnout where everything had happened so suddenly. Rachel offered to stay in the buggy and hold the horse. It is apparent she has had about all she can stand for one day. Tim and I step down into the mud, followed by Uncle Jeremy and Dunn.

The body is lying where we left it. Seeing it brings home to me again that I have killed another human being, and it is setting hard on me. Marshall Dunn turns the body face up so he can get a good look at the face. He opens the man's coat and shirt and looks at the hole the big rifle slug made. Then he turns him over and looks at where it has come out his back. I notice Uncle Jeremy does not say anything while the exam is taking place, and neither do Tim nor I. Dunn reaches inside the man's coat and finds a thin leather wallet we had overlooked. He looks at us.

"Did you search the body?" he asks.

"Well, yes, but sure looks like I missed something." I say. "We found his weapons, and they are all in the buggy box."

"Did you find their camp?" asked Uncle Jeremy.

"Yes, sure did, and we'll show it to you. It's out in the woods."

Hunching our shoulders against the rain, we all walk out to the pitiful little camp in the deep shadow of the trees. Again Dunn looks everything over, even unrolling their bedrolls and looking in the ragged haversacks. He has by this time taken a small paper out of his pocket and begins to write some notes on it, protecting it from the rain and from our sight while he wrote. He finds a paper in one of the haversacks which appears to be of interest, and folding it up he puts it in his pocket with the pad.

Marshall Dunn stands in deep thought for a couple of minutes. Then he tells us to give him a hand and we stack all the belongings in a pile under the scant protection of the big tree roots. Back at the trace he looks at the dead man again.

"Alright boys, let's get him picked up and put in the back of Jeremy's buggy. Hope that's ok with you, Jeremy."

Nobody says anything as we grab hold of arms and legs and lift the body into the back of the buggy. Then the procession retraces its steps back to the village. There the Marshall gets some extra help to carry the body into the back room at the jail and office. He will take care of disposing of everything as he sees fit. Then we all crowd into his tiny office and wait while he writes out a witness statement as to what had happened out on the trace. Tim, Rachel and I sign it, while Uncle Jeremy watches. Then Dunn said:

"This feller you killed is a wanted man if I'm not mistaken. This afternoon I'll ride over to Morrisville and send a wire to make sure. Jenk, in the cell there, is a former member of a gang of raiders that used to terrify all the small villages in Tennessee and along the Natchez Trace. I'll also find out more about him. Now the circuit judge will be here next week, about Tuesday or Wednesday. Ross, you plan on spending a little time with him till this is all cleared up."

We all walk back in the rain over to Uncle Jeremys shop.

"Well, you young folks have had quite a day so far. What are you going to do now?" Jeremy asked as we walked into the warm shop.

"I was headed over to Tim's place when this all happened" I said. "He was taking Rachel over to stay with Lena and help out there while she's sick. So maybe I'll just ride along with them and come back to Tim's house with him. I sure appreciate your help and would like to leave the gold with you for now. Would you look at it and see what you think?"

"Sure will. Now you get going and I'll get back to work."

Tim, Rachel and I climb back into the buggy again. It is just about two miles on to Lena's place. Rachel chattered all the way, but she made one comment which stayed in my mind and I remembered and pondered over because I had the same feeling.

"Ross, that Marshall Dunn is something more than just the Marshall of a little old village. I can't put a finger on it, but I'll bet we hear more from him."

We drop off Rachel with her flour sack of personal stuff at Lena's. Tim and I don't go in the house because of the sickness there. As she gets out of the buggy, Rachel puts her hand on my arm and looks me right in the eyes.

"You did a brave thing, Ross!" Then she ran into the house.

CHAPTER 3

We head back to Tim's place, and on the way I tell him the reason for this trip all started about a month ago. I was hauling rocks on the stone boat with the team of mules. The stone fence along the back of the corn field was down and I was rebuilding it. It was close to dinner time and the mules and me both needed a rest. Just as I was unhitching them I saw a lone man at the other side of the field. I stepped up between the mules and reached for the rifle slung on their harness. The man had come out of the woods on an old trail instead of the trace and I was taking no chances. He watched me a minute and started toward me. He was carrying a long-barreled rifle and was dressed in buckskin. He raised a long arm as he got closer and I recognized Uncle Will Bunch, Ma's brother, who had been gone for about three years.

"Hey, Uncle Will!" I shouted.

"Ross, boy, I hardly knowed you. You've done gone and growed up." He grinned and grabbed my hand in a crushing grip. By this time Ma had come out of the house and was standing on the porch waving.

"Let me unhitch and I'll see you at the house, Uncle Will."

By the time I hung up the harness and turned the mules out he was in the house drinking coffee and eating dried apple pie. About then Pa came in. He had just been back from the war in Texas since last fall. Now he and Uncle Richard are getting ready to go after his horses and other mules.

After a company supper of fried chicken and biscuits, we listened to Uncle Will for hours while he told stories. He told about the wide open

13

prairie with the tall grass and the sky that made a person feel like a tiny speck on the land. He told of being able to see the shadows of clouds moving on the prairie for miles. He told of the shining mountains and the scorching deserts. Above all he told of the things a man could do if he was of a mind to. Uncle Will stayed with us two more days, then one morning after breakfast he waved from the edge of the field and was gone.

For a few days after he left I would find myself day-dreaming until Pa would say something to me. Then Pa and I had a talk. Well, mostly Pa talked and I listened.

"Ross, you're seventeen, soon to be eighteen, and growed up to be a strong young feller with a lot of common sense but not much experience. Since your brother left last year to work on the big river, while I was still off at the war, you've taken care of the place. Now I know what you're feeling, about staying here, and I've talked to your Ma about it. Your cousin Tim is probably about like you. So I'm thinking you ought to go over to Richards, visit with Tim, and you young fellers work out a plan to go west." Pa stopped.

I was silent for a minute while this soaked in. Then I let out a wild yell. I saw Ma look out the door and knew she knew what Pa had just told me.

"Pa, that's great. When can I start?'

"As soon as I get back from Virginia. Richard and I are going after the Morgan's and will be gone a couple of weeks. Then we have to get you some horses and get you outfitted. I want you fellers to scout out the land your Uncle Will was talking about. We would like to find some land to raise horses and mules on, and also a good water supply. With all the people starting to think about going west, there's going to be a real need for horses and mules."

That was two days ago. Pa left yesterday. Tim gets just as excited as I am. We spend the afternoon talking about what to take, and soon it is time for me to head back to our little valley. I take a couple of shortcuts, and am back before dark. I don't say anything to Ma about what had happened that morning till all the chores are done and we are sitting by the fire. I noticed her looking at me when I pet the dogs more than usual, and a couple of times start to say something, and then don't. I hem and haw for a while, and she puts down her mending and looks at me.

"Alright Ross, what's the problem."

I start telling her, and when I come to the part about shooting the man, she gasps and puts her clasped hands over her heart.

"Ross, I've always hoped you would be spared anything like that, but I'm proud of you son, for being the man I know you are. We live in a dangerous world, and all I can do is trust in the Lord to see us through."

A week after the fracas on the trace I go to the village to meet with the Circuit Judge. Ma goes into town with me. Tim and Rachel are there and we go over the entire story with the Judge and Marshall Dunn. Nothing has changed and Jenk has nothing more to say. Uncle Jeremy is also at the meeting with the judge. No mention is made of the gold by anyone. There is a small reward offered for apprehension of the man who was killed and the Marshall says he will get it to us as soon as he can. The Judge sentences Jenk to a year in jail and Dunn will take him to the prison at Morrisville.

Pa and Richard get back about a week later, driving twenty head of nice Morgan horses, and half a dozen big mules, They also have a couple of nice cross bred horses they bought. Best of all, they brought Tim and me each, one of the new Colt Paterson revolvers, Model 1839, .36 caliber. From then on, until we left the cove this morning, time flew by.

There is an opening in the trees ahead of me, and through the drifting rain I can see a ridge in the distance. It is lower than we are and between us and it the forest appears to slope down. I rein my horse in and to one side so Tim can come up beside me. We stop and sit looking down and away to a big valley with a river showing in the bottom.

"Tim, that's the Clinch River where Grandpa and Grandma Greenup live. That's as far west as I've ever been."

Tim grins from ear to ear. We have been riding on the trace for about three hours, climbing some steep ridges and then dipping down into some small valleys. Each of us is riding a Morgan saddle horse and leading two mules with pack saddles. It's early April and the animals are soft after a long winter. We swing out of the saddles and loosen the saddle girths to let the horses breath, then walk around to get the stiffness out of our own legs and thighs. We are as soft as the horses, since we haven't done much riding this winter. There has been lots of snow and most of our work has been to cut and carry wood and keep the fire going, at least till it was time for the spring plowing. I look back to the east and north and see the blue haze of the Smokey's behind us, and south of us the rolling foothills.

Ma packed us a lot of food before we left this morning and I had been too excited to eat much breakfast, but suddenly I'm hungry. There is no water here, so I dig into the food pack and get out a couple of pieces of jerky. I toss one to Tim.

"This will hold us till we get where there is a creek or spring. It's a couple of hours to Grandpa's place there on the river."

Pa's father and mother had settled here several years ago so Grandpa Greenup could operate a ferry boat across the Clinch River. Pa's brother Robert and his wife Jane and two sons live with them now. Robert was wounded at the Battle of Horseshoe Bend during the Creek war several years ago and did what he could to help Grandpa as he continued to heal, but he is probably not ever going to be completely well. He had been with General Andrew Jackson's army and told lots of stories about the Walker boys and others he fought beside.

Once in a while some renegade Indians or trouble hunting white men would try to give Grandpa a bad time. They usually were new in this part of the hills or they would have known better. Grandpa was a peace loving man and had a lot of compassion for folks having a hard time. But when he saw trouble was brewing, he usually made the first move and made it so violently it took the starch right out of whoever was planning the mischief.

Two days ago Tim had ridden his horse to our place in the cove. Rachel was with him, and not her usual cheery self. Tim was leading two mules loaded down with his bedroll and an assortment of food and equipment. Pa, Tim and I spent the rest of the day going through everything and sorting and re-packing until we had trimmed the load to carry his gear and mine on one mule apiece. The other two mules are carrying oats, extra shoes, lead for bullets, and some trade goods, including about fifty pounds of plug tobacco. We raise it ourselves and consider it an extra good quality. All this was done under the wistful gaze and plenty of advice from Rachel. Several times I noticed her looking toward me with tears in her eyes, but she would look away quickly.

The mules are big red mules, broken to pack, lead, harness or ride.

They are branded with a G double-arrow G brand on the left hip, for the Greenup brothers. Pa and Uncle Rich always watch for good mules around the country. Sometimes they find a good mule at a sale, or when a mule colt is foaled that appears to be really promising they buy it as soon as it can be weaned. We train mules and horses alike with the gentle method of training. This means the animals are treated with great care, and attention to the personality of each animal. Consequently the Greenup's have a reputation as good, honest trainers and horsemen.

Our horses are fine Morgan geldings, picked out by Pa when they were new colts. We always have at least two Morgan stallions for breeding the Morgan mares, and these colts would have been fine stallions, but we do not need any more stallions at present, and Pa and Uncle Rich are trying to keep the offspring as pure as possible. There are four more geldings in our herd, used as saddle horses, two stallions, and the rest are brood mares.

Uncle Will had walked into the cove again and we listened to more stories around the fire that were just as exciting as the stories a month ago. Yesterday he used a couple of sheets of Ma's precious paper to draw maps of trails, rivers and mountains. Rachel watched just as intently as we had and asked a lot of questions. Ma spread her a pallet to sleep on by the fireplace. This morning Ma fixed us a sizable breakfast of cured ham, fried potatoes and biscuits and gravy. As I said, I was too excited to eat much, but we sat in the warm kitchen and I did manage to put away quite a bit of food. Rachel helped Ma, but I noticed she didn't eat anything. Then we packed the mules, saddled the horses and it was time for goodbye.

Pa didn't say much this morning but it was plain he wished he was going with us. Last night we had talked for a long time by the fire and Pa said a lot about what we were starting out to do. Ma fried some little fruit pies and fussed around, stopping once in a while to pat me on the back and wipe a stray tear from her eyes. Now she grabbed me in a big hug, held on for a long minute, then turned and walked up the steps to the porch. Excited as I was I felt a pang of loneliness as I watched her. Rachel walked over to me and started to say something, then touched my face gently with the tips of her fingers, closed her lips firmly and walked over to stand by Ma. She put an arm around Ma and Ma hugged her.

I figured as soon as we left, Ma and Rachel would walk up the hill behind the house to the little grave. I well remember the tiny girl who was a bright spot in all our lives. She lived for three years, and then scarlet fever came to the mountains, and when I was seven we buried her under the big tree. This is a fairly common happening in the hills, but Ma has never quite recovered, even though it's been ten years ago. Each year on the baby's birthday Ma puts fresh flowers on the grave, and is real quiet for several days.

Tim and I mount up, and Pa hands us the mule's lead ropes. His big hand slaps me on the knee. Then he turns abruptly and starts toward the corral.

"Hey, you dang dawgs, get back on the porch." He shouts at the hounds. Something in his voice surprised them and they quickly slink under the porch.

Tim and I clatter out of the yard and onto the wagon road. The small pastures on each side of the road have several nice Morgan brood mares and a Morgan stallion is in the corral. I take a last look back and then we are around the bend and in the trees.

CHAPTER 4

W|e left Grandpa's farm, up on the hill above the river, about an hour ago. Tim and I are each riding our Morgan geldings and Caleb is on a big gelding of unknown ancestry. We spent all the day before at Grandpa's, talking to Uncle Bob. Pa had already mentioned the trip to him, but he was still reluctant to let Caleb go, and Caleb's Ma pitched a fit. Then just before dark last night Uncle Rich, Tim's Pa, rode into Grandpa's place.

"Ross and Tim, and you too, Caleb, had better be extra careful. That feller you killed, Ross, has got some friends interested in finding you, and I figure they'll want to raise your scalp."

Now I sure appreciate Uncle Rich making that long ride to tell us, and we are going to be careful. Everything finally calmed down, and this morning we left Grandpa's on our three saddle horses, with each of us leading two big mules. In addition to the oats and tobacco, we have several pounds each of lead and gunpowder. Grandpa also insisted on us taking a big rough looking dog, named Buck. He is brindle colored, and not any particular breed that can be identified, except he is part Plott Hound. Old Man Plott raises a special breed of hound for hunting bear. They are tough and courageous, and having one of them as an ancestor sure don't hurt this ugly dog any. Unlike most hounds, his tail curls up over his back. One ear hangs down a bit, but he sure does not have any trouble hearing. He appears to be about fifty pounds of solid muscle and teeth and is not real affectionate. Last night I fed him a little corn pone soaked in bacon grease, and it appeared he might be friendly to me, though definitely not looking for a close friend.

As we ride up to the ferry landing there are three rough looking men standing by the dock, with their horses tied to the hitch rail. As I start to lead the mules up to tie them one of the men steps toward the mules.

'Buck" I say. "Watch!"

That big dog just moved easily over between the mules and the man and sat down, never taking his eyes off the man. The big red mule looked around at the dog with his ears back, than he turned back and looked at me and settled down. Caleb is off his horse now, but Tim is still in the saddle. The long barreled rifle is held easily in his big hands and pointed in the general direction of the two other men who are watching the situation.

Buck growled.

"Mister, unless you are hankering to lose a leg, you better not get any closer to that mule." I warn.

"I'll kill that dog!" he snarls.

"Well now, you just go right ahead, if you think your scrawny neck is worth the price of a dog, cause that's what it's gonna cost you."

He glared at me and turned back to the other men. One of them laughed out loud, showing a mouth full of black, broken teeth.

"That tough kid just called your hand, didn't he, Jake!"

The man called Jake snarled something in reply and walked over to stand with them. Tim is still sitting on his horse and obviously going to stay there. Caleb and I walk around the mules and check all the pack saddles and equipment. I pat the mules, rub their necks and talk to them and their long ears waggle back and forth. Tim sits easy on his horse, and the ugly dog Buck lies flat with his nose between his paws. He didn't go to sleep.

I look over at the ferry and see it is started back to our side of the river. The river is muddy and high, and it is going to be a slow trip. Since the ferry would be crowded with the other men and their animals, and us and all our horses and mules, we will just wait for another round trip before we board. That will give us time to talk to Uncle Bob, Caleb's Pa, who is running the ferry. I'm thinking this is our last contact with kinfolk for a while and would like to make the most of it. I'm sure Caleb feels the same.

"Ross, there's an outfit just coming into the main road!" Tim says quietly.

About half a mile back along the main trace we had noticed a road joining it from the north. Now I can see a team pulling a covered wagon turning on to the main trace from the side road. A man and a woman and young girl are on the front seat, and I can see at least one other person behind them in the wagon. The three men have now noticed the wagon and are talking about it in low voices.

"Hello the dock!"

There is a hail from the ferry boat. It is now approaching the dock and Caleb moves over to help with the lines. Uncle Bob is handling the sweep and knows just how to get the boat right against the dock. There is a buggy pulled by one horse on the ferry. As the flat bow of the ferry touches the dock a black deck hand tosses a line to Caleb, who takes a fast turn around a cleat on the dock. He then pulls a short wooden ramp from the deck of the ferry to the dock so there is a solid walk from the boat to the dock. The driver of the horse and buggy leads them across the ramp onto the dock. He is a thin, scholarly looking man, dressed in a worn suit. He speaks to me as the buggy crosses the ramp and it surprises me. I have been keeping an eye on the three men and their horses, who have moved up to get on the ferry.

"Howdy Ross. I was just talking to your Uncle Bob. Sounds as if you boys are off on quite a venture."

"Howdy, Rev. McClaren."

Rev. McClaren is the Baptist circuit rider and knows just about everyone in the hills. He is at all the weddings, funerals, auctions and anything else where there will be a bunch of folks together. I take hold of the bridle of his horse as he starts to climb into the buggy. I noticed the three men look sharply at me when the Rev. called my name. The man who had been backed off by Buck a little earlier stops and stares.

"You the Greenup that kilt a feller a few weeks ago over on Little Creek?"

I didn't bother to reply. Tim, who was still on horseback, turned his rifle generally in their direction and they moved toward the ferry.

"We're goin to keep an eye on you, Bub." said the man with the broken teeth, and then they all clatter over the ramp and onto the ferry.

21

While all this is happening the covered wagon with the man and woman on the front seat has driven up. The man hands the woman the reins and steps out onto the hub and onto the ground. He had heard the exchange between the circuit rider and me, and then noticed the comments from the three riders. He is about my height, probably at least ten years older, and looks about as stout as an oak tree.

"Howdy!" he says as he walks over toward me. "Guess I already know your name, Ross." He nods in the direction of the wagon. "My woman and me was talking to your Pa a couple of days ago. He said if we hurried we might catch you here. We'uns are headed over in Kaintuck by the Wilderness Road and would like to travel a way with you fellers."

I immediately start to protest as I think of slowing down to stay with the wagon.

"We planned on moving mighty fast." I say.

"I knowed that, but I've been over the Wilderness Road several times. There's a couple places past the Gap where those fellers ahead of you might give you some trouble. It's not just them. Everybody in the hills knows you killed that feller a few weeks ago and there's a rumor of some gold being involved. Besides that, I've got two little ones and my wife's younger sister in the wagon. I'd sure admire to have some company till we get over in the bluegrass."

I looked at Tim and Caleb.

"What do you fellers think of that kind of a deal?"

About then I notice they aren't looking at me. They are looking at the wagon. A girl moves out from under the canvas cover and onto the front seat. We all stare. She has long, curly black hair, a freckled face, and smiling red lips.

"Well now, I reckon we could take the time to let these mules settle down." drawled Caleb.

Rev McClaren laughed.

"Ross, it looks to me like the decision was made for you."

I grinned at Rev. McClaren's view of what Caleb said.

"You know, I think you are right, Reverend, and it appears the other member of this party feels the same way."

I am not going to admit I agree with them. I watch Tim and he is all of a sudden real interested in the river. Girls scare him some, and his red haired step-sister is a continual source of surprise and irritation. He sits in the saddle with his rifle across the saddle horn, and comments on how much drift wood was in the river. Drift wood is usually a sign the water is rising. The ferry pulled away from the dock with the three riders and their horses.

The strong young man turned toward me.

"Guess I didn't tell you our names. I'm Jeff Clark and that's my woman, Ruth. Her sister's name is Naomi. They were named after those two women in the Bible story. The boy is David and the girl is Elizabeth. We know the Reverend and he will probably vouch for us."

Rev. McClaren was looking us over and he spoke right up.

"Ross, you just made a good bargain to trail along with Jeff and Ruth. They are mighty fine people. As for you, Jeff, you've got some good companions for the trail. These boys are all cousins and they may seem a bit carefree at times, but they can be as tough as an old hickory limb. The Wilderness Road is rough on wagons and animals, as well as people, and sometimes there are toughs like those three ahead of you to put up with."

When he said that about the carefree part I figure he remembers the time I'd tied old man Johnson's leg to the table leg when he was asleep at the church dinner. Then I yelled that his horse had run away. Old man Johnson jumped up and jerked the table over. It had some food left on it from the big dinner, and all the women folks were mad at him, till they saw what had happened, then they were glaring at me. Then Ma had a talk with me, and Pa made sure I took some good apples over to the old man the next day and apologized to him.

"Well Jeff, that's Tim on the hoss, and the feller grinning at your family is Caleb. How are you fixed for weapons?" I asked.

"Ruth and Naomi are both good shots, and there are three long rifles hangin in the wagon bows. I always carry a Bowie knife, and I've kinda got used to this tomahawk in my belt."

Jeff said this quietly, and I'm beginning to like him more. Besides, if Pa had told him to catch up and travel with us, he must be all right. Pa is a real good judge of people. Their wagon appears to be in good shape, and there is a saddle horse and milk cow tied behind it. Their horses are not Morgan, but are slick and shiny and look well cared for.

23

Ruth and Naomi and the two little ones get out of the wagon and are running around. The small boy and girl appeared to be twins. The little boy starts toward Buck and I start to yell at that ugly dog, when suddenly his tail wags and he stands up. He is almost as tall as the boy. The boy stops and looks at him. Buck walked over and licked his face.

"Caleb, look at that!"

Caleb looked toward Buck and David and said something under his breath, and then we all watch as that big ugly dog just crowded right against the little boy.

"I've got a feeling nobody better bother those kids while Buck is around," I said.

We talk a bit more, then Rev. McClaren waved goodbye and started his horse. He will probably stop at Grandpa Greenup's and have a bite of dinner, then go on his busy rounds. The ferry is on its way back and when the ramp is out Uncle Bob walked ashore.

"Ross, we need to hurry. There is more drift coming down and I think there has been more rain up in the mountains."

"Sure, Uncle Bob. Why not take Jeff and his family over first? The mules are standing good, and it might crowd us too much to try getting all of us on."

"Good idea. Let's go, Jeff. Better drive your wagon on and let one of these fellows lead the horse and cow on."

Jeff got up on the wagon seat, while Caleb untied the horse and I untied the cow. She was a small Jersey cow and appeared to be gentle. Ruth and Naomi and the kids watched while Jeff drove the team and wagon across the ramp and onto the ferry. Caleb led the horse up behind the wagon and I started across with the cow. Her eyes were rolling as she looked at the muddy river and just as she stepped on the ramp, the ferry moved and the ramp heaved. The cow backs up suddenly, and when she crowds me my feet slip on the ramp and I am in the water. The water is about waist deep right at the edge of the dock and ice cold. It takes my breath and I lose my grip on the lead rope. The cow whirls around, jumping and plunging right into David and Elizabeth, and knocks David into the river. Ruth screams and runs to the edge of the bank. Caleb takes a quick turn of the horse's lead rope around the wagon ring and makes a running jump into the river where David has disappeared. Then they are both out of sight in the muddy water.

Buck runs to the edge of the bank and launches into the water. Suddenly Caleb's head appears and then he is holding a choking, sputtering David out of the water by his shirt collar, and they are spinning down the river with Buck right by them. Ruth, Naomi, Elizabeth, and the deck hand are running along the bank. I have a grip on the ramp and pull myself out of the water. I'm furious at the cow and wishing it was me pulling David out of the water. A small stream runs into the river about fifty yards below the ferry landing. Suddenly there is Tim on his horse racing into the stream and wading out into the river. As Caleb and David come whirling into him he reaches down and grabs Caleb's hand. Then he turns the horse and drags the two of them up the bank of the stream and drops them. Ruth rushes to David and grabs him in a tight hug, muddy water and all. Buck is right there by her, licking any part of David he can find. Naomi grabs Caleb and hugs him. Tim goes after the cow and I stand dripping cold river water. I'm cold, wet, and mad clear through.

While this is all going on Jeff has jumped off the wagon and is holding the team and keeping them quiet. He sees right away there is nothing he can do to help. Tim grabs the cow's lead rope and drags her back to the ramp and the boat. He hands the lead rope to me and then gets behind the cow with his horse and together we get her across the ramp and tied fast to the back of the wagon. Ruth, Naomi, David and Elizabeth cross the ramp and move up by Jeff. Jeff puts the cold, wet boy in the wagon and then they all watch Caleb, and Ruth keeps thanking him. I walk off the boat and the deck hand pulls the ramp over and shoves the boat off. Uncle Bob is working the sweep and talking to Jeff as they start across the river.

"Caleb and Tim, that was mighty quick thinking" I growl as the water drips off me. The spring sun is nearly overhead by now and feels good. I reckon my bad humor shows some. We are a cold, wet bunch.

"No use building a fire to dry out now. By the time we get to the other side we'll be about dry."

Tim suddenly breaks into a laugh.

"Shall we gather at the River?" he sings and soon the three of us are laughing.

"One old fool of a cow sure put us in a mess for awhile. Tim, did it hurt your rifle when you dropped it back there?" I asked.

He held it aloft in answer. Buck sat on his haunches and actually appeared to have a grin on his ugly face. We walk around and talk about some of the things we can imagine lie ahead of us, until the ferry gets back. Working carefully we get all the horses and mules on the boat without any upset.

"Say fellows, Ike here has something to tell you." Uncle Bob says, as he indicates the black deckhand.

"Yas suh, Mr. Ross. I heared dem white men talk about ya'll, an dey said dey was gonna get you over on the other side of the Gap, or before dat, if dey gets a chance. Dey's mighty mean men, Mr. Ross, and dey said some turrible things about dat nice fambly."

"Thanks Ike. We'll keep a close watch."

I watch Ike as we start across the river. He is a powerful young black man, about thirty years old. I know Grandpa Greenup bought him and his wife and two children a couple of years ago from a plantation in Virginia. His purpose was to free them and work them as hired hands. Grandpa and none of his family had any truck with owning slaves. It turned out Ike did not want to be free right then. He said it was safer for him and his family to be owned. So they work for Grandpa Greenup, and he has papers which show when he dies, Ike and his family will be free, and gives them a piece of land. Aunt Jane has taught the whole family to read and write, so they are better off than most of the black slaves in the country.

There is more drift wood in the water now, and Caleb and I join Ike in fending off the big pieces as they sweep down on the ferry. Tim hangs on to the lead ropes and quiets the horses and mules. Finally we land on the other side. Uncle Bob shakes hands with all of us. Then he takes off his hat and bows his head, and with a break in his voice asks the Almighty God to protect us and bring us back safely.

"Amen!" says Ike in a loud voice.

CHAPTER 5

We check all the packs and saddles again and get some jerky out to chew on while we catch up with Jeff and his family. They have started on. The sun continues to shine, but I notice a few clouds in the southeast. As we mount up and line out we all seem to feel we are cutting some ties to home which will never be the same. I notice Caleb, who was last getting started, stop a moment and look back at his Pa. Uncle Bob quietly raised his hand, palm out, the Indian sign meaning "Peace", with the additional meaning for us "The Lord Bless You." Caleb raised his hand, turned slowly and started after us.

If this first day on the trail is any indication of the rest of our journey, it's going to be quite a trip. It takes us about an hour to catch up with the wagon and the Clark's. They moved right out, but they already had a couple of days on the trail to get everything tightened up and trail broke. The trace is badly rutted from the spring rains and the heavy wagon traffic. We try to keep the horses and mules away from the worst of the ruts as we travel southwest across the Clinch River valley and get into the foothills. We start climbing soon as we come to the ridge that separates the Clinch River valley and the Powell River valley. The wagon team begins to strain as they climb the winding road. We pass several farms set back from the road. The three toughs we met at the ferry probably did not make many friends as they went through earlier, and it's just as well we are traveling with the wagon. In fact, as I think it over, it's a good thing to be traveling with the women and children. It appears to be a family unit instead of just three young bucks that might be looking for trouble. It's been quite a few years since the terrible Harpers brothers had terrified all travelers and settlers along the Wilderness Road, and the Natchez Trace, but there are still often enough men like the three in front of us to make life dangerous.

"Hey, Tim and Caleb, my belly's about to eat my backbone," I say as we stop to breathe all the animals.

Jeff is checking his harness and wagon wheels and the kids are running around, looking at things and enjoying the sunshine. Buck has assumed a kind of casual attitude, just trotting along behind or in front of the mules or sitting on his haunches with eyes, ears and nose alert.

"Jeff, what would you say to making camp as soon as we find a good place. We can get used to camping close to you folks before it gets too dark."

"Good idea, Ross. Maybe you could scout ahead for a way, and see what you can find."

I mount up, and leaving my mules with Tim, start on up the trail. Mules tend to get a bit excited if their lead horse goes off and leaves them, but Tim got them quieted down. I haven't gone a mile before I come across a nice meadow with a stream running through it. There is a farm house at the side of the meadow, with a rough trace leading to it. I see a woman working in front of the house in a garden patch. As I start up the trace to the house she sees me, and calling out to someone, she hurries in the house. Right then a tall, thin man, dressed in ragged overalls and a slouch hat comes out of the barn behind the house. He is carrying a double barreled shotgun in both hands.

"Howdy! I'm friendly!" I shout.

"Jes stop where you air." He growls.

"I've got a wagon with a family, and my cousins and a few horses with me. We're wondering if we can camp down at the end of your meadow for the night?"

He spits a long stream of tobacco juice as he considers the question.

"I reckon so, but it'll cost you half a plug of baccky and half a horn of powder."

These are two of the items we have in our packs, thanks to the sage advice of Pa and Uncle Will. I still ponder it for a moment, then tell him we will bring it to his cabin when we get camp set up. It's a high price, but this is our first night on the road and we need to get things straightened out and ready for an early start. About then his woman comes to the door and stands watching me. She is thin and worn looking, with a ragged dress and no shoes. I ride back to the main road and hurry to meet the others. When we get to the meadow we turn onto the grass at the edge of the oak and pine timber. There have been camps there before, as we can tell from the many old fire rings scattered around, and we will have to forage for wood.

Jeff and his family have their chores all lined out. Jeff unhitches the team, takes their harness off and leads them over to the creek to water. They drink long and slowly, lifting their heads to look around, then put their muzzles back into the cool water again. David and Elizabeth start collecting small pieces of firewood around the trees, and Ruth and Naomi get out their pans and food. Jeff hobbles the three horses and stakes the cow close to the creek.

Caleb, Tim and I each take care of our horses and mules, watering them and then hobbling them with chain hobbles. Its early enough they will have time to graze for a couple of hours before we tie them for the night. We brush them all, as their backs are still tender, and we sure don't want to get any sore backed animals. The packs are piled on the ground, and it takes us a while to get things sorted out.

Ruth has invited us to their fire to cook but we have our own grub and don't want to be beholden to them for any supplies. A bit later Naomi comes over to our fire and, real shy like, asks if we would care to join them in eating some Dutch oven dried apple cobbler. Good thing I wasn't sitting between Tim and Caleb and their fire, or I'd surely have been trampled in the rush. Buck and I follow along behind the other two. We are eating that good hot cobbler with some rich cream that came from the Jersey cow, when suddenly Buck stands up and growls out toward the darkness. I set down the pie and pick up my rifle which is leaning against the log I am sitting on. Then we hear a hail from the dark outside the firelight. Jeff hails back.

"Come on in, if you're friends," he calls.

The tall farmer appears in the light, carrying the shotgun and trailed by the thin woman I had seen at the cabin.

"Pull up a log and set a spell," Jeff says.

The farmer and his woman sit down on the log Jeff indicated. Elizabeth got closer to Naomi. Buck walked stiff legged over to David and sat down by him on the ground. Ruth jumped to her feet from the wagon tongue where she was sitting.

"Now you could both stand a bit of apple cobbler, couldn't you?' she asks.

The woman looked at the man, and he spit, considered the question, and finally nodded yes. Ruth handed them each a bowl of pie and a mug of coffee.

"I've got your tobacco and powder over by our fire." I say and get up to get it.

Buck goes right along by me. When I come back, Ruth and the woman are quietly talking. I hand the farmer the tobacco and powder, wrapped in a piece of burlap. He opens it, looks at it and seems to relax a little, especially when I tell him we raised the tobacco ourselves over on the other side of the mountain.

I had a couple of bites of pie left and pick up the bowl to finish it off. The bowl is empty. Now I know Buck did not eat it, because he's been with me. I look at Tim and Caleb. Caleb has a big grin on his face, and Tim is looking the other way.

"Why, you worthless cuss! You ate my pie!" I shout at Tim.

Dropping my bowl, I jump right at Tim, knocking him over backward, and we roll in the grass. I'm thumping Tim and he is howling with laughter. David and Elizabeth run to Ruth, and Naomi has her hands over her face. Buck is jumping back and forth and barking at us. Jeff and Caleb are laughing and watching the show, and the farmer's wife has crowded close to him. In a couple of minutes we quit rolling around, brush off and come back by the fire. Jeff looks at his family, then at us.

"You can tell this family is not used to being around boys." he said. "David and Elizabeth, there is nothing to be afraid of. These guys are just acting like boys do everywhere." He laughed again, and everyone settled down.

While we sit and talk the woman keeps her head turned so one side of her face is away from the firelight, and it appears to me her face is bruised on that side. She also doesn't have many teeth in front, and appears to be older than she probably is. This is fairly common among the mountain people, and many of the women don't live to be old. They sit for a spell, and then the farmer pulls out a long knife and whittles a small chunk off the plug of tobacco. He hands it to the woman, who immediately pops it in her mouth. Then he cuts himself a larger chunk and starts chewing it. He chewed a few times, and then spit a long stream of tobacco juice into the fire.

"Mighty good baccy. Just so ya'all know it, there were three rough fellers here earlier today that allowed as how one of you young fellers is a killer that murdered one of their kin, and to keep an eye on you if you stopped here. Reckon me and my woman has done that, and we wish ye well. Mam, thanks for the pie, and thanks for visiting with my woman. Ain't many folks do that."

With that he picked up the shotgun, motioned at the thin woman, touched his hat brim toward Ruth, and they disappeared in the dark, as quietly as they had come. Naomi looked at Ruth.

"Ruth, that poor woman made me so sad. Did you see how her face was bruised? You reckon he did that?"

"Well, we don't know that, honey, but when I see something like that it makes me thank God even more for having such a good man,!" She looked fondly at Jeff, who immediately got busy building up the fire.

"Jeff, you got any chains to tie your animals with?"

Jeff looked startled.

"No, I ain't Ross. Hadn't thought about it."

"Well, Pa and Uncle Will said that's the only way we will be able to keep them, and we will also take turns standing guard. We have a bell we'll put on my horse. The mules and horses will stay with the bell horse. Pa said a thief will usually be in a hurry and will figure on just cutting leather hobbles and tie ropes with his knife and getting away fast. It's a big surprise when they find a chain instead."

Jeff thought about that and allowed as how he would get some light chains as soon as he could. Meantime we would keep all the stock together and under guard, and he would take his turn guarding. We set up the shifts, hobbled all the horses and mules, and then all go to bed for a good sleep after a hard first day on the trail. The sky is clear, the stars shining, and Caleb and Buck have the first watch. I can hear the bell on my horse as he stands at the edge of the meadow. As I lie in my bedroll, I can see the glow of the coals from the fire as it dies down.

In my mind I compare the farm woman with Ruth, Naomi and Ma. Jeff and Pa treat their wives real well. They all work together, and it happens that none of the women chew tobacco. Pa and Richard don't chew, though they both smoke a pipe in the evenings. They all have most of their teeth. I know Pa has never in his life struck, or threatened to strike Ma. One evening, just before we left home, Pa and I were sitting by the fire, talking about the new country we were going to.

"Ross, you have probably noticed how your Ma aged so fast after the little girl died. If you look around at all the women and men here in the hills, you will see they all begin to look the same. They marry young, have children when they are young, work hard to just keep alive, and many of the children die young. Just look at the burying ground down by the meeting house." He paused, and looked hard at me.

"You are young, and you have dreams of a different life, a better life. I've seen you looking at the families here in the hills, and know you are thinking about what might be, but don't quite know what to do. Your brother felt the same way, and he made a choice to leave. We want you to have a chance to see a better life, and not get trapped in the life here, which will have you looking like everybody else, and losing the will to try something different or new. In addition to them wearing out, the land is wearing out. If you see a different life, and choose to come back here and live, that's your decision. But I think the Lord has other plans for you."

We were quiet then, and nothing much was said till the fire burned down and we went to bed.

Now tonight I'm lying on my bedroll, and already am seeing and comparing the lives of different people, and thinking of what Pa said. Then, strangely, my very last thought was of the red haired Rachel. I could feel her finger tips on my face, as I went to sleep.

CHAPTER 6

I woke to the sound of the horse bell, just a quiet jingle once in a while, meaning all of the animals were standing quietly. Jeff Clark had the last watch, so he was probably over by the wagon. Just then I saw his campfire flare up in the darkness, then heard him walking toward our camp. I saw Buck get up from beside my bed and walk toward him.

"Ross, it's time to roll out!" He shouted.

"OK, Jeff."

We all roused up and sat up in our bedrolls. Jeff walked to our fire and stirred it up, so the deep coals glowed red in the dark. I appreciated that, because it meant with just a few dry sticks we soon had a blazing fire. The horses and mules were soon standing around where our gear was stacked. They already knew where the oats were stored and were ready for a handout. We each took care of our own horses and mules, leading them to drink out of the stream, and then pouring them out about a quart of oats apiece in their nosebags and hanging the bags over their ears. For a while there is the sound of chomping and blowing as they eagerly down the oats. We can hear Jeff feeding his stock, and by now it is light enough to see around the camp. We see Naomi milking the cow, which Jeff had tied to the back of the wagon.

We have the coffee pot over the coals and a pot of oats is beginning to boil. Ruth has promised us all the milk we can use, as long as we are with them or till the cow goes dry. The cow is due to calve in about a month, so there should be milk for about a couple of weeks. Caleb waits till the oats are done, then he carries the pot over to the Clark's camp and Naomi pours a generous amount of fresh warm milk over the oats. Caleb then poured in a cup of molasses. We don't believe in getting anymore utensils dirty than we can help, so we all eat out of the same pot. The hot, sweet oats are delicious, and are washed down with mugs of hot boiled coffee, sweetened with molasses. I ladle out a couple of spoons of oats for Buck. When we are done I take the mugs, spoons and pot to the creek and scour them out with sand and water. All of us know better than to leave food in the pots to spoil. It is too easy to get mighty sick. We keep the coffee grounds to add a few more too, and boil again.

While I am doing this Caleb and Tim are taking care of the animals. They pack the nosebags and chains, saddle and bridle the horses, and start packing the mules. Caleb is leading two big, tough red mules, and we soon find out one of them does not like the pack saddle early in the morning. He puts on quite a show, bucking and braying, till suddenly he decides he feels better, and stands quietly while Caleb packs him. Soon everything is loaded and all the animals standing tied. I put out the fire and we all check the priming and caps on our long guns and pistols.

I have a personal liking for all the animals, but especially for the mules. They are smart, and generally will repay kindness with good behavior, so I walk around them and pat their necks and talk to them. Uncle Richard has a large donkey or jack and several quarter horses that are used to breed our mules. All these mules and horses have the Greenup G double arrow G branded on their left hip.

It's broad daylight now, with the sun reaching into the woods, warming the leaves and pine needles. We walk over to the Clark's camp. Buck runs ahead of us and goes directly to David, who hugs and pets that ugly dog. David and Elizabeth had their own little chores to do in camp, and Ruth and Naomi have everything in hand. The wagon is about packed and Jeff is harnessing the team. I noticed he brushed the horses down good last night and again this morning. Tim went to help him finish and hook the team to the wagon. I get the Jersey cow watered and tie her and the saddle horse to the back of the wagon. She is a gentle, good cow, even though she pushed me into the river. The kids and Buck follow me to the creek and back. They are beginning to feel at home with me now. I always like little children, and talk to them and tease them about eating all the fried pies. Caleb helps the women load the last few items in the wagon, and we are ready to go.

We tighten saddle girths, check the packs, and mount our horses. We are leading out. Naomi, David and Elizabeth are walking by the wagon as it pulls out behind us. I pull off to the side and stop and watch as everything goes by. It is quite a sight. Tim and Caleb on their good looking horses and leading the big mules, and then the covered wagon with Jeff and Ruth up on the seat and Naomi and the kids walking along beside it. The cow and saddle horse are following without any trouble. The sun has burned the mists away and we can clearly see the farm house in the meadow. As we pull into the road I see the farm woman step out the door. She stands quietly watching us, then waves with both hands. I wave back and see Ruth and Naomi do the same. Then the woman and the house fade from view as we turn out of the meadow. I briefly remember my thoughts of last night, and what Pa had told me about life in the hills. All of us on this road are started on a new life, but the future of the farm woman does not seem to promise much.

The excitement of the journey is strong on me. We are still in settled country, but on our own, and we are young and tough. A clear, crisp spring morning seems to offer us the world. It took a while to get the outfit settled down on the trace. At the first wide place I pass the wagon and catch up with Tim and Caleb. This is to be our first full day of travel and the animals are a bit skittish. After a couple of hours we come to a good stream crossing where we can water the stock easily. We rest everything here. Naomi and the kids have been in the wagon, but when we stop they get out and David and Elizabeth play by the creek, always under the watchful eye of Buck. We dig some jerky out of the packs, and Ruth gets out some dried apple tarts, so we have a little food to refresh us, along with the cold creek water.

We are now on the northwest side of the high ridge between the Clinch and Powell Rivers. From here it is a downhill run to the Powell, where there is a bridge across the river at a narrow place. After about an hour by the creek we start on. In some places the road is steep downhill and it takes careful and skillful driving of the wagon to keep it from running up on the horses. Jeff does a great job and arrives at the bottom of the long slope without any problem. The pack saddles on the mules all have cruppers, to keep them from sliding forward, but the mules still do not like going downhill.

We pass several farms as we travel, with occasional glimpses of the farmers and their families and livestock. Horses and mules raise their heads and watch us, and at almost every farm there is at least one dog to rush out barking at us. Buck doesn't pay much attention unless they get too close then he will growl low and fierce. They then stand and watch us pass. Most of the fields are plowed and spring planting is underway. The season is a couple of weeks earlier than it is at home. Men, women and children are in the fields, and they usually wave and shout hello. I can smell the soil, and in some fields there are green shoots of corn and tobacco peering out of the black dirt. We also meet a number of travelers, some on horseback, some in buggies or wagons, and some walking. They tell us the Powell River is up some and still rising from rains up north. We are passed by a couple of horsemen going the same way we are.

When we arrive at the Powell River there is some water running around the ends of the bridge, but we are able to cross without a problem. After crossing we get out jerky and some of the cornpone Ma had packed and have a fast break. We are all anxious to keep going. Ever since starting down the long grade to the Powell we can clearly see the high Cumberland Mountain ridge ahead of us. This mountain has always been the main barrier to travel west from the Carolina's and northeastern Tennessee. Since I was a small boy I've heard stories of the 'Gap', and now it's clearly visible, looking like a gun sight cut into the top of the ridge. It will be our way through that great mountain, just as it has been for thousands of travelers for centuries. Buffalo, deer, Indians, white men and slaves alike have used it. My heart beats fast as I think of it.

Before we get to the foot of the mountain we will connect with the main Old Wilderness Road, which had originally been laid out by Daniel Boone in 1775 as the Wilderness Trail. Pa had been here before, and told how many people lived over in Kentucky. It had become a state in 1792, because of the large numbers of settlers. The Wilderness Road was still tough on travelers, despite attempts to improve it.

"Jeff, since you've been here before, can we make it to the Gap by dark?' I ask.

"We can't make it. The road up this side is really steep, with several sharp turns. I want Ruth and Naomi and the kids to walk on quite a bit of it, in case we have a problem with the wagon. With just two horses pulling, it's a long haul, and the less weight on the wagon the better. There is not much room on top, and there might be other travelers camped there. We pass a store and tavern just past this little ridge, where we run into the main Road, and on past them there are some fairly good places to camp, before we start the climb."

"Jeff, it appears to me we might be getting to a place where those three riders ahead of us might want to ambush us." Tim said quietly, with a meaningful glance at David and Elizabeth.

I've been some concerned about this myself, though we all recognize the support we give each other. There sure is strength in numbers, but we were also placing this young family in possibly a very dangerous situation. Jeff looked around at us for a minute, then grinned.

"There ain't many places where they can ambush us on this side of the Gap. Let's get going!"

We check our packs, tighten the saddle girths, and start. Looking up I can see Cumberland Mountain looming above us. It is an awesome sight, even to us who are used to seeing the Great Smoky's. It goes from northeast to southwest as far as we can see in either direction, with the only break the Cumberland Gap. There is brush on the lower slopes, with hardwoods and pines mingling into a dense forest as it gets closer to the top, and with great walls of sheer rock rising at intervals. Going toward it we go up and over a small ridge, and cross another creek. There is a store and rough tavern there, where our road joined the main Old Wilderness Road. We stop while Jeff goes in the store and inquires about the trio in front of us.

Jeff comes out of the store in a few minutes and walks over to where we are checking packs.

"Well, fellows, those three riders spent last night here at the bunkhouse behind the tavern. They told the storekeeper they were headed for the Cumberland River and then south along it, so they will be leaving the Road at Pineville. If they are going to give us any trouble it will be in the gorge along Yellow Creek at the bottom of the mountain on the other side. So if we camp soon we can get an early start to the Gap and get well clear of the worst country before it gets dark tomorrow."

"At least the weather is holding up good for us." I say and swing back on my horse.

Our caravan now turns onto the main Old Wilderness Road. We can expect many more travelers from now on. The Road is rough, with deep ruts made during the spring rains. There are mud holes and then places of solid rock. We have gone about another mile when we come to a small stream that appears to come from the general direction of the Gap. There are scattered trees and plentiful patches of new grass. The area has evidently been used as a camp site by many other travelers. We are already in the shade of Cumberland Mountain, though it will be at least another hour before the sun sets. We pull well off the road to a flat area sheltered from the road. This is our second night to set up camp, and we are beginning to get the hang of it.

I get a fire going while Tim and Caleb start unpacking the mules and stacking the gear. We have all seen outfits that would leave the packs on their animals for as long as three days just to avoid all the work of packing and unpacking. Our Pa's have all trained us differently. Without taking the packs and saddles off and letting the backs of the mules and horses dry out, their backs will soon develop saddle sores, and cause the animals to become very difficult to handle. We take the saddles off, brush and rub down their backs, and if there is a sign of a sore, we apply some pine tar ointment to help it heal. As soon as the saddles are off and they are turned loose for a while the animals roll on the ground and stretch and grunt. David and Elizabeth enjoy the show and soon pick out their favorite mules and horses. We tell them not to ever get too close to any of the mules, and especially their hind feet. A mule can turn and kick faster than you can jump out of the way, and lots of people have been crippled or killed by mules.

Buck prowls around the edge of the camp site and then plays with David or goes with him to gather small dry sticks for the fire, as that is one of David's chores. That suits them both, as David is much safer with Buck along. Soon the fires are going and the camp all set up. We hobble all the animals and turn them loose to graze on the fresh green grass for a couple of hours.

We cook a good supper, with thick slices of ham. Naomi mixed up a big batch of Dutch oven biscuits and we all share food for that supper. We dig out one of Ma's dried apple pies and have that with thick creamy milk from the Jersey cow. We all appreciate the fact that Naomi knows how to cook over a camp fire, but it is obvious Caleb is most interested, and Naomi sure enjoys the attention he gives her. He is right there to keep the fire going and give her a big smile when he can catch her eye. It is dark by the time we have everything cleaned up and are settled around Jeff's campfire. David and Elizabeth are sitting on a saddle blanket close to the feet of their Ma and Naomi.

"The storekeeper said you could probably get a good price for the mules when we get to the Bluegrass Country." Jeff said.

"Well, we probably won't sell them all there, even if we get a really good price. We want to keep at least two for our own packs, and Pa was hoping we could trade them for some land after we leave the Mississippi River and start on west. What he has in mind is for us to start raising more Morgan horses and mules to supply all the outfits going west. My Uncle Will has been out there and he figures there is going to be lots of travel that direction. So Pa wants to be raising a supply right where the outfits start toward Mexico and Santa Fe, or toward California and Oregon." I pause. "What are you folks going to do, Jeff?"

Jeff looked over at Ruth and she smiled at him. Naomi gathered the kids close around her and they are all quiet as they wait for Jeff to answer.

"Well, I'll tell you, and also explain why we were talking to your Pa and then caught up with you. We lived in the mountains up north of you folks. Your Pa and I met a couple of years ago, and then him and your Uncle Rich, Tim's Pa, stopped by when they brought the horses back a couple of weeks ago. We talked about it some then, and we decided your Pa and I would like to be partners in this horse and mule raising business. We took off after you to go on over in Kentuck, buy a farm, and get started. I hadn't said anything to you fellers yet, cause I wanted to see how we were all going to get along. We have six mares due to foal in about two months, and they were all bred to a couple of good jacks. My Pa is keeping them, so we hopefully will have six new mule colts to get started with."

I am totally surprised, and so are Tim and Caleb. We stare at each other in the firelight. There is a long silence, and sure it is apparent neither Tim nor Caleb are going to say anything till I do.

"Well, I'm going to say my say, and if either of these fellers want to argue it, or add to it, they'll get their chance. We've been watching you folks, just because we are careful of who we trail with. We noticed how well you took care of your stock, and how you seemed to not be afraid of work. You and your family seem to get along real well, and seem to be God fearing, decent people, and that's important to us. Jeff, you appear to be a feller we would want to go over the mountain with, and if our Pa thinks enough of you to be partners, I reckon we feel the same way. But how do we know you are telling us the truth?"

With that long speech I am plumb exhausted for the moment. Jeff grinned and nodded to Ruth. She stood and walked over to the wagon.

"Guess I go along with Ross," says Caleb. "And I sure admire Ruth's cooking." He stopped and stares at the fire.

"Appears to me like Ruth's cooking is shore sweetened up a bit when Naomi helps with it." Tim says, and grins at Caleb. "Shucks, Ross, I shore agree with you and Caleb."

About that time Buck gets up from beside David and walks over to Jeff. He reaches out that big ugly nose and licks Jeff's hand, then turns around and walks over by me. He sits down by my feet and actually appears to grin at the group.

"Appears to me we just had the final approval." I say.

Ruth came back to the fire and hands me an envelope. Opening it I find a single sheet of paper, with Ma's handwriting on it. It states Pa and Uncle Rich are business partners, and they have invited Jeff Clark into the partnership. It also said for purposes of the partnership, and business, Tim and me are to be their representatives. Pa and Uncle Rich signed it, with Ma as a witness. In the upper right hand corner of the page are two capitol G's with a double arrow between them, the brand and mark for the Greenup brothers. We all look at it and then hand it back to Ruth for safekeeping.

"You fellows don't know this, but Naomi has been living with us for three years. Our mother died and Pa didn't think he could raise a young girl by himself. Now she is a sweet young lady, and we are mighty happy

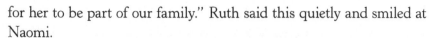

for her to be part of our family." Ruth said this quietly and smiled at Naomi.

We all sit around the fire for another half hour, then catch the horses and mules and tie them with chains, as well as putting chain hobbles on them. Jeff has first watch tonight. We all agreed we each should carry a Bowie, as well as a pistol. I always carry the little dagger fastened by a cord around my neck and hanging down my back until I lie down. I stretched out in my bedroll and thought of Ma, and Rachel. I'm thinking she sure would enjoy this trip.

Caleb has the second watch, and it must have been past midnight when he woke me to take the next watch.

"Ross, it's a mite early, but something ain't right. Few minutes ago the animals got real quiet, and Buck has been prowling around where they are tied." Caleb whispered to me.

I slipped out of my bedroll and grabbed my moccasins, and about then Buck let out a deep growl over by the horses and mules. There was a crash and a yell, then a scream and a shot. Buck let out a yip and then another growl. By now Tim is out of his bed and on his feet with rifle in hand. I can hear Jeff climbing out of the wagon. The animals are jumping back and forth and snorting nervously.

"Call off yore dawg!" came a high pitched yell.

Caleb stirred up the fire. He grabs a stick that is at the edge of the fire and it flames up. Our shadows are tall and moving and fading into the darkness. Excitement makes my heart race.

"Tim, stay here by the wagon." I say, as Caleb, Jeff and I start toward the animals.

We spread out and walk slowly toward where Buck is growling. We can see feet, and Bucks tail sticking out of some thick brush. Holding my rifle pointed at the feet, I call Buck. He backed reluctantly out of the brush. Jeff grinned and pointed a pistol in the general direction of whoever was there.

"Don't shoot." A voice quavered, and a tall, skinny boy scrambled out of the brush.

In the flickering light it is hard to see his face. Caleb walks over close to him and picks up a pistol lying in the grass. Then he motioned toward the fire and the boy stumbled toward it with Buck walking right behind him and growling every step. I could see a bloody crease across Buck's right shoulder. It appeared that if the bullet had been a half inch lower we would have had a totally disabled dog. We get in the brighter light of the fire and Jeff brings a lantern from his wagon and lights it. We can see the boy clearly now. Jeff said:

"You're the boy that was in the store when we stopped there. Why are you trying to steal our horses?"

"Pa told me to see if I could get at least one of them." The boy quavered.

"What were you going to do with it, if you got away?" Jeff asked.

The boy looked down and said nothing.

"Bet you got a holler over here somewhere to stash stolen stuff while the owner tries to find it, haven't ya?" Jeff snarled in his face.

The boy started crying.

"Mister, please don't kill me!" he sobbed.

I motioned Jeff off to one side and we hold a short discussion. Then we walk back to the fire. I get right in front of the boy, where he stands with head down, and feel him all over to see if he has a knife. If he did it is probably back in the brush.

"Sonny, we've been deciding whether to hang you or let you go. We are the Greenup boys, and this here is Jeff Clark and his family. They are real special friends of ours. Don't you ever forget any of this. You maybe heard from those three riders that went through here a couple of days ago that I had killed a man. Well, they were right, and I did it because he tried to steal one of our horses. We are going to keep you right here till daylight. You can sit by the fire, and old Buck is going to guard you. Now he ain't got good feelin's toward you, since you creased him with that bullet, so if you do much more than breathe, you're dead. You got anything to say, sonny?"

I glared as he shook his lowered head.

"Well, then you remember the Greenup boys, and the Clark family, and if we ever happen to have any trouble over in this part of the country, we are going to look up your Pa and see if he had anything to do with it. Sit down! Buck! Watch him!"

The boy dropped to the ground like his legs would no longer hold him.

We all turned and walked to the wagon. Inside we could hear Ruth and Naomi whispering. I speak loud enough for them to hear.

"Jeff and I figured we would just put the fear of God in him, give him a good feed in the morning and let him go home. Jeff thought we ought to take advantage of the reputation we have, whether we like it or not."

Caleb was laughing quietly, and Tim slapped Jeff on the back.

"I'm just right glad we are teamed up with you, Jeff." Tim said, and we turn and walk back to our own fire.

The boy is stretched out on the ground and Buck's nose is about an inch from his leg. I grin to myself as I put more wood on the fire. The night is still velvet dark, though a thin sliver of new moon is showing and the stars are winking at me as I put on a light jacket and wait for dawn.

CHAPTER 7

A faint pre-dawn light is showing in the east when I put a big armload of wood on the fire and rouse the camp. The boy is stiff from lying on the ground under the watchful eye of Buck.

"Sonny, you walk around here and loosen up some, but don't try running or anything like that. Buck will drag you down in about two steps." He nods and walks off to the edge of the trees, then eased back in a couple of minutes, sits down by the fire, and watches intently as we get breakfast and break camp. We figure we have a tough day ahead of us, so Ruth baked biscuits in the Dutch oven, and we have more of the thick ham and dried apple pie, along with lots of hot coffee. Ruth told the boy to help himself and he sure did. Acted like he hadn't eaten for a week. Jeff and I talk some more, then Jeff calls him over. He looks scared as he walks toward Jeff.

"What's yore name, boy?" Jeff asked. "Butch McGuire." He stammered.

"Well, Butch, here's what we are going to do. We're going to let you go home and tell yore Pa what happened, and that it better not ever happen again. Then if you are a mind to, you can catch up with us and give us a hand getting through the "Gap" and over the mountain. We'll feed you good if you do, and then you can come back home. If it works out real good and yore Pa says it's all right, we might even be able to use you later on over in Kentuck. It appears you have worked around horses some."

Butch had tears of relief in his eyes as he thanked Jeff and all of us.

We hand him his pistol and the knife we found in the brush. Then his skinny legs took him off down the road at a run.

I am working with the horses when I suddenly stop and look. The first rays of the sun have just touched the top of the Cumberland Ridge and Gap, and the dark of night is retreating down the steep slopes of the mountain. I stand in wonder and awe, and then thank God for creating such a marvelous sight. Soon all of us are watching, and it's perfectly quiet for several minutes.

It is still early morning when we start. The sun has been shining on top of the Cumberland Ridge and the 'Gap', for some time, and gradually moving down the slopes, till now it's shining on us. The animals can feel our excitement, and are all bright eyed, prancing around, and anxious to go. Buck is right out in front as we pull back into the road, with me leading the way, and Caleb bringing up the rear. Within an hour we are beginning to climb. The road has deep ruts here in the low lands, but Jeff said it gets better as we go up on some rocky stretches. We are still in heavy pine timber, but the great bluffs are clearly visible, towering above us. The road makes a sharp switchback, and I can look down on the wagon and Caleb below me. It makes another switchback, and then begins to get really steep. Switch backs or sharp turns are hard on the team pulling the wagon. Cramping the front wheels of the wagon around makes it hard to pull, and if something breaks the wagon is in a tough place to fix. The creek is hidden off to our left, in a deep little ravine, which seems to come from the Gap. The rushing, splashing sound of the water comes to us clearly.

Jeff stops the team and lets them rest to get ready for the long haul. Ruth, Naomi, Elizabeth and David get out of the wagon prepared to walk and push if necessary. The road has dried out considerable since the last rain. Ruth and Naomi have both put on deerskin leggings with a plain long skirt over them, and leather moccasins. Ruth still looks mighty young, as she doesn't have the stress of frontier life showing on her face yet. Their arms and hands are getting tanned, but they always wear bonnets to protect their faces.

"Elizabeth and David, you are to lead the cow and go ahead of the wagon and team all the way. I don't want you to be behind the wagon if it happened to get away!" Jeff said sternly. "But don't get too far ahead of us. Stay in sight all the time, and if anyone comes down the road toward us, get on the uphill side of the road and stay quiet."

They are so excited they can hardly contain themselves. They take the cow's lead rope and go ahead of the team and wagon. They feel mighty important to have the responsibility of the cow, but they are still laughing and patting the cow's neck. Ruth and Naomi are not near as happy about the idea of helping push the heavy wagon, but they knew it would help the horses and speed things up. We don't have harness to put on our horses and mules, so we can't hitch them to the wagon and help, but we can tie a rope to the wagon, take a dally around the saddle horn and let the horse pull. It seems like we can use only one horse at a time so Caleb will take care of that, Tim will lead all the other animals ahead, and I will help push the wagon. Jeff will walk by the wagon and drive the team.

Looking around at the little group makes me feel mighty good about working with them. Naomi is a slender little gal, but mighty spunky, and is sure going to pull, or push, her weight. With all of us working together, we should get the wagon to the top and over in half the time it would have taken the Clark's by themselves. Caleb tied a rope to the end of the wagon tongue, took a turn around his saddle horn, and was ready.

About then we hear a yell from down the hill below us. Looking down, who should appear but Butch McGuire. We wait till he catches up with us. He is carrying a tow sack and the pistol he had this morning.

"Pa said he would be glad to be shut of me for a few days." He said softly. Ruth looked at him.

"What about your Ma, Butch?" she said.

Butch dug in the dirt with the toe of his moccasin.

"She died with a fever a couple of years ago. Pa ain't never been the same. My older brother is working on a big river up north. He couldn't stand it around Pa anymore." It was quiet, with just the sounds of the horses breathing, and the wind blowing in the tops of the tree.

"Let's go!" I say loudly. "Butch, tie your 'possible' sack on top of one of the mules, then you and I are pushing at the back of the wagon. Ruth, you and Naomi don't push unless Jeff tells you to. With Butch and I both pushing, we probably won't need you."

The women look mighty relieved to hear that. Caleb took up the slack on the rope in front. Tim is already a hundred feet up the road with the horses and mules. Jeff untied the reins from the wagon seat, snapped them and the stout horses lean into their collars. We start toward the Gap. Nobody wastes breath talking. The road gets steeper. Soon Butch and I are both pushing hard, and the wagon moves steadily. We have gone almost a mile when we come to a level place. We are all glad to stop for a rest, and Tim is waiting for us. Elizabeth and David are there with the cow.

"Ross, there is someone ahead of us. The horses are watching." Tim said as we pulled to a stop.

Buck growls. About that time Elizabeth points up the road, and we can see and hear several riders coming down the hill. I grab my rifle from the back of the wagon, where I kept it while we were walking and pushing. The thought of the three hard case riders ahead of us is always on my mind. The riders coming toward us are moving slowly, and we can see there are at least two women in the group. We relax a little, as there would not likely be any shooting, but it sure irritated me they have gotten as close to us as they have before we were aware of them. They hail us as they ride up and stop.

"Where are you folks headed?" was a question asked by a stocky, erect, middle aged man on a big roan horse. He has a white mustache and when he takes off his southern plantation style hat it reveals a shock of white hair. The men are all riding English style saddles, with no saddle horns, and the women are riding well-made side saddles.

He is well dressed and has an air of authority about him. I don't see any reason not to answer him, so I tell him we are on our way to Kentucky, and want to get through the Gap and down the other side before it gets dark. The two other men in the group and the two women are younger and do not appear to be settlers. They are all evidently experienced riders. The men are heavily armed, with each carrying a pistol on the saddle and a long rifle slung over their shoulders. They are leading one pack horse.

"Would you by any chance happen to be the Greenup boys? is the next question.

It surprised me.

"Yes we are, Sir, but how did you know?"

47

"There is an Inn and Roadhouse where a road goes south from the Wilderness Road toward the Tennessee settlements. We stopped there last night and overheard some talk about something Ross Greenup had done over on the Great Smoky side of the Clinch River. From the description I just figured it might be you young fellows. It sounded like you were a salty bunch that might be tough to tangle with. I happen to know a Christopher Greenup that owns a ferry on the Clinch River, and we plan on visiting with him tonight on our way to the coast. I also knew his father, the Christopher Greenup that was the third governor of our great state of Kentucky."

"That's our Grandpa that owns the ferry!" I tell him. "Would you mind telling him we are on our way through the Gap, and haven't had any trouble."

Then I introduce Jeff, Ruth and Naomi to the group, and we have a short, pleasant conversation. The man's name is Jeremiah Allbright and he owns a twelve hundred acre horse farm back in Virginia. He is trying to get something started in Kentucky, where the bluegrass is supposed to be the best horse pasture in the world. We tell him very briefly what our plans are, and that Jeff planned on getting a place of his own in Kentucky, while the rest of us went on west. Jeremiah Allbright has been watching us all closely while we talk. We have been doing the same, noticing the fine horses they ride, and how pretty the women are.

"Ross, I know a little about your family, and it appears you folks have a good partner in young Jeff and his family. I'm going to get in touch with your Pa, Ross, and when I get back in about two months would like to tie in with your operation. Jeff, about three days travel on the Wilderness Road from the bottom of the mountain will put you close to my land. If you are interested in what you see, talk to my overseer, tell him what you want, and let him help you. John, write a note for Jeff to take to Jason, and we will get on our way."

Jeremiah indicated one of the pleasant faced young men sitting his horse, apparently much interested in the conversation. While John was getting a paper out of his saddle bag the rest of us briefly talk. The two women are encouraging Ruth and Naomi and talking to Elizabeth and David.

"Five years ago we were doing the same thing you are." The women tell Ruth. "It takes a lot of hard work, but there are good folks to help you if you settle in the valley where we are."

John finished writing, showed the paper to Jeremiah Allbright, and handed it to Jeff, who in turn handed it to Ruth. You could see that made a good impression on the women and Jeremiah. Waving goodbye, and telling us to keep a sharp lookout, they start on down the steep road.

In the meantime, I am getting a very uneasy feeling. We have spent a lot of time talking, and it is still a way to the top. I sure want to get through the Gap and over the mountain as fast as possible. We could talk about all this later, around the fire. Tim started ahead with the horses and mules, followed by Elizabeth, David and the cow. Jeff started the team, with Caleb pulling with his saddle horse. It did not take long for the horses to be blowing and straining in the harness, and Butch and I are pushing as hard as we can. We stop wherever there is an indication of a level place and rest. At one point we can see the mouth of a cave over at the base of the huge bluffs. The sun is past noon when we hear Tim give a whoop of joy. He was on top. The rest of us soon follow.

As the animals rest we stare in wonder at the land before us. It is new to all of us except Jeff and Butch. Excitement grew in me as I looked west across the miles of ridges and valleys, with an occasional clearing showing through the trees, and a few wisps of smoke from the fireplaces of cabins. Not far out to the west is a line of dark clouds that look like they would have thunderstorms in them, and that made it even more important to get off this high mountain and down where we could get shelter. We sure do not want to be on top of this rocky ridge when the lightning starts popping.

Tim ties the horses and mules to some handy trees, and I tie the milk cow to a tree. We rest, and Ruth and Naomi get out dried apple pies and jerky, which we wolf down with cold water. Buck has a big piece of David's pie. We will water the animals where a stream crosses the Road down the hill.

I look down the road to where it disappears into timber which is much thicker and larger on the shady northwest side of the mountain.

"Let's keep someone on watch all the time from here on." I tell the others. "Every time we stop one of us needs to be watching, with rifle in hand, and we need to all be careful, including Elizabeth and David."

In the meantime Jeff has been busy checking and tightening harness, and looking carefully at the wagon wheels and the brake. Then he walks over to the edge of the open area with his axe and cuts a couple of stout poles. He lays them on the running gear of the wagon. As we start down the mountain the weight of the wagon will push the horses hard, and he will wedge the poles under the axles to drag and help slow the wagon. If necessary he will stick the poles through the spokes of the wagon wheels so they could not turn and would have to slide.

Soon we start, and Butch and I continue to walk with the women behind the wagon to be ready to help Jeff. Caleb and Tim are close ahead with the horses and mules and Elizabeth and David are leading the cow behind the wagon. For a short distance the road is not steep. We see below us where the road evidently makes a switchback. The animals all prick up their ears and Buck looks over the edge and growls. The top of a buggy became visible coming up the mountain toward us. In a few minutes the horse and buggy draw alongside and stop as we stop. The lone driver is a middle aged man, and he is also well armed, with a long rifle and two pistols in the buggy by him.

"That's some mighty good looking horses and mules you folks have." He said as he pulls off his hat. "I'm a trader, and might be interested in making a swap with you."

"Sorry, Mister. They are not for sale right now, but keep in mind the names Clark and Greenup and come over in Kentucky in a couple of years. We might have something for you." Jeff said.

About then I had an idea.

"Butch, if this fellow wouldn't mind, you could probably ride with him back to your Pa's store." I said.

Butch looked startled, then he looked around at the women and Jeff. He looked at the ground and dug his toe in the dirt. Buck walked over to him and licked his hand.

"If you folks don't care, I'd sure like to stay with you." He said. "I'll work hard and earn my keep."

Jeff grinned and looked at Ruth.

"What do you say to that, Honey?" he asked Ruth.

Ruth smiled at Jeff and then at Butch.

"I think that will be just fine." She said softly. "Just tell the man to let your Pa know so he won't be worried."

Butch did that and the driver whirred on up the road in his buggy.

We finally get started again, down the steep road and into the dark trees.

The road has more deep, muddy ruts on this north west side of the mountain, since it is in the shade a lot more. Going up would have been a tough trip on the horses, but the mud slowed the wagon down and Jeff did not have to use the drag poles. We are soon down in the big trees and it is cool and dark. We come to an opening in the trees and stop to rest. Suddenly there was a gust of wind high up in the tops of the trees. The horses and mules tossed their heads and I was startled. Looking up I see the long, thin, white clouds that are often ahead of a storm in the spring. Then there is another gust and the wind began to moan and sigh like a lost spirit, through the trees on the mountain above us. About then Buck barked and looked down the side of the slope below us. When I look I see another rider coming up the road. There is evidently another turn, back around the mountain, but he is moving fast and in a few minutes is up to us. He wears buckskin and carries a long rifle. His broad brimmed hat hangs down low and shapeless, but does not conceal his piercing blue eyes that take in everything. His horse is small and tough looking, and he pulls it to a stop.

"You folks better start looking for a place to tie up right soon. It's fixin to rain like fury," he growled. "There's a level spot about a mile down the road, and iffin you hurry, you kin get there before it hits."

He started on, then stopped and turned.

"Ain't you the Greenup boys?" he asked me.

"Yes, we are, and these are our partners, the Jeff Clark family." I answered. "How do you know who we are?"

"Well, I heard some talk on the Road. I just come up from Tennessee. If I was you, when you go on tomorrow I'd sure want to get past Yellow Creek and the turnoff that goes south to Tennessee before I stopped again. Might save yourselves a lot of trouble. I know your Uncle Will Bunch, and think highly of him."

With that bit of information he was on his way, the little horse moving carefully up the muddy road. We didn't waste any time. Tim moves out ahead and we pull out after him. By the time we have gone another mile and found the flat area the dark clouds are already rolling in above us. Their shadows are moving fast over the ground and we can hear the mutter of thunder a long way from us. The animals can feel the storm and hear the wind and are getting more nervous, rolling their eyes and switching their tails.

Jeff and I look around carefully at the trees to make sure there were no dead tops or snags that might blow over on us. The trees are not very thick growing, and with all the cold remains of fires it looked like there have been lots of camps made here. We have the two poles Jeff has been carrying on the wagon, and with several others that are lying around have enough to throw up a lean-to. I start Butch on that while we take care of the stock. Elizabeth and David are gathering firewood, and we place the shelter close to the wagon so we will have just one fire. We start a fire and the shelter is reflecting the heat on one side and the wagon is reflecting on the other side. We grain the livestock and Naomi milked the cow. We help Butch cut enough pine branches to put over the roof of the shelter, and the four of us will sleep there, though we will probably have Buck right in the middle.

We smell rain all the time we are working, and just as we have everything snugged up the best we can, there is a flash and almost instantly a sharp roll of thunder. The first few drops to hit are huge and cold. The tree tops are swaying wildly and the wind is shrieking and moaning. Then we can see the curtain of rain as it sweeps in above us. Jeff and his family are buttoned up in the covered wagon. The four of us are under the lean-to and have our tarp riding slickers over us, except for Butch, who just has a light jacket. So we put him in the middle and cover him as well as we can, and Buck squeezed right in with us.

I love it. The wildness of the storm was wild in my heart as long as I can remember. When there was a storm Pa used to take us out on the porch from the time we were babies and tell us to not be afraid of the storm. I could remember him holding me close, wrapped in a furry coat, and listening to the sound of the wind and the rain and the thunder. I could smell the rain, and the wet leaves, and the funny smell after a lightning strike. Pa's arms were strong, and he smelled like leather and horses.

"God made the weather and we need to enjoy it when we can." He told me.

Then Ma would come out on the porch and tell us both God made us a brain and not to do foolish things. Pa would wink at me and smile at Ma, and sometimes she would stay with us for a while. Then we would go inside and have a mug of hot tea, sweetened with wild honey.

These memories flood through my mind while we huddle under the shelter, and I wonder what Pa and Ma are doing right now. I think of what has happened in just a few days, and then it occurs to me that many of the happenings have been because of some action we have done. The Bible tells us actions speak louder than words. The thought of the red haired Rachel comes to my mind for a moment, and then we all go to sleep.

It is dark when I stir and we all wake. The rain has slacked off to a light sprinkle, and we need a fire to warm up and fix some supper. I realize we have not kept a lookout while the storm raged and we all slept. It was sure easy to get careless, and we will have to be more careful. I dig down in the pile of firewood to find some dry pieces, and there are some live coals under the wet surface of the fire. In just a few minutes the fire is roaring and we all start moving around. Jeff and Ruth join us, but the other three are sound asleep in the wagon. It has been a hard and exciting day, and they are exhausted. Buck walked all around the camp, sniffed at the other animals, and after deciding all was well joined us at the fire. It seemed like the perfect time to have some buckwheat flapjacks, with a big slab of ham and some homemade cane and maple syrup. We dig into the packs and get out all the makings, and Ruth starts heating the griddle. It isn't long till we are all filled to the brim, sitting around a hot fire, and ready to talk. Jeff started it.

"Well, Greenup's, this has been an interesting day. There sure are a lot of people hearing about you, thanks to the three toughs ahead of us. It appears to me this can be used to our advantage, if we go about it the proper way. As I remember, we will be at the bottom in about another hour. Then in another couple of miles we will hit Yellow Creek and about half a mile past it the Old Road goes on to the northwest, into Kentuck, and another road goes south into Tennessee, and to the Tennessee River. There is a general store and trading post there, and I think if we are going to have trouble we will have it there."

Tim spoke right up.

"Since you think that might happen, do you think those three are smart enough to expect us to be prepared there, and if nothing happens, drop our guard after we go through the village? Then they wait for us half a mile the other side."

After this exchange we talk for a while. Our main concern is being delayed, and some one of us getting hurt or killed. Caleb remembers no one on this side of the Gap knows we have Butch with us.

"Suppose before we get to the village, all of you stop and I go ahead to see what's going on. I've been there before and know how to get back around the village without being seen." says Butch, in a low voice.

"It just might work, if you take your tow sack over your shoulder." I say. "You can tell anyone who wants to know you are leaving home, which is the truth! Check out the village, including the general store and pub, and get back to us. Then we will decide what to do."

The fire has burned low, the clouds are gone and the stars are bright when we end the talk.

"Look!" I say. Through the tops of the trees to the southeast, a huge yellow moon appears with the "Gap", that major milestone on our journey, silhouetted against it. Cumberland Mountain is safely behind us and the unknown lies ahead. We watch for a few minutes as the moon climbs higher, and the moonlight is bright enough we cast shadows. Shadows of the tall trees are all around us. It seems like a good omen to me.

"Let's thank the Almighty for our safe trip so far, and to help us as we go on." I say. I pray a brief prayer out loud.

Caleb takes the first watch as the rest of us crawl wearily into our bedrolls. I sleep a dreamless sleep.

CHAPTER 8

At daylight Butch stirred the coals and threw fresh wood on the fire. Soon it flared up and the rest of us are up and doing chores in preparation for the day's journey. We have hot coffee and jerky for breakfast, feed the animals, and pack up camp. We go over the plan again, then line out on the road. In about an hour we reach the bottom of the long slope. There was a valley with scattered clearings, but the road stays in the edge of the timber. We go on for another mile, then pull off the road into the trees and stop. Butch got his sack of belongings off the mule. We figure it will take a couple of hours for him to walk into the village of Yellow Creek, look around, circle and get back to us. We tell him to be sure and stop at the livery stable. He pets Buck, waves goodbye, and goes out of sight down the road. Buck whines and lies down by the wagon.

The morning is getting warmer. More leaves are beginning to show on the white oak, tiny purple violets are showing everywhere, and spring is definitely well along. We all sit around on a grassy spot and talk of the things that have happened in the last few days. Meeting the Allbrights on the other side of the Gap could be a real blessing for Jeff and Ruth as they look for land. In the future it will probably help all of us. Right now I would be glad to get this business behind us of the three riders, and get on down the road. At least two riders and one wagon pass going toward the Gap. Suddenly Buck jumped to his feet and dashed through the trees. Butch is coming at a trot. We all gather around to hear what he says.

"I didn't have to look around much," he says. "There was no one in the general store, then I went to the blacksmith shop and livery stable and visited with the smithy. I told him about the three riders who stopped in Pa's store a few days ago. He said they camped out in the trees for a couple of days at the edge of Yellow Creek, then just yesterday two of them saddled up and went on west. He said the third one was sitting around in the pub, but this morning he saddled his horse and left it in the livery stable right by the blacksmith shop. Then he went back to the pub. Two of them are the Allen brothers from Alabama and the third is from Georgia. They are all mean and not much liked around here."

"It's just like we figured," says Jeff. "If that scoundrel is waiting for us, as soon as he sees the wagon he will hightail it out of town to warn the others we are coming. Then they can ambush us."

"Pa always said "forewarned is forearmed," I say. "We don't want the wagon or Ruth and Naomi and the little ones involved in this. Let's try this: Caleb and I will ride ahead a little. Tim is best with the livestock, so he will follow a hundred yards behind us leading the mules, and you folks wait for several minutes and then come on in the wagon. Caleb and I are going straight to the livery, because that fellow is going to be looking for the third rider and the mules. When Tim comes in sight the thug will come straight to his horse in the livery, and we will be waiting to escort him to his friends."

"That's good," says Jeff, "but let's change the odds even more. The rider should be drunk by now, and probably easier to handle. To make sure, I'll have Ruth drive the wagon, with Naomi on the seat by her. I'll ride my horse in with Tim and the mules, and as soon as the three of you 'help' the rider away, I'll tie the mules at the livery, and go right back to the wagon. They don't know Butch is with us, so he can stay with the wagon, and keep one of the rifles handy. Buck will stay with them, and then we can take care of picking up some supplies and getting the mules and horses hooves and shoes checked by the smithy."

We all agree that plan is about the best we can do for now. I give Ruth some coins to buy supplies for us and to replace all we have eaten of theirs, and to buy some candy for the little ones and some ribbon for herself and Naomi. Then we start in the order we have planned, with Caleb and I in front on our horses, Tim and Jeff next with the mules, and Ruth driving the team and wagon after them, with Naomi on the seat beside her. The kids are in the wagon, the cow is tied behind, and a very serious Butch is walking behind with the long rifle over his shoulder, and Buck at his heels.

Just before we come out of the trees in sight of the village, Caleb and I spur our horses into a fast trot, and Jeff and Tim stop. We ride straight to the livery stable, and just as we get to it a rider steps out of the pub, which is about two buildings down. Just then Tim and Jeff come in sight with the mules. The rider cursed and starts for the livery stable at an unsteady run. We slip off our horses, pull them inside and pull out our pistols. As the rider runs through the door I put the barrel of the pistol right against his side.

"Put your hands high!" I tell him.

As he did Caleb stepped behind him, and reaching around pulled the riders pistol out of its holster. Then he jerked a big knife out of the riders belt scabbard.

"Look at that cord around his neck." I said. Caleb did and pulled out a short slim knife.

Caleb then grabbed a lead rope which was hanging by the door. Putting a fast loop in the end of it he slipped the loop over the man's head and around his neck. This started a new round of cursing, which Caleb promptly stopped by tightening the rope.

"As I remember, your name is Jake. Best way for you to keep from getting your wind shut off is to keep your mouth shut!" Caleb said.

Right then Tim and Jeff rode up with the mules. The smithy also came around the door corner from the blacksmith shop, and looked at what was going on. He grinned real big and turned back to the shop. Several men were walking toward the mules as Tim and Jeff tied them to the hitch rail in front. Looking back down the street we could see the team and wagon coming, with Ruth driving. Jeff rode back to meet them. Tim talked to the smithy a few minutes about the mules, and told him we would soon be back to settle up. Caleb pulled the riders saddled horse out of a stall and holds the reins. I motion with the pistol for him to mount up.

"Jake, we are going to ride out of here with you right in the middle. You try anything and we'll jerk you off the horse and drag you to death,"

I tell him. I take his pistol and rifle, pull the percussion caps off the nipples, then walk to the soft mud around the water trough. With him watching I stick the barrels of the guns as far into the mud as I can and then give them back to him. He is considerable sobered up by now and his face is an ugly sight to watch. He knows the guns will have to be cleaned before they can be safely fired. We all mount and wait for Jeff and the wagon. It soon pulls up. Jeff ties his team and horse, and Ruth and Naomi and the kids start for the general store. I tell Buck to stay by the wagon and then the four of us ride down the Road. Several people watch.

We keep Jake in the middle. He started to say something but a quick tug on the rope around his neck silenced him. The road entered the woods again and we are mighty careful. Soon there is a clearing and the road forks, with a road leading off to the southwest and the main Wilderness Road going on to the northwest. We stop and look it over carefully.

"Jeff said, if he remembered correctly, just on a little way past the fork there is a narrow place where they could ambush us easily," says Tim. There is lots of brush and heavy timber on the right side, so Tim and I tie our horses, leave Caleb with a firm hand on the rope around Jake's neck, and go ahead on foot. We go as softly as we can through the brush and trees, keeping a sharp watch all around. Excitement is high in us, and this is something we are both used too, as we are both hunters. Suddenly we hear low voices and the sound of horses stamping the ground and rattling their bridles. We creep closer and can see the two thugs sitting under a tree, waiting for their partner Jake to come along. Then we heard a yell, which sounded like it was choked off in the middle. The men started to stand up.

"Stop right where you are, and get your hands high!" I yelled. "We'll blow you to bits if you make a move. Don't look around."

Tim and I move up fast. Tim moves around and gets their pistols and big knives, then their long rifles, which are leaning against trees. Then he steps out in the road and halloos for Caleb. Soon Caleb and Jake come trotting up the road, with Jake looking a little worse for wear.

"He tried to yell, and I had to choke him down a bit," Caleb explained.

The Allen boys are getting tired of holding their hands up, and when I step back behind them, one of them suddenly whips around and quick as light has a knife in his hand and takes a vicious swipe at my throat. I duck and the blade tip went across my right cheek, making a shallow cut which immediately started pouring blood. I lost my balance and fall backward, and as he starts to follow, the barrel of Tim's pistol hits him in the head and he goes down in a heap. The other Allen was started toward the horses when Tim's pistol roared and the man's leg collapsed under him.

Meanwhile I am getting back on my feet. I grab up the knife the man dropped. It had been hidden in his jacket sleeve and my carelessness almost cost my life. The man Tim shot has a bullet through the calf of his leg, which is not a threat to his life, but is going to be mighty sore for a long time. We quickly go over all of them again, finding one more knife in the top of the other Allen's boot. We unload their guns by firing all of them and then stick the barrels deep in the mud at the edge of the road. Caleb and Jake have watched the entire show from their saddles. Caleb has a big grin on his face.

"You boys are sure some entertainment." He drawls.

We tie all three men's hands behind their backs, help them on their horses and then tie their feet together under the horses bellies. They curse and snarl the entire time, swearing vengeance in terrible ways. We slung their disabled long rifles over their shoulders. The three of us discuss our plan.

"This is the last time we are ever going to be really nice to you boys," I tell the thugs. "We were brought up to believe in the Good Book, and it says "Thou shalt not kill." That feller I shot over in Tennessee this spring didn't give me any choice, and I sure felt bad about killing him. Right now we would have been justified in killing all of you for what you planned on doing to us. You probably don't understand us letting you go, but remember this, any time we ever see you again we will think you mean to harm us in some way, and we're going to kill you. Right now we are going to take you down the road toward Tennessee a couple of miles and turn you loose. Figure you won't need these pistols and knives, so we're keeping them. We've got relatives and friends on the big rivers, and we're going to pass the word that you boys don't like the

Greenup's. So anytime you hear of one or meet up with one, you might want to take another trail."

With that note of warning I mount up and ride back toward town, while Caleb and Tim gather up the reins of the three riders and start leading them back to the road that went southwest to Tennessee. They will take them down that road for a way, then turn the horses loose and come back to Yellow Creek. When I ride into Yellow Creek the Clarks and Butch are waiting for me, along with the smithy and several other residents. They had heard the shots as we unloaded the Allen's guns, and Ruth cried when she saw my face and immediately got a pan of warm water from the general store and starts cleaning my wound. Another woman in town gave her some dried herbs and told her to make a poultice and put on my face to keep it from getting infected.

I tell them what happened, and that we would be coming through Yellow Creek later on as we got established. We are there another hour while the smithy finishes looking at our animals feet and shoes. During this time Ruth and Naomi get to visit with the women folk of the town and spread the word about what we are planning to do. When we finally get all harnessed and saddled back up and ready to leave, there are waves and calls and invitations to come back. I notice several pies have been put in the wagon under the watchful eye of Ruth.

Arriving at the junction and place of the planned ambush, we find Tim and Caleb just getting to the junction from the other road south. They have big grins on their faces, and we are all glad to join up again. Naomi hands them each a big stick of horehound candy.

"Let's go west!" yelled Caleb, and we line out down the road.

Three hours have gone by, and we are getting close to the larger village of Pineville. The road is much better, though still muddy with some large mud puddles. My face is sore, and it's a welcome relief when Jeff suggests we stop at a nice open meadow. There is a small stream crossing it, and lots of fire wood around the edges. There are the remains of a fireplace and some charred logs at the edge of the meadow. There is no sign of the storm clouds which we had yesterday. That means there will be some moonlight tonight, and the animals will be easy to watch. After camp is set up, Ruth cleans my knife wound again and puts a poultice on it.

"Ross, you are going to have a scar." Ruth said.

This immediately draws several sarcastic comments from Caleb and Tim, and even Jeff has to say something. We have a good supper, and after all is done and we are sitting around a big fire, Caleb tells us about the Allen boys.

"We rode fast after we left you, and had gone about four or five miles, when we rode into a camp of troops who were going to Texas. After we explained what happened, they laughed at the Allen's, and said they sure needed some help going south. So we didn't even untie the Allen's, just left them on their horses, and headed back up the road. It looked to me like the troops could sure handle them, and definitely were not afraid of them." Caleb laughed at the thought.

We spend another hour talking about the past and the future, and finally go to bed. I do not think of anyone, as my head hit a saddle blanket and that's all I remember.

CHAPTER 9

We are on the road early this morning. It's been four days since we had the encounter with the Allen boys at Yellow Creek. It's a great relief to not have to worry about them any more, and we did not want to waste any more time. With the Gap behind us, I wanted to get over in the Kentucky bluegrass country as fast as we could. The road is much better and we are making good time. For two days we put one of the mule teams pulling the wagon and let the horses rest. The road wound up and down over hills and valleys, crossing numerous small creeks and then the Rockcastle River, with another ferry crossing. It has not rained in this part of Kentucky like it did when we were crossing the Gap, and the water is lower in the creeks and river.

Ruth has been singing since she is no longer worried about the Gap and the Allen boys. She has a beautiful clear voice and Naomi is learning from her. Jeff even breaks into song once in a while, and so do I if it's a song I learned at Meeting House. We have talked about the different jobs facing us on a horse farm. Ruth and Naomi have decided they have to be able to ride horseback, as part of the operations of the farm. I remembered Ma was a good rider, though she did not ride a lot. Rachel, Tim's red haired step-sister, could ride about any horse we had, and usually rode a man's saddle. We don't have a side saddle with us. I have really begun to enjoy traveling with this family. Unless we meet strangers, both women travel with their sunbonnet's pushed back and long sleeves pushed up. Their arms and faces are getting as brown as hickory nuts. Having them along is definitely keeping the three of us cousins from some of our rowdy ways. We have not tossed any gunpowder in the fire, or thrown any food at each other.

Our saddle horses and mules are now in shape and trail wise, so they need little rest. Buck is lean and has proved he is fast enough to catch a cottontail rabbit, which he promptly devours. Our main concern is the milk cow, who does not give any milk and is due to calve any time. Butch is now driving Clark's wagon most of the time, so Jeff is able to ride his own saddle horse.

A rider caught up with us a couple of days ago, and after visiting a few minutes, rapidly left us behind. He was on business for Mr. Allbright and told us to contact Jason Campbell when we got in the vicinity of Crab Orchard. Last night a farmer told us we were about ten miles from Crab Orchard. As we ride this morning the country is opening out into larger pastures and more prosperous looking farms. A rider on a fine looking bay thoroughbred approaches us. As we meet he reins in and calls out:

"Are you the Greenup boys?"

"Yes, Sir." I reply. "And who might you be?"

"I'm Jason Campbell, the Overseer for Mr. Allbright. I had word you would be here, and have been looking for you."

He turned his horse and rode beside me.

"There is a turnout right ahead where you can pull your wagon and stock out and we can talk."

Campbell is a wiry, ruddy complexioned man, about my size, with an intense look about him. He ride's the big bay with ease, and soon we are all stopped on a grassy knoll overlooking a small valley. Across a pasture is a small frame house and log barn, with two smaller log outbuildings. The grass in the pasture is already tall and does not appear to have been grazed. We all dismount. Butch, Ruth, Naomi and the kids get off the wagon and walk to where we are standing.

Campbell pointed at the pasture and farmhouse.

"The man who owns this has left to go back to Virginia. He was a personal friend of Mr. Allbright." said Campbell. "He brought a beautiful young bride with him and worked very hard to make this a good horse farm. You can see there have not been any horses on the pasture this spring. His wife died in childbirth at Christmas, and he took the baby girl back east to his wife's parents. He sold the horses he owned, and gave Mr. Allbright the Power Of Attorney to take care of his affairs. This included selling the farm. I know Mr. Allbright has not offered it to anyone, and you must be some special folks for him to make the offer."

"Mr. Campbell, How much land and money are we talking about?" asked Jeff.

"There is a quarter of a section of land, one hundred and sixty acres. The pasture you see here is about fifty acres in prime bluegrass and timothy. The house and corrals take about five acres. There are about fifty acres of prime hardwood timber, and the rest is brush and cane, and a few acres that have been plowed. You see the creek running through the valley, and there are two springs. One is right past the house and runs into the creek. The other is to your right where you see the willows in the pasture." He paused, then looked at Ruth.

"Mrs. Clark, there is a nice garden patch just past the spring house. It's not too late to plow and plant it."

I look and we all look at the rolling green country side and the small farm. Campbell watched us. Finally I turn to Jeff.

"Jeff, when we left Pa, and Uncle Rich, our directions were to go west and find a favorable place to raise horses and mules. Then you talked to Pa and Uncle Rich, and caught up to us with the news we were all partners, and you were going to find a place in Kentuck to stop and start horse farming. We haven't heard from Mr. Campbell yet how much this would cost us, but it sure looks like it could be the place we need here as a start."

We all look at Jason Campbell. A big grin split his ruddy features.

"You lads are in luck. Mr. Allbright took a real likin to all of you. Ross, when he was a boy he personally met your Great Grandfather Greenup, who was the governor of Kentucky at the time. He is a friend of your Grandfather Greenup, who owns the Clinch River Ferry. He heard about your fracas with the hoss thieves over in the Tennessee mountains, and was mighty pleased to meet you. He wants five dollars an acre for the pasture land, and the timber land. That's five hundred dollars. He wants another hundred for the house and land it's on. For the rest of it he wants one hundred dollars. So the price is seven hundred."

He paused again and let that sink in. I'm thinking about how we are going to manage all of this. I have no idea how much cash Jeff has, since we have never discussed this. No one else knows I have eighty gold US eagles in the bag with my personal gear. There are also twenty gold coins of France. These came from the gold we found in the money belt of the man I killed. Pa, Uncle Rich, and Uncle Jeremy had a long discussion about the gold we found in the money belt. It has not yet been claimed and they decided we would use part of it for the time being, until there is an inquiry or some indication of legal ownership. No one except our family know about it. The money I'm using for the trip is mostly from the cash reward we got for the man Jenk.

Mr. Campbell spoke to us again.

"You don't need all that in cash now. The owner is no longer here and will not return. Mr. Allbright will be back the first of July. You will need one hundred dollars for him at that time. I can tell you now he will give you a hundred dollars for any one pair of these mules, as long as he can leave them on this pasture. The remaining five hundred is payable at one hundred dollars a year, starting a year from now, but he has enough work on his own farm, which is just over that ridge, for you to earn most of the payments. Now I doubt you will ever find a better bargain in this part of the country."

I breathe a sigh of relief and grin at Jeff.

"You folks might want to drive down to the house and look it over, then you can walk over the ridge behind it on the wagon road to our house. The Missus would like to have you for supper tonight."

Jason Campbell walked back to his horse, mounted, and cantered off on the Wilderness Road. I can't hold it in any longer. I let out a wild yell, and so do Caleb and Tim. Jeff grabbed Ruth in a bear hug, and Naomi, David and Elizabeth joined them. Buck was barking and jumping. Butch watched it all with a worried look on his face.

"Let's go!"

I mount up and wait for the rest. We ride out on the Wilderness Road about a quarter of a mile to where we can see a wagon track across the pasture to the farm house. Here there is a split rail fence between the pasture and the road, and a gate in the fence. We follow the track to the yard of the house. There is a split rail fence around the yard, and a hitch rail. We all dismount again and started exploring. There are several flowers blooming in the yard, and Ruth smiles as she looks at them. I follow Jeff, Ruth and Naomi into the farmhouse. There are curtains at the windows and it appears most of the furnishings are still there. The farmer must have been handy with tools because everything is handmade and well done.

In one bedroom is a bed frame with wooden slats and no bedding. I noticed Ruth as she looked around. It occurred to me she might be thinking of the young wife suffering in this room. Her eyes filled with tears and she hugged Jeff hard. I thought of the farmer, facing the future with a tiny baby, and having to move fast to keep it alive and get it back to family. He had to leave behind all the things he had worked so hard to make for his wife and their home. It made me think of how fast our lives can change, and I thought again of pulling the trigger and seeing a man die. I think of how important it is to tell my family how much they mean to me, and to take the opportunity to help ease difficulties of others, whenever I can.

I turn and walk out of the house. Elizabeth and David are running around in the yard and behind the house. There is an outhouse back against the fence on one side, and on the other side is a small stream coming from under another low building which is the spring house. I walk out to it, then farther on to the barn. The inside of the barn is as well made as everything else, with four horse stalls on one side, and a tack room and storage room on the other side. There is a hay mow overhead, and a door at each end big enough to drive a loaded wagon through. Another building appears to be a corn crib or smoke house, and next to it a chicken coop. There is a strong pole fence corral, with a pole gate which can be closed and chained.

It's about noon and Naomi is getting some food out of the wagon. I take a bucket from the kitchen and bring a bucket of cold water from the spring. We all gather by the wagon, and pass around a tin dipper, with each person getting a fresh dipper full of the delicious water. I look at Jeff and the others.

"Jeff, can you see anything wrong with this place, or with the offer from Mr. Allbright?"

"No, I can't. Since this is a partnership, I'm prepared to give Mr.

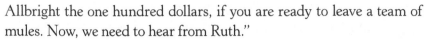

Allbright the one hundred dollars, if you are ready to leave a team of mules. Now, we need to hear from Ruth."

Ruth's sweet smile lit up her face.

"Jeff, and Ross, and all of you, I think the Lord is really watching over us. We have had some hard times, and will have more, but I'm a firm believer if we trust in the Lord, he will see us through." She paused and then said shyly,

"I would feel honored to keep a nice home in honor of the woman who started it. I think that's her grave over there." She pointed across the creek to where a wooden cross showed under a tall tree.

We were all silent for a few moments while we thought this over. Again I looked around at the others, then bowed my head, closed my eyes, and silently thanked God. I've done this a lot since killing the man on the Trace.

After we ate, the other fellows and I walked out to the barn and looked it over to see what needed to be done soon. One more stall could be added before winter, and the roof extended out for a shelter without taking on a major construction job. Jeff planned on bringing his horses from Tennessee before they foaled. He would have to know where he could get hay in the fall. He also would have to get several acres plowed and planted to oats right now, or be able to buy some later. I think Pa and Uncle Rich will want to come out to look the property over and help some. The garden patch has a rail fence around it and will be easy to plow and plant. Across the creek and behind some small trees and brush is a field of about ten acres which had been plowed last fall but not planted. It will be best for the oat crop.

We look and talk and walk. Then we go back to the house. Ruth and Naomi are in tears. They found a small book which the young wife had written in, telling of her joy at becoming a mother. Jeff stays with them to console them, and the rest of us hurry to unhitch and unsaddle. We hobble all the horses and mules and turn them out on the good pasture. I put the bell on my Morgan, and soon they all busy cropping the good bluegrass. Jeff examined the cow carefully and decided to fasten her in one of the stalls. We talk about leaving Butch to keep watch, but decide to let him go along to the Campbell's with us. I tie Buck to a wagon wheel and tell him to watch. Then we all walk out along the road which leads over the ridge.

When we get to the top of the ridge, we stop and take in the view. A split rail fence separates this property from the Campbell's. Ahead of us to the west, is a large pasture with several others visible through hedges. The sun is getting low over a large frame farmhouse which can be seen about a mile away, and closer to us and just below the top of the ridge we are on is a smaller log house with a number of outbuildings and corrals. This is evidently the Campbell's place. I look back east, at the farm which lay behind us in the evening shadows, and think of all that can be done. It sure looks like a place where a person would never be out of a job.

We are greeted at the front gate by a small, motherly woman with a big smile.

"I'm Belle Campbell," she said, as she welcomes us all, and gives the kids a big hug. We go into the spacious house, where a long table is set for the grownups, with a small table on the porch for David and Elizabeth. I noticed it made Naomi feel important to be included with the rest of us. A big, six foot tall young man comes in with Jason Campbell, and is introduced as Stewart. He is sure the image of his father, and as good natured as his mother. A small, middle aged black woman named Lucy is working in the kitchen. We are not used to sitting in chairs and it sure feels awkward, but a table full of good food had us all comfortable in a few minutes. Jason Campbell asked a short blessing for the food, and we dig in to the stack of fried chicken, heaping bowl of mashed potatoes, and huge biscuits.

All of us are soon full. Mrs. Campbell gestured at the black servant, and told us she was nursing her own child when the farmer's wife died, and had immediately volunteered to nurse the new baby. In fact, she and her husband accompanied the farmer and the baby back to Virginia, and then returned.

Jason suggested we were all tired and excited, and it would be best if he came over to the farm the next morning with the papers, and we could work out details then.

"That will be fine." I replied. "The three of us are going to stay at least a couple of days and help Jeff settle in."

We thanked Mrs. Campbell for the delicious supper, and started back over the hill. When we got to the top of the ridge we hear the cow bawl. Jeff listens a moment, then starts at a run for the barn, with the rest of us trailing behind. Jeff lights a lantern and shadows from its light move on the walls as he goes in the stall where the cow is. We start getting our bedrolls out. Ruth and Naomi elect to sleep in the wagon till they have time to get the house cleaned and in the order they want it. The horses and mules have their heads down, still eating the good grass. I untie Buck and he makes the rounds and comes back where we are putting the bedrolls down. We're too tired and full to build a fire. I am just stretching out when Jeff walks over with the lantern. I hear him call out to Ruth and Naomi and the kids.

"We have a fine little heifer calf!" he says. "Tomorrow you can think of a name for her, and in a couple of days we will start getting some milk again."

It takes me awhile to go to sleep. I think of all that has happened in the past few weeks, and especially in the past nine days since we left Pa and Ma. I think of them, and know they are wondering if we are alright. I remember Rachel touching my face with her fingertips as we were leaving, and how her eyes had tears in them. What a great time she would have, helping on a new place like this.

CHAPTER 10

It's barely light when I wake. Nobody else is stirring, but when I move and raise my head from the saddle blanket, Buck is right by me. I scratch his ugly head and he grins with those big sharp teeth shining, then trots off to check the camp. The sky is clear and I see the first rays of sunlight touch the ridge west of us, then start marching down. It's going to be a warm day. Walking to the spring I get a long drink of the clear, cold water, and wash my hands and face. Probably Pa is doing the same thing at the bench in front of the kitchen right about now. He and I would be talking about the weather and what work we had for the day. This time of the day I feel a little lonely without him, and sure would like to get his ideas on what we are doing here. Wide awake now, I see the horses and mules standing by the fence watching me. They nicker at me as I walk into the barn to see the new calf. She is lying on straw in a corner of the stall, and her huge liquid brown eyes and fawn color are just like her ma's.

The stock nicker again and crowd around me as I go through the gate into the pasture. They nuzzle my hands and pockets, hoping for oats or an apple. It's a pleasure to not have to get them saddled and ready to go. I pat their necks and dodge flying hooves as they jostle for attention. They cavort and toss their heads as we walk toward the stream and spring in the middle of the pasture, and Buck runs in front of us. The spring is at the edge of the stand of willows, and with a little shovel work and a few rocks can be developed into a good water hole.

The sun is up now, and shining on the house. I see smoke rising

70

from the kitchen chimney. Ruth said she and Naomi would fix breakfast for all of us in the house, and I see her and Naomi carrying a sack of flour and a side of bacon from the wagon. Ruth is singing and her clear voice carries in the cool air. It appears to me she is mighty happy to have a house to move into. I guess maybe most women are like that. David and Elizabeth are rubbing their eyes as they walk to the house. Jeff, Caleb, Tim and Butch are filling nosebags with oats for the animals. The horses and mules see them and leave me in a wild thunder of hooves as they race to the fence. Watching all this fills me with a great feeling of pleasure, and I walk slowly to join the others.

After a good breakfast of bacon, hot biscuits, and dried apple pies, all of us, including Ruth and Naomi, settle down outside with a mug of hot coffee, to wait for Jason Campbell. The flowers smell good as they open in the morning sun, and there is the hum of honey bees and several big black and yellow bumble bees.

"Jeff," I say. "Lets get a plan going. Ruth is going to need some help, and there is a lot to do before we leave. I figure we need to stay at least two days, and more likely five or six days."

Ruth smiles at me as I say this. She and Naomi are both dressed for some serious house cleaning, with their dresses tied up and their hair tied back out of the way. Their eyes are shining with excitement at starting a new home. Jeff waits for her.

"First, I would like the big iron kettle in the back yard filled with water, and a fire built under it. Naomi and I need Butch with us today. He can help us move bedding and food supplies out of the wagon and keep the fires going."

Butch looked happy with that announcement from Ruth, but Caleb spoke right up, volunteering to help them whenever he could, and grinning at Naomi.

"Ross, I guess you and Tim and me better plan on staying right here till Jason gets here, and we can get all the paper work done. We can use one of your mule teams to start plowing the garden, and let my team rest a couple of days." said Jeff. "There comes Jason and Stewart."

Jason is on his big horse and Stewart is driving a team of nice roan colored mules, hitched to a farm wagon. As they rattle into the yard we can see plow handles and a harrow sticking out of the wagon.

71

"Mornin Folks," Jason shouted as he dismounted and tied his horse. He grabbed a leather saddlebag and walked over.

"Mornin Mr. Campbell. We are just having a council of war." I say.

Ruth hurried to get them a mug of coffee.

Briefly outlining our plans, I tell him we are ready to start. Butch starts filling the kettle with water, and building a fire under it. Caleb went to take his team into the barn breezeway and get them brushed down and harnessed. Then he will hitch them to the plow and start on the garden. Ruth, Naomi and the kids start moving food supplies and bedding out of the wagon. "Stewart is going to start on your oat field," said Jason, "and you can buy the seed from us. Its in the wagon."

Stewart grinned and left, and Mr. Campbell, Jeff, Tim and I start going over the papers. It is a good thing Ma had schooled us boys, and I have no trouble reading the land description, deed, and contract Mr. Campbell had with him. We show him the letter of partnership between Pa, Uncle Rich, and Jeff Clark, showing Tim and I represent our Pa's in any business transaction. The contract spelled out all Mr. Campbell had told us the day before. We sign and date it, and Ruth, Naomi and Butch witness it.

A wild yell from the barn brings me up and grabbing for a pistol. We are all on our feet when Caleb comes racing out of the barn, and from the inside we can hear mules braying and hooves thudding. Ruth and Naomi come running from the house and David and Elizabeth are running toward the house, with Buck right by them. Caleb is wildly waving his arms and slapping with his hat, and I instantly know what the problem is.

"Don't come over here," I yell, and about that time two big mules, one with a collar on, come running and bucking out of the barn.

"Get in the house and close the door," I yell at everyone, and we all crowd inside. We watch through a window as Caleb races along the road, and the mules scatter into the pasture. In a minute Caleb slows down and stops the wild waving. He waits a few more minutes, then starts toward the mules. We all cautiously walked back outside.

"He got into a hornet, or a bee nest, and he is going to be hurting," I say. Ruth immediately takes charge.

"Oh that poor boy. Naomi, find the baking soda. Jeff, or one of you fellows, get a chaw of tobacco going. Get Caleb over here and we'll try to keep him from hurting as much as we can. Butch, get a bucket of fresh water."

Everyone hurries to do her bidding. Tim and I start to help round up the mules. Jeff cautiously goes into the barn to see about the cow and calf. Caleb is a sight. There are huge welts on his face and arms.

"One of the mules kicked into a bumble bee nest," he said. He goes to the house while Tim and I take care of the mules.

When we get back to the house Caleb is enjoying the attention of both women as they cover his stings with baking soda solution, and where they can, hold chewed tobacco in place over the stings with a cloth bandage. His shirt is off and they counted over twenty big welts on his body, arms and head. I told him the mules were stung as bad as he was, but wouldn't get sick. We have the mules harnessed and hitched to the plow. Tim volunteers to do the plowing, as past experience tells us Caleb is probably going to be sick for a few hours. Jeff said the big bees had missed the cow and calf while they concentrated on chasing Caleb.

We finish our business with Mr. Campbell, and he leaves for home, after offering to help in any way he can.

"Mr. Campbell, what is the danger of thieves or rustlers here?" I ask him, as we walk out of the yard. "We stay armed all the time, but I wondered if we need to put the stock up at night, or keep a watch."

He frowned as he thought about it. "Always have a side arm, and I always put my stock in a locked corral at night. That dog of yours is priceless." As he started to mount he looked around and grinned. "You have a bumble bee nest to get rid of before you put anything back in the barn."

With that bit of advice he mounted the big horse, waved goodbye, and went up the road.

I'm busy at the spring in the pasture when I hear Naomi's sweet voice calling us to supper. Jeff and Tim and I smoked out the bumble bees right after Mr. Campbell left. It was a big nest and we had each been stung a couple of times. We tore out the nest and killed all the bees we could find.

Tim is just now finished plowing and harrowing the garden. I see him un-harnessing the mules. Stewart Campbell went home about an hour ago with his mules. He will come back in the morning, and he and Tim will finish plowing and harrowing the oat field. Then we can all help plant the oats and get it done in a hurry.

Jeff has worked on the barn all day. He put the Jersey cow in the pasture to graze, but kept the calf in the barn so the mules wouldn't bother it.

I pick up my tools and walk to the house. It's been a warm, clear day, but there is a cool evening breeze starting up. Caleb is sitting on the porch when I walk to the house. His face is flushed and his eyes are bloodshot and tired looking. Naomi has kept applying cool wet cloths to his head, but it's going to take some time to get all the bumble bee poison out of his system. David and Elizabeth have been kept busy, and are now sitting on the edge of the porch by Caleb.

I walk around to the back door and stop in amazement. Everything I can see in the house appears to have been scrubbed. I pull off my muddy boots and walk inside. Oak wood is blazing in the fireplace, and pots are hanging on the andirons. Ruth had soaked a pot of beans and they are simmering with a ham hock from our supplies. There are biscuits ready to put in the dutch oven, and I smell cooked apples. Coffee is bubbling. It all smells like home and my mouth waters.

Ruth and Naomi look exhausted. Wisps of damp curls cling to their flushed faces. They are smiling, and I walk over to them and give them each a big hug. All at once there are two pairs of soft, young arms around my neck. Ruth kisses me on the cheek and Naomi smiles shyly. *I'm going to miss these women more than I thought.* The others are in the room now, and it's sure enough crowded with Jeff, Butch, Tim and I. Caleb and the children are still outside. Ruth looked around at this room full of men, and her eyes are shining again.

"I just love all of you," she said, as Jeff put his arm around her. "The biscuits will be done in a few minutes, so help yourselves to the coffee and beans, and go on outside. Naomi will bring the biscuits out. There's stewed dried apples in the other pot." We loaded our plates and went out on the porch with Caleb and Buck. Soon Naomi brought out the biscuits and a plate for Caleb. There was no more talking. We finished and Butch gathered up all the plates and hardware and put them in a pot of hot water. Ruth sure had things organized.

"David, Elizabeth, Naomi and I are going to take baths tonight. Butch is going to keep the big black kettle full of hot water for several days, so you fellows can take a bath whenever you want." announced Ruth.

She and Naomi and the children immediately went inside to the back bedroom where they had set the copper washtub. The rest of us sat around for another hour, watching the last light of the sun fade out, swapping yarns and relaxing, before rolling out our bedrolls. We made sure the horses and mules were in the corral, and the cow and calf in the barn, and then no more voices were heard. As I lay in my bedroll I hear a Whip-poor-will give its lonely call, and another answers, and then an owl hoots. A few night insects are beginning to call, and I drift into a deep sleep.

As usual it's first light of dawn when I wake to a clear day. I hear somebody moving around in the house. A big red tail hawk is circling above the buildings, barely moving his wings as he looks us over. Back in the woods the hoot owl is saying goodnight, and Buck growls a friendly growl.

The cold spring water sure makes me wide awake. I call to Caleb and Tim as I walk to the barn. All the animals crowd to the corral fence to watch and Buck eases over to touch noses with them. Jeff walks out and looks at the cow and calf. The others are up by now and we get oats to the animals that are working today. I've been here two days and am already beginning to feel at home.

After breakfast we all sit on the porch, drink coffee and talk about what needs to be done. Caleb feels better this morning and is ready to go to work. He and Stewart will finish harrowing the oat field and then we will all help get it planted. Butch will help Ruth and Naomi, keeping water hot in the big black kettle, and whatever else they need. David and Elizabeth will help hang wet clothing on the fence and all the other chores Ruth has for them.

"Jeff, how soon are you going after your horses?" I ask. "We need to get word to Pa and Uncle Rich about this place and see what they want to do."

"If we get the oats and garden planted and everything fixed we can in two days, I think I ought to be able to leave in about four days. Since Butch is here I feel easier about leaving Ruth and Naomi and the kids. Here comes Stewart."

Stewart is driving his team of mules ahead of him as he walks through the pasture. Another man is with him and is carrying a sack over his shoulder. Butch growls and paces toward the barn till I call him back. Stewart leaves the team tied at the barn and he and the other man walk to the porch.

"Mornin', everyone" Stewart shouts. "This is my Uncle Jake, my Ma's brother. He lives on the place the other side of us. Missus Clark, Ma sent you a present. It's a couple of things you might need."

Jacob tipped his big, floppy brimmed hat to Ruth and Naomi. Strange noises came from the sack as he took it off his shoulder. Kneeling, he reached in the sack and drew out a squawking, flopping, red hen with her legs tied together. Then he brought out a small, covered, woven hickory basket. Opening it he showed Ruth eight chicken eggs, nestled in grass.

"Missus Clark, this old hen has been sitting on these eggs for a week, so they should hatch in another two weeks. Belle wanted you to have them so you could get a start on a flock."

Elizabeth and David clapped and squealed.

He pulled another basket out. "This is a dozen fresh eggs for all of you to enjoy."

Jacob stood and bowed to Ruth with a flourish of his hat. Ruth clapped and smiled her thanks.

"One other thing," Jake said. "We're having a hoe-down at our place tomorrow night. You are all invited, and it's a good time to meet the neighbors."

This was exciting news to all of us, but it immediately makes me feel a little uneasy. Pa and Ma and my brother and me would go to the shin-digs at home, but we usually left early. Often there would be some hard liquor brought to the party, and sometimes there would be trouble because of it.

One of the few times I saw Pa really get angry was at one of the dances, when a fellow from over on the next creek, who had been drinking, made some comment about how pretty Ma was, and it was a shame she didn't have a "man" to take care of her. Pa is about five-feet-ten, and has been either logging or breaking horses since he was a little feller. His arms are big, and hard as iron. First thing I knew he picked up the man in a bear hug, walked out the door holding the kicking, yelling drunk, and threw him bodily over a fence and into a creek. Everybody cheered when he walked back into the room.

In a few minutes it got real quiet. The drunk came in with a rush, and had a Bowie knife in his hand. Pa looked at some of the drunk's friends and asked them to take him away. They made another huge mistake by laughing. The drunk lunged at Pa, who easily stepped aside, and as he did, reached out and grabbed the man's arm. Pa jerked his arm behind his back and clamped down with those big hands. I heard bones break, and then a scream from the drunk.

On the way home Josh and I got a strong lecture on the evils of alcohol, and how it made men do crazy things.

"Oh, Pa and Ma may come over awhile after dinner," said Stewart as he and Jake struck out for the oat field.

Ruth, Butch, David and Elizabeth hurried to the chicken house to fix a nest for the hen and eggs. Buck was there to protect them. Naomi went in the house to clean up the breakfast dishes. Caleb harnessed the team to help Stewart finish the oat field. Jeff, Tim and I poured some more coffee and went to lean on the corral fence while we discussed our plans. Caleb left the mules standing and came over.

"Say fellows, I've been thinking. You know, my Pa and me are not legal partners in this deal. The three of you have a personal interest because of the horses and mules. The team of mules I have belong to my Pa and me. They are good mules and I brought them to sell or trade for land. Pa is not interested in raising mules. It's really hard work and most of the time he does not feel like it because of his war wounds. So I've got a proposition for you."

He stopped, and sure had our attention as we drank coffee and waited. "Let me go to work for you right here, and keep my mules here, to either sell or trade. I would like to work into some kind of partnership with all of you, because I'm sure feelin left out. I could go with Jeff to get his horses and help bring them back here, along with Uncle Jim and Uncle Rich's horses and mules. I could work to help pay for this place, or whatever you like. Think it over and let me know."

Caleb left for the field. I watched him go and said;

"Guess I'm not too surprised at that little speech. I've been expecting it." I said.

Jeff grinned. "I think we all have. What do you think?" he asked.

Tim spoke up. "I think it would work. Caleb is a good horseman, and understands the animals, but it would need to be all right with our Pa's. Family agreements can get kinda sticky sometimes, and Caleb's Pa is sure not interested in joining us."

"Tim, if it's OK with Jeff and Ruth, lets you and me leave the morning after the party." I said. "I'm anxious to get on the trail."

"Let's all go to Crab Orchard that morning, get acquainted with the town, buy some supplies, and you fellows go on from there." said Jeff.

"Meanwhile, let's ride the property line this morning and make sure the fences are all in place. Then we will have a good idea of the lay of the land."

We took our coffee mugs to the house. Naomi was bustling around in the kitchen, but had taken time to set a small mirror on the table. I bent down and looked at my reflection, and was shocked. I suddenly realized I hadn't seen my face since leaving home, and that's been almost two weeks. My hair looks like a haystack, and my few whiskers sure need shaving or trimming. The knife scar on my right cheek is barely healed and shows red through the dark skin.

Jeff sees my expression and laughs.

"Guess you boys need a little shaping up. Maybe tonight and tomorrow we can all get trimmed and curried. I've got a pair of shears with my horse shoeing outfit, and I bet Ruth would be glad to help."

Naomi was laughing, and about then Ruth walked in.

"Sure will. You boys look like a bunch of curly wolves."

They all laughed and I felt my face growing red as I got out the door fast.

About noon we were all back at the house, except Stewart and Jake. Soon we saw a buggy coming from the Campbell's, with Jason Campbell driving and his wife Belle sitting by him. Ruth came out in the yard to greet them. Belle gathered Elizabeth and David up in a big hug and they all went in the house.

Jason Campbell appeared mighty pleased with the work done around the house and barn.

"I met Stewart on his way home and he told me the oats were in and the garden plowed. Belle brought some cabbage and onion settings, and some radish seeds for your garden. I brought some tobacco plants so you can at least raise your own." he said.

We walked toward the barn and corral, and he looked at the sky.

"It's getting mighty sticky this afternoon. We can probably expect some thunderstorms to build fast."

Naomi called from the porch.

"You men come and get some of the cake Mrs. Campbell brought."

There was a near stampede as we headed back. While we were eating cake and drinking coffee we told Mr. Campbell of the change in plans with Caleb. He grinned and took another huge bite of cake.

"Ross, you and your cousins are already known here. I was in Crab Orchard this morning picking up supplies, and the storekeeper, Julius Rubin, asked if I had seen you yet. You may even have some kin folk here."

Another bite of cake.

"Something else you need to know. Belle's brother Jake and his wife have three daughters, and the two oldest are sure looking for husbands. You lads better watch careful, or they might put a loop on you. There's not many young bucks around here."

"Now Jason, you stop that." said Belle, but she grinned and winked at Ruth. "Why don't you folks come over after chores tomorrow afternoon, and we will all go together. We can introduce you around. Ruth told me she taught some book learnin where they used to live. We haven't had a school-marm since last winter, so maybe she can have the job for next fall."

After some more talk they climbed in the buggy and left. I looked at some big thunderheads building in the southwest.

"Ruth, if you want to we could all help you get your garden planted before it rains." I said.

"Oh yes, lets do that. Then if Jeff will get his horse shears I'll trim everyone's hair."

By time to light the lamps we were done with the garden and hair trimming.

"Tim and Caleb, let's go through all our tack in the morning and sort it out." I said. "I'm sure going to miss having you along, Caleb, but I've been thinking it over and think this is a good way to do it. It's sure safer with three of us, but we will have Buck, and Tim and I are going to have to be extra careful. Now we can take whatever you brought, since our loads are all getting lighter, and carry everything on our four mules."

Lightning flashed and thunder rolled and we all made a dash for the barn, getting there just as a solid black wall of rain marched across the pasture and slammed into the barn and house.

CHAPTER 11

This morning the storm is passed and we are sorting through equipment, packing and re-packing. I still haven't told Caleb or the Clarks about the gold. I tell Tim about it now and we agree to say nothing more. It's divided in packages in two bags of lead for casting bullets. Finally everything is together. Our four mules are going to be carrying heavy loads for awhile.

The six mules we brought are all about the same size. We decide to leave the pair Caleb brought as the part payment for the farm. Caleb will be here with them till our Pa's and Jeff decide what to do. Our teams will carry our packs. They are good mules and I look forward to working them. Butch has been keeping the big kettle full of hot water. So we move the tub out to the barn and get cleaned up. Finally we are ready. Jeff took the cover off the wagon and is driving it with his family. Butch is riding Jeff's saddle horse, and Tim, Caleb and I are on our own horses. The mules are in the corral, with the gate chained and Buck on guard.

The Campbell's are ready when we get there and we make quite a procession. We ride on about a mile to the other side of the valley. We see light and hear music coming from a big barn. I look carefully at the saddle horses and wagons and buggies parked around the barn. A few months ago I would not have even been concerned, but recent happenings have made me mighty cautious.

"Tim and Caleb, and you too, Butch, look everything over real careful. If any of us see any signs of trouble, let the others know, and we'll get out of here."

Plank tables are set up, with mounds of food. I smell fried chicken, and see platters of sliced pork and venison, and baskets of corn pone. There are a lot of folks here. Sure enough, here comes Jake and his wife, with three pretty, yellow haired girls trailing behind. They are all well filled out, and their dresses show them off in grand style. We get introduced to Jake and then Jason Campbell leads us onto the dance floor and stops the music. There must be at least fifty men, women, and children, with more coming.

"Folks, these are our new neighbors, just bought the James place, next to ours."

He then went through the introductions, and the music started again. Before I can even get to the food, a slim, pretty young woman, with curly black hair and blue eyes grabs my hand.

"I'm Samantha Ellen Corbitt, and we are probably cousins," she announced, and we were dancing.

Now I'm built like Pa, though not as strong, but well coordinated. I can't say I'm much of a dancer, but managed to get through the first round on the hard packed dirt floor. Then I headed for the food, with Samantha right by me.

"You and me have the same Great-Grandpa Greenup. My Ma was a Greenup, but from Great-Grandpa's Cherokee wife side of the family."

Now this is news to me, but while I loaded my plate with fried chicken, sliced pork, cucumber pickles, and hot corn pone, she talked quietly, and directly to me. Her face is most amazing. She beams and her eyes sparkle, but I figure they would snap if she got upset.

"The Allen knife left you with a permanent reminder, didn't it?

I stared at her in amazement.

"How did you know about that?"

She smiled at me.

"You are really well known here. Mr. Allbright's son, Matthew, returned about a week ago. He was with Mr. Allbright when they met you at the Gap. He heard what you boys did to the Allen's and has told the story around here. My Pa is one of the fiddlers, and he and Ma keep track of the Greenup's. So he got out the family Bible, and right away knew who you and your kin were."

My surprise didn't keep me from piling on more food. Samantha continued.

"Don't look directly at them, but see the thin, dark man and his wife. Their name is Quintara, and they came here from the Spanish colonies. They own a small horse farm, and seem to always have money. He is a trader, mostly of horses. He seemed to have a lot of interest in the story of you killing someone, and is not happy with the Greenup boys."

This really got my attention. We walked out the big open doors into the warm spring night. I am still carrying a plate and was making good use of the food on it. From the friendly comments of others its apparent Samantha is a favorite around here. When we are out of hearing of anyone else, Samantha said:

"Ross, my Mother and Grandmother both had the 'gift' of understanding some things other people didn't. It has been starting to happen to me in the past year. We are all strong Believers, and think this is a gift from God."

She stopped again, and I realize I haven't said a half dozen words since we started.

"Ross, I'm telling you to be careful. You don't know me, but I feel you are going to have trouble, starting with Quintara. Always keep a close watch, and always be armed and ready! Oh, and just call me Sammie. Everyone else does."

Sammie reached up and touched the fresh scar on my face, then took hold of my hand. Her hands were strong and firm, and the touch on my face made my heart speed up some. The last touch like that was when Rachel said goodbye.

"Ross, the Quintara's son, Roberto, has taken a liking to me, and keeps pushing to court me. Since the word of you killing the man came out, and then you showing up here, he has really been giving me a bad time, and I'm getting scared. The sooner you leave here, the better. He hasn't been here yet tonight. Are you sure everything is alright at your place?"

I thought this over.

"Sammie, introduce me to your Pa and Ma as soon as you can. Don't tell anyone else, but Tim and me are leaving in the morning. And don't be surprised if we kinda fade out of here."

I take one last huge bite of dried peach cobbler and we go back inside. When the music stops, Sammie brings her folks over where Tim and I are standing. She looks a lot like her Ma. Instantly I like her folks, and see the strong family resemblance between her Ma and my Pa, even with the evident Indian blood. When the music started again, I look around, see Caleb with Naomi, and David and Elizabeth with some other children. Caleb and the family were all leaving early. I drift around where Tim is, say a word to him, and we both ease out, walk our horses a little way along the road, then mount and ride hard for our place. There is no moonlight and we get to the top of the ridge above the house. When we stop we hear a horse coming hard behind us. We both grab our pistols and wait.

"Ross, it's me, Sammie!"

I am sure surprised but don't say anything. We dismount, and tie the horses. Buck is howling from inside the barn. We walk quietly down the hill toward the barn. Sammie is holding her skirts tight so they won't catch and make noise. She stays behind me as I go around one side of the barn and Tim the other. I hear a horse move right in front of me, and can dimly see it tied to the corral fence. Then I see a sudden glow of fire and hear a yell from Tim, and a string of Spanish words. Running around the corner of the barn I run straight into someone running my way, and we both go down. About then Tim piled right on top of us, and there is a mad scramble. Next thing I know Tim has the other person by the throat and is clamping down. Soon it gets quiet, except for hard breathing and the crackle of flames.

"Get the water bucket from the house, while I pull this hay out." I yell at Sammie.

Tim is fully occupied with tying up the person we captured, and who is still unconscious. We soon have the burning straw separated, and with plenty of water have the fire out. We can hear Buck jumping and snarling from the stall where he is shut up, and in the stall next to it a lantern is burning. I let Buck out and have to keep a tight hold on his collar to keep him from the throat of the unconscious man. When Tim holds the lantern up where we can see his face, Sammie exclaims:

"Roberto!

The stall with the lighted lantern is where all our packs are. We can see they have been gone through, though it does not look like the gold was discovered.

"Samantha, thanks to you, we haven't lost anything, but if we had been two minutes later it would all have gone up in smoke." I say. "Now you get back to the dance as fast as you can, and we will be along in a few minutes."

She nods with immediate understanding, and slips out into the dark. Tim gets some more water and we pour it on Roberto's face. He begins to moan and gasp, and finally comes around. By this time I'm beginning to work up a real temper tantrum. I take a pistol and knife from the Spanish style sash around his waist, then grab him by the front of the shirt and shake him hard.

"I don't know who you are, but we shore intend to find out. One yell out of you and Tim will finish what he started!" I growl in his face. "Tim, get that rope over the rafter, and let's string him up till he decides to talk a bit."

Tim throws the rope over the rafter and in the dim lantern light I make a crude loop and drop it over the man's head. Tim pulls up on the rope, and as he does I put the point of the knife against the man's throat.

"What's your name?" I snarl.

He chokes and Tim slacks off a bit.

"Don't kill me." He quavers. "I'm Roberto Quintara."

"So, Roberto, you know we should slit your throat. You were trying to rob us and burn our barn. We are going to take you to the dance and tell everyone there what you just did, and see what they want to do with you."

He moaned.

"Let's untie his feet, and get him on his horse. Then we can decide what to do with him." says Tim. I can tell he is afraid of what I'm going to do to this scoundrel.

We keep his hands tied behind him, then set him on his horse and lead him up the hill to where ours are tied. He does not talk, but moans quietly as we mount and start back toward the dance. We stop when we are some distance from the dance and discuss the situation. I'm cooled down a bit, and we decide since we are strangers it would not be good for us to take him in front of everyone. So Tim stays with him and I ride on to the dance and ease in the door. Jason Campbell is close, and I get his attention. We step back outside and I quickly describe what happened.

"You did right" he exclaims. "There would be hell to pay if you disgraced his father by bringing him inside. Let me have him now, and you folks go on home. I know Jeff is getting anxious to leave. I'll get the Quintara's and they can take the boy home."

We step back inside and I walk around, saying goodnight to folks till I find Samantha.

"Thanks for making me feel at home. We are probably going to be on the road in the morning, but will see you when we get back."

I take her hand and hold it a moment as she smiles and her eyes search my face. Then I turn and leave, as Caleb and the Clarks are also leaving. Caleb and I walk along till Jason Campbell catches up with us. Mr. Quintara is with him and we walk to where Tim is holding the horse with Roberto sitting on it. I get right in front of Mr. Quintara.

"Mr. Quintara, Mr. Campbell and your son can tell you what has happened this evening. Now the Clark's and us Greenup boys are peaceful, God fearing people, and we don't get riled up very easy. What your son has tried to do to us tonight has got us considerable upset, and if it had been someone else's property he tried to steal and burn, he would probably be dead. He's young and foolish, but if we have anymore trouble around here the first place we are going to ride to is your place. We just want to be good neighbors, and hope you will do the same."

As I finish the Clarks and Butch ride up. Caleb and I mount, and we start back to the farm, describing everything to the Clarks as we ride.

Early the next morning we leave the place in the care of Butch, figuring no one is going to bother anything now. Jeff and I have a discussion about leaving Buck, but with both Caleb and Butch staying with them I feel we need Buck with Tim and me. I do think Jeff needs to get a dog as soon as he can. Jeff is driving the empty wagon, with Ruth and Naomi on the seat with him, and the kids behind them. Tim and I are each leading two mules, with heavy packs on each of them. It takes a while to get to Crab Orchard, and we are ready for a bite to eat when we do. It doesn't take long to find a boarding house, and the lady cooking there soon has a big feed on the table for us. She is mighty friendly and her and Ruth are soon chattering away. Jeff, Tim and I look around at the general store, and get acquainted around town. There is a big blacksmith shop and livery stable. We make a point of meeting the town Marshall, and letting him know who we are. He is another who has already heard some stories about us. Tim and I lay in some corn meal, bacon and coffee and other supplies.

Then its time for Tim and me to leave. We sure hate to say goodbye to Ruth and Naomi and the kids. David and Elizabeth cry, and hang on to Buck, but Jeff promises to get them a dog as soon as he can. We hug everybody, then mount up and ride slowly out of town. When town is well behind us we start moving faster till we find a pace that seems to suit all the animals and then settle down to a steady ride.

CHAPTER 12

It's good to be on the road again. I've sure enjoyed the family company for the past few weeks. Since we are in business together it makes it all the more important for us all to share the same beliefs. At the same time, I'm ready to get on with going west. Tim appears to feel the same way, and I think the animals sense it because they are stepping right out. Buck trots behind the mules or occasionally comes up by me. It's a warm spring afternoon and we can smell new plants and leaves as we ride.

This is the first time we have really had a chance to talk since we left Grandpa Greenup's on the Clinch River. We go over all that's happened in the last three weeks, and it's hard to believe. Pa has always taught me most things don't happen by chance. They are all part of God's plan for each of our lives, and we need to continually learn from every experience. I've got enough stored up to think about for a long time. For instance, finding the farm in the valley where the price was right, and where we already have good neighbors. It shore doesn't seem to me just a chance we stopped where there are Greenup relatives we didn't even know about.

We still have the gold to think about, and I wonder if the Quintara's know something about it.

It's almost dark when we see a farm house with several horses in the pasture, just a short distance from the road. The farmer is friendly, and willing to let us put our stock in the pasture and our packs in the barn. We pay him, and before we get our bedrolls spread in the hay his wife comes out and offers us some cold cornbread and buttermilk. We sure aren't slow about accepting that offer, and she gives Buck a big chunk of cornbread and some meat scraps. Soon after we are rolled up and sound asleep.

This morning before the sun is up we eat bacon, eggs and biscuits with the farmer and his hired hand. They are curious about what we are doing, so I give them a brief explanation. When we give them our names they start telling us of the Greenup's they personally know. So it's with a friendly goodbye that we leave the farmer and get back on the road. I sure have a lot of time to think as we travel. I think of what the Bible tells us about being truthful in our contacts with other people. It makes it clear we should not always expect justice and honesty in the world, but at the same time should always be just and honest.

Tonight we are camped in a grove of trees on a ridge top close to the road. We keep a close watch. I miss having Caleb along, but am sure glad we have ugly Buck with us. This is our third night out since we left Crab Orchard, and we should reach the Ohio River tomorrow. There is a lot of traffic, going both ways, and its been several days since rain, so there is lots of dust.

I take first watch, then wake Tim just after midnight to take second watch. I'm sound asleep but wake instantly when I feel the touch of Tim's toe against my ribs.

"Ross, wake up. I heard horses on the road just now, but they have stopped and seem to be just standing. Listen!"

I sit up, and as I do Buck growls, and the horses start nickering.

"Ross! Tim!"

Buck barks once, and his tail wags. Then we hear the call again, and this time I tell Buck to go. He barks again and tears off down the hill to the road. We hear him whining and jumping around and the voice talking to him.

"Whoever you are, come up slowly!" I shout, as I climb out of the bedroll and slip on moccasins.

Tim is holding his rifle and I grab my pistol. Whoever it is leaves his horses. We can hear him coming slowly. We don't have a fire, and it's hard to see him.

"Don't shoot, Ross. It's me, Sammie!" gasps a tired voice.

I can't believe my ears.

89

"What are you doing here? Is there anyone else with you?" I growl.

"No. I've been chasing you, trying to catch up, and I'm so glad to find you, and I'm so tired. Let me rest."

And with that she collapses to the ground. I kneel by her and call her name, but there is no movement. Tim grabs one of the pack covers and we gently move her onto it, and fold it over to cover her. I pull off her boots and she doesn't stir. Tim goes down the hill and brings her horses up. He ties them with ours and slips off their saddles. Samantha doesn't move. Buck lies down close to her with his chin on his paws.

"I reckon she'll be alright till morning." I say.

I crawl back in the bedroll, and my thoughts are in a whirl for a few minutes, then I'm sound asleep.

I wake when Tim stirs up the fire. It's getting light in the east, and a slight breeze is rustling leaves high up in the oak and sweet gum trees. Tim has already walked down to the creek we crossed at the foot of the hill, and has a canvas bag full of water. I wash in the cold water, then get out the coffee pot and skillet. We figure on a hot breakfast to start this day. Buck is making the rounds, touching noses with the horses and mules, and generally checking everything. Soon bacon is frying and coffee is boiling. The first rays of the sun just start to touch the tree tops, when I kneel down by the still form of Samantha. Her head is resting on her tanned arms and hands, with a battered felt man's hat lying by her. A mean looking red welt is across her cheek. Tim walks over and looks down at her.

"Poor little gal, looks like she has had a rough time."

Without touching her I call her name. There is no movement. I call her again. This time she stirs, then suddenly raises her head with a look of bewilderment, which quickly turns to a smile.

"Oh, I'm so glad to see you both! I've been really scared, and was afraid I would miss you."

"If you feel up to it, there is a bucket of cold water over there, and you can wash and then have some cornbread soaked in hot bacon grease, and plenty of bacon and hot coffee."

She smiles again, then starts slowly getting up. She is dressed in worn buckskin pants and shirt, and because of her slender figure could easily pass for a boy, especially if she kept the old hat pulled low over her face. She walks off into the trees, then returns in a few minutes and splashes cold water onto her face. After brushing her curly black hair into place with her fingers, she turns to us.

"I'm ready for that hot grub." She says with another big smile. "I'll tell you why I'm here while I eat."

Buck grins up at her while we dish her up some bacon, cornbread, and a big mug of hot coffee. She sits cross legged on the ground and takes several bites, and a swig of coffee. Then she smiles again, and starts talking, between bites and drinks.

"I knew you were all going to Crab Orchard the morning after the dance, and that you were both going on from there. I told you how Roberto had been really pushing to court me, and I didn't want him around. After noon that same day he rode over to our place. Pa was gone, and just Ma and me were there. You could tell he had been roughed up some, but he did not remember I had been there at the barn when he tried to burn it."

She paused and took a few bites and drank some coffee.

"He didn't mention what he had done. He told me he was going away for a week, and when he came back, I would have to plan on him courting me and us getting married soon. When I said I was not interested he got really ugly and said I would find I wouldn't have much choice. Then he cursed the Greenup's, the Allbright's, and Campbell's and rode away."

Tim poured us all some coffee. Samantha blew on the coffee till she could take a drink, then started talking again.

"Ma and I talked about it till Pa came home, then we all talked about it some more. We have some Greenup kin folks over in Missouri, and it's a long buggy trip over there. I've been wanting to visit them for a long time, and figured this would be a good time to do it, but it's dangerous for a girl to be out alone on the Road."

She stopped again and her lip trembled. We didn't say anything.

"Then I figured if I could just catch up with you fellows, I could travel with you, if you would let me. If I'm real careful, I can pass as a boy, and I've got my own little saddle mare and Pa let me have one of his horses. I've got some money of my own, so don't think I would be burdensome." She stopped.

"How did you get that mark on your face?" I said.

Tears came to her eyes.

"Roberto slashed my face with the end of his leather quirt. He apologized and said it was an accident. Pa said a man who would do that would also beat his wife. He said that would never happen again, so I figure Roberto is in for trouble with my Pa."

I thought about that, and how the Greenup's I knew treated their women folk. I looked over at Tim. He had a grin on his face.

"Well, Mr. Ross Greenup, whatcha gonna do now?" he said.

I threw a stick at him, and said;

"What are WE gonna do now?"

Then I get serious.

"This puts us on the spot. We are traveling fast, and I don't know if its best for you to try to pass as a boy, or a girl. If you are going to be a boy, you may see and hear a lot of things you wouldn't if you were a girl. On the other hand, it may be less dangerous than if you are a girl. Tim, if its alright with you, lets give it a try, and see how everything works out."

Tim grinned again. "Why not."

Samantha threw down her cup and plate, jumped up and gave me a hug, then did the same to Tim. "My Pa told me he figured I couldn't find two better people to travel with, because from what he had heard, the Greenup boys were not much afraid of anything, and besides that were God-fearing, honorable fellows. I left home early the morning after you left Crab Orchard, and didn't camp. When I could find a safe place I would stop and rest, and let the horses feed and rest, then keep going."

Another long pause, and more coffee.

"I was so scared late yesterday, afraid I had missed you, and didn't know what I would do. Then I stopped and prayed, and asked the Lord to help me find you. Right before dark I met a farmer and his wife in a buggy, and they said they had seen you about two hours before, so I rode hard for three hours, and started looking for a place you might be camped."

"We sure have to figure another name for you," Tim said. "Then we have to practice using it."

We sat around for awhile, thinking about that while we finished the coffee, then came up with "Curly". That was obvious, because of her curly black hair, and wouldn't arouse any suspicions. After cleaning up the cups and pans, we repacked our gear, and saddled up. Tim and I watch Curly as she saddles her horses, one with the man's riding saddle and the other with the pack saddle. They are light and she does a good job. Watching makes me think of what we are facing.

"Tim and Curly, lets talk. From now on, we have to treat you like a boy, Curly. It's going to take some doing, and you are sure going to have to play your part. Try not to talk more than you have to when we are around other folks, and if we are with others, and you talk, try to make your voice as husky as you can. Are you armed?"

"I've got this," and she reached to the top of her boot and pulled out a slim knife with a five inch blade. "Pa gave me a pistol, but it's so big I put it in my pack. I can shoot, but it's so heavy I can't hold it up long."

"That's good. Leave everything like it is for now, and we will have to get you a better pistol and belt knife." I stopped.

Tim had a worried look, and finally said;

"As long as we can get away with you being a boy, I guess you better be a cousin, then we won't have to change any more names. But if we get in a tight, and you get found out, then we need to think about whether you are a girl cousin, a sister, or a wife. Remember the fix old Abraham in the Bible got into when he lied about his wife." Tim's face got red as he said this, and then we all laughed.

"If everybody's ready, let's ride out." I said.

It's still early when we are back on the road. We begin to meet a few people, some on horseback, some in wagons or buggies, and a few on foot. Curly is a good rider. We ride over the top of a rise and I stop in amazement and wonder. I've always heard about the 'big' rivers, but had no idea they were this big. Ahead of us is the Ohio, and it is immense. So this is where Josh came to work!

We get in the edges of the Ohio River town of Louisville, Kentucky, about noon. The streets are wide and rutted, with many mud holes. They are crowded, with farm wagons, covered wagons, buggies and carts, being pulled by horses, mules, oxen and donkeys. There are riders going through the crowds, and horses and mules tied at hitch rails in front of various stores. There are pack strings of horses and mules standing patiently, and dogs of every size, shape and color. The smell of manure, leather, sweat, hay and smoke is almost overpowering after being in the clean air of the trail for so long. The boardwalks are crowded with men, women, and lots of children, talking, laughing and hurrying about their tasks. I hear a steamboat whistle and see smoke coming from its stacks. We pick our way to the waterfront and tie our animals at a crowded hitch rail. Buck has stayed close and now sits down right under the hitch rail.

"Tim and Curly, you both stay here with the animals. I'm going to the ferry landing and see when we can cross and how much it will cost us."

I walk down to where I can see a ferry boat tied to a dock. There are also two steamboats tied at the docks and there is mass confusion. The river is running full, but not over its banks here. There is driftwood in the current, so it must be rising. I see a big, bearded man talking to a couple of riders and pointing at the ferry. I figure he is running it, and start toward him. Just then a rough hand grabs my shoulder and spins me around. I grab for my bowie when another hand grabs my wrist and the bearded face of my brother Josh is grinning at me.

"You sure are getting slow in your old age." He growls at me. "What are you doing here? Does Pa know you are here, or did you run away from home?"

While he is asking questions he is pounding my shoulder. Then he pulls me over to the edge of the dock.

"I've got to hurry. We are loading a barge below here that's going down river in the morning."

I explain to him as fast as I can what has happened.

"Ross, that may explain part of the gossip I hear on the River about us Greenup's. There are quite a few Greenup's here in Kentuck, what with our Grandpa being the third governor a few years back. But I hear something about a Spanish or Mexican messenger with money who was going to pay for raiders to go into Texas from the east. Something happened to him because he tangled with a Greenup over in Tennessee. The money has disappeared and some folks are looking for it."

Josh stopped and looked hard at me.

"Bub, you are a wanted man." He laughs and grabs my arm.

"Come with me. I've got an idea."

We hurry through the crowd to the main road running along the river. We pass piles of split firewood, stacked for the steamboats. Black slaves are unloading wagons of more wood. We go around stacks of crates, and stinking piles of animal hides, all bound down river to the Mississippi and New Orleans. It takes careful walking to stay out of the fresh piles of horse and cow manure. There is continuous shouting, swearing, dogs barking, and slaves yelling at each other. Over all are the smells of sweat, wood smoke, leather, tobacco smoke, and the river itself.

A large river barge with high sides is tied to the bank, and black men are crossing four gang planks, carrying crates and bales from the stacks on the bank. There is one area visible on the deck with some canvas awnings set up and two or three women and several children sitting under the shelter.

"Captain!" Josh hails a powerful looking blond man standing by one of the shelters. The man strides over.

"Judging from your looks, and the company you keep, you've got to be a Greenup." he says to me by way of greeting and holds out a ham sized hand.

"Captain Bradley, this is my brother, Ross, and he has two cousins with him. We needed two more hands, and the third one can help cook and generally help with the lines. But they have eight horses and mules. Could we rope off part of the deck and take them with us down river, at least to the Wabash?"

I hadn't thought of this, and if we went all the way to the Mississippi I didn't know how far up river we would have to go to get to the Missouri. But if Josh said it was a good way to go, it should be alright. The Captain thought about it and looked around the barge.

"We could probably do that, if they will take care of the stock and keep the deck clean. We can put them right amidships. Since you are all Greenup's, I figure you are armed to the teeth and good shots!"

"Yes Sir," I said.

"Get your animals down here. I want to be loaded by dark, and shove off by first light. Josh, give them a hand, but hurry it up."

We hurry to shore and back through the crowds. Getting close to the hitch rail where we left Tim and the others we see a small crowd gathered, yelling oaths and encouragement to someone. Pushing through we see

Curly lying face down in the dirt by the hitch rail, not moving. Tim is pointing his pistol at a burly, bearded man backed up against the rail, with Buck standing right in front of him. Buck's hackles are standing on end, his big fangs are shining, and a savage growl is coming from his deep chest. The man's right hand is dripping blood.

"Tim, what happened," I said, dropping to my knees by Curly. Her shirt is torn back off the right shoulder and I can see blood on the side of her face.

"This rascal tried to get into the pack on one of the mules, and Curly tried to stop him. He smashed her in the nose and grabbed her shirt front and tore it half off her, and about then Buck had him by the hand, and I had my pistol out, and was ready to shoot him if he moved."

I pull Curly's shirt up over her shoulder and gently turn her face toward me. Her eyes are closed and her nose is dripping blood into the dirt. I jerk my neckerchief off and begin to wipe her face, and about then Josh steps over her and grabs the big man by the shirt front. Now in the year Josh has been working on the river he has filled out some. He is about five feet eleven inches tall, and built like a white oak tree trunk. His shoulders and arms bulge with muscle, and his hands are hard as iron. I didn't see what he did, but suddenly the big man is lying on the ground by the hitch rail and Tim is holding Buck by the collar to keep him from attacking. The crowd is yelling and hooting, enjoying the diversion.

I turn Curly more, pulling her shirt over her small breasts that are covered with dirt. Her eyes began to flutter open, and she instinctively and protectively crossed her arms over her breasts. A fury was beginning to rise in me, and I fought to control it. After all, Josh, Tim and Buck had everything under control. I helped Curly sit up, and kept my arm around her shoulders as I wiped more dirt and blood off her face.

"Hey, that's a little gal." someone in the crowd shouted. Then there was a general chorus of boos and shouts of derision directed at the man on the ground. Josh let him get to his feet, and with a well directed kick at his rear, told him to get, and never let us see him again. Tim holstered his pistol and joined me by Curly while Josh kept an eye on the animals and packs. Buck crowded right in by us and tried to lick Curly's face. Tears start and run down her face as she hugs Tim. I wish she were hugging me. We help her to her feet, and steady her while she arranges the torn shirt. We get her on her horse, retrieve her hat, and with Tim mounted and leading the mules, Curly riding behind them, Josh and I bring up the rear, walking and leading my horse. While we walk back toward the barge, Josh and I discuss the situation. We stop by a pile of freight the blacks are loading on the barge.

"Tim and Curly, Josh and I have been talking this over, and think it would be best if we let the barge crew know Curly is a girl. That way she can bunk with the other women and kids, and it will be a lot easier to handle. She can keep the deck clean where the animals are, and help with cooking and anything else, including handling lines. When we get to the Mississippi we can decide what to do after we leave the barge and are traveling up the river. So let's get loaded. Josh will tell us what to do. All we have to do about this is tell the truth."

Curly looked at us with evident relief and a small smile.

"Just keep calling me Curly," she said. "That way I'll get used to it."

With that we all get to work. My anger faded away, and within an hour we have the packs and animals in a roped-off place amidships, and Buck has become friends with the entire crew. Curly is visiting with the women and children, and it is evident has a lot of sympathy from them. Tim and I begin to learn what our duties are, and figure this is sure going to be an interesting trip. The black hands work hard under the eye of a stern overseer, but I noticed he gives them frequent breaks. I overhear one of them telling the others about what had happened at the hitch rail, so word traveled fast.

"Dats dem Greenup boys, so don't mess wit dem!" I heard one of them say to another, and they would grin as they passed us.

By dark everything is aboard, guards are posted, and the women are cooking supper at the stone fire pit amidships. Tim and I are assigned on the guard list, and are now considered as a regular part of the crew. I feel a huge sense of relief as we eat, and visit around the fire. The Captain, Big Jack, as the hands call him, is a friendly, talkative fellow, and we tell him the entire story.

"No wonder you boys are getting such a reputation." He laughed about all that had happened to us in the short time we had been gone from home.

"One things for sure. Curly made a good decision when she decided to throw in with you." He grinned big at his wife, a pretty black haired woman, who looked as if she could hold her own in a brawl.

"Nancy will sure try to marry her off to one of you, so watch your step."

Nancy smiled back and didn't say anything. She is one of the three women aboard, and two of the children are theirs. This is their third trip to New Orleans with freight. They will sell all the freight at Natchez and New Orleans, and sell the boat for lumber, then buy horses and a wagon to travel back home on the Natchez Trace. There they will build another barge, and do it all over.

There are two of us on the first watch. One of Big Jack's partners, Jim, is the other hand on watch, and he gives me some pointers on what to watch for. We are both armed with pistols and rifles. We had built two fires on the bank so we could see any activity around where the lines are tied. There is a three quarter moon shining white, which sure helps. I notice an orange ring around the moon, which means we have some weather making. Buck joins me, but I figure he will go back and forth, from me to the horses, and where the others are sleeping.

"Keep an eye on the water and bank, close to the lines. One of the most common tricks is to cut the lines and let the barge drift. Then there will be a gang waiting a little way down the river to board it, kill us if they have to, and take the barge. They tried this the first year we went down. We had a small barge, with just Big Jack, our wives and two black deck hands. One of our hands was killed, and we killed one of the bandits."

He stopped to spit a stream of tobacco juice over the side.

"Nancy threw one of the bandits into the river, one was dead on the bank, and the rest skedaddled."

Armed with that information, I take one end of the barge and he takes the other. Other barges and numerous boats are tied up along the bank, and camp fires are burning all along the river bank above and below us. Dogs are barking, and there is lots of shouting and singing hymns and field songs among the slaves, who are bedding down on the bank. Mosquitoes are thick, and the night is warm. Except for the whine of mosquitoes, I listen with real pleasure to the sounds, including frogs and other sounds from the river. I'm not sleepy, and keep thinking back over the day. Sure seems to me like Tim and I have taken on a huge responsibility with Curly, but I don't regret it right now. I'm beginning to feel real protective of her, and can still see how small and helpless she looked lying there in the dirt with blood on her face.

I wonder how the Clarks and Caleb and Butch are doing. They sure have a lot of work to do, but Pa should soon have some more horses and mules on the way to the Kentuck farm. I think of Ma and Rachel, and the way they looked when we left. Buck licks my hand and I feel a bit homesick. Its been about twenty days since we left home, and we sure have crammed a lot of experience into them. One of the horses stamps and blows gently. I walk over and move easily around them. They seem to be settled in and content. It gets quieter, and before I know it, two hours are past, and Big Jack is telling me to get some sleep. I walk cautiously to my bedroll, crawl in, cover my head to keep the mosquitoes off, and instantly go to sleep.

CHAPTER 13

ON THE RIVER

All Hands Up" shouts Big Jack.

I don't waste time. Pulling on moccasins and shirt, I notice there is a little light in the east, and clouds are building. One of the women has dipped a couple of buckets of water and it doesn't take long to splash cool river water on my face and wake up. The women have a private place set aside by the rail with a head-high canvas hung around it, and they are all up in a few minutes. A black hand has the fire going, and in a short time there is coffee boiling, and bacon frying. A tub of hard biscuits is set by the fire. By this time the bedrolls are tied and stacked out of the way. When the coffee is done we each grab a biscuit, dip it in the hot grease, fish out a piece of bacon, fill a big mug with hot coffee and start eating. It is sure good.

I look around as the light gets better. It's a good sized crew. Besides Big Jack, and Jim, his partner, and their wives and three children, there are Joshua, two other white barge hands who work for Big Jack, and two black hands who belong to Jim. The third woman is the wife of a steamboat officer who is going to Natchez to meet him. She is also a good friend of Nancy. Tim, Curly, and I make a total of eleven adults, and three children.

"It's a good thing you were available," Big Jack said to me. "I hadn't been able to get any other hands and was going to try to find at least one more before we cast off." He looks around. "Listen up, everybody.

Bow your heads, and we are going to ask the Almighty God for a safe journey."

By now its good light. Looking around, I see some heavy clouds building in the southwest. We are sure going to get some rain in a few hours. Joshua shows Tim and me how to rig the big yokes on the sides of the barge, which hold the sweeps. The sweeps are used to control the barge, and in addition there is an extra big steering sweep at the stern, and another on the bow. I've always heard how these sweeps make it possible to handle one of these big barges, and I'm about to see how it works. I also notice a small skiff setting on the stern of the barge.

Time to go. Big Jack is at the stern steering sweep, Josh in the bow, Jim overseeing the lines, and Tim and me are waiting to grab the lines when they are untied, or cast off, from the bank. The other four men are at the side sweeps. The women and kids are perched on top of freight, watching all the excitement, and Buck is barking at dogs on the dock.

"Cast Off!" shouts Big Jack.

"Wait, Wait!" screams a voice from the bank.

We all look around, and see a skinny, dark little man running toward us, wildly waving his arms and hat.

"Hold Up!" shouts Big Jack. "What do you want?" he roars at the little man.

"Sir, Sir. I have two mules loaded with trade goods, and my knife and saw sharpening tools." He catches his breath and then continues. "I'm going to the Mississippi, and will make it worth your while if you can carry us!"

A woman who is about twice his size appears, trotting along the bank and pulling on the lead ropes of two heavily loaded mules. They are not cooperating and she is swearing at them in a shrill voice. I notice she is carrying a large pistol strapped around her waist. Big Jack stares at them, then turns to Nancy.

"What do you think, Honey?" he asks.

Nancy stands and walks closer to the rail.

"Can you cook?" she shouts at the perspiring woman.

"Sure, I can cook, and shoe mules, and handle a sweep!" is the loud reply. Nancy grins, and looks at Big Jack.

"Looks to me like you might have hired another hand." Jim directs the hands to run out one of the gangplanks and help get the mules aboard. They don't appear nervous, so apparently have been on a barge or boat before. The little man and the woman take them to where the other animals are tied, and immediately start unpacking them. Jim gets the gangplank back aboard, and Big Jack tells the hands again to cast off. Jim directs them to untie the down stream lines first. As they toss them aboard the bow of the barge swings out, helped by the action of the sweeps. Tim and I both watch this operation carefully, so we will know what to do with the big sweeps. Then the stern lines are cast off and tossed aboard, and we really go to work.

In half an hour I'm soaked with sweat. Josh comes by and laughs at my efforts.

"You and Tim are both working too hard. You need to let the current help. Here, let me show you." Josh grabs the long handle.

I step back and watch my strong brother handle the big sweep with little effort. We are now mid-stream of the huge Ohio River, and moving about three to four miles an hour. Big Jack turns the barge over to Jim, and we float along with a man at one sweep on each side, and one at the big steering sweep in the stern. I watch Jim, and notice he is watching ahead constantly, and talking back and forth with the men at the sweeps. We will stand duty about an hour at a time, and the rest of the time is ours, to do whatever we want or need to.

I smell coffee and walk to where there is a big pot of hot coffee by the fire. Curly gives me a big smile. Buck is standing by her, and grins at me with those big fangs showing. He is already the pet of the kids and the black hands. The women are talking and laughing. The little man has a sharpening stone set up, and is busy sharpening a pile of knives. He stands up and holds out a small hand. I'm surprised at the power in his grip.

"I'm Diego Vasquez, preferably known as Fierro, cause I work with iron, and that's my woman, Liz. We are headed for the Santa Fe Trail or the California Trail, or any trail that looks good. We know a lot about you Greenup boys, and figure it's a pleasure to travel with you."

"Howdy." I reply. "I've got a Bowie in my belt that could sure stand a touch up with a fine stone. Maybe you might have a good belt knife for Curly."

"Sure do. We have plenty of time to do some trading.", and with that he bent over his work.

Curly's eyes shine as she hands me a mug of steaming coffee. I breathe deeply of the smell, thank her for it and sit down on a box by Big Jack. He is busy working on a slate with a piece of chalk. He glances at me, and hands me the slate. I see it's an inventory of everything we have aboard, and a list of all the hands and passengers.

"Can you read that?" he asks.

"Sure." I reply. "Tim could too."

"Well, it's not uncommon for people from the Tennessee or Carolina mountains to not be able to read and write. We hired your brother Josh because he can, and he helps us with everything. In fact he is now a partner with Jim and me."

Well that sure surprised me some, and I sat and thought about it while sipping down that good hot coffee. Then I noticed all the women were watching me, and it made me a little nervous. Nancy laughed at me.

"Ross, you better watch your step, cause if the word gets out you have some kind of book learnin, there's going to be a passel of females trying to rope you. Course, they are going to have to get past Curly, and she can read and write too."

I can feel my face getting red, and Curly laughs out loud. Just then Jim calls:

"Big Jack, looks like we might have some company."

Big Jack hands the slate to Nancy, and jumps to where he can see the river. A row boat with three men is cutting across ahead of us from the Kentucky shore. As the boat gets close the man in the bow hails us.

"Who is the Captain of that barge?"

"I am!" shouts Big Jack, "and who wants to know?"

Ignoring the question the man shouts again:

"You got any blacks on board?"

Big Jack looks around at us. He motions and Nancy hands him a rifle. I stand in plain sight with my rifle, and Tim does the same. By this time the boat is close.

"I said, who wants to know?" shouts Big Jack, "and don't you think of putting a line over!"

The man in the bow is watching all of us and getting mighty angry.

"I'm a sheriff in Kentuck, and I'm looking for some runaways. I'm coming aboard."

"Mr. Sheriff, you see the only two black men working on this boat, and you are not coming aboard. I know all about you, and know we are not on your side of the river. You just want to see how many people we have and what kind of cargo. If you so much as put a hand on this boat, you are going to be the first one dead!"

As Big Jack said this he raised his rifle and aimed right at the man in the bow. The oarsman frantically backed water and sheared away. The man in the bow was shaking his fist and screaming curses as they started back toward the Kentucky shore. Big Jack lowered his rifle and looked around with a grin. Jim came climbing over the cargo to the fire and got a mug of coffee.

"We've seen him before." he said. "Don't ever let one of those thugs get aboard. They murder and rob, and get away with it. What Jack did is the only way to handle them."

I watched all this and am reminded again of killing the man on the trace, and what Grandpa said about there were some times a person just had to be more violent than the person you were dealing with. I looked at Tim and figured he was thinking of the same thing. Curly's eyes were big and she was kinda pale looking. Nancy was smiling with pride at Big Jack, and Fierro and Liz were commenting they had sure picked the right outfit to throw in with.

Nancy was on her feet and digging through a box of grub. She held up a cloth sack with a shout:

"It's only the first morning, but the Lord has been with us, and its time to celebrate. If Jack will offer a prayer of thanks, and safety for the rest of the trip, we will have a fried pie with our coffee."

I bow with the rest of them, and then dig in. This is going to be some trip.

We spend the rest of the day taking turns on the different sweeps, and learning to read the river, with its different currents and constant changes in banks, low places, and floating dangers. Jim and Big Jack are the experts, but the black hands are about as good, and Josh has learned a lot in his short time on the river. There is lots of drift in the river, so it's still rising. We can see where it has spread over some low lying areas where there are no levees. I notice the sounds of the water are completely different from the boat than they are from the bank. I hear little water sounds from the side of the boat.

Curly and Liz have been taking care of the animals, cleaning the deck and washing down so the smell and flies won't get too bad. The clouds have been getting darker all morning, and now a slow, steady rain has commenced. It's fairly warm, so we don't put on oil skins. Since the river is high we have not had to stay right in the center channel with the shallow draft barge. Josh told me the river is getting close to flood stage.

"We are a couple of miles above Otter Creek on the Kentuck side, so we need to get close to the shore before we get there." said Big Jack. "It's a good landing, there is some pasture close to the river, and my friend has a mill where he grinds feed and saws boards."

This sounds good to me, since the animals are getting hungry, and we don't have hay aboard to feed them. Jim watches the river and Big Jack directs us at the sweeps till we are close to a high rocky bank. As we swing in we see a dock sticking out just above a large creek flowing into the river. By careful maneuvering and hard work at the sweeps, we go right in against the dock and the black hands on the dock tie our lines fast. As soon as we are tied secure we put a gangplank over to the dock. The mill owner is at the dock to meet Big Jack, and makes us all feel welcome. Liz, Curly, Tim and I lead all our horses and mules ashore and to the pasture the mill owner points out to us. Buck goes right along. Tinker is already busy setting up his knife sharpening equipment, and soon all hands are busy.

When all the animals are busy eating the new grass I walk to the mill and watch it operate. The big water wheel is turned by the stream from Otter Creek. It either turns the stones grinding grain, or turns the big circular saw which is sawing boards from logs piled in a log deck close to the mill. Teams of mules drag the logs from the deck to where they are rolled up onto the carriage. The carriage then carries the log into the big saw blade, where it is sawed into boards. Workers are shouting, and the saw has a high pitched whine when a log hits it. There are several large stacks of lumber drying. The fresh sawed lumber smells good. Big Jack and the mill owner are busy discussing price, and Josh and Jim are listening. I listen for awhile, then get Josh attention and we walk back toward the pasture.

"Josh, it sounds like you could make some profit if you had the money to buy some of that lumber." I say.

"That's right. We can make room for a stack of it on the barge, and would like to get the business started, but we are just simply stretched thin."

"Suppose Pa and me, and of course Uncle Rich and Tim, were to lend you some money?"

"That would be fine, but I need it now."

I laugh and tell him to go ahead and make the deal, and let me know how much he needs. I walk back to the pasture, and we watch the sun setting red. The rain has quit, the clouds are thinning out, and the stars starting to shine. The smell of wet grass combines with the smell of the river. It's a pleasure to be with Tim and Curly, and I tell them what Josh is doing. We walk the horses and mules back to the mill, water them at the creek and load them aboard the barge. I buy some hay from the mill owner so we won't have to depend on getting ashore for pasture. Then we all settle down and have a good supper on some fresh beef Nancy bought at the mill. I walk over and stand watching the river flow. Josh, Tim, and Curly all come to stand by me, and Buck crowds right in by Curly.

"Ross, I need sixty dollars." Says Josh.

"OK, watch my back, and I'll get it."

I walk to where the packs are stacked and dig down in the bag with lead in it. I dig the gold coins out, and a couple of plugs of our good tobacco. Then I hand the tobacco out to all hands, so they think it was what I was looking for. In a few minutes Josh, Big Jack and Jim go ashore again. Soon they are back, and ask Tim and me to join them on the river bank.

"Josh, Ross and Tim, we appreciate what you have done to finance the lumber we just bought." said Jim. "But from what Josh tells us, we think you are making a mistake by not making real clear what your terms are. Now I know you are family, but experience has shown Jack and me that money sure can ruin a family if it's not handled right."

This catches me by surprise, since Josh and I had agreed we would let Josh take care of the details. I stammer around, then say lets get it taken care of right now. So we work out all the terms of the trade, and agree with a handshake all around. I will get out a sheet of the good paper Ma gave me and write it up tomorrow. Then we sit around the fire telling yarns, or stand our watch. Curly and Tim and I talk a while about what the day has brought, then turn in to get what sleep we can. I'm exhausted and don't stay awake tonight.

Somebody stirring the fire wakes me. I'm stiff and sore from working the sweeps yesterday. I sit up and put my hat on, and suddenly a small hand is holding a steaming mug of coffee in front of me. Its still dark, but in the light of the fire I see Curly smiling shyly as she hands me the coffee.

"Thanks," I mumble, as I grab the hot mug.

She watches me a moment as I take a cautious swallow. Buck is right by her, with his big white fangs smiling. I reach out and pet him, then they both return to the fire. I get up and walk to the rail. The river is rolling past, with the sound of the water loud right below me, and the smell of the river strong in the mist rising up from it. Light is showing in the east, and the sky is clear. The black hands are eating and talking and laughing. Big Jack calls out:

"Listen everybody. We need to all help load the lumber, except the women and Fierro. Josh will get everything moving at the lumber piles, and Jim and I will stack on the boat. So grab a biscuit, and a cup of coffee, and let's get moving."

Josh leads us across the gangplank and up the bank to the lumber piles. By the time its light enough to carry and cross the gangplanks safely we are moving boards. Working hard, carrying a load of boards on our shoulders, dropping them where Big Jack or Jim tell us, then trotting back up the bank, it doesn't take long to break a sweat. An hour later the lumber we have bought is aboard, tied down, and we are shoving off. The women have pans of bacon and stewed dried apples waiting for us, with another gallon of scalding hot coffee. In a few minutes we are out of the eddies close to shore and moving downstream in the strong current of the river.

Its past high noon and we are getting close to the mouth of the Blue River. Josh is teaching me to use the big steering sweep. He tells me the

Ohio makes a big turn to the south through the bluffs, after we pass the Big Blue. For a couple of miles it actually flows back to the east.

A steamboat passes us going downstream. We hear its whistle before it comes in sight, and are steering off to one side of the main channel when it sweeps through, making a big bow wave that rocks the barge. The horses and mules stamp and snort as they keep their balance. Passengers line the rails of the big boat and wave as they pass.

"It's a good thing they caught up and passed us here." said Josh. "A series of sharp bends takes us more south than west for several miles. It's a dangerous stretch of the river, because of currents and whirlpools, and with a lot of drift and the water high, it is at its worst." Josh is telling me all this as we work at the big sweep. "It's also a place where robbers like to hide and watch for victims on the river."

As we approach the Blue another barge comes out into the main stream of the Ohio. We have noticed another barge at least a mile behind us, and moving about the same speed we are. The one in front of us is smaller than we are, and also loaded heavily. I see at least two women aboard. They steer to get close to us and Big Jack gives them a hail as they close.

"Who is your captain, and where are you headed?"

"I'm the captain," shouts back a burley, red bearded giant. "The name is Angus Stuart, and we are headed for New Orleans. And what about you?"

"Same here. I'm Big Jack. We have families, and a stout bunch of riflemen aboard." About then Buck jumps on a box and looks across at the other boat.

"And a mean dog!" adds Big Jack, which makes me smile.

"Have ye been down the river before?" roars Angus Stuart.

"Yes, this is our third trip." replies Big Jack as we close to within a few yards of the other barge.

"We'd be obliged if ye would let us travel with you down river. It's our first trip." shouted Angus.

"Sounds good! We'll visit some when we tie up." said Big Jack, and with that we floated on.

I am sitting on a bale, drinking coffee, resting and watching the river go by. The water is murky, with more drift wood, and it swirls and splashes. I'm amazed at how far it is to either bank, and can hardly imagine what it's going to be like when it joins the Mississippi. Curly, Tim and Buck all join me. Curly looks at me.

"Ross and Tim, its hard for me to believe we have been on this barge almost two days, and its only been three days and nights since I caught up with you. I don't remember if I told you, but Pa and Ma told me if I didn't catch you before you crossed the Ohio to come back home." She shivered. "I was so scared, but I sure feel safe now. If they hadn't met you fellows, and heard about you, they sure would not have let me go. In fact, I wouldn't have wanted to do it, but the Gift was strong in my mind." She stopped.

"You keep talking like that, and Ross won't be able to wear his hat." drawled Tim. "Sides that, you done stole our dog!'"

I laughed at Tim.

"Curly, you have sure got that Tim trying to clean up a bit. Ruth Clark was working on both of us to get our hair and beards trimmed, and use the curry comb on ourselves as much as we did the horses and mules. Guess we get a mite careless without some women folks around. Anyway, I've been thinking a lot about all this business, and kinda arrived at the conclusion we have a bunch of getting used to each other." I could feel my face getting red.

"Anyway, I've got to admit I sure enjoy your company. It sure beats talking to Tim and Buck all day. And I bet the women folk are sure giving you a lot of advice." I stopped and petted Buck.

Now it was Curly's face that got red.

"You are sure right there. But their hearts are as big as this river, and I already love all of them, and especially that rough Liz. I feel there is something dark hanging over her and Fierro, but am not sure what it is. I am going to pray for them, just like I pray for all of us." Curly said in a clear strong voice.

I thought about that, then suddenly remembered we needed to get a knife for Curly, and also see if Fierro had any pistols. We walked over to where Fierro and Liz were sitting quietly by their packs. They greeted us warmly, and I reminded Fierro of the need of a knife for Curly, and asked if he had any pistols. Curly showed him the knife in her boot, and he started digging in one of the packs.

"Got just what you need!" he said.

He held up a nice leather knife scabbard, with what looked like a miniature Bowie blade and a bone handle.

"This is what I call a ladies knife, and the feller that owned it doesn't have a need for it anymore. I think I have a small pistol somewhere in here, and tomorrow I'll dig it out for you."

We visited for a while, and then it was time for Tim and me to get back to the sweeps. The hours went by, and so did quite a few miles of river bank. We fended off several entire trees floating in the river, and lots of smaller drift. We have traveled at least forty miles from where we started this morning, when Jim shouts to Angus Stuart we are going to tie up above Sinking River. Again all hands get hard at work manning the sweeps, and we manage to tie up at a high bank with several large trees above the water level. The water is deep and we should have no trouble, even if the river were to drop several feet. Stuart's barge ties up about fifty yards below us, after a struggle with the current. Big Jack and Josh grab their rifles and go ashore as soon as we are made fast. They walk down stream to the other barge and help Stuart's crew secure all the lines. The sun is setting behind the tree tops across the river, and casting long shadows over the water.

I'm watching the shore carefully, and see a movement up the hill above where we are tied. Buck is sitting on a bale and sees it as soon as I do. He growls and looks around at me.

"Jim!"

Jim looks around when I call. I motion up the hill and pick up my rifle. Jim picks up his rifle and calls softly to Big Jack. About then two men, dressed in buckskin, and both armed, show themselves and hail us.

"We're friends. Have ye got any 'baccy' aboard? We shore would like to trade."

Now I know some of the merchandise aboard is bales of dried tobacco leaf from the hills of Kentucky, so I wonder what Jim is going to tell him.

"What ya got to trade?" shouts Jim, and quietly says to the rest of us; "All of you get your rifles and be ready for action!"

The two men are looking us over carefully. They talk to each other

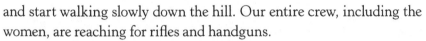

and start walking slowly down the hill. Our entire crew, including the women, are reaching for rifles and handguns.

"I heard him ask what ya got to trade!"

The deep bass voice bellowed it out, and the two men stopped and their heads jerked around at the sound. They instantly saw Big Jack, Josh, and Stuart standing among the trees by the other barge. I knew the two strangers hadn't seen the three boat-men before, and they looked shocked. I laughed to myself, and thought Pa would surely have had some strong words with me if I was not any more careful than they were. The spokesman stammered a bit, then in a voice a bit more shrill than while ago said;

"We really got nothin to trade, but thought we might get some baccy, as we are plumb out."

"Tell ya what." said Jim. "I'll give ya some baccy. First you boys put your rifles on the ground where you're standing, then just skedaddle up the hill a bit. My man will bring the baccy up the hill and put it with your guns, and you wait till he gets back here before you go after it."

Now I sure admired that kind of a move on Jim's part. He was one to do some fast thinking, and had probably seen his share of hard knocks. The two men hesitated, looked over at Big Jack again, than carefully put their rifles on the ground. They moved back up the hill a little distance, and stopped. Jim motioned to me, and I followed him over to one of the stacks of bales. He opened one end of a bale and it showed cut, dried tobacco leaves packed in tight.

"Ross, this is trading tobacco, and not the best quality. We have some in that stack of bales next to it that is high quality tobacco, for cut plug or even cigar grade. Don't ever hesitate to get a bit of this out to keep the peace."

He spoke to one of the black fellows standing nearby.

"Here Joe, take this up the hill to where those rifles are, put it by them, but don't touch them. Keep your eyes and ears open and come back here fast."

"Yas Suh, Mr. Jim" His white teeth gleamed as he took the loose bundle of tobacco leaves and left.

Jim and I then crossed the gangplank to shore and joined Big Jack,

Josh and Stuart. We watched Joe as he climbed the hill through the trees. He dropped the little pile of tobacco and came back to us fast.

"Mr. Jim, I sees two mo mens up de hill. Dey got guns too."

"Good work, Joe," said Jim. "You go back on the boat and keep your rifle handy while we work on this."

"Yas Suh." said Jim and he trotted over the gangplank to the barge. We watched as the men came down the hill to retrieve the rifles and tobacco. Angus Stuart nodded at Jim.

"That was good thinking, Jim. I'm sure glad we tied in with your outfit. I can see we are going to be a lot more careful than we have been."

Jim looked at me then at Big Jack.

"Jack, Ross saw them first, and he seemed to have the idea they were not here to just visit. I'm thinking we need to be better prepared for tonight. What would you think about drifting our boat down a little closer to Stuart's boat, then the people on watch tonight can have a better chance of protecting both boats."

I can see Big Jack is thinking over the situation.

"Let's do that. Let's double the watch, and Angus, you need to make sure all your folks sleep in their working clothes. That includes the women. We will do the same. It's starting to cloud up, and going to be a dark night, so we may want to have a good fire burning on the bank between the two boats."

He paused and looked around at the trees and the river.

"Angus, do you have enough people to stand watch? We could loan you another, and I'd suggest one of the Greenup boys. They are kinda salty, and don't put up with much foolishness. We can all gather around the campfire tonight and work out who does what."

"Lets do it." Angus deep voice boomed out.

Jim calls his hands and Josh, Jim, Big Jack and I join them in moving our barge downstream till we are just a few yards above Angus boat. We tie fast, and then gather enough fire wood to keep a good blaze going on the bank all night, enough to keep the fires going on the barges without having to go ashore. By now it's twilight and the women folks have a good hot supper ready. The black kettle has been on the fire all day, and I can smell beans and ham, and see pan bread. Both crews gather together around the fire, after first putting the black hands and Tim out on watch in the woods, a little back from the barges. Angus has his wife, his sister, who is a bit of a homely young, red haired woman, and two sons, who are in their early teens, but are both huge, like their Pa. Also there are two young farmers, one who appears to be mighty interested in Angus sister.

As we eat we talk about who will stand what watches and where they will be stationed.

"I reckon they probably won't try anything till they figure we are asleep, so lets go easy on the watch till about midnight, then double all the guard." said Big Jack. "Make sure all the kids are under cover."

I said: "Just in case someone got in where the horses are, we will chain them tonight. Another thing, whoever has the watch, remember to not look directly at the fire. Watch the dark and the shadows, and move real slow. A quick movement will give you away. Buck will be on a light chain and with whoever is on the side of the boat next to the bank. He will probably be the first to know something is wrong, and don't let him go, cause he will be right in the middle of someone and might get killed."

Jim spoke up:

"Ross, as soon as we break up, why don't you go over to Angus barge and bed down there, then start watch about midnight. Angus can put the rest of his people where he wants them, but we need to keep in touch between the two boats."

"I'll stay at the end of our boat next to Mr. Stuart's boat, and keep in touch with Ross, or whoever is on watch," said Curly. Nancy grinned at this.

Suddenly there is a shout from the bank just above our boat, and Buck is on his feet with a growl.

"Mister Jim, look what I jes cotched!" shouted Joe.

"Let me loose!" screamed a shrill voice. Joe dragged a struggling young boy into sight. Jim walked over to him.

"Let him loose, Joe." Joe turned him loose. The boy stood with his head down.

"What ya doing here, boy? " said Jim.

"Jes putting out a trotline" said the boy. Jim looked at him, then gave him a push.

"Git out of here, and if I catch ya here again I'll jerk down your overalls and whip your bottom!" Jim growled. The boy ran.

This reminds me of catching Butch trying to steal one of our horses and the scare we put into him. It sure seems like its been a long time ago, but it's just been a few weeks. Jim makes the rest of the watch assignments and after visiting around the fire awhile we go back on the boats. Curly, Liz, Fierro, Buck and I go to the horses and mules and change their ropes for the light chains. Fierro has the same for his mules. It's a warm night and I don't take my bedroll when I start over to the other barge. Curly puts her hand on my arm.

"Be careful, Ross. We sure need you."

Now that sure makes me feel good.

CHAPTER 14

It's well after midnight and I'm at the far end of Stuart's barge. There is hardly any light from the fire at this end of the barge, and few shadows. I'm wide awake and listening when I hear a change in the sound of the water right below the barge, and next to the river bank. It's just a slight difference, but something has changed. Then I hear a growl and a bark from Buck. My rifle is leaning against a bale close to me, and I've got my pistol in hand. I pull out the big bowie knife, raise up a little, and watch the low rail. Soon I hear hard breathing, and a hand reaches and grabs the rail. When it does I swing hard right across it with the Bowie, and let out a bellowing yell.

"All hands!" I yell, as Josh told me to do.

At the same time there is a scream from under the end of the boat, and it continues as someone flounders in the water and struggles toward the bank. A shot is fired from our barge, and then several more from the bank. There are more yells. Against the light of the fire I see the outline of Angus Stuart as he swings down with a huge club at someone trying to climb over the rail. There is another scream as the club connects and a splash alongside. Then there is the sound of a person struggling up the bank and crying out in pain. I hear Buck raging and growling as he struggles to get at the pirates. Tim is holding him on a leash.

It's over as fast as it began. We hear the sounds of running feet, and cries of wounded and scared. Big Jack is ashore throwing wood on the fire and as it blazes up we count the damage. Fierro has a knife slash across one arm. Joe has a bullet crease across the top of his head, and blood is pouring over his face and shoulders. I see Tim checking on the animals. I don't see Curly. My heart jumps.

Curly! Are you alright?" I yell. There is no answer.

"Ross, here she is!" Nancy cries, and moans deeply.

I jump over bales in the dark, and hear Buck whimpering. Nancy is seated on the deck with her back against a bale. Curly is on the deck by her, lying between piles of bales. Buck is licking her face and whimpering.

"Bring a light!" I shout.

Curly is not moving, for the second time in our short acquaintance. Nancy is moaning and I see dark stains on her shirt.

"Tim, Jack, come here!" I shout.

Jim rushes over with a lantern, and Tim is right there by me. Big Jack crowds in and kneels by Nancy. Tim and I both gather up Curly and rush her to the fire on the barge. We place her on her bedroll and start trying to find out what is the matter, and get her to respond. Liz pushes me out of the way. Jack and Jim carry Nancy to the fire and place her on a bedroll, and Jim's wife and the other woman start attending her. I back off and sit down on a bale. Then I bow my head and pray.

Its half an hour before Curly finally begins to move and cry quietly. The only outward sign of injury Liz can find is a huge, egg shaped bump on the back of her head, and now Liz has turned her attention to Fierro and the knife slash. Nancy is quiet. Under the attention of the other two women they have removed her shirt, and determined a bullet has gone clear through her upper arm, apparently without hitting a bone or major artery. What a relief, that it is no worse. Jim has put a bandage around Joe's head, and he is drinking coffee. Tim and I take Buck on his leash and join Josh and the other hands who are patrolling the bank along both barges. We walk over to Stuart's barge to see how they fared.

Stuart and one of his deck hands are standing on the bank. As we walk over, Stuart turns to me and holds out his huge hand. It fairly hides my hand as I hold it out and he grabs it in a massive grip. I'm thinking I'm sure glad we are friends.

"Thankee lads!" he booms. "Hate to think what would have happened if we had been alone. Those miserable bastards might have

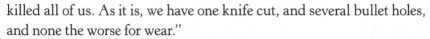

killed all of us. As it is, we have one knife cut, and several bullet holes, and none the worse for wear."

"I don't think they will try us again," I say, "but as soon as I check on Curly again, I'll be over to spend the rest of the night on your boat."

Curly is sitting up by the fire, drinking a cup of coffee and not saying anything. I sit down by her and put my hand on her shoulder and Buck gives her a quick lick on the face. Liz is standing watching her.

"Ross, as near as I can figure, she was turning from the rail when one of the pirates grabbed her from behind. How he got there so fast, I don't know. I was trying to get to her, and suddenly he yelled, she was down and he was back over the rail. She shore got a crack on the back of the head." Liz exclaimed.

"I had my new knife." Curly said in a weak, trembling voice. "I tried to stick it in him, and don't remember anything else. My knife is gone."

I grinned at Liz.

"Curly, we are just glad you are alive. We'll look for the knife when daylight comes. I'm going back to Stuart's barge, and keep watch the rest of the night, but I don't think they will try another attack. You get some rest. I'm telling you the same thing you told me. We need you." I squeezed her shoulder, and got up.

"Liz, and the rest of you." Curly looked around as she spoke. "If any of you have any honey, it is one of the best things you can use for an open wound. Spread it right over the wound and put a bandage on it to keep it from getting on everything else, and to keep all the bugs off it."

"I've heard of that." said Liz. "but never tried it. We have a small bag of honey in our pack." She went to get it.

I walk over to the other barge, taking Buck with me this time. I tell Stuart what Curly said about the honey. Then he and I sit and talk till the sky began to lighten in the east. I go back to our barge, and then all hands are up on both barges and we get underway, but not before we find Curly's knife by the rail. It is covered with blood, so she had evidently made contact before she got hit. She is now sitting on her bedroll, leaning against a bale, and gradually getting more color in her face. I watch her carefully.

The day has passed slowly, but we have been moving rapidly right in the center of the channel. Twice today we saw smoke and then tall stacks as steamboats passed us. One was going upstream, and black smoke was billowing as it labored slowly under a full head of steam. It had a single big wheel and as it passed we waved and exchanged hails with the passengers. The other boat was moving fast downstream. The sound from their steam whistles echoed off the cliffs.

I think of the discussions Tim and Josh and me have had today. There is a lot happening, and we are all anxious to be in the action, and as I think about it, it seems to me like we are. Curly has listened to some of our talk, but has not felt well enough to share much. We are going to tie up close to the steamboat docks at Owensboro, Kentucky, tonight. Josh says that's an important stopping place. Then we will take two more days to get to Paducah, Kentucky, where the Tennessee River comes into the Ohio. My day dreams end when Jim calls me.

"Ross, take the big sweep on the starboard side."

He gives everyone their assignments, and Owensboro comes into sight ahead of us. For the next half hour we are all working hard. Sweat is pouring off me, and I'm glad when we crunch into the big dock. Stuart is right behind us, and for the next few minutes there is bedlam as all of us and the hands ashore get us properly tied to the dock. Buck is now getting to be a know-it-all dog and keeps everyone encouraged with frequent barks.

A short, clean shaven little man hails us and asks for the captain. Big Jack talks to him a few minutes, and I see them looking at our manifest. Later Big Jack, Jim and Josh leave the dock and walk toward the main street of the town. I'm hungry and join everyone else in eating another big pot of stew, with cornbread and dried apple pie. Later I go ashore and manage to buy some more hay for our horses and mules.

Tim and Curly, Fiero and Liz, and me are all sitting by the fire, talking quietly with Nancy. She is leaning against a bale, drinking some hot liquid Liz has brewed for her from sassafras root and ginger. I know from past experience it will sure make her feel better. She says the wound in her arm is very sore, but Liz says it looks good. About then Big Jack, Jim and Josh return to the barge. Jim calls all hands to gather round, except his two black hands, who remain on watch.

"Nancy, Honey, I'm sorry you couldn't be with us, but here is what we have done" said Big Jack. "We have sold the entire barge; cargo, boat

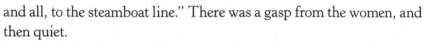

and all, to the steamboat line." There was a gasp from the women, and then quiet.

I look at Tim, and then Curly. They look about as surprised as I feel. Big Jack continues.

"The little man who came to the dock when we were tying up is one of the owners of the steamboat company. He is opening several stores on the river, and one of them is at Paducah. When he saw the size of our barge, and the stacks of bales and lumber, he figured we might have the kind of cargo he needs. He is willing to give us a good price, probably as good as we would get in New Orleans, if we will deliver it to Paducah. That will save us several weeks of work on the river, as well as the danger. We will unload it for him."

I'm now thinking of all the different plans this will change. I look at Josh.

"What are you going to do, Brother?" I ask him. He grinned.

"Jack hasn't told you everything. He told Mr. Wideman of my work, and put in a good word for me, and I've already been offered a job on one of the big steamboats."

"I've got more." said Big Jack. "Nancy and me will have free passage on one of the steamboats up-river as soon as we are done at Paducah. This will give her more time to heal properly. Jim and his wife can do the same if they want to." He looked at the other woman, the wife of the steamboat officer who was going to join her husband.

"You will have free passage to the Mississippi to join your husband." She smiled a huge smile and gave Big Jack a hug.

"It sure looks like we have to do some planning tonight and tomorrow." I said to the others. "Jack, can we cross the river at Paducah and go across to the Mississippi without going on down to where the Ohio and Mississippi join?"

About then Fierro spoke up.

"Ross, you are right. We have a lot of planning to do. Will you boys be willing to let Liz and me throw in with you, for a while anyway?

Before I could answer Jim said;

"Ross, there is a ferry at Paducah, and I'll draw you a map which will get you to the Mississippi and on up the river, or across the river."

I look at Curly, and then at Tim, then back to Fierro.

"Sure, Fierro, we'll talk with you. Right now I've got about a dozen ideas, and I'm sure Tim and Curly do too, and we haven't heard a word from Buck!"

At mention of his name the big ugly dog showed his fangs in a huge grin and licked Curly's face. She gave him a hug and a pat. For a moment all is quiet while we think of what there is to do. Then Jim spoke again:

"I know the rest of you are wondering about the partnership. When we are all done at Paducah and are paid off, we will settle all our accounts, then everyone is free to do whatever they want to. We may or may not keep the partnership. Josh will probably work for the steamboat company for awhile, but if he wants to stay in the partnership, there might be some benefit later."

This comment gives me a new idea, but I've got about all I can handle for now. I sit back and watch this group of friends and families talk about what has happened. As I often do now, I think back over the past few months and what has happened. I know Ma would tell me,

"Don't sit around and talk about what you are going to do – Do it!"

And once again, I thank the Lord for our safety.

It's almost noon, the second day after Jack's announcement of selling the barge. Yesterday passed rapidly, and we had lots of conversations about what we are going to do. Right now, we have Paducah in sight, and I'm manning one of the big sweeps. Stuart is right behind us, and is going to try selling his barge and cargo here. There are two steamboats tied at the docks, and lots of activity. Jim is directing our landing, and we are working hard. Our entire crew is either manning sweeps or sitting on top of the cargo, watching our approach. I don't have time to look, but Curly tells me Mr. Wideman is standing on the dock. We bump hard, the lines are over, and I think to myself, we have had one more adventure to tell Pa and Ma about.

We get Stuart tied up, then we receive orders for all hands to stay close to the barge till Big Jack and Jim get everything sorted out. I see them motion to Stuart to come with them, and they all leave with Mr.

Wideman. I get Tim, Curly, Fierro, Liz and Josh with me on the river side of the boat, where it is quiet, and we sit down.

"Here are some of the things we need to consider." I say. "I want Josh to hear all this, and I want all of you to speak up with any ideas we need to hear. First, I'm going to write a letter to Pa and Ma and the Clarks and tell them a little of what has happened. If they are at the Clarks farm they will all know at the same time. Curly can write her folks, and then Josh can take the letters and make sure they get sent." Josh nodded in agreement.

"Next," I say. "We need to get a place to put our horses and mules till we are done here. Fierro and Liz, will you work with Curly and get that done as soon as we break up? We will all help move them, and it would be good to get them some green pasture." They all nodded in agreement, and Fierro said;

"I need to find a place where I can set up shop, and I may just know a couple of fellers here. So we should get something worked out."

Watching all of them makes me wish again Pa was here to do a lot of this planning, but he's not, so it's up to me. So far we have fared well, and I pray it will continue. We must not for a minute forget to be on our guard. Too much can happen.

"Tim, and Josh, and Curly too, I've been thinking about our experiences on the river. We have needed hay, and pasture, and because Big Jack and Jim have friends along the river, we have been able to get what we need. What would we have done without them?" I pause, and Tim jumps right in.

"You are right, Ross. So we need to work out some way to have hay and pasture available at landings along the river, and I'm thinking we need to keep that in mind from now on." He looked at Josh. "Josh, you could do a lot of that right now if you are going to keep working on the river, and you could be part of our partnership with our Pa's."

It was plain Tim was doing some thinking, and Josh spoke up.

"If I start doing some looking around on the river, and talking to people, we might be able to work something out." he said.

I'm proud of my brother."Lets talk about it some more, and while we are waiting for Big Jack, lets get these horses and mules ready to go ashore. Ready, Curly?"

While we have been talking Curly has started looking worried, and I'm curious to know why. She does not say anything, just nods and she and Fierro and Liz start toward the dock. She tells Buck to stay and he walks back toward me.

Its half an hour before we see Big Jack, Jim and Stuart coming back. Big Jack shouts at all hands, and we gather around.

"Mr. Wideman will have a crew here in an hour to show us where to unload. Several of his hands will be along with some wagons, and we'll get right on with it. Josh, we will all settle our accounts tomorrow night. Its going to take us that long to get unloaded. Ross, there is a ferry that will take you and all your animals to the other side of the river the morning after that. I'll pay for that as part of your wages for working for us. You and Tim and Curly have been a real help to us."

Just then Curly shouts from the dock.

"Ross, we have a pasture for the horses!"

We all pitch in and soon have the horses ashore and in the middle of fresh green pasture. Fierro and Liz then go off to take care of their business and Curly, Tim and I go back to start unloading the barge. Curly gets us all a fresh cup of hot coffee, and we drink it while we wait for the wagons.

"Ross, and Tim," Curly says in a quiet voice. "I've been getting a real bad feeling about Liz. Every time we go ashore she knows quite a few folks, and they are all a rough crowd. But it's more than that. She has asked me questions about you, and I fear we are going to have trouble. Fierro doesn't say anything. I think he is a bit afraid of her."

Just then we hear a shout from Josh that the wagons are coming.

"Tim and Curly, keep your eyes and ears open!" I tell them. "I'll tell Josh to do the same, and when we are done here we can decide what to do!"

With that last word, the hard work begins.

*

"Ross, just one more load!" shouts Tim, as he walks beside a wagon load of freight.

I've been supervising unloading the wagons, Curly has been keeping the accounts of all the freight as it is unloaded, and Tim has been going back and forth with the wagons between the warehouse and the barge. Josh and Jim have been handling loading the wagons at the barge, and Nancy has been keeping the books at the barge, recording everything loaded there. She and Curly get together when they can and compare notes. They are just coming back from a stroll around the docks as this wagon pulls up.

"Ross, Ross, and Tim! He's here!"

Curly grabs my arm. She is pale and shaking.

"Who is here?" I demand.

"Roberto! I just saw him talking to Liz. They didn't see me. Ross, I'm afraid."

"OK. Just stay out of sight as much as you can. Put on a sunbonnet and pull it around your face. When we are done go right back to the barge and stay on it. Don't let on to Liz you know anything. Tim and I will go get the horses. Tim, we need to let Josh know about this, and then we need to be packed and ready to go on the first ferry in the morning."

An hour later Tim and I are leading the horses and mules from the pasture to tie them at the barge. Josh and Big Jack said we can keep them on the barge and then they will be ready to go when we get them packed in the morning. Fierro and Liz have their mules ready, and have acquired a saddle horse for Liz to ride. Fierro will ride one of our mules. That makes me nervous, but for now will have to do.

We have a big supper tonight with the barge crew. Nancy got some fresh pork ribs, and Joe has cooked them over coals. There is fresh baked bread and two dried apple pies from Paducah, a pot of beans, and another pot of new turnip greens, procured by Big Jack from a steamboat. It's been a great week with them, and we have learned a lot. Josh has our mail, and we have made a lot of plans. Josh pays us back the money we loaned him. It almost doubled, and he gives us ten dollars extra. He would give us more, but agrees to keep it to apply to the business on the river. I think about tomorrow, and wonder what the future has for us. Curly knows what I'm thinking, and she is wondering the same thing. We go to bed early, and as we say goodnight Curly gives Josh a big hug. He grins at her, and says:

"Bet I see you again soon."

I lie on my bedroll, and listen to the river, and think of Pa and Ma, and the mountains, and then of Rachel. I wonder if I'll see her again, and if she will get married while I'm gone. Then I feel lonesome, and think of Curly, and how pretty she is. Things are really getting complicated. It comes to mind I need to talk to God, so I do, and especially ask for a clear mind and a strong heart tomorrow and in the days to come. Then I fall into a deep sleep.

CHAPTER 15

Josh wakes me for the last watch, but as soon as there is light in the east I rouse Tim and Curly, and we start getting the packs on the mules, and the horses saddled. Fierro and Liz are up, doing the same, and then Nancy has a fire going and a big pot of coffee boiling. She hands each of us a big piece of flat bread, with bacon and dried apples rolled in it. Pa says the Mexicans call them burritos, and they hold together better than corn pone or biscuits. We eat hurriedly, and drink the hot coffee, and by then its daylight and time to go. One last round of goodbyes, and we lead the animals off the barge and mount up.

It's a mile to the ferry dock, and we find the ferryman already up and ready to go. Jim had evidently talked to him last night and paid him well to take us across. It's a big, wide river, but we cross it safely, and once on the other side, tighten all the straps again, mount up and are on the trail again. I feel good, and ready to face what ever happens.

I'm leading out, and go slow for an hour, till we get away from the river traffic and where there are farms scattered over the hills and valleys, like we had on the Kentucky side. One difference here is Illinois is a "free" state, where there are supposed to be no slaves. I don't understand all this means to the common farmer here, except there is no cotton here. It appears to be mostly corn and some tobacco, and the new plants are just showing above the ground. Some folks we heard talk on the river had some real strong ideas about slavery, and I listened closely, but didn't say much. I still hold with the idea its wrong to have someone else do the dirty work and not get paid for it. Way back in the Bible there was lots of discussion about how slaves should be treated, but if we live like the Bible teaches us, there would not be slaves.

After about an hour on the road we stop and look the animals over and adjust straps and buckles. Fierro seems to be doing real well on top of the pack on one of our mules, and Liz is able to stay in the saddle, but she is rough on her horse. Tim and I have agreed one of us will always lead out, and one behind. Whoever is behind will keep a close watch on our back trail. Curly is her happy self again, singing and chatting as we ride along. Buck stays close to her horse most of the time. We meet or pass a number of travelers, and always check with them about the road conditions ahead. When we get to the Mississippi we will decide whether to stay on the east side of the river, or cross and go up the west side. Last year the government soldiers brought a lot of the Cherokee's through here, and Curly knows some of her relatives were with the group.

As we ride I keep thinking of Liz and Roberto, and wondering what they are planning. It seems to me the longer we put off knowing, the more danger we could be in. I feel the strain of being in charge again, instead of just riding along on the big barge. Early in the evening we come to a nice meadow by the road, and a well set up farm. There are rolling hills and lots of forested land, and numerous creeks. I ride to the farmhouse and ask for permission to camp in the trees at the edge of the meadow, and let our animals graze some in the meadow. The farmer is an older man, with a kind appearance, and tells us to be careful with the campfire. I offer to buy some eggs, but his wife says she has too many and we can have some. She said she really appreciated us asking, instead of trying to steal them, like some travelers did.

I select a place by the edge of the trees where we can see down the road in both directions, but stay back out of sight ourselves. We unload the animals and turn them out to graze, and I get a chance to tell Tim my plan. We have a good supper, thanks to some of the eggs we got. Then we have a nice little fire, though it's a warm, clear night. Just north of us the Big Dipper is showing bright. Buck is lying by Curly, and I'm sitting where I can keep an eye on the road. Caution is really getting to be a habit, much more than it was before we started on the trip. I notice Tim does the same, and Curly is beginning to be more aware of what is going on.

Fierro is telling one of his endless stock of funny stories, and Liz is sitting close to him on a saddle blanket. I very quietly ease my pistol out of its holster and lay it beside me, out of sight.

"Fierro," I say quietly. "Before you and Liz came aboard the barge with us, had you ever heard of the Greenup boys?"

Fierro looked a bit surprised at the question. There was a moment of silence while he thought about it. Then Liz spoke up.

"We had heard some of the blacks talking about "dem Greenup's", and then we saw the scrap about Curly. That's when we decided to join with you, if we could."

My next question shocked her, and surprised Fierro again.

"Liz, how long have you known Roberto?"

Her face changed expression, and neither of them said anything. Curly is watching first me, then them. Tim is quietly putting more wood on the fire, and moving around closer to Fierro, and Buck is suddenly on his feet. I speak softly.

"We know you have talked to Roberto, Liz, and wonder what he has to say to you? It makes us real nervous, and not sure we can trust you and Fierro. Tim and I have a reputation, and have about decided to live up to it, and now Curly is with us, and we are apt to be a mite touchier than we were before. You both need to know, if you and Roberto are planning some kind of cussedness while we are traveling together, one of you is going to get the first bullet or knife blade!"

I surprise myself at my little speech, and sit back to see what the result will be. Curly is not moving, and Tim is watching the couple closely in the flickering firelight. Buck moved closer to Curly, and a low growl rumbled in his chest. Then all is silent, except for the snapping of the fire, and the sounds of the tree frogs and other night sounds in the woods.

Then Liz turns slowly to Fierro, puts her arms around him, and begins to sob.

"Fierro, I'm so sorry. You were right, and I was wrong, and now we are going to pay for my stupidity." She turned to the rest of us. "You need to hear my story, then we will go." She gulped. "I was married, had a baby born dead, lost a fine man to a river accident, started drinking, and ended up last fall on a river boat, dealing cards, drinking, and selling myself to any and all." She paused and wiped her eyes, then went on. "There were people from all over, riding the boats and gambling, and I heard talk about everything going on. There was one man by the name of Quintara, who seemed to have a lot of money, and a lot of luck with the cards. He and some other men were talking about money from Spain that was going to help Mexico in its fight with Texas. I was with him in a bar in Natchez, and there was a fight, and I was beaten and knocked out."

She stopped again and looked at Fierro. Fierro smiled at her and nodded, then gave her a hug. She hesitated again for a few seconds, then coughed, a deep hacking cough, before continuing.

"This man, Fierro, found me lying outside the bar. He is stronger than he looks, because he dragged me off the street and to the livery stable. When I came to he was wiping my face with a grooming rag he dipped in the water trough, and was talking to me in a low voice. I was so sick, and hurt all over. He helped me sit up, then stand, and got me to a bed he made in the hay, covered with his blanket. I guess I passed out again, because the next thing I knew it was daylight and he was sitting by me, holding a mug of hot coffee and a slab of cornbread and bacon. Well, that day I left Natchez with Fierro and his outfit, and we've been together ever since. He saved my life."

Before she could say anything else Buck growled and jumped and I had my pistol in hand and was right behind Buck. Curly yelled and Tim was looking around and had his Bowie out. Fierro pushed Liz over and was on his feet with a pistol in his hand quick as thought. Buck had jumped past the fire and was growling and snarling at the stack of wood. I had seen the same thing Buck had, but he is faster, and reaches the big black timber rattler before I do. I see the fire light glint on its back just as Buck jumps. The snake coiled, and the firelight is reflected in the eyes of his big head. I yell at Buck, and grab his collar. By now Tim has seen the snake. He grabs a stick of firewood, and while I hold Buck proceeds to pound it to death. Its body is as big around as my arm, and it has fourteen rattles.

Finally we all settle down, after building the fire up, and looking around carefully. Liz sits down again by Fierro, and is looking at all of us with a sad face.

"Now I'll tell you what happened at Paducah, and you may not believe it, but I can't help that. When we first got there, I was walking around looking at the shops and waiting to begin unloading the barge, and saw Roberto. I knew him because he had been with his father once on the river. I did not know he knew you, until he told me he was there on an errand for his father, and he was looking for the girl he was supposed to marry, who had run off with the Greenup boys. Not only that, but he suspicions you have some money, because you killed a man who was working for his father." She sobbed again.

"I didn't tell him we knew you, but I was going to see if I could find out if you had a lot of money hidden. I watched you when you got stuff out of your packs, and tried to look in them when you were not around. I hadn't told Fierro about it either, till we were making camp, because I knew he would be angry. Then I noticed Curly watching me, and with a look on her face that made me think she suspected me. That's all, and Fierro and me will be moving on by ourselves in the morning. I'm so sorry, Ross, because I really like you folks. I don't know what I was thinking." She buried her face against Fierro's chest, then started coughing real hard and deep.

I sit and think about the situation. Nobody is saying anything. Curly turned once and looked at me, then turned away. Tim put some wood on the fire, and walked around camp with Buck, looking for more snakes. I think of Curly telling me to be careful of Liz, because something is not right. Then I think of what Pa and Ma might say. Then I stand up, because I can sure think faster and talk better when I'm standing.

"Tim, and Curly, listen to what I'm about to tell Fierro and Liz, and if you disagree with any part of it, speak up right now. Will you do that?"

I look at both of them in turn. Tim comes over to stand by Curly, who gets up. Buck leans against her. They both nod, and Buck shows those fangs. First I tell them the reason we are traveling, right from the start, when I was on the way to see Tim about going west, and killed a man. I don't mention anything about money, except to say we received a reward for the capture of one man, and that is the money we are using on our travels.

I stop and take a drink of cold water, then tell them of the Clark family, and the farm in Kentucky, and the Allen boys, and about Roberto trying to burn our barn and supplies. I tell them about Curly, whose real name is Samantha, and she is also a Greenup, and just as tough as the rest of us. Then I stop, and look around in the fire light. Nobody else moves.

"Liz, and Fierro, as I figure it, you know about us, and we know about you, and the best thing for us to do is go on with our plans. I firmly believe the Lord has blessed us and protected us. We know greed and money can sure get in the way, and ruin peoples lives in a hurry, and we would like to forget all this and be friends. Is that all right with everyone here?" I look at them as I finish.

"Ross, and Tim, and Curly, I'll speak for us." said Fierro. "We have no reason to think you are not completely honest and dependable. You may not feel the same about us right now, but we agree with you. Lets put it all behind us. We would like to keep traveling with you. We are safer in numbers, and want you to learn to trust us."

Liz put her arms around him again. Curly smiled at them, Tim put more wood on the fire, then Buck walked over to Liz and licked her hand.

"Looks to me like it's a deal," I said. "except for one thing. Liz, did Roberto say anything about following you and Fierro?"

"No! He said he had business down toward Natchez." The tears started again. "Thank you all. You are so kind to me!" She stood. "Let's go to bed, Fierro."

CHAPTER 16

urly had the last watch, and got us all up early. It's been three days since we crossed the Ohio, and we are camped on a high bluff overlooking the Mississippi River valley. Last night I could see lights in farmhouses, and lights reflecting on the water along the river. The weather has been clear, but change is coming, and this morning a mist is rising from the water. There are fields of corn and oats across the flat valley, which has deep black soil. I look at our small group sitting around the fire, drinking coffee and talking about what is ahead of us today. We constantly slap at mosquitoes, but they are not as bad here as down by the river. Tomorrow we will cross the Mississippi on the ferry at St. Genevieve, then probably follow the west side of the valley to the Missouri River.

This is about where the Cherokee came through last year, and they crossed the river on a ferry boat close to where we are. We have been pushing hard since leaving the Ohio. It's been several weeks since we left the farm in the hills, and is now late spring. I think of the distance we still have to go to Westport, which is where the wagon trains are staging and leaving for the Oregon Trail or the Santa Fe Trail.

During the night the fairly cool evening breeze changed to a warm, gusty wind, and this morning there are deep black thunderheads building in the southwest. The horses and mules are nervous, and Buck is prowling around like something is bothering him. The air is getting heavy feeling. All of us are wearing the thinnest shirts we have, and the women have their hair tied back, to try and stay cool.

Last night I was worried about Liz. She has been very quiet since our confrontation about Roberto three days ago. When she and Fierro first joined us I noticed she had a frequent deep cough, and this has become worse. I've noticed Curly watching her closely, and Fierro has been very careful with her. Fierro brews a hot drink for her whenever we stop. I can smell sassafras and ginger when it's brewed, and this morning she has had a couple of mugs of the drink. Fierro looked around at us now.

"You probably have guessed by now that Liz has 'consumption'. Sometimes it's not so bad when its cool and we are away from the river. We heard if you go west toward the shining mountains you can get better. So that's the reason we are trying to get there, before it's too late."

He gently patted Liz shoulder, and she smiled at him, and then coughed a deep, harsh cough. Fierro spoke softly.

"Maybe we can buy a buggy here on the river. Riding is getting too rough for her."

For a few minutes the only sounds are the crackling of the fire and the noise of the animals finishing their oats. I think again of the different things which keep coming into our lives, and wonder what is next in store for us.

"Let's go!" I say, and start packing things up.

By the time the sun is well up we are on the trail, which is in deep woods, and starting down the hill toward the big river. Two hours later we are at the village of Chester, Illinois, where we are advised to follow the main road north up the river to the ferry at St. Genevieve. We are also told to watch the storm clouds real close. Evidently tornados go through here about every summer. As we stand and talk to a fellow about the clouds, the sky begins to turn a sickly yellow, and what looks like a curtain drops down from a cloud between us and the river. I watch it a minute, then the fellow turns to me.

"You folks tie your animals and take cover. There's enough room in our cellar for us all to crowd in, and you are about to see a funnel cloud. Just hope it misses us!"

It sure doesn't take us long to get the horses and mules tied. They are all tossing their heads and crowding into each other. As we run to the cellar door, I look back and see a long, wicked looking funnel drop from the cloud to the ground. I can't tell which way its going, and then we are in the cellar and the door is closed. Curly crowds close to me, and Buck is crowding at our feet. Then I can hear Curly praying, and the sound of the wind outside sounds like a huge fire. Suddenly the doors of the cellar fly open, and then are ripped away. The sound gets less and the wind dies down.

"All clear!" Shouts the owner of the cellar.

We all climb out and look around. My first thought is for the horses and mules. One of the mules has broken loose and is standing about a hundred yards away, grazing at the edge of the road. The house, which is close to the cellar is alright, but the barn, which was on the other side of us, is gone. The owner looks around, then sees his mules and a milk cow standing in the pasture. He grins real big.

"Well, Ma, we didn't loose much. I've been intending to build a new barn, anyway!"

"I know, Pa, but we lost the house last year, and the barn three years ago. Maybe we should build somewhere else."

We travel all day, and tonight we are camped in a woodland, right at the base of the river bluffs and well away from the main road. It's just a mile to the ferry landing. Today we talked to several travelers, and they assured us the road on the west side of the river is well traveled and a good road. We also stopped at a farm house close to where we are camped, and I traded two hours work with the team of mules, early in the morning, for two dozen eggs, a bucket of fresh milk, a side of smoked bacon, and several big beef bones for Buck. What a feast we have tonight.

The farmer is down with a bad back and would like for us to stay for several days. I told him we were trying to get on across Missouri to Westport. I didn't say anything about trying to find any of our Cherokee relatives, because some people are not apt to be friendly concerning Indians.

Dawn is just breaking with a weak light, when Tim and I go to the farmhouse with the mules. Mist is rising from the fields and the grass is wet. We left Fierro, Liz and Curly in camp to rest some and take their time getting packed to go. Using the farmers harness, we hitch the big mules to a plow and in two hours have turned a large garden patch, and got it ready to plant. It's late for corn planting, but he is mighty pleased and his wife gives us two loaves of fresh baked bread and a sack of dried apples as we leave. We heard a steamboat whistle as we leave.

We go back to camp, load everything on the mules and start for the ferry. It's getting hot here in the river valley, and the sun is brassy looking in the damp morning. I'm getting real anxious to get out of this valley, and I know the others are feeling the same.

When we get to the ferry it's getting ready to cross, but they have room for all our animals, and the sight of a two dollar gold piece convinced the operator to wait for us to crowd on. I stood close to him as we started across.

"You fellers wouldn't happen to be the Greenup boys, would ya?" He asked. I looked closely at him.

"As a matter of fact we are, but what have you heard about us?"

"Well, a steamboat stopped here last night, and a young feller by the name of Josh Greenup told me if I saw ya to give ya this letter."

He reached in a wooden box sitting close to the steering oar and pulled out a packet, wrapped in a piece of oiled canvas. It was addressed to us, in Ruth Clark's handwriting. I handed it to Curly, and said to hold on to it till we got ashore. I was mighty excited when we finally had everything unloaded, and could tell the others were too. I put Buck on a leash and led the way through the crowd of people and animals to a quiet spot. Curly handed me the packet and I cut it open with my bowie. I read slowly.

"Dear Ross, Tim and Samantha. Hope you are well. We are all doing fine. We got one letter from you, and several travelers have stopped to tell us where they saw you. The last one told us they saw you on a barge at Owensboro. Ross, your Pa, and Uncle Rich brought 25 mares and mules to the farm here. There are already 2 new horse colts, and 3 new mule colts, and more on the way.

Caleb is making eyes at one of the neighbor girls, and Naomi is being courted by young Stewart Campbell. Butch is too bashful to even look at a girl. Ross, your Pa said your Ma was mighty lonesome without her boys

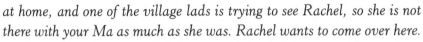

*at home, and one of the village lads is trying to see Rachel, so she is not
there with your Ma as much as she was. Rachel wants to come over here.*

*Your Pa said you are all doing a great job, and they are anxious to hear
from you again. Samantha, your folks are sure happy you tied in with Ross
and Tim. Roberto has not been seen since you left, and now his Pa is gone
too. We know now they are involved some way in the war with Mexico,
and you are all to stay on your guard and armed because they think you
have some of their money. Stay close to that ugly Buck, Samantha.*

*David and Elizabeth miss all of you, but they have a fine new puppy
to play with. We pray for you, and trust in the Lord to guide you. Your
Friends, Clarks."*

I look up from the letter and around our little group. Nobody says
anything for a few moments, and I know their thoughts are on home,
just like mine. I fold the letter, and give it to Curly. She tucks it in her
saddle bag.

"Let's find Fierro and Liz a buggy." I say. "Fierro, do you want us
to help you look, or just stay here till you find one."

"Liz and I will look," says Fierro, and the two of them leave us.

"Tim, why don't you and Curly look around and Buck and I will
stay here with the animals." I say. "See if you can find us something to
eat. My belly is about to eat my backbone, and Buck is going to tear into
one of these chicken coops if I don't hang on to him." They laughed and
walked off.

I make sure the horses and mules are tied, then lean back on a
hitching rail. Buck lies down at my feet, and we watch the scene around
us. There is a long, solid dock where we got off the ferry. Several horses
with riders are waiting to board the ferry for the trip back across the
river. Wagons and buggy's are lined up, either with freight or empty, so
there is evidently a steamboat due in a short time. Several black dock
hands are standing at the other end of the dock, and there is a large
stack of split wood on the bank behind them. This is evidently a major
refueling dock for at least one steamship line. I wonder if we will see Josh
again, this soon after leaving him on the Ohio.

A dusty, crowded street goes up the hill toward town, and several
side streets go off from it. The smell of horses and mules is strong,
combined with wood smoke, leather, tar and the river. A board walk

is above the street, along the bank of the river, and several people, including some well dressed ladies are standing there, watching all the activity. When I see them I suddenly realize its been a long time since any of us has seen hot water, except to make coffee, and it would sure be nice to scrub off some of the layers of sweat and trail dust. I'm going to find a place to do that, and keep it as a surprise for Curly.

Several small boys in ragged overalls, with no shirts or shoes, come running down to the dock, and one of them comes over to where I am standing. I suddenly realize I miss having David and Elizabeth running around. Buck is on his feet, with his big fangs showing in a grin.

"Can I pet him, Mister?"

I laugh.

"If he will let you, it's alright with me."

He reaches cautiously toward Buck, who rewards him with a lick. The boy laughs with delight. I watch them, and then become aware I'm being watched myself. A medium size, dark swarthy man is standing on the other side of the mules, looking intently at me. I reach for the butt of my pistol, and think to myself, I've got to be more careful. He stands a moment, then walks around the animals toward me. He looks like a half breed, with straight black hair, but with bright, piercing blue eyes, just like Curly. I notice he is wearing Cherokee style beaded moccasins. Buck pays him no attention, which is unusual. The boy wanders off with his friends, and the man speaks.

"Are you a Greenup?" By now I'm getting used to this greeting.

"Yes, and who wants to know?" I ask.

"My name is Aaron Greenup. Is Samantha Corbitt with you?" he asks.

"Hold it right there, Mister. I don't know you from Adam's off ox, and you be careful where you tread." I drew my pistol, and it suddenly got quiet around us. Buck was right by me, and a quiet growl rumbled.

His face flushed and he held up his right hand, palm toward me.

"I'm sorry. Samantha is my niece and I've been waiting for her for three days. Her mother is my sister, and a week ago we got word Samantha was traveling with you, and that there were dangerous people who might want to hurt her and you. So my brother and I hurried here to meet you and travel with you till we get to our home. We live here in

Missouri. There are several Greenup's in this part of the country, some of them from the all white side of the family, and some like me. You looked about tough enough to be one of the clan, and judging from your actions just now, can probably take care of yourself."

I stared at him a moment, and then realized we were once again about to enjoy a special happening we had not planned for. I holstered my pistol, and reached out and shook his hand. He had a grip of steel, and his muscles bulged under his leather shirt. Buck sat down, grinned his toothy grin, and everything got noisy again. I immediately liked Aaron, but before we could say anymore, a young giant of a man, with blue eyes, like Aaron's and Curly's, but with blond hair, came striding toward us.

"You found them!" His deep voice rumbled in his chest.

"This is my baby brother, Seth." said Aaron.

I shook hands again, and was sure glad these two were going to be my friends. They could break a man in two with those hands and arms. I then told them briefly about Tim and Curly, or Samantha, and about Fierro and Liz. I also told them we sure needed to find a place where we could get some hot water and a scrub down, and maybe sleep in a bed before we went on. They laughed at that and told me they had made arrangements for us to stay tonight at a friend's Inn. We would put our packs in a barn, and all the horses and mules in their pasture. Suddenly there was a scream of joy.

"Aaron, Seth. Where did you come from?"

Curly came running right into their arms, and they all hugged and grinned at each other. This was most unusual for Indian folk to act like this, and I noticed some surprised, and some angry looks at Aaron. It did not seem to bother him. Tim was walking slowly behind Curly, with a cloth sack in his hand, which I hoped held something to eat. Finally all the explanations were over, and we stood around the hitch rail and ate flat bread with bacon, and some different food called 'tamales'. They were made of meat cooked in corn meal and wrapped in cornhusks. I'd heard Pa tell about them, and they were sure good.

Before we were finished, Fierro came and got their saddle horse. He had traded some knives and a little gold for a buggy, and was going to get it and come back. Liz was waiting for him. Seth decided to go with them to lend a hand, and I could tell Fierro was pleased with that. It looked to me like Fierro was about worn out, what with trying to take care of Liz, the animals, and all his equipment. Curly and I went on with Aaron as a guide, and Tim stayed to take care of Fierro's mules till Fierro, Liz and Seth got back. Aaron was riding a big, raw boned gelding, and I noticed Seth's horse was also big. They both looked like good stock.

We were about two miles out of town when Aaron turned into a lane lined with big white oaks on each side. There was a good pasture on one side, and a field of young corn on the other. About half a mile down the lane we crossed a small stream, stopping to let the horses and mules water, then on another hundred yards up a slight hill to a large, two story log cabin. As we rode up we were announced by two large red hounds, who came bounding out to meet us. I commanded Buck to stay with me, and he walked right by my horse, growling a bit, but not too excited.

As we rode up, a middle aged woman came out onto the porch, wiping her hands on her apron. She waved at Aaron, and told us to go on around to the barn with the animals. Then she saw Curly, and told her to get right down off that horse, and let the men take care of the animals.

"You look plum tuckered out." She told Curly. "It's still early in the day, but there is lots of hot water, and more heating. You can just go in the back room, and I'll get the wash tub there with plenty of hot water, and you just soak some of that trail dust off." She looked at me. "Young man, get her some clothes and bring them."

I grinned at her, said "Yes Mam." and rode to the barn.

Aaron laughed and said that the lady was a distant cousin, and her husband was the owner of a trading post in St. Genevieve. We had all the packs off and in a shed, and the animals turned out to pasture by the time the others arrived. As they came up the drive Fierro was driving their horse, hitched to the buggy, and Liz was leaning against him. She had a cloth pressed to her face, and I could see it was bloody.

Supper was served late, and all of us except Fierro and Liz were gathered around a table for the first time since Tim and I had left the Clarks in Kentucky, and met Curly. I had a big helping of fried potatoes and roast beef, and was looking toward an apple cobbler in the middle of the table, when a thought came to my mind.

"Tim, and Curly, we have never been together around a table before.

We have eaten standing, or sitting around a fire, or looking over a boat rail, or riding a horse. In fact, we have not slept in a house, Curly, since we met you." She smiled at this thought, and then went on eating and talking with Seth and Aaron.

I was not so hungry now, and leaned back to think, and watch. Tim was putting away the food like it was his last meal. Aaron and Seth were also doing their share. Curly was a different story. She had eaten very little. She was smiling, talking to her Uncles, and appeared more like the girl I had first met at the barn dance. So much had happened since then, and it occurred to me she had been living in a very uncertain, dangerous world since then. It had taken a great amount of courage, and faith in God, for her to even think of leaving her family, and throwing in her lot with two strange young men.

For a month she had slept every night where there was danger, and on a couple of occasions it had almost taken her life. Now, tonight she would be safe behind walls, in a protected place, and not have to worry. The Uncles had told her we would be staying in a house each night till we got to their home, where she intended to stay. She looked to me like a weight was taken off her shoulders. She had obviously washed and combed her hair, and the dark curls framed her face. I noticed she helped the lady with putting the meal on the table, and they were getting along fine.

I had enjoyed the hot water and even managed to trim my hair and what little beard I had. Clean clothes and now a meal sure made the world look a lot better. The owner of the Inn has been most helpful in taking care of all of us, thanks to the brothers Seth and Aaron.

Curly turned toward me, and I suddenly realized I was staring at her.

"Is everything alright, Ross," she said.

I felt my face get red.

"I was thinking of all the things we've been through since we met at the dance in Kentucky. You and Tim are sure the best to travel the trail with. And I have to include Buck, even if he likes you best."

Curly's white teeth flashed in her tanned face as she laughed, and Tim chuckled between bites of cobbler.

"I've been telling Aaron and Seth about some of the things that happened to us. They are impressed." She smiled again.

I reach for the cobbler.

Later I walk out to the pasture fence to check on the animals, and Buck goes with me. It's a warm evening, and definitely feeling like the beginning of summer. There is a half moon, and its light enough to see shadows on the ground. I see the mules and horses and hear them eating the good pasture grass. Even though they are behind a fence I insisted they all be hobbled, and put my little horse in the barn. Aaron and Seth put their horses in the barn also. As I'm looking I hear soft footsteps and Curly walks up beside me. She does not say anything, and we stand quietly, listening. An owl has been hooting, there are several frogs croaking, and suddenly the beautiful, mournful cry of the whip-poor-will floats out over us. Curly takes hold of my arm, and we are still. Buck sits right in front of Curly.

"Ross, I'm really concerned about Liz. She is coughing up lots of blood, and there is nothing we can do to stop it. Fierro is scared and worried."

Suddenly the mules stop eating and raise their heads. They are all looking toward the back of the pasture, past the barn. Curly's hand tightens on my arm. I reach over slowly with my other hand and touch her lips with my finger. Now all the animals are staring. I look closely in the direction they are looking, but don't see anything. Then I notice all the night sounds have stopped but the Whip-poor-will. Now I take Curly's hand, and start walking slowly and carefully toward the barn. When we reach the edge of the barn I stop, and look toward the animals. They are lowering theirs heads and starting to eat again, except for one of our mules, which continues to look.

Something is not right, and my heart is beating faster, but I think it's partly because Curly is standing so close to me. We walk back to the house, and I whisper to Curly that I'm going to stay in the barn tonight. She nods, reaches up and gives me a big hug, and goes into the house, where several lamps are still burning.

I hold Buck close and stand right by the door in the shadow for several minutes, then go around the side of the house and out to the fence, which I follow to the barn yard. As we get close to the barn Buck stiffens and I can feel the hackles rise. I hold him tight and stop. We look and walk around, but there is nothing there. I go back to the fence again and watch the animals and listen to the night sounds. I stand for some time, not being anxious to go in and lie down. I keep thinking of Curly, and how pretty she is. Lights are still on in the house, and suddenly I hear a cry. I turn and walk rapidly to the house. Curly meets me at the door.

"Liz just left us. I talked to her some more this evening, and she told me she had made her peace with the Lord long ago, and she was ready to go to Him. All she asked was that we help Fierro, cause he was going to be a mighty lonely man without her." Curly burst into tears, and I hold her close.

CHAPTER 17

We are on the road again. Its Tim, Curly, and me on our horses, with Fierro driving his buggy, and the Greenup men, Aaron and Seth, along with us.

Liz died night before last, and we buried her this morning, in a family plot belonging to the Innkeeper, at the back of their property. Fierro said he had never been able to find out about any kinfolk, and so we had a minister come out from St. Genevieve, and have services over her grave. Curly and I have talked about that first night at the Inn, and decided there was a presence which we could not understand, and Buck was aware of it. Curly said she had seen this happen before, and I knew of such things in the hills at home. Fierro told us he wanted to keep traveling with us, if that was alright with us. He has not gone through her belongings, and wants Curly to help him. She has comforted him through all the sad ordeal of Liz dying and the burial.

As I ride I think about Liz. I'm going to miss her cheerful voice around the fire, and as we travel. For all the troubles she had been through, and all the rough treatment, she still was able to look on the bright side. She sure 'mothered' all of us, and I know Curly was glad to have another woman along. This thought reminds me of Curly, and I think how much I liked the hug she gave me, and how I like to be close to her as we travel. Pa and Ma always liked doing things together, and Ma always was a strong voice of reason in our daily lives.

We come to an open meadow and decide to stop, check the packs, and have a cup of coffee. Aaron and Seth told us they need to talk to us before we get to their settlement. That won't be for another day, but they seem to be concerned. While we are going over all the packs and rigging, Curly fixes a big pot of coffee, and soon we are all sitting around with a mug of steaming liquid. I watch Fierro carefully. He took it real hard to lose Liz, and seems to be in kind of a trance. Buck has licked his hand a couple of times. That ugly dog surprises me. He seems to have a sense of what a person is feeling. It appears to me Curly and Buck are both mighty good to have along. Aaron looks around the group and speaks.

"We are all Greenup's, except for Fierro, and I don't know much about him, but you boys appear to trust him, and that's good enough for me. Now I know Samantha, or Sammie, or Curly, is planning on staying with us for awhile, since we are kin. You boys have a reputation for being tough as a hickory nut, and as long as you are there, we won't have any trouble." He stopped and took a long drink.

"But soon as you leave, there is going to be a crowd of fellers around wanting to court Curly. So you better have it all worked out before we get there. If she is spoken for, let us know, and we can kinda watch out for your interest. Otherwise, you can ride on west and never give it another thought."

What he said hit me right in the wind. I looked sideways at Curly, and she was all red faced and looking the other direction. Tim had a serious expression on his face, and then it changed to a big grin. "Ross, he's saying you are going to have to fish or cut bait. Which will it be?"

Fierro spoke up.

"Ross, don't answer till you think it over good. This little gal is a special person. My Liz told me to keep a close watch over her while I can, and I intend to do that as long as she will let me. So let's ride on out of here, and think about it."

About then Curly got to her feet. Now her face is really red.

"You stuck up men, stand around and discuss me like I was a piece of property for sale. That's not the Christian way men treat their women, and I'll make up my own mind whether or not I'm spoken for. I'm just as tough as any other Greenup!"

With that she stomped off and started gathering up her horses and getting ready to go. I have not said a word.

As we ride on, I'm deep in thought. I think of Pa and Ma back on the home place, and how thin and worn Ma is, just like most of the other hill country women. I think of how Pa treats her differently than most of the women there get treated, and of the little grave out on the hill. I think of Rachel, and that she is already being courted by some feller from another cove. Well, most of the hill country gals get married when they are as old as she is, about sixteen, and by the time they are twenty already have some little ones tugging at their aprons. Either that, or some little graves on the hillside. Then I think of what may be ahead in my life, and wonder if I'm headed where the Lord wants me to go.

I'm riding last, and Curly rides back along side me. Nothing is said for awhile, but I can glance sideways at her and see how nice looking her figure is, even in the rough clothes she is wearing. Dark, curly hair peeks from the edge of her hat. She turns to look at me, and speaks.

"Ross, I've been thinking. I sure put a load on you boys when I joined you. I'm mighty grateful for you helping me out of a bad place, and always will be. But I sure don't want you to think you have any obligation to me. For all I care you can just ride on your way, and I'll take care of myself."

Her lip began to tremble as she said the last, and she spurred her horse to ride ahead. Then she wheeled back, and crowded close to me.

"That's not true," she said. "I do care. A lot!"

With that statement, she was gone ahead of me, to ride with the two brothers.

We get in late at the farmhouse of another cousin, and this time we will all bed down in the barn. The cousin invites us to a late supper, then we sit around on their front porch and visit for awhile. I ask Aaron if we can spend a couple of days at one of their places after we get there. I need to do some work on horse and mule shoes and hooves before we get to Westport. He agrees to that, and asks Fierro if he can set up shop for a couple of days. We all finally go to the barn and get some much needed rest, but not before Curly walks close to me and says,

"Ross, lets pray about this matter of you and me."

This morning I'm up early, and getting the packs ready. Fierro is lending a hand, and hitching to his buggy.

"Ross, I'm sure the last person to tell you what to do, but I've been all over the world, and can sure tell you Curly is a rare find. Ask her if she knows Proverbs 31." He turns away as breakfast is called.

Now I don't remember what Proverbs 31 says, if I ever knew. I eat in a hurry, walk over to the fireplace mantle where the family Bible is lying, and open it to Proverbs 31. I am some amazed as I read it. Curly sees me reading and walks over to look over my shoulder.

"Did you ever read this?" I ask her. Her answer was swift.

"Sure have. And did you ever read the fifth chapter of Ephesians?"

With that she turned and walked away. Well, I'm sure stumped again. I find the book of Ephesians, and by now the rest of them are watching me. I read chapter five, close the book, and walk outside, without saying a word.

For two hours, as we ride north, I'm in deep thought. I'm amazed at Fierro, knowing about Proverbs 31. I agree with him, that Curly is sure an unusual person. I think of the days we have spent on the trail together, and what I know of how she acts. I think of the way she treated Liz, and the various things she can do. I think of Rachel, and I think of Ma, and how she would probably like Curly. I try to think of what Pa would tell me to do. He would tell me to follow my heart, and the teaching of the Word, and not put too much stock in advice from other people. I think of the mountain women, and the hardships they face every day, and the hopelessness of so many of their lives.

All the thinking just about wears me out, but it also makes me realize what Aaron said is probably true. If I ride away without any kind of agreement with Curly, she is going to either be gone back home, or be married to someone else when we come back from the shining mountains. Thinking of the shining mountains, reminds me of one of the real reasons for making this trip. I want to see the shining mountains of the west. What will Curly think of that, and how will we work out what to do. To myself, I say, Lord, help me do this right.

Last night I prayed, and asked for answers. I sure didn't hear a voice, but then Fierro is giving me a Bible passage first thing this morning about the virtues of a good wife, and then I get a reminder from Curly of what it means to be a good husband. Maybe those were answers.

The sun is high noon when Aaron announces we are going to be turning west into the Bourbeuse River valley, and then it's about a three hour ride on to their village of Mosette, on the Miramac River. We stop, build a small fire, and put on a pot of coffee. Curly is singing and cheerful, apparently her usual self, but I'm scared, because I've made up my mind. I would rather take on a wild panther than do what I'm about to do. I know Curly is not going to like any bold announcements, and I've got to do this right.

"Curly, can I talk to you a bit?" I ask her.

Her reply was not exactly as excited as I thought it might be, considering what had already been said. I see Tim and the brothers grinning at each other, and Fierro had to go check his buggy wheel. I lead the way over to some big oak trees some distance away from the others.

"Curly, I've been thinking this over." I start, and stop. She is cool as a cucumber, staring over my shoulder at something. I wait a few seconds, then plow ahead.

"I've been thinking about all the times we have had together, and it appears to me we could really get along good, if we got hitched." I stammer and stop again, and she still doesn't say anything. It is real quiet. I think of the way I had intended to say this, and I have just made a mess of the whole thing. Her eyes brim with sudden tears.

"Ross Greenup, is that all you've got to say! If it is, you can just go take care of your old mules, and don't ever bother me again!" She turned.

"No! Wait!" Now I am desperate. "I've been watching you all these weeks, and how pretty you are, and how you get along with people, and help, like you did with Liz, and," I stop again, and she wipes her eyes on her sleeve. "and I don't like the idea of living without you. Will you marry me?"

There, it is out, and I have made a perfect fool of myself, and she is glaring at me.

"Ross Greenup, is that the only reason you want to marry me, because I get along with folks, and help out once in a while?"

I am sinking fast. Finally, I gather my wits together for one last try, look right into her eyes, reach out to take her hands, and in a low, shaking voice, say:

"Curly, I want you to marry me, because of those other things, but mostly because I love you!"

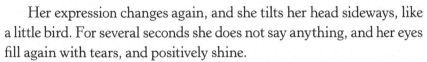

Her expression changes again, and she tilts her head sideways, like a little bird. For several seconds she does not say anything, and her eyes fill again with tears, and positively shine.

"Oh Ross, I love you, too, and have since the first time I saw you. Yes, I will marry you, but we sure have a lot of talking to do."

Then she said something which made me immediately know I had made the right choice.

"There are so many things to consider, like your trip to the shining mountains, which you must finish, and when will we get married, and where we will live."

She stopped, partly because I have gathered her in my arms, for the first time since I met her. It sure seems right for her to be there, and her slim arms slide right around my neck, and we whisper to each other.

We stand for a few moments, then turn back toward the fire and the others. Tim lets out a yell, and throws his hat in the air. Aaron and Seth grin and clap their hands. I see Buck walk over to Fierro and sit down by him. Fierro patted his big head, and I know it is a bittersweet time for Fierro. They all stand then, and wait for one of us to say something.

"Reckon all of you knew this was about to happen!" I say. "Anyway, Curly and I have agreed we are meant to get married, and it appears to be in God's will. We don't know exactly when or where, but we will work all that out."

Curly looks at me, then at all of them, and speaks.

"I know that all of you are the best family a girl could travel with on the trail. I know I probably seem like a tomboy to you, but now I'm an engaged woman, and would you mind calling me Samantha, or maybe Sammie for short?"

While the others are shaking my hand and hugging Curly, or Sammie, Fierro suddenly rushed to one of his packs in the buggy. He digs into it and retrieves something, then comes over to me.

"You folks have been so good to Liz and me, I want you to have this, and I know Liz would want the same thing," he says and holds out his hand to me. In it's a gold ring, with a beautiful stone setting. "Sammie can wear it to show she's spoken for."

I turn to Sammie and she immediately holds out her left hand. I slip the ring on her finger, and it's a fit. She smiles shyly at me, then rushes to Fierro and hugs him tightly, as the tears flow freely.

After a cup of strong, black coffee, we are in the saddle again, and moving at a fast pace. There are now so many things Sammie and I have to tell each other. Lots of them are just between her and me, but even now as we ride along we begin to talk about how Tim and I are going to keep our eyes open for good land to raise horses on, as we go on to Westport, and then on west. Aaron and Seth get real excited as we talk about the possibilities, and I can see they are just busting with ideas. The time flies by, and we are across the Merimac and close to the village where the Greenup's trade. Then we ride up in the yard of a nice one story log cabin, set in a grove of trees, with a big pasture being cleared on one side, and a barn and corral below the house on the other side. Arron looks at Samantha.

"Well, Sammie, this will be home for you for awhile."

About then the door of the house flies open and a sweet faced young woman runs down the path toward us. She is followed by a small child, then two more children appear out at the barn. They are yelling that Daddy is home.

CHAPTER 18

It's late in the afternoon as Sammie and I walk slowly down the path from Aarons house to the spring, where ice cold water is trickling from the wooden spring box and over the rocks. The water then goes over a series of limestone ledges and small falls, deep pools, and through a narrow, wooded little ravine to the creek. Water cress and mint grow along its edges. We have been here five days, and this quiet, cool place is one of our favorites. There is a split log bench close to the stream. It has been a busy five days, but Sammie and I still managed to spend several hours by ourselves. Tim and I have been taking care of the horses and mules, getting their hooves and shoes in good shape before going on to Independence. Fierro set up his shop and tools, and has been sharpening knives and trading with the local folks. Sammie has taken care of repairing some of our clothing, which is beginning to show wear and tear. Tim is smiling real big at one of the teen-age girls, and her folks invited him to supper.

One afternoon several of the boys and young men start wrestling on the grass in front of the blacksmith shop. The girls, including Sammie, were watching, cheering and clapping for their favorites. I watch for a while, then one of the fellows, about my size, grins at me, and motions for me to join them. Off comes my shirt, I hand it to Sammie, and now I'm in my element. He is quick and strong, and throws me on my back, but I'm right up, and throw and pin him twice. We have a great time, and when I glance at Sammie I see her eyes shining.

All of us have been talking with Aaron and Seth, about the possibility of raising horses and mules here, and establishing trading posts for the move west of the settlers. We have a need for horses that are strong and rugged for the trail, not the long legged racing breeds. Since Pa and Uncle Rich are raising Morgan saddle horses, and big mules, that's what we have with us. Just this week I saw one of the Quarterhorse breed of horses. They are big, strong saddle horses, and we may want to look into raising them also. One of the Greenup cousins is building wagons and wants us to try one of his new wagons on the Santa Fe Trail. He has one already at Independence, where his shop is located, and will give it to us to use. There is good land available here.

One of the relatives here is a banker, and Tim and I spent some time with him, and got some valuable advice about trading. He also gave us a letter of introduction to a friend in Independence. With his help we did some re-arranging of the packsacks which held our lead shot and the gold, and I did some replacing of the gold with some other coin, which he suggested.

This is the Sabbath, and Tim, Sammie and I went to the Meeting House this morning. It's just through the woods, on the far side of Aaron's place. There was dinner on the grounds, and then some singing. I put Buck in the barn, figuring all the food might be too much temptation for him. Right now, I'm getting anxious to get on the trail again. Sammie turns to me, and I gather her in my arms. She puts a finger on my lips.

"Ross, my heart is going with you. We have known each other for just a few weeks, but I feel like this has been ordained and blessed by God. I love you, my sweet, and pray for your safe return."

Her lips tremble as she looks at me, and I kiss her eyes closed.

"Sammie, I love you too, and I'm sure going to do my best to get back soon and in one piece!"

"Ross! Ross!" I hear Tim shout, and there is alarm in his voice.

As I turn and look back along the path, two men appear right behind us, both with drawn pistols pointed at me. I push Sammie behind me as I face them. They look about like the Allen boys, but even more dirty and ragged.

"Ross Greenup, do exactly as we tell you, or both you and the gal are dead. Put your hands behind your head, and walk back up this path by yourself. Leave her here. If she tries to warn anybody, you will be dead. Our partners are with Tim, and its too bad he tried to warn you."

A red fury rises in me as I start back up the trail. I can feel the handle of my hidden knife between my shoulder blades, but there is no chance to do anything now. I hope Sammie stays calm. As we walk out of the trees I see Tim struggling to sit up, with blood pouring from a cut on his head, while two men stand and watch him, both holding guns pointed at him.

"Greenup, take us where your gear is. We are going to search it. We know you are getting ready to leave tomorrow, and you better cooperate with us. You don't, you may not ever see the gal alive again."

I struggle to stay calm. I figure there is no use stalling, since they seem to know what we are doing, and they didn't hesitate to knock Tim down. They know our names, so this has been planned by someone.

"Did Quintara, or the Allen boys pay you to do this?" I growl.

I get a sharp prod in the back from a pistol barrel.

"We ask the questions!" one of them snarls.

We walk toward the barn, where all our gear is packed and ready to put on the mules in the morning. As we get to the stall door, the pistol is stuck in my back again.

"You wait here."

By this time Tim and his two escorts have caught up with us. Tim is holding a bloody cloth to his head. I hear Buck scratching at a stall door and growling. One of Tim's captors and one of mine enter the stall where our gear is stacked, and the other two watch us closely. I wonder why nobody has seen them, but evidently they have been waiting till everyone is gone or out of sight. I hear them going through our equipment, then an exclamation.

"Here it is, just like Roberto said it would be!"

They come out of the stall, carrying a heavy leather bag, and step out into the light. They set the bag on the ground, and open the top. The four of them crowd around the bag. One of them reaches in and pulls out a handful of coins. There is silence for a few seconds. Then they both turn on me.

"Where is it? Where is the gold?"

I look at them and laugh.

"Did Roberto and his Pa tell you the same lie they told the Allen's? What gold? Bet Roberto told you Sammie was his girl. Well, guess what! She and I are getting married. You better have collected some pay in advance, cause you sure wont get any when you get back without the gold or the girl. Go ahead and take a handful of that money. In fact, take the whole bag. It's not gold, and it never was gold."

I hear the sound of a horse running, then another. Then Aaron appears walking toward the barn, and suddenly there are a dozen men, all heavily armed, walking toward us with drawn pistols or rifles. A horse skids to a stop and two armed teenage boys jump off. I jump back and grab Tim, who is still groggy and in pain, and pull him away from the group of four thugs.

"Drop your guns!" shouts Aaron. "You are surrounded and we'll shoot you to pieces if you even raise your hand."

Another horse is pulled to a halt in front of us. Before the four toughs can do more than drop their weapons, the rider has thrown a braided leather lariat loop, and it settles around the shoulders of one of the four. The rider is one of the Greenup cousins. He jerks the loop tight, and spurs his horse. As the tough hits the ground on his back the other three go to their knees and begin to plead for their lives. Dragging the man to a large oak tree standing nearby, the rider stops, throws the loose end of his rope over a low limb, and jumps off his horse. The two teenage boys run over with a short rope and tie the tough's hands behind him, and stand him on his feet. Then they put the loop of the other rope around his neck. He is now screaming and crying for mercy. The boys look at me and then at Aaron. Aaron walks toward me while other men gather up the weapons of the thugs. Aaron looks at me and winks.

"What do you want to do, Ross? Hang them?"

"Sure!" I say. "I'm getting tired of these shenanigans by these crooks. First, let's find out who is paying them, then hang them all. Did Sammie tell you what was going on?"

"Yea. She came tearing into the church yard, screeching like a gut-shot panther. Didn't take long to get action out of this bunch."

I walk to the man with the rope around his neck.

"Who paid you to do this?" I ask.

His answer was to spit at me.

I motion the lads holding the other end of the rope. They really get into the spirit of the moment, and putting their weight on the rope, tighten it and haul his feet off the ground. He begins to kick and struggle violently, and we let him hang for about five seconds. I motion them again, and they let him down to the ground. I loosen the noose around his neck.

"Now I'm going to ask you the question again, and if you don't give me the right answer, we are going to put you on the horse, and run him out from under you. Then we are going to do the same with the other three. All of you listen up. Who paid you to come after us, and where are you from?"

This time there are three rasping voices answering. The man with the rope around his neck can't talk. They all say the same name.

"Roberto Quintara and his Pa, and we're from St. Louis!"

I step over to Aaron and we walk out of hearing of the group. By this time Ben is here, and another older man, who is also a Greenup, and a Deacon in their church. My fury has cooled down, and I listen carefully to their wise counsel. Then I turn back to the group, and speak loudly, so they can all hear me.

"This is what we are going to do. We are going to turn you loose, but we are keeping your weapons. Your horses have been found where you left them tied. You will be given a handful of the money you tried to rob from us, and you are to take it to the Quintara's and tell them that's what you found. Is that understood?" They stood silently, and nodded. I went on.

"About everybody that lives here is a Greenup or relative. There are Greenup's working on the steamboats and on the river fronts. We are going to pass the word if any of them see you doing anything that looks suspicious, to shoot first and ask questions later. Tell the Quintara's the same goes for them." I pause and let it sink in.

"We are generally a God-fearing people, and want to love our neighbor, but that sure does not mean we let our neighbor abuse us. I will be the first one to come for you if anything else happens. Now, get the ropes off that bum, and all of you, *GIT!*"

There was a rush to untie their partner, then with him slightly staggering they leave. Aaron tells the young men with the horses to follow them and make sure they get well on their way. That order is carried out with great glee.

Sammie comes running to us, and after giving me a hug goes to Tim, and starts looking at his head wound. I thank the entire group for their help, and I am really serious. I think they saved us from serious injury, or possible death. I go to Sammie and Tim, and we help Tim to the house. The thugs had hit him with a short, heavy club, which seemed to be a common weapon among them for close fighting. No doubt they were used to doing this sort of thing. I watch Sammie clean and care for Tim's cut. He is sure going to have a headache. I'm mighty proud of her.

"Sammie," I say. "I was sure hoping you would do just what you did. They were watching us so closely we would not have had a chance of doing anything, if you hadn't sounded the alarm."

She looks at me and gives me a warm smile. I know she can hear the pride and admiration in my voice. When she is finished Tim lies down on the porch, with a blanket under his head, and soon is asleep. Sammie and I decide to spend the rest of the evening with each other and with Aaron's family. Right away we had found out we both liked children, and have already talked about having a family of our own. Aaron's three small children remind me of the tiny little girl back in the hills, who came into our lives for such a short time, and whose grave Ma goes to frequently. Aaron's children have already adopted Sammie as their own, and it appears Aaron's wife is glad for the help. Also, we discovered the local school has so many children, the two teachers there already would be glad for help, and the school board will be asking Sammie if she will be interested in teaching.

Sammie and I finally kiss goodnight when everyone else has gone to bed, and a whip-poor-will is calling. I go to the barn to sleep close to our gear and animals. We will need to repack a little in the morning, and Fierro will join Tim and me with his buggy and horses and mules. Then we can get started once again.

It's getting light when I wake. Buck had slept near me, but he is not around, and I figure he went to the house to greet Sammie. I slip on pants and moccasins, and walk down the path to the spring and pools below them to take a quick dip before breakfast. It's going to be a warm day, but there is a faint cool breeze blowing in the trees by the spring. I pass the spring and then hear something down below me in one of the pools. I stop and listen and look. Then I faintly see the form of Samantha standing waist deep in the pool. She is naked, and I catch my breath sharply at her beauty.

I've never seen a grown woman without clothes on, and she is standing sideways to me, with the outline of her small breasts showing in the soft light. I'm speechless. My heart is pounding, and my mouth instantly dry. Just then Buck sees me and starts wagging his tail. He is lying by her clothing at the side of the pool. He is probably supposed to be guarding her, and afterward I tell her he is so taken by her beauty he forgets to keep watch. Samantha sees him look around, and she sees me. An involuntary "oh" escapes from her lips and she instantly folds her arms over her breasts. I continue to be speechless and entranced.

"Oh Ross!" she says faintly. "Will you please look away while I get my clothes on."

I look the other way, and hear her step out of the pool and dress. Then she appears beside me, and takes my arm.

"Sammie, you are so beautiful!" I stammer.

She squeezes my arm, and we walk up the path. About then we meet Aaron walking down the path to get a bucket of water. He says "Good morning" as he steps off the path to let us go by, and watches with a little smile on his face as we pass. I nod, and don't say anything. Buck is racing ahead to see if the kids are up, and greet the other dogs. We go by the barn, and I put on a shirt, then we go to breakfast.

While we eat Sammie will hardly look at me, and her face is flushed. I figure mine is the same, and I eat in a hurry. I leave the table and Tim and I start packing the mules, and get everything ready to go. It just doesn't seem right to be leaving without Sammie. She comes to the barn to watch, then Fierro shows up with his animals and equipment. We are leading six mules, including Fierro's, so have them in a single string, pulled by one rider. Fierro is using his saddle horse to pull the light buggy, but can trade off for a mule if needed.

Now there is a small crowd, as the family gathers around to wish us God-speed and safety. The sun is getting hot. Insects are buzzing around, and flies are beginning to get bad. The father and mother and young woman who invited Tim to supper drive up in their buggy. Finally we are all set to go. I stand by Sammie and put my arm around her. The older Greenup is there, and he looks around the group and speaks.

"Let's all bow our heads, and ask the Lord's blessings on these young men and Fierro as they travel. They have just come into our lives, and we already think of them as part of our family."

Hats come off, and heads are bowed, as he prays. When he finishes, I kiss Sammie, and she slips a little package into my shirt pocket, then reaches to touch the knife scar on my face.

"Be careful, and don't forget me, Sweetheart."

We mount up, and are on our way. We leave with a clatter and a jingle of harness and equipment. The animals are anxious to move, and Buck licks Sammie's hand, and takes his place at the front of the procession. I'm in front, Tim is next, leading the mules, and Fierro brings up the rear with his buggy. As we go around the last bend, where the barn is still visible, I turn and look back. Sammie is standing alone, and we wave, with palms out, wishing each other farewell, and God's Blessing.

CHAPTER 19

Six days ago we left the little village, where Sammie was staying with other Greenup's. We have been traveling fast, and not really looking for farm land. So far there has not been much trouble with roads, and since we are traveling with horses, mules, and one light buggy, we have been able to cover many miles a day. Based on information from other travelers, we are cutting across some of the great bends the Missouri River makes. The river itself is never stable, with the main channel moving back and forth as flood waters, bank cave-ins, and other things alter its course.

One traveler told me of a village on the south side of the Missouri, called Hermann, where a group of German settlers were planting vineyards and establishing wineries. Several travelers told us we should follow the river from a village called Jefferson City to a boat landing on the north side of the river called Roche-port. It sounds like a wild place. We were in a hurry, and kept moving. The river takes a big bend north there.

Tonight we are camped by the road, on a high bluff overlooking the Missouri. Tim, Fierro and I are sitting around our campfire, talking about the trip. Buck is stretched out at my feet. He is one tired, ugly dog. In the morning we will ride into Independence, and there we will find a wagon built by one of the Greenup's. We passed a group of wagons and settlers yesterday. I talked to one of them. Their leaders said they were going to try the Oregon Trail. Evidently not many settlers are going that way. Right now it's mostly traders and trappers going to Santa Fe.

"Tim, I reckon we have bit off quite a chew, considering what we have in mind." I say.

Tim grinned and looked at Fierro, who was sound asleep.

"We shore have, but I'm looking forward to getting away from the crowds and on our own. One thing sure, there is a lot of good land in this part of the country. We haven't had any trouble with the animals. Not one of them has gone lame, and we have been moving fast."

I pull a small leather pouch from my pocket. It has the name Ross done in beadwork, inside a heart branded into the leather.

"This is part of the reason." I say. "Sammie is praying for us. I know she is praying we will be safe, but I know she is also praying, when we do have problems, we will be strong and wise enough to handle them."

Buck stretched and looked around at the sound of Sammie's name. I know he misses her, and I sure do. Never thought I would be lonesome for someone so much. During the long hours of riding I've thought a lot about what we are going to do when I get back. I stretch out and go to sleep.

This morning we are up early and ready to go before the sun is well up. I lead the way, and soon we are in the midst of mass confusion. Dust is in the air, mules, horses, oxen and wagons are going in every direction, dogs barking, and people talking or shouting. There are at least two blacksmiths working, and there is smoke and the smell of hot iron. A horseman pulls up by us, and I ask the way to Danny Greenup's stables.

"Turn right past the Jefferson Hotel, and you'll see it right in front of you." he said.

We do that, and there is a good sized barn and stables, with a yard full of used and new wagons of all kinds, shapes and sizes. We tie our animals, and put Buck in the buggy where he can see and tell him to stay. He knows what that means, and watches everything carefully. We walk into the barn. The smell of fresh hewed lumber fills the air, and boards, shavings and tools are scattered around the floor. In the back of the barn is a blacksmith shop, and there is one man busy at the anvil. Smoke is rising from the forge, and a black boy is pumping the bellows.

"Is Danny Greenup here," I ask an old timer who is busy painting a wagon box.

He jerks a thumb toward two men standing by a stack of boards. As

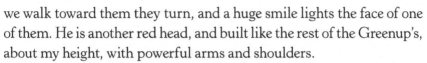

we walk toward them they turn, and a huge smile lights the face of one of them. He is another red head, and built like the rest of the Greenup's, about my height, with powerful arms and shoulders.

"You've got to be Ross and Tim!" he yells, and grabs my hand.

"I've been expecting you, and you must be Fierro." He shouts again, as he about lifts the slight Fierro off the ground.

We soon find we are hearing his normal speaking voice, at least while we are around the barn. Before I can say anything he and the other man lead us out into the wagon yard.

"This is about the best wagon maker around these parts." says Danny, indicating the slender young man with him. "His name is Burl Johnson, and he knows all there is to know about wagons. I think he already has one picked out for you. Heard you boys had a little trouble at the village."

By now I'm not too surprised at how fast news travels along the river.

"Well, yes, we did, but the clan sure took care of us. Let's look at the wagon." He grins and slaps me on the back.

"We are on a kind of a trial run, testing our mules and horses, and not interested in pulling a big wagon across the prairie to Santa Fe." I say. "Can we have a small wagon, that four mules can handle, and carry enough trade goods to make it worth our while?"

"We already knew that." Said Burl. "Its right here, and we have a supplier who is willing to give you a load of trade goods at a good price. We didn't know what Fierro wanted to do, but if he has in mind traveling by buggy, we can get him a load of goods that's not too heavy. With this wagon you can either sell it at Santa Fe, or load it with whatever you want to and bring it back."

That sure sounded good to me, and Tim, who had a good eye for wagons, walked around it with a big smile. Fierro was looking at it closely, and I could tell he was trying to figure out what to do.

"What do you boys figure my buggy is worth, if I was to trade it for a new wagon?" he asks Danny.

This really surprised me, as I knew Fierro for a canny trader, and he usually was the one to say what an item was worth. Then I realized he was really showing a lot of trust in Danny, and figuring Danny would be fair with him. Danny looked at him, then bellowed:

"Let's look at your buggy."

We all walk back to the front of the barn, where our animals and equipment are tied. When we get there Buck is standing with his feet on the side of the buggy, growling at a man on horseback who is looking over our outfit. He has a star pinned on his vest.

"Howdy Marshall." says Danny.

The Marshall looks at me, then at Tim and then back to Danny. He shifted a big chaw of tobacco from one cheek to the other, then spit a long stream of tobacco juice in the dirt. I already knew part of what he was going to say. I spoke sharply to Buck, and that ugly dog sat down in the buggy and gave me a big toothy grin.

Sure enough, the Marshall said what I figured he would.

I gotta hand it to you Greenup's. Ya'll are built about like some of these oak trees around here. I also know you are tough to handle in a mix-up. I already got the word you would be in town, and to keep an eye on you."

The Marshall grinned at Danny as he said this, and Danny promptly introduced us to Marshall Von Baer. He has a hard, powerful handshake, about like Danny, and the two brothers, Aaron and Seth.

"Pleased to meet ya," I said, "and I surely hope we won't be any trouble." The Marshall laughed as he shook hands with Tim, and then Fierro.

"Well, considering it was one of them girl Greenup's, Samantha, I believe, that passed the word, I reckon we won't be too worried. I've got all I can do just keeping track of Danny." He rode off down the street.

I felt my face get red, and Danny gave me a slap on the back that was like a bear paw, and a roar of laughter. Then we got down to business. He looked at Fierro's buggy, and told him if he loaded it light, and was real careful, it would be worth quite a bit in Santa Fe or Taos. He reminded us there was a difficult, high mountain pass between Trinidad and Raton, in New Mexico territory. It was still safer than going the Cimarron Cutoff. In the end, Fierro traded the buggy for the wagon, deciding to pull the wagon with his two mules, then sell wagon and mules in Santa Fe. He might ride his horse back with us, or do something else.

It is dark when we have everything ready to load. I'm a bit concerned about four mules pulling the wagon day after day with the load we have.

Danny takes us to a small group of wagons located about half a mile away from the main rush of people. All the wagons are small like ours, or medium sized, and some are already loaded. There are no oxen, just mules. This is strictly a fast moving freight outfit. I notice a couple of dark looking women in the camp. Danny introduced us to the wagon master, a tall, lean, capable looking fellow. He looks us over, especially our horses.

"What breed of horses?" he asks.

"Morgan's." I say. "Bred and raised them ourselves, in the Great Smoky's. Pa used one in the Mexican War in Texas. Been raising them about ten years. We raise our own mules, too."

He looks at Fierro.

"You the feller that has your own shop along?" he asks Fierro.

He seems real pleased to know all Fierro can do. He has evidently already talked to Danny, and has just one more comment.

"I see you boys are well armed, and hear you ain't afraid to take care of yourselves. Well, I'm the boss here, and what I say goes, but I sure don't mind good advice, and don't never turn down help. Glad to have you join us. We leave day after tomorrow, early." He turned and walked off.

We ride back toward Danny's barn, where we are putting our bedrolls for the night. We are going around another group of wagons, when we hear a terrible scream from one of the wagons. We stop as a woman jumps from the wagon to the ground, falls, gets up, tries to run, and falls again. Then she lies moaning on the ground. A man hurries around the wagon and runs to her. As he tries to help her up she hits out at him, and screams again. Another woman comes running from among the wagons, than others. She starts sobbing as we sit silently watching.

"I can't go! I can't go!" she moans. She looks up at the man.

"Please take me home. Please take me home!" He gathers her in his arms as she clutches at him.

We start on, quietly go to the barn, and spread our bedrolls. Tomorrow is going to be mighty busy. I feel pain for the poor anguished woman, and pray a silent prayer for her. Then I think of Sammie, and smile as I go to sleep.

Buck licks my face before I'm fully awake. It's not quite full light yet, and I can see a man standing close to our bedrolls. Buck does not growl, but sure wants us awake. I sit up, put my hat on, and look at the man. He comes closer, and asks if the owner is here. I look around and don't see Danny, so tell him to just wait a bit. He appears to be agitated, and walks nervously back and forth. His face is red, and scratched, and his eyes are bloodshot. I get up, and go to the horse trough outside, where I wash my face and hands in the cold water. Tim is up now, and we get ready to walk down the street to an eating place.

Danny comes in, and the man rushes over to him. We listen as he tells Danny about his wife. It turns out he is the man we saw trying to calm the woman last night, out by the wagon train. His name is Jenson. He tells Danny they have been on the trail a month, from Indiana. His wife was pregnant when they left, lost the baby two weeks ago, and has gradually become totally despairing. He is afraid for her life, and wants to sell everything they have, so he can get steamboat passage back to their home. Other families in the group will buy their household goods, but he wants to know if Danny will buy his wagon and mule team. I have a good idea Danny is thinking about the sad scene last night, as he listens to the desperation in the man's voice. Danny looks at Tim and me.

"Would you fellers be interested in working out some kind of a deal with me, if I buy this wagon and team?" he says.

Now I'm already thinking about how we have been blessed, and when I look at Tim know he is thinking the same thing. I know Sammie would not even hesitate to say yes to this plan of Danny's.

"Danny, you and this fellow work it out, and when you are done, you can find us at the nearest place that serves hot coffee and biscuits and gravy. I can sure think better after breakfast. Bring him along if you want to. Looks like he could stand a little grub under his belt." We walk out.

Well, I'm not surprised when Danny and Jenson walk into the Inn right after we get our first cup of hot coffee. Jenson gets a cup of coffee and after speaking to Danny, the woman running the place lets him take it and another cup for his wife, along with some hot biscuits and bacon. As he is leaving he stops by the table and thanks us with tears in his eyes. Later Tim, Danny and I go out to the camp and get the wagon and mules. We are going to use the mules, with Fierro's wagon, and add some more trade goods to his wagon, since we will be pulling with four mules, but will have two extra mules to switch back and forth.

The man has taken his wife to an Inn in Westport, and is waiting for the next steamboat down river. I give him a letter to give to Josh, if he can find him, and another to Pa and Ma and the Clarks. I figure it will give him something to do. Tim, Danny, Fierro and I finish eating. We have got our work cut out for us.

For two days we have been fixing harness, loading and reloading wagons, making sure of every detail we can think of. Now Fierro, Tim and I are standing around a big fire with the rest of the people from the wagon train. This caravan is equipped to move fast. The wagon master, Jason Furson, stands on a crate and tells everybody to quiet down. He reminds us to take care of our stock, and to try to get along with each other. He sounds like a Believer to me when he says we need to look out for each other, as it tells us in the Bible. He reminds us we have two women with us, and to act accordingly. Then he asks each of us to tell our names, and if we want to, where we are from. The two women are Mexican. One is the wife of Furson, and the other the wife of a teamster who appears to be French. Only one American white woman has ever been over the trail. As soon as we are finished a rough talking, bearded, middle aged man, pulls a jug and half a dozen tin cups from a wagon. He pours whiskey into the cups and hands them out.

"A drink for the trail!" he shouts, and there is a chorus of yells.

He hands one to Fierro, who takes it and drinks it down. Then he hands one to me. I don't take it and just shake my head no. He stops and stares at me.

"Ho, what have we here!" he shouts. "A softy!" It suddenly gets quiet. I look right at him and don't move a hand. Suddenly Jason speaks up.

"Guess I better finish the introductions." He says. "Ross and Tim Greenup are the two youngest members of our caravan. They are first cousins. They may be the youngest, but be careful about making a snap judgment. A few months ago a thug tried to hold up Tim, and steal his horse and buggy. He ended up facing Ross, and got hisself shot dead." He paused and let it sink in. "Then a boatman roughed up Ross's girl, and is still recovering from that fracas. Latest was just a few days ago when four thugs from the big city of St. Louie tries to steal these lad's equipment. The lad's hung one of them from a tree limb, and the rest of them took his body and ran. If I'm not mistaken, that's a knife scar on Ross face. Guess I'd think twice about calling them names." He stopped and looked around.

"Now to make sure you don't take this wrong, I got all this story from some of the black hands on the steamboats. They think dem Greenup boys and dat Fierro man is de best, and they told me not to mess wif dem."

There were chuckles at this, and the man with the jug got a little red in the face and moved back. Then a lanky, dark faced man with a bad limp called out.

"Ross, do you have an Uncle Will Bunch?" I nod yes.

"Wal I'm dammed if he ain't one of the finest mountain men you could ever know. I membered him talking about his family back in the Tennessee mountains. I'm Alex Laroux, and you already met my old lady. Pleased to meet ya, lad."

He limped over and gave me a powerful handshake and slap on the back, and the same with Tim. Everyone started talking, several shook my hand, and we rode back to the barn where Buck was waiting with our wagons. I told Tim and Fierro I didn't see any use correcting the small errors in Furson's story about our actions, and all it did was make it easier for us.

The Wagon Master, Jerry Furson, waves his arm, shouts "Lets Go!" and the mules of the lead wagon lean into their collars. The second wagon moves in behind it. Tim, Fierro and I have worked two days since making the trade with Danny Greenup for the extra wagon and mule team. They are good mules, almost as big as ours, and make a fine four mule team. The wagon is loaded, but not too heavily, so the four mules should be able to handle it easily. This gives us two wagons, with two teams of four mules each, and two extra mules.

The wagon Fierro is driving has all his tools and supplies, as well as quite a lot of trade goods. We are carrying bolts of cloth, rolls of ribbon, sewing supplies, such as thread and needles, trade beads, small tools, bridle bits, lots of tobacco, several pounds of sheet lead, and even two kegs of molasses. We have our bedrolls, cooking kit, oats for the mules and horses, a small keg of gunpowder, and the heavy bag with lead for our weapons and what little gold is left, under that. The gold and tobacco are for dealing with the Mexican authorities, and I have an extra package Danny told me to get, in case of unusual trouble with the Mexicans. Then this morning Danny gave me a letter addressed to a Mr. James Magoffin, an American merchant in Santa Fe. After loading yesterday we hitched up and drove the mules a couple of miles out of Independence and back to make sure everything fit and get the mules used to the idea.

With Danny's help and recommendations, we deposited all the French gold we brought, and most of the American gold, at a bank in Independence, as security for our supplies and the mule trade with Danny. Only the banker knows how much, but he assured Danny it was enough to cover everything.

Tim and I are both armed the same as usual, and have agreed to watch more closely than we have been. We have been a bit careless. I'm driving as we start, sitting on the high seat, and Buck is on the seat by me, till we get out of the crowd. Tim is on his horse, riding close to us. There are eighteen freight wagons total, with about thirty five men and two women. There are also twenty mounted US troopers, and two more women who are wives of their two officers. They are going across Kansas to Bents Fort on the banks of the Arkansas River. There are three army supply wagons and two army ambulance wagons, and the women are riding in them. This is a small caravan, but heavily armed, and with the soldiers along we can expect a minimum of trouble crossing the plains.

All extra horses are herded in a remuda, which is Spanish for extra or spare, unless a saddle horse is kept tied to the back of a wagon. One horseman is in charge of the remuda, and the rest of us take turns helping haze them during the day. At any time there are about fifty horses and ten mules being herded in the remuda.

A crowd is gathered to watch us off. There are shouts of encouragemint, guns are fired into the air, dogs are barking, and even Buck gets into the spirit by letting out a couple of barks. The mules and horses feel the excitement and are stepping out. I watch as the line of wagons straightens out and gets underway. We were the last to join the caravan, and so are last to start. Fierro starts his mules and pulls out. I slap the mule's backs with the reins and shout at them. They lean into the collars, and we fall in last. This is exciting, and I wish Sammie and the whole family could be here to see it.

Just a few miles west of the settlement we begin to leave the wooded areas and see open stretches of grassland. Then the grassland areas become larger, and the caravan pulls up to rest the animals and adjust harness and wagon covers while we look ahead. I stand on the wagon seat and stare. It's just the beginning of what Uncle Will told us about. Deep grass rolls in waves like I would picture ocean waves. Here the trail is wide and there are some scattered cabins, but I can see to the far horizon. The bright blue sky is like an immense blue bowl upside down over us. There are birds flying and calling above the grass. They are Meadowlarks, and have a clear, penetrating call which is pure music. There is a delicious smell of crushed grass, and a breeze is blowing from the west into our faces. I feel a great freedom, and longing to go, and go and keep going, to the far mountains.

Its late in the afternoon and the Wagon Master is leading us in a circle on a flat plain close to a creek. We will do this every night for the rest of the trip. The wagons will be placed with each wagon tongue turned in enough to overlap the next wagon in line, and the first wagon will be by the last wagon. A rope corral will hold most of the animals, with some saddle horses brought inside the wagon circle at night.

We unhitch, and lead the animals to the creek to water. This does not take long with three of us working at it. Then we feed them each a quart of oats and hobble them. Afterward they are turned out to graze on the prairie under the watchful eyes of two riders. Later they will be put inside the rope corral.

We are using chain hobbles, and some of the teamsters look at them and say that's a good idea. Others don't hobble at all. I would rather be safe. My horse and Tim's horse are kept inside at night. We also have Buck, and he is becoming more important as a guard dog.

When the animals are taken care of we build a small fire and fix our supper. Fierro is a fair cook, and Tim and I are only too happy for him to do the cooking. We take care of the fire and cleaning up afterward. Meanwhile Buck is making friends with the two other dogs in camp. It doesn't take long for him to become the boss dog. This first night we are all exhausted, and soon after eating and seeing to the animals we are rolled up in our bedrolls under the wagon, except Fierro. He has fixed a small space on top of his load of freight, under the canvas, and sleeps there. None of us have guard duty tonight. The Wagon Master appointed the crippled mountain man, Alex, to set up a roster for guard duty and enforce it. He may not be able to walk well, but he sure can ride, and I have an idea he can shoot just as well.

It's still dark this morning when the Wagon Master rolls us out. The first thing I'm aware of when I sit up is the breeze. It carries the smell of the prairie, of the grass and flowers, and makes me feel strong, and alive. Uncle Will told us it hardly ever quits blowing, but if it does, be ready to take cover. Tim and Fierro and I are used to early morning wake up, after the days on the trail, and we have the animals fed and harnessed while Fierro gets the coffee going, and some bacon and grits ready. Furson walks up about the time we are finishing eating and we refill his coffee cup. He looks around and nods.

"You lads have done this a couple of times already, it looks like." is his comment. "Mighty glad to have you along, and if that dog gets enough to eat, he can probably do a good job of guarding."

He turns and goes to the next wagon. Last night he told the group the days would be long, but he prefers to start early and quit while there is plenty of time to make a strong, secure camp. He also said we needed to be careful of the sudden violent storms which are common on the plains. Soon we hear his yell, to "Lead out!" to the first wagon, and we are on the trail again.

Tim is driving this morning, and I'm horseback, so it gives me a chance to ride along beside the other wagons, and riders, and get acquainted. Alex Laroux's wife is driving their wagon. Her name is

Flor, and the other woman, Jason's wife, is Maria. At noon we take a rest stop, without circling wagons. We are traveling generally southwest, staying well south of the Kansas River. We pass a long caravan, pulled by oxen. They are mostly families, and have a small herd of cows with them. They are turning north to cross the Kansas River and follow the trail to Oregon, or maybe California. We are going to travel as fast as possible, without hurting the animals. Our first major stop to rest and repair will be at Council Grove, about one hundred thirty miles out, or six days travel. At noon I relieve one of the remuda wranglers.

CHAPTER 20

It's our fifth day on the trail, and about a hundred miles out. It's almost noon, and all morning we have been watching heavy dark clouds gather from the southwest. There have been huge swirls of hot wind, that pick up dust and weeds, as they move rapidly across the prairie. I know now they are called dust-devils, and mean we are probably in for some stormy weather. Jason has told us to stay away from lone trees when there is a storm, and especially to keep the animals from sheltering under them. They attract lightning. He had seen five big mules killed by one lightning strike when they gathered under a tree.

I'm driving the wagon, and Tim is herding remuda. There are occasional groves of trees, but we stay in the open, and on the trail. Now the wind is getting stronger, in violent gusts. The air is sticky and close. The clouds have a yellowish tint, and now ahead of us a solid black column of water begins to fall from the clouds to the ground. Lightning is flashing through the clouds, and some of the flashes are striking the ground. Suddenly we feel a blast of cold air. Jason stops as he rides down the line of wagons.

"That cold air means hail is falling. If we get hit with hail the animals are going to be hard to control. I'm going to stop the caravan, so get ready to protect yourself and probably hold the lead mule's bridles."

He gallops on up the line of wagons. I've already got my oilskins out, and when we stop get down off the high seat and slide into them. I walk to the lead mules and talk to them. Buck is right by me, pacing back and forth. Many of the wagons have two people holding the bridles of the lead animals. The soldiers are all gathered around their supply wagons, and dismounted. An ugly, yellowish curtain of cloud like a wall starts hanging down from the main cloud, and then while I watch, a long white tube extends from the cloud to the ground. I know I'm seeing a tornado for the first time. It is going from right to left, in front of our line. There is a tremendous roar. It hits a grove of trees and suddenly the tube is black and spread out, as it picks up limbs, leaves, and brush. Then the wall of water hits us, and we can see nothing in the solid downpour of water.

Ouch! A hail stone the size of a marble hits my arm, then I'm pelted with hail stones. They come down harder and the mules are jumping and plunging. I hang on to their bridles, and one of them begins to scream in terror. Neither the animals nor us have ever been where we could see the entire storm before, like we can on this open prairie. Suddenly it's over. The trembling mules are staring wild eyed at the white ground, and I can hear and see the storm as it moves on east of us. My saddle horse was tied with a stout halter rope to the back of the wagon, and is still there. The saddle is on him, and protected his back some. We can see the back of the roiling clouds as they race away, and there is no sign of the funnel. A yell startles me. It's Alex, coming in from where the remuda is being held.

"Jason, Ross!" he yells, as his horse slips and slides on the slick hail. 'Tim is gone. He got caught in the tornado."

My heart jumps in my chest.

"Fierro, watch my mules!" I yell, and run to my horse.

In seconds I'm in the saddle, and as Jason comes running we follow Alex as he turns back toward the remuda. Jason yells at the troops as we pass, and they mount and start after us.

Two other riders are rounding up the shivering, nervous horses and mules. They had scattered widely, but are gradually wandering back to the herd. One of the riders trots over to us.

"We were right close to the edge of that stand of cottonwoods!" he says, and points. "Suddenly it looked like the funnel swerved almost right by us. Tim was closest, and I saw him jump off his horse and hold its reins, then I couldn't see anything. After it passed I found Tim's horse down in a little ditch, on its side. He's standing over there by the trees with his saddle on. Don't appear to be hurt."

Jason took charge.

"OK, everybody, spread out, and lets go through these trees real slow. If we don't find him on our first pass, we'll go get more riders."

We spread out, and start moving, and yelling his name. While I'm yelling I'm praying. Suddenly there is whoop from one of the other riders. There is Tim, caught high up in the branches of a big cottonwood. He isn't moving, but I'm sure happy to see him. I soon have my boots off and start up the tree barefooted, just like we climbed trees back in the Smokys, but this one is wet and slick. I've got a sixty foot lariat from Jason's saddle over my shoulder. When I finally reach Tim he is beginning to move a little, and I tell him to lie still. I put a loop around his chest, and under his arms, that he won't slip out of, like Josh showed us on the boat. Then I put the lariat around a big branch and use it to lower Tim slowly. The others catch him, and place him gently on the ground.

By the time I get to the ground he is sitting up and looking around. I talk to him, and he begins to look at me, but soon makes it clear he can hardly hear. In a strained voice he tells us he couldn't breathe in the storm, and does not know what happened. His hat is gone. We let him rest a bit, then help him on his horse and take him back to the wagons. Buck whines and licks his hand. Tim sure is not hearing, and I fix a place in the front of our wagon for him to lie down. After all the horses and mules are accounted for we start on. Its muddy going for awhile, then dries out and we move faster.

Skies are clear when we make camp close to a small stream. Tim is sitting in the wagon. Flor comes over with a big mug of hot soup and Tim takes it with a smile. When it's finished he climbs down and we walk over to his horse. Tim looks him over and the horse knickers and nudges Tim. Tim still can't hear much, but is feeling better. I've thanked the Lord a dozen times that Tim's life was spared.

We got to Council Grove last night, and this morning Tim, Fierro and I are checking all the mule and horse shoes. We replace them if we need to, but are careful to save the used ones. Tim is still having some trouble hearing. The Army Captain, Tom Nelson, walks over and visits us. He wants to know if Fierro is going to be able to set up his grindstone, and other tools. He pats Buck, who is getting plum sociable with about everyone. He looks at Tim, then at me.

"Ross, Alex said he knew your Uncle Will Bunch, a mountain man. Now I think I knew your father, Jim Greenup, who fought in Texas, against the Mexicans." He paused.

"Well, my Pa sure was in Texas a couple of years ago. Is there a problem with that?" The Captain laughed.

"No, but there is more to this. In my written orders is a comment to keep an eye open for the Greenup men. After the comment Jason made at our first meeting with the teamsters, I took another look at the orders. Evidently the man you killed, and another man who was involved, by the name of Jenk, were being hunted by the Pinkerton's. They had been involved with a Spanish man by the name of Quintara, who is stirring trouble with Mexico."

I drove the last nail in the shoe I was putting on a mule, and straightened up to face the Captain.

"That's the first time anyone has told Tim and me what all the trouble is about. There was some gold involved, and we were given some reward money for the capture of Jenk, but did not know why these people keep coming after us. Let's get a cup of coffee. Buck, stay."

Tim and I walk with the Captain over where they have a fire by the Army wagons. His wife and the other Army wife have a big pot of coffee going, so we have a mug of hot coffee, and his Lieutenant, James Murray, joins us. Tim and I are introduced to their wives, Elizabeth and Rebecca. They are both young women, compared to Flor and Maria. I tell them all why we are here and all that has happened to us. I end by saying:

"Captain, we are Believers, and we don't think these things are just coincidence. I personally think it's all a part of God's plan for our lives, and so just try to take each day as it comes. We plan for tomorrow, knowing it may not happen the way we plan."

Nothing was said for a few minutes. We replenish our cups, then the Captain spoke again.

"I agree with you, knowing sometimes it is necessary for us to do

172

things we don't agree with. Apparently we are to be aware of where you are, and possibly to be a protective element. We can do that till we get to Bent's Fort, but after you cross the Arkansas River you are on your own. I suggest nothing more be said about the previous trouble." He took a long drink.

"One thing the Army is always interested in, is acquiring good saddle horses and draft mules. You might want to look into contracting with the Army to provide either horses or mules, or both. When we get to Bent's Fort let's see if we can get started on that, if you are interested."

Now that was something I had not thought of, and for the rest of the day Tim and I discussed it. We said nothing to Fierro or anyone else about it, but I'm started thinking it's one more of those happenings which are not just coincidence. Fierro has his shop set up, and is sharpening knives and selling a few things to the teamsters. I walk to the edge of the grove of trees and shoot a rabbit for Buck. It's what's called a jackrabbit out here, and has long hind legs, and long ears. They can sure cover the ground in a hurry.

There are several Indians camped around the area. Alex said they are mostly of the Kansas tribe, and not very impressive. There are also a few Cherokee and Choctaw, who are actively involved in horse trading.

While here we cut two spare axles and a spare tongue for our wagons, and also several single and double trees, for use when one breaks. There may not be many trees where we travel now.

I continue to be amazed at how much can be seen on the endless miles of prairie. In the hills at home a cloud shadow would pass over us, but it could not be seen ahead of time unless it came across a field. Here I can see a cloud shadow for miles and watch it, as it either crawls slowly across the grass, or comes racing towards us and passes silently over or around us. One shadow from a big fluffy cloud came toward me, and I managed to stay on the edge of it by walking slowly. This morning the wind was blowing hard, and when a cloud shadow came across, I only managed to keep up by putting my horse to a gallop. There are many shadows racing across the prairie, and the patterns are constantly changing.

We are now six days past Council Grove, at the great bend of the Arkansas River. We have overtaken a freight caravan of about fifty wagons, which was slowed by heavy rains, and are camped just ahead of them. We seem to have missed the rains, had good traveling conditions, and really covered the miles. Just ahead of us is Pawnee Rock, where there have already been a number of incidents with marauding Indians. I'm happy we have the troops with us, and they are prepared for a fight if necessary, but hope we don't have one.

Tonight we are all making sure our firearms are working properly. Tim is back to his usual happy self. His hearing appears to be normal again, after the brush with the tornado. It happened Fierro had a new broad brimmed hat in his pack, so Tim is feeling good. Tonight, and from now on, we will double the guards on the remuda, and bring them inside the wagon circle if it looks like there might be trouble. Tim and Fierro and I are using the chain hobbles now, and I notice some of the other teamsters are doing the same.

We are invited to the Captains campfire tonight, and are joined by Lt. Murray, their wives, Alex, his wife Flor, and Jason and his wife, Maria. Its another mild, late spring evening, with the steady, soft breeze blowing from the west. A half moon is shining bright on the prairie, and the wind carries the smell of the tall grass. Cottonwood limbs carried from the trees along the little creek make a bright, crackling fire. Buck walks around the group, making friends and showing his big fang smile. I'm really lonesome for Sammie and don't have much to say tonight. Maria says, turning to me,

"Ross, don't you have a gal back in Tennessee you are sweet on?"

I know I turn red, and stammer around, till Tim speaks up, and tells the group the whole story. The women love it, and the men give me a bad time. Finally the Captain says its time for Taps, and we go to our wagons. I have trouble going to sleep tonight.

It's really early this morning, and the camp is on the move. We are going south, and will actually pass Pawnee Rock to our west about mid-morning. Captain Tom has sent scouts ahead of us, and out on each flank, and Jason is keeping the wagons close and moving a little faster than usual. The mules sense there is something going on, and are nervous and jumpy. The remuda wranglers are keeping the animals close to the train. The troops are in single file, between the wagons and Pawnee Rock. All weapons are loaded.

Suddenly a scout on our right flank, whirls around and waves and points. Just then a horse with an Indian rider appears right on top of Pawnee Rock. The scouts pull back in closer to the wagons, and we keep moving. No one is talking. The only sounds are mules and horses panting, harness and wagons rattling and squeaking, and the quiet prairie wind blowing across the grass.

We travel like this for four hours. Pawnee Rock is now behind us, and we are beginning to talk, but the Army scouts stay out, and the remuda stays close. Late in the day we come to the Pawnee River, just above where it flows into the Arkansas River. The crossing is made with no major problems, and we make camp on the south side of the river. We have seen only the one lone warrior today. Tonight we have a council meeting to decide whether we take the Cimarron Cut-off to Wagon Mound, or go to Bents Fort and across the mountains at Raton Pass.

Tim, Fierro and I have been talking about this as we travel. There are two major problems. One is water, for us and the animals. On the advice of Danny we each have an empty hogshead in our wagons. They each hold about thirty gallons. The other problem is the threat of Comanche's.

We join the council around the fire. At the request of Wagon Master Jason, Captain Nelson and Lieutenant Murray join us. Jason asks each of us to tell how much water storage capacity we are carrying. Most of the wagons have at least one empty hogshead, and some have two. Jason speaks.

"I've asked the Captain and Lieutenant to join us tonight. If we decide to take the Cut-off, they will leave us as soon as we cross the river, and go on to Bent's Fort. So we lose their protection. We may possibly catch up with a train which left a week before we did, and they have oxen, so are going slower. We don't know if they took the Cut-off. In our favor is the early, still cool weather, and we might catch some rain. Also, the Comanche's are not as bad in the spring, as later." He paused and let that sink in.

"Tomorrow we are going to take a short cut from here to the Arkansas, which will take two days, and give us a chance to see how things are going to work, if we decide to go south. Alex has been over this route before, and I've asked him to answer questions?"

"How long will it be between waterholes, at the worst?" I ask.

"Remember, in the past few years there have been several caravans over this trail. There may already be one caravan ahead of us now, and they are the first ones this year, but they will be using the water. If we were a month later, I would not want to go, but we have a good chance. Anyway, from the time we leave the Arkansas, we will have two dry camps, at the worst. The third night out we will have water, unless" he paused. "we are attacked!"

Captain Nelson then reminded us the troops would not be with us, but felt because we were not a group of settlers, we would not have as much trouble with the Indians. He suggested we go in three rows of six wagons each. That way we could form a defensive circle faster than if we were in a single file. After this there was general talk, and finally Jason suggested we do as planned, and take the shorter road just ahead of us, and see how we fare. He also told Flor and Maria they should tie their hair up and wear men's clothes and a man's hat, so it would not appear there were women with us, to a scouting Indian.

Tim and I are both carrying the new Paterson revolvers, which are six shot, and each have long barreled "Kentucky" rifles. Fierro has an Army carbine, single shot, and two single shot pistols. He asks Flor and Maria if they have personal pistols. Flor does, and Fierro gets one for Maria out of his supplies. Jason starts showing her how to load and shoot it. He says she is a good rifle shot.

This morning early we are driving about three or four wagons at a time close to the Pawnee River and loading our water barrels. They have to have a tight fitting lid. Once everyone is full we line out, driving in three lines, six wagons in a line wherever possible. Jason and Alex are scouting ahead, and directing the lead wagons. They are careful to not let any wagon get separated from the others. I'm driving, and Tim is herding remuda. At Jason's suggestion, I've got Buck tied on the wagon seat. The troops are riding on each side of the caravan, and their five wagons are first in line. Their two wives are also wearing Army hats.

Stopping when the sun is high overhead, we eat some dry jerky, drink a little water, and give each mule in harness about a half gallon of water. Resting the animals an hour, we start on. I'm riding herd on the remuda with three other riders, and Tim is driving our wagon, when suddenly the horses and mules start looking toward the west, and their ears prick up. Buck starts growling. Jason notices all this, and is watching. Before he has decided to take action, the Indians are on us from the right flank, and behind us. With shrill whoops and yells, they come up out of a shallow ravine about a quarter of a mile from us, and are running their horses at a full gallop. There are about thirty of them, and apparently two or three have guns, and are shooting.

The ten troopers on our side are returning the fire. Jason is turning the two outside lines of wagons toward each other and the inside line is dropping back to close the circle. The four of us with the remuda start hazing them into the open area between the wagon lines. I'm at the back of the remuda, running my horse back and forth, yelling at the top of my lungs. The last of the horses are running past the last wagons, into the circle, and the leading Indians are a long arrow-shot away. I don't see the first arrow shot, and it hits me in the left shoulder. It has lost a lot of its speed when it hits, but its still enough to go through my shirt and bury half the arrowhead length in the muscle of my upper arm. It hurts, and I reach around and jerk it out.

Dust is flying, guns are firing, and all is turmoil. I jump from my horse, grab my pistol and turn just as the closest Indian, maybe the one who shot me, gets inside the line of wagons. He has a tomahawk in one hand, and comes right at me. There is no time to think. I pull the hammer back, point the gun at him and fire. He is hit, and knocked off his horse, but comes up swinging. I jump back, trip, and go down on my back, with him on top of me. He raises the tomahawk again, and I grab his wrist and hold it. He is strong and slippery, and I'm putting everything I've got into holding his wrist away from me. Looking right into his eyes, in the painted face, I see hate, and fury. I try clawing at his face and eyes, and bring a knee up into his groin. A gun goes off right by me, and the Indian collapses. Pushing him off me, I see Flor, standing close to me and holding a smoking pistol in both hands.

Guns are firing and horses are galloping back and forth, but the circle of wagons is complete. Buck is howling in a frightening manner. The attack is over as suddenly as it began, and the prairie swallows up the Indians and their horses. Captain Tom said at least one of the Indians was killed, and several wounded, but their companions grabbed them up and took them away. The only dead Indian we can see is the one lying at my feet. Two troopers have been struck by arrows, neither seriously. Several mules and horses have been hit by arrows, and one of the mules has to be shot. The owner has an extra mule, and it is soon harnessed and ready to go. All the wounds, including mine, are treated by pouring whiskey, then hot water into and over them, and then an application of pine tar, to keep flies and infection away. I thank Flor, and promise to get her something in Santa Fe.

I look closely at the dead Indian. He appears to be about my age. Then I look for, and find the arrow which hit me, and the Indian's tomahawk. The arrow point is stone, but the tomahawk head is iron. I wonder where it came from. I think about this being the second man I have been involved with which resulted in their death. In my own heart I think of the futility of their deaths. Did this young warrior have someone like Sammie waiting for him? In the eyes of most of the people here he is a savage, but I think of him as another human being. It makes me think of my friends, or even relatives, the Cherokee, who have suffered at the hands of the white man. As the other teamsters slap me on the back, and congratulate me, my heart is heavy. The arrow and tomahawk are stored with the knife the Allen man tried to kill me with.

CHAPTER 21

nce again we are standing on the banks of the Arkansas River. Its been three days since the attack by the Indians. My arm is sore, but there is no infection. Our caravan is taking the Cut-off route to Santa Fe. We believe we can make it, with careful use of the water, since we gave it a try already for two days. Tim, Fierro and I are planning on selling our wagons in Santa Fe, packing our mules with whatever we are bringing back, and coming back the mountain route. We talked to the Captain, and when we get to Bent's Fort on the way back will start working on a contract to sell horses and mules to the Army. He also suggested we might be interested in guiding other caravans across, since we will have traveled both ways.

Right now we are looking at the river and wondering how deep the water is, and how Jason plans on getting us across. Its afternoon and we need to work fast. There is still a lot of water coming out of the shining mountains and the water extends from bank to bank, but there is no drift wood, so it apparently is going down. It definitely is not in flood.

First Jason sends Alex across on his horse, and we all watch carefully. Alex leaves his weapons in his wagon, and rides into the river. The bank is shallow, and is obviously where other wagons have crossed. It appears to have a gravelly bottom with a gradual slope. The horse wades out several feet, then suddenly Alex is out of the saddle, hanging onto the saddle horn, and the horse is swimming, and being swept downstream. It swims for about fifty feet, then hits bottom and begins to walk and climb onto the far bank.

Jason thinks that does not look too bad, and Alex, on the far side agrees with him. Tim and two others ride their horses into the river, each carrying the end of a long rope, and cross to the other side. The ropes are fastened to the front of the first wagon. The teamster drives his mules into the river, and when they start swimming the riders on the far side use their horses to pull and steady the wagon till the mules get their footing again. All the wagon boxes are tarred and tight, so they float some, even with the heavy loads. Most of us have our merchandise packed in oiled canvas, so we don't have much damage. Fierro and I drive our wagons, and don't have any trouble. I keep Buck in the wagon. At the end of three hours all the freight wagons are across, leaving the five Army wagons to follow the Arkansas to Bent's Fort.

The Captain told us they would be there in about seven more days. We hate to leave them, but we are busy now filling all the water casks. The water is a little muddy, but the mud will settle. We make camp close to the river, eat supper, let the remuda graze, then bring them close to the wagon circle for the night, with a double guard. We have four guards around the wagon circle all night. It's a warm night, with the moonlight bright across the waving grass. We are all anticipating the unknown tomorrow, and I'm excited about it. Tim and Fierro and I sit around the fire for a while. I'm getting ready to crawl into my bedroll, since I have remuda guard duty about midnight. Fierro looks at us, and asks us to wait a minute. He goes to his wagon, rummages in the box, and comes back with a small bundle.

"Ross and Tim, we are headed into a strange place, and a dangerous place. In case anything happens to me, this paper authorizes you to sell all my belongings, and it gives you the address of my granddaughter, in St. Louie. I would like for you to get the money to her. It authorizes you to keep some to pay you for your trouble and expense." He pauses, then goes on.

"She's all the family I've got left. You boys and Samantha have been about as close to family as I've had, and you were good to Liz in her last days. Not only that, but you aren't afraid to stand up for your faith. I sure admire you for that, and if we get through all this in one piece, maybe you might consider one more partner."

He hands me the paper, says goodnight, and goes to his wagon. I stow it carefully in one of our packs, and go to bed. My thoughts are of Sammie, and the strange turns our lives take. I think of what the Bible says about being honest, and treating others as we would like to be treated. I miss Sammie, and pulling the little buckskin bag out of my pocket I hold it close and say a silent prayer. Just as sleep is beginning to close my eyes, a far off flash of lightning shows in the west. Sitting up, I watch till more lightning shows, reflecting against towering high clouds. Then sleep comes.

A crack of lightning and instant boom of thunder wakes me, and I get my boots and slicker on. Alex comes by and says all the riders available are going to be up to keep an eye on the animals. In the flashes of lightning the huge towering clouds are seen almost overhead, and the smell of rain is strong. Wind is gusting in all directions. Horses and mules are moving nervously, and again I feel a cold breath of air, meaning hail is falling. Soon we are pelted with hail, not as big as it was in the storm by Council Grove, but lots of it. The storm lasts for almost an hour, and leaves about three inches of hail on the ground. Thankfully, there is no tornado funnel.

As first light shows on the eastern horizon, we are already watering the animals, and getting them hitched to the wagons. The river is at least two feet higher than it was yesterday, and I'm sure thankful we are across. We all eat a quick breakfast, take a long drink, and soon the caravan is lined out, and moving. Its slow going at first, because of the soft ground, but as it dries out the wheels turn faster through the tall grass. The caravan is moving southwest, and Jason reminds all of us we are now in another country.

It's late afternoon and I'm riding as lead scout. Topping a rise, my view takes in a long expanse of prairie sloping down and to the southwest. The slopes look almost like water flowing, as the steady wind ripples the tops of the prairie grass. There are no signs of human habitation as far as I can see, and I feel my heart swell with freedom. Stopping to take in the huge amount of land in front of me, I see immediately in front, and a mile away, a black mass of animals. It appears the entire mass is moving slowly, and I realize it's a herd of buffalo. My first! What a sight! Stories about these wonderful animals have been told in the hills since I can remember. Uncle Will Bunch told us of hunting them, and how they supply the Indian with everything he needs to live in the wild lands of the west. They furnish meat, hides for shelter, clothing, sinews, campfire fuel, and many other uses.

I'm still sitting my horse in wonder and excitement when Alex rides up beside me.

"Ain't that a sight for sore eyes!" he exclaims. Then we are both quiet for a short time.

"Ross, this is one of the things that makes this country get in your blood, and you are always homesick for it when you are away. Let's let Jason know and see if he wants any fresh meat." As we turned away he said,

"Ross, always remember, where there are buffalo, there are also Indians, and may be wolves."

Jason stopped the caravan and we rode back to the top of the rise. He looked it over, then detailed Alex and me to try to get close enough to get at least two of the animals down. He would start the caravan again when they heard our shots, and since the buffalo were right on the trail, we hopefully would not experience much delay. He said ordinarily we would have seen the dust cloud from the herd, but there had been rain, and the grass was green, so there was little or no dust.

Jason went back to the wagons, and we rode a little southeast to get downwind of the herd. We were both watching the country on all sides for Indian sign. In a short time Alex signaled we were far enough, and we turned directly toward the herd. When we rode in sight of the herd they were slowly moving north, away from us, and Alex said that was good. We would ride quietly behind them, till we got within easy rifle shot. Each of us would pick a young animal, either bull or cow, and he would say about when to shoot.

We did just that, and got within close range without apparently attracting any attention. We eased out of our saddles, and each picked a buffalo to shoot. Alex cautioned me to reload immediately after I shot. The smell of the animals was really strong, like a huge barnyard, and the noise of the herd was a constant murmur, with frequent high bleats from the little calves which were dashing around.

Alex fired first, and before the powder smoke had cleared I fired. He said to aim right behind the front shoulder, and a young cow was standing almost broadside to me when I fired. I kept my eyes on her while I reloaded. She didn't move, and I thought I had missed. Suddenly she collapsed and was down. Alex rifle boomed again. Now the entire herd is standing still, listening and looking. Then they start slowly moving away from us. They are continuing north, and apparently the boom of rifles is not a real danger signal to them. A young bull is down, and just past him another young cow is standing on unsteady legs. Alex reloads, we mount, and ride toward the buffalo.

"Don't ever approach a wounded buffalo on foot," he says. He rides close to the cow and fires into the vital spot with his pistol. She slumps to the ground.

"Now the work begins. If we get right on it, we can have them gutted by the time help gets here."

Tonight we are in a dry camp. We have given all the pulling mules about a gallon of water, and the remuda animals about a half gallon apiece. Tim and I are drinking from our canteens, and really being careful. The smell of roasting buffalo meat comes from every fire. It doesn't take long to know its delicious meat. Tim is envious of my good fortune at getting my first buffalo. Buck is gnawing happily at a huge leg bone, and I put a couple more in the wagon for him to work on later.

After a long day we are in our second night in a dry camp. The lack of water is beginning to tell on the animals. There is still plenty of grass. We are staying away from the trail made by the caravan ahead of us. Jason and Alex say we will reach the north fork of the Cimarron by noon tomorrow. As we made camp tonight I could see faint purple haze on the far west horizon. Alex said we are seeing some of the lone peaks which are east of the Sangre de Cristo Mountains. Sitting here by the fire tonight, my excitement is probably obvious. In the past few days I've seen and been a part of things that were just stories around the fire till now.

First, I will never forget seeing the broad, beautiful open prairie, with the splendid grass and the tremendous expanse of sky. With it goes the sound of the wind, the birds, and the smell of the grasses, flowers, and fresh rain. Across the prairie in Kansas Territory we had seen hundreds of acres of sunflowers. Now we are where there is not so much rain, and the grass is shorter, with lots of bluebells, and a beautiful, short plant called Indian Paintbrush. It is sure well named. Thinking about these, the fast moving white clouds and their shadows, the rolling black clouds, the hail, and even the tornado, makes me want Sammie and Pa and Ma to see the same things.

My stomach grumbles for some water, and my mouth is dry. Then I see the telltale flash of lightning far off in the west, against a background of dark clouds.

"Hey, Tim, maybe we will get water right away."

About then Alex strolls by.

"What we may get is what we call dry lightning. There will be dark clouds, lots of lightning, and even rain falling from the clouds, but never reaching ground." He pats Buck and walks on.

I don't have any guard duty tonight, so stay awake and watch the storm move toward us. Tim is sound asleep, but Buck stays close to me. The huge black clouds are moving fast, and lightning is almost constant. In the lightning flashes I can see rain falling from the clouds, but as they come over us, there is no rain. I go to sleep.

This morning we are moving down rough slopes toward the North Fork of the Cimarron River. The ox-drawn caravan can be seen several miles ahead of us, on the other side of the river. I'm riding lead scout again, and keeping a sharp lookout for Indians. Suddenly I see the caravan ahead of us has started to circle their wagons. Since its not even noon yet, that can mean only one thing – Indians. I turn back to our caravan, and tell Jason. Jason calls up Alex and a couple of other teamsters who are experienced. We all ride up to where we can see the caravan ahead.

"Right now we need to get to water," says Jason. "It's probably a good thing for us the other caravan was first. It gives us more time. Alex, you take these two fellows and go to the river. If you can find standing water, we will be lucky. Anyway, find us a good place to get across, and we may have to dig some wells. Ross and I will keep watch on the caravan, and move it to the river as fast as we can."

Jason and I ride back toward our wagons, and start talking to the drivers. He goes to the remuda wranglers and tells them to move in a little closer. It looks like we have about a mile to go to the river. There is brush and small stands of cottonwood along the stream, but I can't see any water.

The soil is soft and sandy here in the river bottoms and the mules are working harder. Some of the larger, heavier wagons are putting a real strain on their animals. I go ahead of the caravan again, and soon see Alex waving a little way off to our left. Turning toward him we soon reach the river bank. It is low, and the river bottom appears to be rock. From the signs the caravan ahead of us crossed here. Jason wants us to cross the river right now, and the lead wagon goes ahead. As soon as several wagons are across Jason starts them in a circle and has the remuda driven across. Then all the wagons are across and circled, with the remuda inside.

As soon as everyone is in place, several of us take shovels to the river. We find where there were apparently wells dug by the caravan in front of us, but the Indians had caved the sides in. Finding a place where there is no rock and the sand appears moist, we start digging. We are down about two feet when the first water appears at the bottom of the hole. Then we spread out and start several shallow wells. First we drink. Then we bring the mules and horses down, a team at a time, and let them drink their fill. We keep one well upstream just for us, and let the animals have the others. It's late afternoon when everybody has had plenty of water, and the hogsheads are full again. We are going to camp here, and let the remuda graze on the opposite side of the river, with heavy guard. We have doubled the camp guard, and everyone is nervous, as the evening wears on. Jason explains there was not much use for us to try to help the caravan in front of us. Our animals were thirsty and tired, and if we went rushing off to help the other caravan it would thin us out too much. We will probably catch them tomorrow, and see what the situation is.

Meanwhile, we need to take care of ourselves. So tonight Tim, Fierro, Buck and I eat cold buffalo and tortillas, washed down with water from the North Fork of the Cimarron. Then Buck enjoys a buffalo bone for dessert. Alex and Flor come by with some cold dried apple pies, and visit for awhile. Alex likes to tell of some of the tight places he and

Uncle Will Bunch were in together. Along with the stories we pick up a lot of information on what to expect in some of the places we might be in as we travel, and I get more of an idea on the general feeling about Indians.

I've got guard duty from midnight on, and Alex tells me to be careful just as the dawn light begins to show. That is the favored time for sneak attacks, especially to steal horses. I don't sleep very much before its time to go on duty. If the caravan ahead of us was attacked, then it seems like the Indians won't miss a chance to hit us. As I sit my horse and watch the faint light of morning appear, I sure wish Buck was with me. He would be, but having him prowling around at night makes the mules nervous, so Buck is tied at the wagon. All the horses and mules are inside the circle, and it's quiet.

I'm close to our wagon when I hear Buck growl, and a sudden commotion on the far side of the circle. Suddenly the shape of an Indian appears on the back of a mule, and just as suddenly is gone. I fire a shot from my pistol and yell. Men are coming out of wagons or from under them, wherever they happen to be sleeping.

"Everybody be careful. There are Indians inside the circle!" I yell.

In a few minutes of searching no Indians are found, and everyone is getting ready to move out. I tell Jason what happened. Several of us start looking at the chain hobbles on the mules, and soon find one which has a bright streak, like a knife blade had been used on it. Jason laughs when he sees it.

"That young brave jumped on the mules back while his friend cut the hobbles. Except they didn't cut, and you sounded the alarm, and they both took off. What a surprise for them.!" He laughed and walked away.

It takes us an hour to climb to where the other caravan had circled yesterday. They had been gone for a couple of hours when we got there, and there is plenty of sign to show they put up a stiff fight. Fire pits are still warm, and the ground is churned up where they and their horses ran back and forth. It appeared a couple of oxen had been killed, so the caravan is probably having fresh beef tonight. We look a little and then move on. I'm driving the wagon and Tim is with the remuda. Fierro does not draw guard duty, since he is alone, and one of the older drivers.

Its about noon when we reach the top of a long, low ridge and stop to rest the animals. Ahead of us I can see the other caravan going down the slope to the main branch of the Cimarron River. Alex is riding point scout today, and is about half a mile south of us. I see him stop, get off his horse and walk around, looking at something on the ground. Mounting again, he trots back toward us.

"Ross and Tim, get your horses and come with me!" he shouts.

We ride toward him, and to where he had been looking around. He points. There is a large ant hill, of the big red ants we see frequently. Scattered around it and on top of it are a number of white bones, and a close look shows they are human bones.

"That's what the Comanche do to their enemies when they capture them alive." Said Alex. "Probably it was a Mexican rancher, or even a white trapper crossing the country alone last fall, and got caught. There is no sign of a wagon or anything else, so he was horseback. He might have been wounded, so they just staked him out on the ant den, and left him. Tough way to die."

I look at the bones, then all around at the waving grass. The blue sky reached out over the hills, and far away in the west we can see the tops of mountains. South of us several black, cone shaped peaks are beginning to show, and Alex said they had been volcanoes, and are called cinder cones. The breeze is warm, and meadow-larks are singing as they balance on grass stems. I look at Tim, and he was staring at the bones. I wonder to myself, how could human's do this to another human. We quietly ride back to the wagons.

Tonight we are camped close to the other caravan on the banks of the Cimarron. Since there are no families, the camps are fairly quiet. We have plenty of guards out, and there is some visiting back and forth between the two camps. Two of the wagons in the other caravan were built by Danny Greenup, and we make some good contacts for future use in selling Greenup horses and mules. When I crawl into my blankets I don't spend a lot of time thinking about all the things we saw today. It's not long till morning.

It's been a week since we camped on the Cimarron. I can see the ruts made by wagon wheels ahead of us, coming from the north. We followed the Cimarron awhile, then turned over into the Canadian River valley. We left the ox drawn wagons far behind us, and now the hump of Wagon Mound hill is to our right as we pass it. I don't see any sign of wagons coming on the trail from the north, so we are probably going to be the first caravan into the Mexican villages. Tim killed an antelope, which was really small, but delicious, when roasted in small pieces over the fire.

Alex and Flor have been visiting our campfire often. Alex has more stories of the things he and Uncle Will did together, and I keep thinking of questions about the country they were in, and wanting to go there. The excitement rises in my chest, and looking up at those shining mountains, and breathing deep of the delicious air, makes me feel like I could go on forever. Tim seems to feel some of my excitement, but is far more cautious about saying what he would like to do.

Its getting late, and Jason has signaled to circle the wagons. I'm driving today, and as we start the circle, notice we seem to be on a level bench, beyond which the land rises more rapidly to the west. We have been watching ahead at hills covered with brush and then trees, and now we are close to them. I see willow trees along a stream, and looking east I can see back down the long slope we have just climbed. The endless waves of grass are rippling in the west wind, and again it looks like water rushing down the long slope toward the river bottoms. A pair of small hawks are circling close above the grass and the meadowlarks are quiet.

Tim has been riding scout, and he comes up as I start unhooking the mules. Fierro's wagon is next to ours, and he stops unhooking and looks at the hills and all around. We are at a high elevation, and the air is crisp, and one has to breath deep to satisfy the lungs.

"Ross, this is the kind of air I have heard about, and this is what would have cured Liz of consumption!" Fierro exclaims.

I agree completely. As I finish unhooking the mules, I'm thinking again I want Sammie to see this, and Pa and Ma, and Josh. It's not far to the creek, and some dead limbs for the fire, and there are some clumps of oak brush beginning to show. They usually have a lot of dead branches. So in a few minutes I've got a good fire going, while Tim and Fierro water the animals. Soon all the fires are burning, and the caravan settles down to its normal evening routine.

There is a brilliant sunset, with the rays of the sun shooting out over the tops of far distant peaks, which we cannot even see. First there is red and orange, and then the entire sky turns pink gradually. Then in the east there is darkness moving slowly toward us, and it can clearly be seen, like a curtain being pulled over us. There is a chill in the air, which we did not feel out on the plains.

Jason keeps a heavy guard on the horses and mules. We have had only the one attack, when Flor and I shot the young Indian who got inside the wagon circle. The arrow wound in my shoulder has completely healed, thanks to prompt attention by Flor and Maria. Fierro cooks our supper, and we have a last cup of coffee when Alex and Flor, then Jason and Maria join us. We have all become good friends. In addition to the stories and knowledge of the country I've been storing up, Flor and Maria have been teaching me some Spanish. Tim is also picking it up, and Fierro already has a fair use of the language.

I notice Flor has been watching me, and tonight when we are all settled in for some good story telling, says:

"I need to give you boys some instruction on how to act in Santa Fe. I grew up in these villages, then went to Chihuahua. Finally I was back in Taos, where I met Alex, and your Uncle Will." She laughed at my surprised look.

"Yes, I knew him, and he helped me learn English. Alex and I traveled back to Missouri, and I learned a lot of things there." She paused.

I think back to the stories Uncle Will told at our farm, when I really got an urge to travel to the shining mountains. That was just last winter. I don't remember him mentioning any women he met in his travels. Probably there were lots of things he didn't tell us about. Flor spoke again.

"You and Tim are the youngest in this outfit. Alex and Jason will help you as far as trading, selling and buying your freight. Now you listen real close to me! We are going to go through a couple of villages that are real poor. Don't do any trading there, but just keep your eyes open. There will be girls, some not so young, who would give anything

to grab a young American with money and go back to the US with him.
Don't even smile at them. When we get to Santa Fe it will be worse.
Women, single and married, will flirt with you, and offer to sleep with
you. Don't do it!" She stopped and grinned at Alex.

"See what it got him."

All of us, including Alex, laughed at this. Fierro got up and put some
wood on the fire. Sparks flew, the smoke drifted up lazily, and all of us
were enjoying the evening. Maria had been listening with great good
humor, nodding and smiling.

"Listen to Flor, boys. What she is saying may save your life."

Suddenly I'm aware of a strange feeling about what these two women
are telling us. Is the Spirit in this telling, and is there something critical
to what we do here? I look at Tim. He is taking it all in, and interested,
as we all are. I draw a deep breath, and watch Flor.

"Everyone of these women will have a boyfriend or husband. If you
are at a dance, the girls will flirt, and try to hug you, and snuggle up.
They may get beaten when they get home, but that won't stop them.
Then one or more of the men will try to pick a fight with you. Again,
don't do it. Before you are well out the door you will have a knife in the
ribs. Always be armed. There are some fine people here, but there are
some real bad people." She paused again for a moment, then went on,
in a completely different tone, with a strong sense of warning to me.

"Alex and Jason will be busy, and if there is something which seems
strange to you, find me or Maria. We will be available, especially if there
are Mexican soldiers involved."

She stopped talking. There is silence, except for the crackle of the fire
and the low sounds of the rest of the camp. Horses and mules are quiet,
and there are few other men talking. Buck came over from where he was
lying under the wagon, and lay down right against my feet. Suddenly
there is the howl of a coyote, and then a whole chorus of them. Alex got
to his feet to make sure the guard was changed, and Jason growled:

"We need to talk about this a little more before we get into Santa Fe."

All said goodnight and we got ready to sleep. I know there is more
to this than what we have heard tonight, and I don't sleep for awhile. I
think about Sammie, and wish she were here to talk to.

CHAPTER 22

It's another beautiful, early morning on the trail. Sunlight is shining red on the snow capped peaks of the Sangre de Cristo mountains above us, and the Sandia's south of us. Flor tells us the shining red peaks are common, and the name 'Sangre de Cristo' means 'Blood of Christ'. A warm breeze is sweeping up the slope toward us, and the air is strong with the smell of the pinyon pine and juniper forest which surrounds us. We camped last night with the lights of Santa Fe shining in the hills below us. Jason and Alex have ridden ahead into the village.

We are traveling along a heavily used dirt road, and small mud brick houses are beginning to appear. They remind me of the village of Vegas we went through a couple of days ago. It was the first village of any size where all the buildings were made of "adobe" bricks. The residents here appear to be about as poor as those in Vegas. Small children are beginning to run along beside the wagons. Tim is driving ours, and we were warned last night to keep everything inside the wagons, or tied down. Small items have a way of disappearing before you know it.

There is a whoop and a yell, and three horsemen appear, riding at a full gallop toward us. We watch as they skid to a stop at the lead wagon. Maria and Flor are there, and after a lot of rapid fire Spanish we continue into the crooked, narrow streets of Santa Fe. We pass a church, with thick adobe brick walls. It reminds me of the ruins of the ancient pueblo we saw yesterday on the other side of the pass. One of the horsemen rides past to the remuda which is trailing us. Then all the remuda is driven into a corral and the gate closed. We cross a creek, past another church, and suddenly we are at the Santa Fe Plaza.

On the far side of the plaza is a long, low adobe building, which is the Palace of the Governors, and is the office of Governor Armijo. There are several officials in uniform, and a Catholic Priest waiting there, with Jason and Alex. Jason directs us to circle our wagons till all are parked around the plaza. We are to unload our freight in the plaza, leave it under guard, then take our wagons to a horse pasture by the creek where we can park and camp for the night. Early tomorrow we will get together with the merchants and start the trading. Tim, Fierro and I work together, unloading first our wagon, then Fierro's.

There are plenty of mosquitoes at the camp area, but the horses and mules are mighty glad to see the tall lush grass. They are turned loose and are soon rolling and feeding. I know there is going to be a shoeing job before we leave. We still have our personal gear in the wagons under cover of the canvas. Fierro builds a smoky fire to help keep off the mosquitoes. We are going to eat in the village. At Jason's direction we have three of the freighters on guard at all times. Fierro is on first shift, I'm on the next shift, and Tim has the early morning shift, so Tim and I go to town with the rest of the freighters.

Walking to the Plaza, we are greeted with smiles and "Hola". We stop at a cantina and sample our first real Mexican food. It's good, and has a lot of green chili's which really heat it up. Then we walk around, looking at the few small shops. We are offered glasses of strong beer, which I cautiously sample. I would really like a hot bath. We go to the Governor's office and are invited in to walk through it. Then Flor appears. I tell her I would really like a hot bath.

"Come with me." She says.

We walk across the plaza, past the big church, and into a narrow, crooked street, where all the walls are adobe and right on the street. Some doors open directly onto the street, other places there are gates in adobe walls. We enter one of these gates, and are in a small courtyard, with flowers, a small tree in one corner, and a roof made of small poles, which I learn are 'vigas'. Flor calls out, and a cute young Mexican girl appears. After a brief discussion, the girl smiles at me and beckons. Flor tells Tim to wait here in the courtyard.

We go into a small room at the back of the house, and find a tile tub set into the floor. The girl yells at two small boys to start filling the tub with hot water from an iron kettle over a fire in the back yard. She looks at me and motions for me to take off my clothes. I stand and stare at her, waiting for her to leave. She giggles, and finally turns her back. I'm just about undressed when Flor walks in. Flor laughs when she realizes I'm really not used to being naked in front of women. After what she had already told us about what to expect in Santa Fe, I guess I should not be surprised. I lift the leather string over my head which holds the narrow scabbard and slim knife. Their eyes widen a little when they realize what it is.

"Ross, you are getting a real treat. There are only a couple of tubs like this in Santa Fe. Now you just hop in, and don't worry about Rosy scrubbing your back. I may even help her!"

Now they both giggle as I try to get my naked self in the tub with them watching me. Rosy has a brush and wash cloth in her hands.

"Ross, she is my niece. She is fifteen, and was supposed to be married when she was thirteen. Second, her father, my brother-in-law, is a cruel, jealous man who will beat her without reason. He almost killed the man who she was to marry, and probably for good reason. Anyway, you go ahead and enjoy your bath, and pay no attention to her." Flor grinned again as she said this.

Half an hour later, I'm cleaner than I've been for a long time. It feels like some of the hide is gone off my back, but Rosy did a great job. As I dry off she calls Tim, and its my turn to laugh when he walks in and finds me naked, with Rosy pouring more hot water in the tub, and Flor supervising the show. I tell Tim what Flor told me, and he gets in the tub. When we are done I ask Flor if we can do this again before we leave, and give Rosy a handful of coins. Her eyes get big, and she claps one hand over her mouth, before giving me a big hug.

I had a good sleep after standing guard duty, and tell Fierro about the bath while we are having a cup of coffee this morning. We don't have to hitch the mules to the wagon this morning, and they are sure enjoying the pasture. We are all ready to go when the rest of the drivers start for town. I have the letter written by Danny Greenup for Mr. James Magoffin. Jason and Alex are at their own houses in Santa Fe, and we meet them and Flor and Marie as we enter the Plaza. I tell them I have the letter for Mr. Magoffin and we go to his store.

Mr. Magoffin is an imposing man, and is here, instead of in his store in Chihuahua, because the traders are due to start rolling in. Since we are the first caravan, we get quite a welcome. I give him the letter and he immediately reads it. Then he invites Tim, Fierro, Jason, Alex and me into his office, and we get to the business of trading.

"Jason and Alex already know this," he says, "but the Governor is the Mexican Government Representative, and he will charge you an import tax. If you like, I will be your 'bondsman', and handle the transaction. It helps if you have a little 'mordida', or separate gift to give him." He looked around at us.

"We were told to expect that, and we have some money, in American gold." I say. "How much will be the right amount?"

"Perfect. Let me see your trading stock, and then we can figure it out. If you have gold, it will probably be a small amount."

"I also have a gift to give to the commanding officer of the local Mexican Army unit." I told Magoffin.

"They are not here, but in case they show up, a gift will come in handy. Let's go look at trade goods."

It is late afternoon, and Tim, Fierro and I have traded or sold most of our merchandise. I've learned a lot, and am sure thankful we are with Mr. Magoffin. It was also mighty helpful to have Flor and Marie along, and at their suggestion we have kept back some of our good tobacco, and other goods. Packed in saddle bags we have quite a supply of Mexican silver pesos, or dollars, and we have four large packs of nice beaver furs, or pelts, along with some martin and lynx pelts. These are in the back room of Magoffin's store. Tomorrow we are going to get two big Mexican donkeys, or jacks, that will be great for producing the big mules we are going to raise at home. We sold the four mules we bought at Independence, so Tim and I will be leading our four mules, and the jacks, all loaded with our packs as we start back on the trail to Independence. Fierro has sold his trade goods, but has not yet decided what to do about the wagon.

It's been quite a day, and Mr. Magoffin invites all of us to a party, or 'Fandango' in the courtyard at the Palace of the Governors tonight. Before we go back to camp to take care of the animals, including Buck, he asks the three of us, Tim, Fierro and me, into his office.

"I'm real interested in Danny Greenup's proposal about building and selling wagons. I'm also wanting to know more about the horse and mule business you were telling me about," he says.

I tell him about the entire plan, and he assures me he will look into it, from the Mexican side, but there may not be much he can do till the US takes over all this part of Mexico. We shake hands and go our way. Outside I hear a bugle, and people start moving toward the Plaza. We watch, and in a few minutes a troop of Mexican cavalry ride into the Plaza, with flags flying, and people shouting welcome. Flor appears, and suggests we go back to camp, and this evening we can bring our gifts, and meet the troops at the fandango.

I give the chained Buck a big, fresh, beef bone retrieved from a butcher shop in town. He is overjoyed, and retreats under the wagon to work it over.

The courtyard is crowded when we get there.

"Tim and Fierro, keep your eyes and ears open. I have a feeling there is something going on, and it may have to do with the soldiers."

I start moving around through the crowd. There is a lot of drinking going on already, and it's early. There are tables loaded with hot tortillas, roast lamb, beef, and a tomato sauce called 'salsa'. There are pots of soup made with hominy and pork, called 'posole', which is delicious. There are small cookies or 'bollitos', and different pastries. Even with the open courtyard it's getting hot in the crowd. Flor crowds close to me.

"Remember what I told you!" she warns, with a big grin.

About then a small arm circles my waist. I look down into the dancing black eyes of Rosy, and right behind her a dark, scowling Mexican face. I smile at Rosy, then she slips away, leading the Mexican by the hand, but not before he snarls something which sounds like 'gringo'. Governor Armijo's Aide stands on a table and waves for quiet.

"We welcome our brave soldiers to our Fandango. The Captain would like to express his welcome to our guests, the Americanos."

He said this in Spanish, and used a lot more words, but Flor translates for us. Then he introduces Captain Cruze. The Captain is in uniform, with his sword and a pistol hanging on his belt. Again Flor translates as he speaks.

"We welcome the Americano traders with their wonderful trade goods. The Mexican government hopes we can continue to have peaceful dealings with you." He looked directly at me. "Some of you have not been here before. Do not forget we require a tax before you are allowed to trade."

Immediately, Mr. Magoffin speaks up, in Spanish.

"Captain Cruze, there are three new traders here. They are Ross and Tim Greenup, and Fierro. They are personal friends of mine, and the first thing I did was inform them of the tax. The Governors Aide informed us of the amount, and they have paid it with American gold coin. I am holding it in my safe until the Governor requests it." He does not mention the extra gift of gold we had given the governor. Captain Cruze looks irritated.

Then I speak, and Flor translates.

"Captain Cruze, we have heard of your excellent command. I would like to present you with a gift from the Greenup Boys, as we have become known, and that includes Fierro."

I walk toward him, holding the gift in the air. At the suggestion of Alex and Flor, and based on what they told me of the Captain's girl friend, it is wrapped in a fine, red linen shawl which was part of our trade goods. Handing it to him, I say:

"The wrapping is for the one you love. The gift is for her protection."

He unwraps the shawl, and there are oohs and aahs from the women in the crowd. Then he holds up the big, shiny bowie knife, pulling it from it's scabbard. There is a yell from the crowd, and lots of cheering and hand clapping. His hard, dark face breaks into a huge grin, and he jumps down, throwing an arm around my shoulder.

"Mi Amigo!" he shouts, and the party is on.

Alex stops by and tells me I have just pulled off a 'coup' with the Captain. He tells me to be careful, and wandered off. About half an hour went by, and I tell Tim I am leaving. He says he is ready to go, and we tell Fierro we are going back to camp. Most of the other traders are really whooping it up by now. Maria joins us as we walk.

"You boys need to get up early, and pack your goods to carry back home. I sure don't know who you killed, but the word is out to make sure you don't get back in the US alive." She paused and looked around.

"I really wanted to look around at this country, and I know some of the freighters are not leaving for several days." I say.

She grabs my arm.

"Listen! I'm telling you this to save your lives. You and Tim. Fierro don't count. I never told you this, but Flor knows it, and now Alex. Before we left Independence I had been contacted by a couple of Mexicans, who paid me a small sum to get rid of you, and promised me a lot more when the job was done. I agreed to it, and I never told Jason." She stopped and took a deep breath.

"But I took a real liking to you boys, and Flor loves all of you. Early in the morning Flor and Alex and me will be where your stuff is stored. We have a plan." With that comment she was gone.

Tim and me talk by the fire awhile after we get to camp. Buck was pacing around, looking worried about something. Fierro walked up to the fire light a little later, and was greeted by Buck with a big toothy grin.

"He's been worried about you." Tim said.

"Well, so have I!" Fierro exclaimed as he sat down. "A couple of those Mexican boys were getting kinda nasty, and Jason told me he thought I should leave. So I did. Much as I like this place, it seems like some of the local blacksmiths are a bit jealous of their territory. And their women!" he added, with a laugh.

I tell him what we had been told by Maria. He does not seem surprised, and sits quietly, petting Buck, and staring at the fire. Then he looks at me, smiles, and speaks.

"Ross, remember when Liz died, and I decided to keep traveling with you lads." I nod. "Well, I figured the people that contacted her would keep trying to get you, so I've been watching. I knew Maria was under some kind of strain, and now we know what it was. I've decided to go back with you. Tomorrow I'll sell my wagon, and figure on loading my mules."

We are all in the warehouse, looking at our pile of saddle bags, and bales of furs. It's going to be quite a load, but we have the four mules, and will have two big jacks. We tell Alex, Flor and Maria about Fierro's change of plans. He has his mules and saddle horse, and is carrying back mostly Mexican silver, besides his personal stuff and tools. Alex looks it over, and turns to us.

"You fellers have done mighty good, for your first trip. We have been talking it over, ever since Maria told us about her deal to get rid of you. Jason and Maria will be staying here till the caravan is ready to start back. Flor and I want to get back to Missouri, and will have enough capitol to start some kind of business there. Then we will freight again next year, but I'll plan on working as a wagon master like Jason." He stopped and Flor took over.

"We know you need to work some on shoeing your horses and mules. So do that today and tomorrow, and roam around the village some so everyone knows you are here, but make sure all your packs are ready to go. We will do the same, but tomorrow night, as soon as its dark, have all your personal gear packed, and bring the mules here, and load them. Alex is going to bring his saddle horse and four of our mules. Then he will lead you out of here, and up the Rio Grande Norte. He is going to take you to the Rancho de Taos, to my relatives. I'll catch up with you there."

Maria has been listening to Flor, and is clearly excited about this adventure.

"Don't tell a soul about any of this. Flor and I will know a lot more by tomorrow night. Now lets all go to her house and have some hot chocolate and bollitos."

CHAPTER 23

It's been two days since our meeting with Alex, Flor and Maria, and Tim, Fierro and I are in the warehouse loading our mules. Mr. Magoffin is here, and we have been talking about what may happen.

"Ross, you and the rest of your family are getting in on a good thing with the different business ideas. Things are going to change around here, but we just don't know when." He looks around at the packs. "Right now you just need to get out of here. The Mexican soldiers left for Las Vegas last night, and they may try waiting for you there. I trust Alex and Flor to get you to safety."

The sun is down when we tighten the last ropes, and lead the mules outside. I shake hands with Mr. Magoffin and mount up. With Alex leading, we move as quietly as possible out of Santa Fe, going south and east like we were going toward Las Vegas. After a couple of miles we turn back toward the north on a trail which gradually climbs the slopes of the mountains. We don't talk much as we travel, and it seems like the animals are happy to be on the trail again, even though they are carrying loads. It's better than being hitched to a wagon. Buck follows the last animal, but occasionally comes up by me if there is room on the trail. The air is getting thinner and colder.

Light is beginning to touch the mountain tops to the east when we turn off the main trail to a ranch hidden in a small valley. We are welcomed by a short, thin little Mexican who is Flor's father. Quickly the packs are pulled off the mules and they are turned into a small pasture behind the farm house. We are fed hot coffee, chicken burritos and delicious apricots from their orchard. In a few weeks there will be peaches, then apples. Then we lie down in the cool interior of their barn and go to sleep.

I'm awakened by the sound of horses coming into the barn yard. Buck is on his feet, but stops by me when I speak to him. Sitting up I place a hand on my pistol and watch through the door. Then I see Flor getting off a nice saddle horse, and right by her is Rosy. I reach over and hit Tim on the shoulder.

"Wake up, sleepy head, we have company."

Fierro wakes and rolls over in his blankets. He looks out the door, sees Rosy, and shakes his head.

"What is she doing here?" he growls.

Getting up I walk to the door. Alex is there in the barnyard, helping Flor and Rosy. They each have a saddle horse and Flor is leading a mule with a pack. They wave and smile. Alex comes over and talks quietly.

"They will rest a couple of hours, then we will pack all the animals and ride out. We are taking a trail to Rancho de Taos and will ride all night. They have good horses, and are good riders, so we plan on getting to Taos in the morning. You boys make yourselves at home. These folks are mighty nice, and won't say anything about us being here."

I go to my trading pack and get out a small plug of our good tobacco, then two gold coins. The little man and his wife are talking to Flor and Rosy, and smile as I approach. I hand him the tobacco and one of the gold coins, and give the other to his wife. He breaks into rapid Spanish, and she claps her hand over her mouth. Then he grabs me, hugs me, and plants a kiss on each cheek. She hugs me and then hugs Tim and Fierro, then comes back and hugs me again, and gives me several kisses.

Alex laughs at this show, and they all talk in Spanish for several minutes. I go to the pump by the house, pump some of the good cold water over my hands and face, drink some of it, and then go to get the horses and mules. Tim and Fierro follow me.

"Ross, you made some friends just now," says Tim, "but I bet they would be friends anyway!" I sure agree with him.

We are quite a procession as we enter the outskirts of Rancho de Taos, after a long hard ride through the night. Sun light is shining on

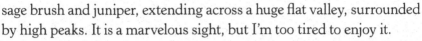

sage brush and juniper, extending across a huge flat valley, surrounded by high peaks. It is a marvelous sight, but I'm too tired to enjoy it.

All of us are on our good saddle horses. Alex is leading five mules, followed by Flor and Rosy; next is Tim, leading four mules and two big donkeys, and then Fierro, leading two mules. I am riding last, watching carefully the side hills and our back trail. I see Alex is well known here, as several Mexican people wave and shout greetings. We ride through a high gate into an enclosed courtyard, where immediately Flor and Rosy are grabbed and hugged and kissed. Then the packs are stripped off our animals again, and they are turned into a small pasture.

We are all given cold ale, and there are bowls of melted cheese, with pieces of hard toast to dip in the cheese. I start getting sleepy and am shown to a pile of soft hay in the barn. The rest of them soon follow.

The soft voice of Rosy calling us wakes me. Its late evening and there is the sound of music from the courtyard. It does not take long to get washed and attack the delicious food set on the long tables while we were asleep. There is posole, trays of tamales, roast chicken, bowls of cheese dip and piles of hot tortillas. I really enjoy the friendliness of the Mexican folks, and am amazed again at the amount of powder and red color the women put on their faces.

There is a shout and four riders come through the gate. They are all mountain men, friends of Alex, and they also know Uncle Will. Soon the homemade ale is flowing, and the stories are getting wilder. I enjoy every minute of it, and wish Pa and Uncle Will were here. Then I think of Sammie and how she would like to be here, and yearn for the day I can see her again.

I think of my first sight of the wonderful open Taos plain as we came up out of the Rio Grande canyon this morning. It is miles and miles of grey sagebrush, with mountains on every side. On the north and east are the high, shining peaks of the Sangre de Cristo. Right through the middle of the plain is the tremendous deep gorge of the Rio Grande River. Alex told me it was about seven hundred feet deep. North of the Rancho is the Taos Indian Pueblo. The air is thin and cool, and makes me feel like doing a lot of things.

It's after midnight when the group thins out. Before we go back to bed in the barn, I walk out along the trace, and look at the immense show of stars, from horizon to horizon, and the mountains, with dark, tree covered slopes, capped by thousands of feet of rock, and shining snow. It's my land. I can feel it, and understand Uncle Will's faraway look as he describes it.

Daylight finds us up again, and on our way to the small village of Taos and then the Taos Pueblo. After a day spent there, we are almost completely out of trade goods, except for some tobacco, and some trade beads and trinkets. Instead we have several packs of fine furs, and Tim, Fierro and I are decked out in new buckskins.

Sitting around the fire tonight, after another delicious supper of pit roasted mutton furnished by our hosts, we are listening to a Mexican man, who is Flor's Uncle. He tells us of the Mexican and Spanish settlement of this land, and the difficulties of living here. He also tells us it's much better since the Spanish are gone, and the Americanos can bring in trade goods. He tells us they are afraid the Americanos will want their land. We talk about this and the troubles in Texas. Last, he tells us we are going over the mountains in the morning, and will come out on the Santa Fe Trail close to the village of Cimarron.

CHAPTER 24

On the way home at last! We are strung out in a long line on a narrow trail through the mountains east of Rancho de Taos. Alex is leading now, and behind him is Rosy, with Flor leading their mules. Next is Tim with all our mules and donkeys, Fierro and his mules, Buck, and me bringing up the rear. We are traveling fast, and as quietly as possible. The Mountain Men told us the Ute Indians seldom travel this far south, but we are not going to take any chances, and there are lots of Indians besides Utes. Alex has been through the mountains on this trail before, and is looking for a nice, well protected meadow for us to camp in tonight.

Yesterday we had climbed all day, over some very rough country, but now are gradually going down hill, and Alex tells us we are coming into a huge, high basin right on top of the mountain range. I see him stop suddenly, and I rein in my horse. I hear a thump, a gasp, and a fierce growl from Buck. I look at Fierro just as he slumps forward over his saddle horn, and then hear a shrill war whoop.

"Indians!" I yell, and grabbing Fierro's bridle rein, spur into the mules ahead of me. Everyone reacts instantly, and Alex leads a wild rush into a small open meadow, with a rocky bluff on the left, and stream flowing at the far end. An arrow hits the rump of a mule in front of me, and another sticks in one of the packs. Alex heads for the stream, and we are across in a rush, and into a tangled windfall on the far side. Get behind the trees or logs, he yells, and is off his horse and out of sight. Then his rifle roars and there is a wild yell from behind us. Fierro is a dead weight as I drag him out of the saddle and onto the ground behind a rotten log, being careful of the arrow sticking out of his right side. Now I'm behind a tree and looking for something to shoot at. There is nothing in sight.

For a short time I watch closely in front, and all around, moving my head slowly. Fierro moves, and moans softly. Soon Alex comes in sight, crawling cautiously through the windfall. I point at Fierro and Alex crawls to him. He looks closely at the arrow and wound, and shakes his head. He crawls over to me.

"I trapped beaver here one time, and as I remember, just past us there is another rocky bluff where I had my camp. It was under an overhang, where they can't drop rocks on us. Nobody else is hit, but we need to get out of here. I nicked one of them, so it may be a few minutes till they regroup."

Buck turned and looked through the trees and growled. I saw a flash of feather, and then a brown arm showing beside a stump. Quick aim, and I fired. Another yell echoed through the trees, and all was quiet again.

"Good shot!" said Alex. "I'm going to have Flor and Rosy lead all the mules, and you and Tim get Fierro on his horse and lead all the horses and follow us. Its going to be noisy, but there is no other way to do it."

I am already reloaded, and Tim and I are getting Fierro on his horse. We probably sound like a mob going through the trees, but if we are shot at do not know it. Buck is growling and running beside the horses, as we push through the windfall. Sure enough, we come to an open area at the base of a bluff, and there is the overhang just as Alex remembered. Pulling Fierro off his horse, we get him back by the rock, then start piling logs and rocks in front of the bluff. Flor and Rosy are getting the animals tied as safely as possible, leaving packs and saddles on as protection.

When we have done as much as possible in the short time, the rest of us stand watch, with weapons ready, while Flor and Rosy examine Fierro. They are both dressed in buckskins, like the rest of us, and unless the Indians had been watching us for a while, which we doubted, they do not know the two are women. For all her young years, Rosy appears to have seen a lot of rough life, and does not hesitate to help Flor.

The arrow head is out of sight in the wound. Flor grasps it tightly and starts pulling. Fierro opens his mouth in a shout of pain, which Rosy immediately stifles with her hand over his mouth. Flor pulls harder, and the arrow suddenly comes free. When it does a gout of fresh blood wells up in the wound and Fierro moans. Then bubbles show in the blood, and we all know the arrow had penetrated the lung cavity. I hand Flor my bandana, to stop the blood and plug the hole. It's not clean, but will have to do till we can get a clean one. Rosy tenderly wipes Fierro's face with her own bandana, and in a few seconds his eyes open.

I have been watching my friend instead of watching for the foe, and now look around in time to see a small alder sapling quiver as if something had hit it. It's about as far away as I can see through the tangle of trees and brush, but I steady my rifle against a log and watch the area. I don't focus directly on the tree, but instead look a little on each side of it. It appears a rotten log is on the ground by the tree, and soon I notice the top of the log has moved a tiny bit. I sight on the top of the log and squeeze the trigger.

There is a howl of pain as the big slug finds its mark. An Indian jumps violently, and is visible for just a second, as he claps a hand to his buttock and disappears. Tim did not see it, but Alex did and chuckles.

"He shore is going to set easy on his horse for a few days."

All is quiet again, except for the painful breathing of Fierro, and his quiet moans as Rosy keeps wiping his white face. Flor has moved by Alex and has a rifle resting over a log in front of her. Buck is lying by Fierro, and manages to lick his hand occasionally. We wait and watch for an hour, and the sun is beginning to get low over the western mountain. There is no movement and no sound, till a gray jay bird, that Alex calls a Whiskey Jack, lands on a tree limb out in front of us. Then there is another bird, and soon a chipmunk runs across the clearing. We wait longer, till the sun has set, and Alex finally moves.

"I think we are safe till just before daylight," he says. "We have to keep the horses tied right here all night. We can water them one at a time, and let them grab a few mouthfuls of grass on the way to and from the creek. If the Indians are still here, they will sure try to steal a horse, but they probably won't take us on till morning. I think we actually wounded three different braves, and depending on how many there are, and how serious the wounds are, they may have had enough."

It's my mule which has an arrow sticking out of its rump, and it is sure causing the animal some pain. Getting it against a log where it can't kick me, I have Tim hold its halter, and pull the arrow out. It grunts with pain, and I'm sure glad it's against the log, because it delivers a couple of kicks which would have felled an ox. When we have some ashes I'll mix a salve with the ashes and water and cover the wound. I put this arrow and the one we pulled from Fierro in my pack, along with the arrow which stuck in my arm so many weeks ago. This is getting to be a collection.

Flor has built a fire, carefully hiding it from sight, and is heating water. As soon as she has some hot water she takes a clean bandana and bathes Fierro's wound. He is conscious, and thanks her in a quiet voice. Then taking some dry leaves from her traveling bag, she stirs them in a mug of hot water, and has him drink it.

"This will keep it from hurting so bad during the night, and you might even get a little sleep," she says, and soothes his forehead with her cool hand.

We all eat some jerky and then take turns watching the animals and getting some sleep. Buck prowls around, and frequently lies by Fierro. Once I wake and in the dim starlight can see Rosy by Fierro, holding his hand and humming quietly. I get up and sit by him for awhile, but Rosy does not leave him. I think about her troubled life and wonder if her compassion is a result of how she has been treated, or is she a Believer and simply reflecting the love of Christ. Maybe it's some of both.

I have the last watch before daylight, and get everybody up. As the first dawn light touches the mountains, we are all armed, and ready for what comes. Nothing does. An hour goes by. Buck does not seem to be nervous, and that's a good sign. I glance quickly at Fierro. He is not doing well. Finally Alex indicates he is going out for a look, and I move over by Fierro. Tim is keeping watch, and Flor and Rosy come over to Fierro. Flor looks at him and at me.

"We have to get him out of here and where there is better help," she says.

When Alex returns he tells us there were apparently only three braves, and we somehow managed to wound all three. They are gone. We immediately prepare to leave. We tie Fierro loosely on his horse, and Rosy and Flor ride on each side of him when they can. Alex rides in the lead, and Tim and I take care of the animals. All the while I'm doing this I manage to look at this beautiful land, and we talk about what we could do here.

We are going down hill rapidly, and I'm surprised at the sight of so much wildlife. We startle deer and then I see my first elk. The animal is so big and powerful looking it shocks me. It has huge antlers, and they are covered with velvet, or skin. Alex tells us they will soon start shedding the skin and scraping the antlers on trees to get rid of it. We see half a dozen black bear, and I wish we had time to hunt and have some fresh meat.

At noon we stop in a thick stand of pine at the edge of an open meadow. Fierro is having a difficult time and we need to give him some rest from the jolting of the horse. We ease him off the horse and onto a blanket spread over some soft pine needles.

"Ross, come here," he says. "Ross, remember the paper I gave you."

"Yes." I answer in a low voice.

He reaches out his hand and I take it in my hand. It surprises me that it is almost limp and lifeless.

"Ross, I probably ain't going to make it. I want you to be sure and do what I told you, for my Grand-daughter, but would you use some of the money to help Rosy. She has shore been mighty good to me, and I want to help her."

"Fierro, my friend, I sure will, but if you can just hang on till we reach help, you can make it." I say.

He does not say anything, but barely squeezes my hand. Rosy sits down by him and takes hold of his other hand. Buck crowds in close and licks Fierro's face. We don't scold him. I hold Fierro's hand for some time, then it goes limp, he draws a deep, rasping breath, and is gone.

We bury Fierro at the edge of the meadow, digging a deep hole, and wrapping his body with some of his own clothing. Stones are piled over it. I repeat the Twenty Third Psalm over the grave, as we all stand and mourn the loss of a good friend. I select a large, healthy aspen tree standing nearby and scribe Fierro's name and the date he died in the beautiful white bark.

Looking back as we ride out of the meadow, I vow to some day come back and place a marker over that lonely grave. We don't say anything for a long while, then Rosy rides close to me and says;

"He was so good to me, and such a good man."

CHAPTER 25

Its late afternoon when we ride out of the trees and see a cloud of dust, and the lead wagons of a caravan, pulled by mules. Our horses and mules immediately whinny and bray a welcome, and pick up the pace. Its been two days since we buried Fierro and it's a quiet procession coming out of the beautiful mountains. I have not touched any of his belongings, and Tim and I have not talked about what we have to do in following his wishes. Fierro's saddle is still on his horse, and we take it off each night and care for the horse like he did. Even Buck seems a bit subdued as he trots along. Alex has been setting a fast pace, but I still have time to look around as we ride. It's a wonderful land, with fast rushing streams, lots of game, and many open meadows. Alex says most of the meadows were formed over many years by beaver ponds, which had then been abandoned after their food supply was exhausted.

I watch Tim and Rosy as they ride, side by side when they can. They seem to be really enjoying each other, especially as they learn each others language. I asked Flor and Rosy to teach us as much of the Spanish language as they can while we travel, so we are using it all the time. In turn, Tim has been teaching Rosy English. I frequently think of Sammie, and how much she will enjoy this country. It surprises me that my feelings are so deep for her, after knowing her for such a short time, and after being gone for so long. I still in my mind see her bathing at the spring.

We have reached the wagon tracks of the Trail and stop to rest our animals and wait for the caravan. It's now mid-summer and hot. That's

one reason why we are taking the mountain trail instead of the Cimarron
cut-off. The lead rider looks closely at us as he rides up. We are a bit of a
strange looking group, with two Mexican women riding men's saddles, all of
us dressed in buckskin and moccasins, heavily armed, and a large ugly dog
smiling at the rider with shiny white fangs. Also we came out of the trees on
the side of the mountain, not following the wagon tracks. The rider stops.

"Where you folks hail from, and where ya goin ?" he asks.

I tell him, and point out the packs on our mules and donkeys. Alex
asked him if the caravan had any trouble with Indians.

"We did have one short skirmish other side of the mountains."
he said, pointing back toward the dark mountains to the north of us.
"Worst problem was getting our wagons over the pass. Reckon ye won't
have any trouble."

He looks closely at my horse, and then Tim's.

"What kind of hosses are them?" he asks.

"These are Morgan's." I reply. "About as tough as any horse you
can find, and almost as sure footed as a mule. My Pa breeds and raises
them back in Tennessee and now in Kentuck. We finally got a chance
to try them in these Rocky Mountains, and they sure proved how good
they are."

"Who are ye?" he asked. I grinned a bit at that.

"Why, we are the Greenup boys." His head jerked around.

"Ye don't say! I heered about ye in Independence, and then at Bent's
Fort. There was a mighty pretty little Indian gal asking about you boys
at Danny Greenup's, where we had some wagons repaired, and bought a
couple. She said if we saw ye, to let ye know she was waiting fer ye. One
of the black boys had already told some stories about how tough ye were,
and to hope ye were friendly." He laughed. "Guess we hit it lucky, as it
peers ye are in a good mood. At Bent's Fort an Army Captain said they
were expecting ye. Ye Greenup boys throw a wide loop."

He looked around at the level ground where we are standing.

"This looks like a good place to circle and camp for the night," he
says. "Ye folks are welcome to join us if ye care to."

As he says this I have a strange foreboding. Usually Alex decides
where we are going to camp, since he is the most experienced of our
group. But I speak right up.

"We are moving fast and can get a couple more miles under our belt before we stop, and we are anxious to get home," I say. "Thanks anyway. By the way, if you see any Mexican troops at the village of Las Vegas, they might inquire about us. Appreciate it if you don't remember seeing us. We paid our taxes and all, but this goes way back to Kentuck."

Alex doesn't say anything, touches his hat brim to the rider, and starts his horse. The rest of us follow, and as we ride along the file of wagons, we trade greetings and comments with the traders. There are apparently no women with the caravan. I notice they mostly wear black hats, and long hair and beards. Finally we leave them behind, and looking back can see them going into their defensive circle. Alex looks at me.

"What was that about?" he asks. ""I'll wager them is Mennonite folks, and they are generally mighty fine people."

I explain to him the sense of warning I had when the rider invited us to join them.

"It doesn't happen often, but when I have a feeling like this, I've learned to be careful." I say.

Flor and Rosy both nod agreement. In the open prairie we are able to ride as a group, instead of single file as we have for the most part since leaving Taos. We talk about this for a while, and soon our little group is out of sight of the caravan as we ride down into a low valley. After another hour of fast travel we find a place suitable to camp, where we can graze our animals and keep a good lookout through the night. There is a good stream of clear, cold mountain water, and we all drink plenty, and are thankful we are not on the cut-off this late in the summer.

In the middle of the night I'm standing guard, thinking of how good it will be to get back to Sammie, when I hear a far off gunshot, then another. It's quiet until false dawn, and we are up and packing when we hear several more gunshots in the direction of the caravan.

"I wager the Utes had a try at that caravan, but most of those fellers looked mighty salty, and the Utes won't scare them much." said Alex.

We move rapidly away, crossing more of the open grass land, but keeping close to the edges where there is good cover of scrub oak and arroyos coming out of the foothills. Tim is riding rear guard, and we are not stopping. Since the animals are all in good condition and not climbing steep grades its easy to put the miles behind us. Suddenly Tim spurs and comes up beside me.

"Everybody take cover. There are Mexican troops coming below and behind us."

We turn into an arroyo and in thirty seconds are completely out of sight from anyone unless they are right on top of us. The troops would not likely cut our tracks unless they have scouts out. Our little cavalcade does not make much dust, especially since we are not moving in the wagon tracks of the trail. We sit quietly on our mounts while Alex dismounts and carefully moves through the oak till he finds a vantage point where he can watch the trail without being seen. There is no sound but the buzzing of flies, bees and a few mosquitoes. The sun is bearing down hot and there is no breeze in the shelter of the brush. Suddenly Buck growls, and Alex is back with us.

"Ross, it's sure a good thing we followed your gut feeling last night. The Mexican Officer with ten of his men are riding hard toward Raton. I'll bet they got into the wagon caravan late, and were there when the Utes took a few shots. It probably surprised the Utes to find the troops, and they didn't stick around."

He stopped and took a long swig of water.

"Looks to me like we better stay high and out of sight. Not only are they after you, but they probably are some bent out of shape at these two women, for helping you get out of Santa Fe. They figured sure they would catch us camped with the caravan."

He grins at Rosy and Flor. I silently thank the Lord for protecting us, and without wasting more time we trail in single file after Alex. It is good to get moving again, and we soon leave most of the oak brush behind us and are in a stand of huge, beautiful pine. Alex says we are entering an area called Vermejo, which is part of an old Spanish land grant. We cross several fast flowing streams, and see several beaver dams, though there doesn't appear to be much activity around them. Apparently many of the beaver have been trapped out. We see a sow bear, with two cubs. She smelled us before she saw us, and stood on her hind legs for a moment to watch us passing. Then she woofed at the cubs, and sent them scrambling. Once we came to a heavily used trail, which Alex said came from a huge valley west of us, and went into Raton. We stop and sweep away the tracks made by our animals crossing the trail. Then we start up a steep mountain side.

It's starting to get dark when we finally stop in a deep, heavily wooded valley, with a small stream. We find a small grassy area and let the horses and mules graze for a while, then bring them in close and take turns guarding them through the night. Just after we bring them in, Buck growls and the hackles rise on his neck. From his actions I figure it's a bear, and build the fire up a little. We can hear the animal snuffling around outside our firelight, and finally it leaves and all is quiet again. While I'm awake I think of the narrow escape from the Mexican troops and wish we were crossing the Arkansas. Then I think of this beautiful land and want to come back.

Climbing the mountains above the village of Raton does not give us much trouble and we can sure see what a struggle the caravans have going the other direction with wagons. I look at all the work apparently done, and am glad we are riding and leading. Small trees have been cut and laid across soft places, and large trees have been cut just to let the wagons through. At a couple of steep places we can see where the wagons were actually lowered on ropes.

Right on top of the mountain there is a clear area where we can look both north and south. We can see for miles across the plains in either direction. Suddenly my heart jumps. Far to the north of us, above a blue haze of mountains, is a shining, white peak. Its silhouette against the bright blue sky is immense, and there are great shoulders and ridges extending out from the shining peak. I can only sit in awe, and thank God for his creation. This has to be the mountain called "Pikes Peak," discovered years ago by the explorer, Zebulon Pike. Uncle Will had told of seeing it from far out on the plains. Now I get to see it. I can hardly wait to explore the country around it. Looking back to the west there are more shining white peaks, with immense blue valleys, and great cliffs of rock, as far as I can see.

There are white clouds drifting across the sky, and from here I can see their shadows moving on the prairie far below us. The patterns of color are constantly changing, and with the green grass of spring still showing across the plains the contrast is wonderful. Far out on the Cimarron River valley I see a large black area, which can only be a herd of buffalo.

The trail down the north side of the mountains is much worse than what we just came up on the south side. The timber is really thick, with huge fir trees, and lots of dead tree trunks lying around like straw. There are various pieces of wagons lying by the edge of the ruts, and we can see where different routes have been tried. There is an occasional level place where it looks like the traders camped whenever they could. Finally we get off the mountain to a river the traders call "Picketwire", and Flor tells us that's a "gringo" way to pronounce "Purgatoire."

There is a poor Mexican village called Trinidad on the banks of the river and we stop for a while, but I'm getting in a hurry to get back across the Arkansas and to Bent's Fort. Buck quickly asserts his ownership of our mule train. The village dogs bark and growl, but if one gets too close, Buck stops, his hackles rise, and his big white fangs shine. The village dogs leave us alone.

We wait for a few hours for Flor and Rosy to visit some of their numerous relatives. They all know Alex, and it seems the word is already here about Fierro. I'm not sure how it happens, but it's the same way in the Smokey Mountains. Here it's called the ghost whisper.

I notice another strange thing. Rosy introduces Tim, and then me, but it seems Tim gets all the attention. I smile to myself, and think Tim is really soaking this up. That's great, and I just hope they are both happy with the arrangement. Then I think of our folks, and laugh out loud at what they may think when I show up with Sammie and Tim with Rosy. Another thing makes me laugh. Many of the out-houses are along the banks of the river, and their walls are only high enough that the user can look around and visit with the neighbor. Ma would be scandalized. We are invited to spend the night in the village, but the weather in the mountains west and north of us looks grim. Great thunderheads are beginning to roll up over the mountains, and I think even Flor and Rosy want to get across the river before dark. We eat a big supper of beans, deer meat, and tortillas, and leave to cross the river.

CHAPTER 26

rossing the river takes little time, then we move at a fast walk, crossing several small arroyos which appear to drain into a large arroyo. Staying above it and below a ridge top between us and the main trail, we find a narrow bench and make camp. All the saddles and equipment are stacked and covered and the animals hobbled and tied to several small juniper trees. Its pitch dark when the animals and equipment are secured, and we are huddled around a fire with our oilskins over us. Lightning is getting closer and there is a steady drumroll of thunder.

A gust of cold air hits us and Alex says; "hail coming!" In a few minutes a black wall of water and then hail sweeps over us. It probably does not last more than half an hour, and is gone into the darkness. Then we hear another noise from the arroyo, and Buck growls deep in his throat. We walk to the edge of the bench. Below us, and visible in the lightning flashes, is a raging torrent of muddy water. We can hear boulders rolling in the stream bed and see sage brush and juniper trees being swept downstream.

"Thank God we came up here!" exclaims Rosy. We all agree and stand watching the violence below us, then return to camp, set a watch and spread our bedrolls.

When I wake the others early the next morning we are all tired. As we straighten out the packs we decide to have a good hot breakfast since we are well concealed from the trail and any Mexican soldiers. This also gives the flood waters more time to drain away. Then we pack, and travel fast, soon reaching the wagon tracks of the main trail.

We are gradually drawing away from the dark mountains with the shining tops, on our left, and heading more north to north east. Two tall cone shaped peaks, which Flor says they call the "breasts of the world" are on our left between us and the main range. Makes me think of Sammie, standing by the spring, and then I begin to dream of all the things we can do in this country. Time is passing rapidly, and we need to get started.

Two more days passed, and we decided to travel later. The stars are incredibly bright, and it seems like we could almost reach up and grab them. The marvelous warm prairie wind is blowing, I can smell the grass, hear the creak of leather and the sound of the hooves as the animals move at a fast walk. Tonight is our last night to camp in Mexican territory, if all goes well tomorrow. I'm learning to always remind myself to say "The Lord willing" when we make big plans. Too many times they have been changed. I'm constantly amazed at the tremendous expanse of beautiful prairie grasses we walk through. We can occasionally still see a glimpse of a snow covered peak. We sit around our small fire, and watch the stars, and the new moon, and talk of things we expect to see and do. The horses and mules are mostly standing quietly, as if they too will miss the trail we have just come over. We talk of how people will come along this trail if the US takes this land from Mexico. I want to come along this trail, and bring Samantha, and Pa and Ma. I would like to have a family to raise out here where I can see "as far as the eyes can see."

We stopped late this afternoon at Iron Springs, and watered and rested the stock for a couple of hours. Then we moved on for several hours, because we heard the Indians watched the Springs for small caravans to raid. We find a small sheltered arroyo, loosen the packs and saddles, build the small fire, and are going to sleep till just dawn, and start again.

Buck's head comes up, and his ears go to alert. Then a low growl comes deep in his chest. Tim is on watch with the horses and mules, and I immediately figure Indians are trying to steal our animals. I roll over and start to crawl out of the firelight, when a voice from the darkness stops me.

"All of you, don't move, and keep the dog back, or I'll kill it." I settle back to the ground, and tell Buck to "stay."

Now, take your pistols out with two fingers, and throw them out of the light. Then put your hands behind your heads." The voice has a foreign accent that sounds familiar.

We do as the voice says, and wait. There is some discussion from two or possibly three men out in the dark, and its all in Spanish. Then one man walks into the circle of light from the fire, and it's Roberto Quintara. He looks at me and laughs.

"So, Greenup, we meet again. I've been waiting for you to come back from Santa Fe, and this morning my lookout spotted you." He looked around. "So your brother is watching the horses and mules, and you have picked up two nice senoritas to travel with. Where is the Fierro man?"

I don't say a word, just sit and watch him. Alex is watching him, and we are all listening. Then we hear a shout, and a scuffle, and soon two men march Tim into the firelight, with a gun in his back and his hands in the air. I'm sure they know how many of us there are, but are not quite sure about Fierro, and the women are a surprise. Roberto speaks again.

"Greenup's, we are on Mexican soil, and your troops cannot do anything about it. Now you are going to tell me where the gold is, that you took from the courier you killed last winter. If you don't, I'm going to start with your brother, and put him in the fire, like an Apache would do. When we are done here, we'll go back to Independence and take Samantha."

Just then Flor opens up in Spanish, and I don't know most of the words, but they sure don't sound nice. He laughs and steps around the fire and slaps Flor hard. She spits on him, and then Rosy turns into a demon. On her feet like a cat, she claws and scratches at Roberto. He steps back and coolly shoots her in the right arm. It is a mistake. Rosy screams, and grabs her arm. The two hard-cases with Roberto are briefly distracted. Flor reaches inside her shirt, and comes out with a small derringer, which she shoots point blank at Roberto's face. He screams in anguish and goes to his knees. Alex has come up with his own boot gun, and is shooting. Buck is right in front of Roberto and growling his horrible growl, with his white fangs right in Roberto's face. Tim is scrambling for one of our guns. With my hands on the back of my head, I have already had a grip on my slim little knife. I slip it out of the sheath, take a step, and stick it right into the side of the thug nearest me.

"Drop your gun, now!" I yell. He does, and drops to his knees.

The other man is on the ground, apparently hit by Alex's bullets. Not more than thirty seconds have passed, but the scene has sure changed. Roberto is still down, moaning in agony. Tim is collecting guns, and gets some rope. We tie the feet of all three, and build up the fire. Then we look at wounds, starting with Rosy. She has a nasty bullet wound in the upper part of her right arm. It apparently didn't break the bone, but grazed it, and went through, coming out the back. Flor digs into her medicine kit and comes up with some dressing for the wound, so we can clean it with hot water, and get the bleeding stopped. Then she looks at Roberto, who is lying still, with his hands over his face. I pull his hands away, and we look closely at his face. It appears the small caliber bullet must have gone right across one eye, and glanced off the bone at the edge of the eye socket. I figure he has lost sight in that eye, and so does Flor. She puts a dressing over the eye, and holds it in place with his bandana.

The man Alex shot is dead, and the one I slipped the knife into is sick. We can't tell how badly hurt he is, and can't do much about it. I tell Roberto and the wounded man they will just have to tough it out till we get to Bent's Fort tomorrow. We tie their hands behind them and I tell Buck to guard them. The wounded man tells us where their camp is, and we decide to wait till morning to pick up their horses. Finally we fall into the sleep of exhaustion, with Tim standing watch for a couple of hours, then I spell him.

With morning light we have some breakfast, tend Roberto and his man, who appears worse, then Tim and I dig a shallow grave and bury the dead man. We finally find a few rocks to cover the grave with, and tell Roberto he will have to take care of the man's personal belongings. He only moans in pain. Then we pack, go by their camp, which is meager, since they were working out of Bent's Fort. We pick up their three horses, put Roberto and the wounded man on their horses, and lead the third.

The Arkansas River valley is just ahead of us, and it's still a few hours till we will reach the river and cross it. We travel as rapidly as we can. We have not met another caravan today, and may have seen the last of them, as it's getting late in the season to go to Santa Fe, unless they intend to winter there, or in Chihuahua.

Finally, the banks of the Arkansas again. We waste no time in crossing it, and there is Capt. Nelson, with a couple of his troopers. We shake hands all around, introduce Rosy, than start explaining to the Captain why we are leading horses with two wounded men. He tells the troopers to take them to the Doctor at the Fort, then put them behind bars till he can decide what to do with them. His wife and the Lt.'s wife have been house guests of the Bent's this summer, and have invited us to supper. In the meantime we can set up camp in an area reserved for important travelers, which will be under guard by his troopers. When we arrive at the area he has another trooper escort Flor and Rosy to the Dr.'s office to have Rosy's arm examined and treated.

We set up camp, and when Flor and Rosy return we have a large kettle of water heating over a fire. We also borrowed a tub, and after putting it in the tent and filling it with hot water, retreat to the walls of the fort. There we visit with some troopers and a couple of mountain men who are lounging in the shade of the walls. They tell us the large camp of Indians we see east of the Fort are Shawnee's and peaceable, and there have not been any attacks in the vicinity of the Fort for several weeks.

Tim and I take a walk around the inside of the Fort. It's a small walled city, complete with a large adobe room where meetings and dinners can be held. In addition there is a well equipped blacksmith shop, and carpenter shop, where any kind of repairs to wagons, harness, or weapons can be taken care of. William Bent has nice living quarters, and we understand he has two Shawnee wives. This might help explain the large camp of Shawnee's outside. The Dr.'s office is well equipped, and there is a large area for trooper's barracks. There is fur storage, and a fur press right in the open court yard. The horse corral is in good shape, and there is a flock of chickens.

Finally Tim and I walk back to the tent, and taking the tub outside behind the tent proceed to use the rest of the hot water to scrub off some of the trail dirt. Alex has already cleaned up. I still am too bashful to undress in front of the two women, even though they have both seen me stark naked when I took the bath in Santa Fe.

As the five of us walk through the heavy gates of the Fort, I think of Roberto, as he rests either in the Dr.'s office or the small jail cell by the trooper's quarters. I think of catching him when he tried to burn our barn back in Kentuck, then when he paid Liz to spy on us, sent four hired criminals to steal from us, has tried to do us more bodily harm, and has nothing to show for it but the possible loss of an eye. I don't feel any sympathy, because he has tried to kill us, and would apparently have no remorse if he had succeeded.

We have a wonderful evening. Flor and Rosy are dressed in beautiful Mexican outfits, but they sure wear too much red on their faces to suit me. The two military wives are dressed in the fashion of the day back east, but I notice they immediately put Flor and Rosy at ease. Tim and I have on new deerskin shirts. The Captain and Lieutenant are in civilian clothes, and William Bent and both his Shawnee wives are at the table, in native attire. The women have on beautiful, beaded buckskin dresses. Rosy has learned a lot of English in the past few days, the Shawnee wives know a few English words, and with Flor translating for Rosy, and Mr. Bent for his wives, we have a laughter filled evening.

I realize I feel completely at ease for the first time in many weeks. Our horses and mules are with the military remuda, thanks to Captain Nelson. Buck is guarding our camp, with the help of a buffalo leg bone. The Captains wife insists on hearing all of our adventures since we left them on the banks of the Arkansas several weeks ago. We tell them about the death of Fierro, and there is a moment of quiet, before the conversation resumes.

The meal is delicious roast buffalo hump, and tongue, with several Mexican and Indian dishes, and fresh baked bread from the horno, or Mexican oven. It is followed by sweet Flan, or Mexican custard. Then the women go to the Bent's quarters to look at the babies, and we settle down to some serious discussion of horses, mules, wagons and other equipment.

It's late when the officers go back to their quarters. Alex and Tim escort Rosy and Flor back to our camp, and I climb the stairs to the parapet around the entire top of the Fort. It is really well designed, and from the two lookout points on opposite corners, defenders have a field of fire that covers all four walls. I walk slowly around the walls, looking out across the prairie, and across the Arkansas River into Mexican Territory. I think of the wonders of this land, and the blood that has already been shed along the borders.

There is a half moon, and it shines on the tall prairie grass, and the cottonwood trees by the River. I smell the grass, and the river, and the horse corral, and see the dim light of fading campfires, and am overcome by the wonder and immensity of it all. I keep my eyes open, and thank the Creator, the all-powerful God of this universe. Finally I leave the fort, and go to my bedroll, and a sleep filled with dreams of shining mountains, beautiful mountain meadows and streams, and Sammie.

We stay at the Fort four days. During this time we shoe the horses and mules, have all our furs evaluated by Mr. Bent, and put in the fur press. This makes smaller packs, and we are able to add several buffalo hides to fill out the loads on the mules. William Bent looks at all the money and furs we have traded for, and smiles.

"You boys have done real well on your first trip. I'm looking forward to meeting your Pa's, and the rest of the family. Just be careful on the rest of the trip. The Pawnees are quiet, but I'm getting concerned about white thieves. There are horses and mules being stolen, and blamed on Indians, but we know it's not always Indians."

Captain Nelson has decided to hold Roberto Quintara till he is able to ride, and send him back to Independence with a company of troops in an ambulance with his partner. I go in to see the partner, and talk to him about his life. He is still not doing well, from the knife wound I gave him, and may die before he can get back to his home. I suggest he make his life right with his Maker, and find some other kind of work, if he lives,

The last day Tim and I go through Fierro's personal belongings and tools, and decide what to do with them. The trade goods he has left we trade to Mr. Bent for more buffalo hides, except for some calico, which we give to Rosy and Flor. They smile, and cry, and pack the calico with their goods. We decide to sell the furs with ours, retain the money with the rest of Fierro's money, and hold the horse and mules till we find the Grand-daughter in St. Louis and determine her circumstances. We will keep the tools.

CHAPTER 27

The days are still hot when we leave Bent's Fort and start due east. We are carrying a large Army pouch on one of the mules, with mail Captain Nelson has asked us to deliver to the garrison at Independence. From Bent's Fort to Independence is over five hundred miles, and we are all in a hurry.

We are with a detachment of troops for the first two days. They had word a wagon caravan was having trouble, and possibly being harassed by a small band of Indians. Sure enough, we run into them, camped close to the banks of the Arkansas. They are driving mules, and a raid had left them with about half their animals. They were not using chain hobbles or chains to stake out the animals. They are settlers, not traders, so there are a number of women and children. They had reduced their loads, and their number of wagons, and were struggling along. The Wagon Master is not sure the raiders were Indians, though some wore Indian dress. Their intent is to settle on the US side of the Arkansas. We leave the troops to work with them, and travel on. We are moving fast, but stop frequently to rest and water the animals. We are also keeping a sharp watch for anything suspicious.

We have noticed the few household things left beside the trail. I stop and look at some of the items. One is a spinet piano. It was probably an heirloom and a woman was determined to take it to her new home. Finally, after lugging it all these miles, it had come to the point they leave it behind, or turn around. The sun and wind, and possibly some rain, have already ruined the beautiful finish.

We are covering about thirty five to forty miles a day, walking fast. Supplementing the good prairie grass with a measure of oats we bought at Bent's Fort, the horses and mules are holding up well. It's easy to follow the trail, but we are more cautious than ever, after what William Bent told us about white thieves. We stay a little to one side of the heavily traveled ruts, and try to make the rest stops where there is still plenty of grass. I notice the heat is more intense, and the air is damp, and muggy.

About the fourth day out I'm riding high above the others, on the side of a narrow little valley, when I catch a glimpse of riders ahead, coming toward us. I immediately turn to our group, signaling to close up. They do, and by the time the riders get close we are in a tight, box shaped group, with Alex and Tim in front, Rosy and Flor on each side, and me at the back. This makes it impossible to cover us all with one or two guns. We each have a rifle in hand, and as the six men approach make it clear we have them covered. When they are about a good rifle shot, but a long pistol shot away, Alex halts them. He raises an arm, holding his rifle.

"Stop! Who are you, and what do you want?" he shouts.

They immediately stop and talk amongst themselves. They appear to be mostly white men, with possibly one Mexican or Indian. Then one speaks.

"We are friends, who are looking for a caravan of settlers who are on this trail. Have you seen them?"

Alex shouts back.

"We left a caravan yesterday who had lost some of their animals to white thieves. A platoon of troops from Bent's Fort is with them, escorting them on to the Fort. If your intentions are good, go around us, not getting any closer than you are now. If you have mischief in mind, some of you will die right here. Whichever it is, get moving!"

I carefully sight my rifle at one of the riders, and wait to see what they are going to do. I'm calm as I've ever been, because I know what I can do, and will not hesitate. After the meeting with Roberto, I've had a change in my thinking. I can feel it. I'm trusting in the Lord to give me wisdom, compassion, and a clear eye and steady hand. I also remember Grandpa Greenup, saying there are times we have to be more violent than the person we are facing, and be faster. The evident leader, who spoke to us, says something profane, then they turn and slowly walk around us, never getting closer than they are now. I carefully turn and watch them, keeping my rifle on one of them all the time. Flor and Rosy turn with me, but Tim and Alex keep facing the front. In turn the men watch us as they ride. When they finally turn their backs they are completely behind us. We let the animals rest and graze for some time, till the men are almost out of sight, then I ride carefully up the slope so I can watch them longer. I look around in every direction, and keep looking around all the time we let the animals graze.

"Alex, and all of you, did you notice they had very little tied on their saddles. They are probably not more than a few miles from their camp, and are waiting here for anyone they can rob!" I say, when I get back.

We have been out of Bent's Fort six days, and have not met, or overtaken anyone after meeting the six men. I'm leading a string of mules and Tim is riding lookout, when he shouts and waves from ahead of us. We immediately gather all the stock closely and go to our defensive positions. Tim comes riding hard, and joins us.

"I saw a line of riders, coming across the valley from the River," he says. "Look like Indians."

This is a good place to rest, and graze the stock for a while, after we see what we are faced with. I get off my horse and let him graze while we wait. It takes awhile before the first rider appears, and I breathe a sigh of relief. They don't appear to be in war paint, and then we see some women and children.

"Sure looks like a hunting party," says Alex. They are probably trying to get a winter supply of meat dried. Looks like Pawnee."

There are several horses loaded with great bundles of meat, wrapped in the hides of the buffalo they came from. We stand firm, watching as they cross in front of us, and then I remember the young Pawnee who tried to kill me. He may have come from one of these families. The first few Indians have gone out of sight, when suddenly there is a shout and one of the braves comes racing back along the line, yelling at the others.

They immediately start to bunch up, with the women and children pulling their horses and the horses with the meat into a group, and the braves racing back to form a protective circle around them. There are not more than fifty total, with about fifteen braves. They are about a pistol shot distance away, and in a poor place to defend themselves. They no sooner get in a defensive circle than a group of five mounted white men sweep over the hill, rifles in hand, and intent on the small band of Indians. Then they see us.

The white men rein to a halt, and then spur their horses toward us. I mount, and when they are about the same distance from us, as we are from the Indians, I wave my rifle and tell them to stop. Once again we are ready to take action, just like we were with the group the other day. These are different men, but with the same dirty clothing, and nothing tied on their saddles but slickers and small stuff. They stop and one of them yells at us.

"Who are you and what are you doing with these redskins?"

"Just so you know, this is the Greenup party, and we are minding our own business, and appears to us you ought to be doing the same!" I shout back, and bring my rifle up.

There is an outburst of profanity, and some discussion, then another shout. They start to raise their rifles.

"We figure we'll just take care of you first, then the filthy injuns!"

As he said this, five rifles are lined up on them. At the same time, out of the corner of my eye, I see a few rifles and several bows raised from the ring of braves, all pointed at the group of white men.

As I mentioned earlier, I have changed, and there is not a moment's hesitation as I pull the trigger. The man's life is saved by the movement of his horse, but the big slug hits him in the shoulder and knocks him backward over the saddle. At least one of them got off a shot, which hit Rosy's saddle horn, but our sudden shot, and hearing the bullet hit, makes the others hesitate, and that costs them another man, as Alex's rifle booms and their spokesman goes off his horse, hitting the ground hard and not moving. The others, including the man I hit, spur their horses and race away. The Indians have not fired a shot. I fire several pistol shots after the fleeing men, then quickly reload.

We quietly walk our outfit toward the Indians. They just as quietly watch us, and then a large brave signals the others to lower their weapons. Alex says several words to them, and makes movements with his hands. We stop and watch. Alex uses the name "Greenup" several times, and points at the rest of us, including Flor and Rosy. There is some more discussion, and Alex tells us they are on the way to join another group of Pawnee back in the hills. They will meet them tomorrow, so if they can avoid the white men, will be safe. Then they get into single file again, but I notice a couple of braves moving out and ahead of them. They ride by, as we watch them, and I see the black eyes of a tiny papoose, or baby, staring at me from a cradle board.

I ride over where the motionless man is lying on the ground. His horse is grazing a short distance away, paying no attention to what is going on. I get off, and examine the rider. He died instantly from the shot, which apparently hit him right in the heart. He is unshaven, scruffy, with filthy dirty clothes. I think of him again as a man with possibly some loved ones who will always wonder what happened to him. I think some of his companions will come back for him, but I don't feel we can leave him without covering him from the buzzards, which are already gathering above us. Alex is watching me with a half smile on his face, and I know he knows what I want to do. Tim is off his horse, getting the short handled shovel off a mule's pack. Alex and the women sit their horses, keeping a sharp lookout. In a few minutes we roll the man into a shallow grave, covering him with dirt and a few rocks, and sticking a rock up at the end of the grave.

Several hours later we ride over a ridge, and see the crossing over the Arkansas where we left it to take the Cimarron Cut-off several weeks ago. We also see an Army camp, and away south and west is a dust cloud which must belong to a caravan coming toward the river. We ride down to the Army camp, and they have several troops armed and ready to greet us, whether we are friend or foe. A First Lieutenant, apparently the C.O., is waiting as we ride up. I look directly at the Lieutenant.

"Howdy. We are the Greenup's, seven days out of Bent's Fort, and before that out of Santa Fe. We are headed for Independence, but if you are Lieutenant Clay, we have a package for you."

He looks us over with a practiced eye. He sure doesn't look like a greenhorn, and I know he figures right away we are fairly able to take care of ourselves. He grins at us, and tells the troopers to stand easy.

"So you are the Greenup's! You folks have made quite a name for yourselves, and I even had a discussion with a Spaniard, hmm-m-m, his name was Quintara, some time ago, who wanted me to pick you up for grand theft. I tended to ignore his request. Well, you came to the right place, because I am Lieutenant Clay. Get down, and I'll wager my Supply Sargent can rustle up some coffee."

We didn't waste any time doing just that, and soon were hunkered down with steaming mugs of coffee, while we watched some young troopers lead our animals down to the water hole they had developed. Tim and Rosy got the envelope with U.S. Army Dispatches, LT. Clay, printed on the side and handed it to him. He chuckled as he took it, and looked at me.

"Didn't know you had a couple of ladies and a mountain man in your company. Last I heard it was the Greenup's and a Fierro man."

I quickly tell him what had happened to Fierro, how we happened to have Alex, Flor and Rosy with us. I tell him briefly about Roberto, and the dead man we left south of the Arkansas, then about the first party of white men we met, and the Indians and second party of white men we met just this morning. I tell him we left another dead man this morning, and had his horse, and would like to leave it with the Lieutenant.

By this time most of the troops are gathered around listening to the story, and looking with great admiration at our party, especially Flor and Rosy. The Lieutenant reads his dispatches, then gives us another packet to put with the bag of mail we have for Independence. He issues orders for the Sargent to muster the troops and prepare to leave on a short patrol on our back trail, just in case the white thieves have decided to follow us. The caravan coming in from the southwest won't be here till tomorrow, so he has plenty of time to get ready in case there is trouble from either Indians or whites. We down the last of our coffee, shake hands all around, and mount up. Three hours and several miles later we make camp on a small creek, which runs into the Arkansas. It's been a mighty full day.

The next morning we are on the trail early. We are taking the short-cut across the bend of the Arkansas which we took on the way out to test our horses and mules. Now that we are not pulling wagons we are moving fast across this dry stretch, and push the animals hard. I am afraid we are not keeping careful enough watch, but we make Pawnee Fork without any problems. We camp before crossing the river, and Tim takes the animals to water and then graze. We are done eating and I'm about to go to sleep by our very small fire. Rosy sits down by me, and Flor stands by me. Rosy says:

"Ross, do you think Tim really likes me?"

Her English is getting better all the time, and she catches me by surprise. I stammer some, and finally tell her I think he really likes her. Her next question is a bit more difficult.

"Will your folks like Mexicans?" I sit and think.

"Flor, and Rosy, when we are in places like Independence, there are all kinds of people from all over the world. Flor has seen them. In the hills, we are kinda clannish, but my Great Grandfather, who was the third governor of Kentuck, had a Cherokee wife. We have close friends who are Indian, and as you may not know, President Van Buren is working hard to move all the Indians from the East and South to the West."

I pause, and think, then start again.

"Pa and Grandpa have always said we shouldn't be too concerned about another fellers skin color. We should be most concerned about how he is in his heart. Trouble is, most people can't get past the skin color. So, it appears to me, some folks won't think twice about you being a Mexican, and others will curse you. Personally, I think you are just a pretty young lady, who will have to control her temper to get along."

Alex has been listening to me, and now he chimes in.

"Rosy, Ross has it right. Your Auntie has seen lots of different kind of people, but she managed to get along fine. I figure you will do the same. Just try to act yourself, control your temper and your tongue, and be careful about flirting with other men. You can cause more trouble than a barrel full of rattlesnakes, and we don't want that to happen. You won't find many young fellers as good as Tim, if that's where your interest is."

Alex was quiet then, Flor hugged Rosy, and I turned away from the fire and went to sleep.

We passed Pawnee Rock this morning, and are approaching the bend in the Arkansas where it turns south toward Texas. From here on I'm watching carefully for places to locate, where we can raise horses and mules, and where we can raise hay, and transport hay to store and sell. This country is going to settle fast, and if the United States takes the land south of the Arkansas from Mexico, there won't be any stopping the flood of settlers.

We reach and cross the Neosho River, and then on into Council Grove. It's been two months since we were here last, and the grass lands around Council Grove have really taken a beating. The caravans of mules and oxen have grazed the good grass for several miles around, and it's either dusty or muddy in the main area of the Grove. There is a company of US troops here, and I visit some with the First Lieutenant in charge. I don't say anything about the discussions we have had with Captain Nelson about furnishing mules and horses to the US. This Lieutenant makes me a bit uneasy. After talking to him a few minutes, I figure he is jealous of anyone who has been west to the beautiful prairies and shining mountains. I just leave him alone after that. We go over the feet of our animals, making sure the shoes are in good shape, and getting ready for the last push into Independence.

"Hey, Greenup!" There is a shout, and I turn to see who it is. A stocky, black headed young feller is waving at me, and comes trotting over. Its one of the hands Danny Greenup had working at his wagon shop in Independence. He tells me Danny sent him out here to see what it would take to set up a wagon repair and blacksmith shop in council Grove. While we are talking the Army Lieutenant comes over.

"Did I hear him call you Greenup?" he asks me.

"Well, yea, that's my name." I reply.

"Are you one of the "Greenup Boys" I keep hearing about? Did one of you kill a fellow last winter over in the Smokys, and cause a lot of trouble over there?"

"Well, I'm not so sure about the last part, but I did kill a man who was trying to kill me."

He glares at me, and looks at the Private who is following him.

"Go get the Sargent. We need to talk to the Greenup's."

I bristled up a bit at that.

"There is nothing for you to talk to us about. We have spent several days on the trail with Captain Nelson, who is now at Bent's Fort, and he is aware of all that's happened. He has trusted us enough to send dispatches to the Commander at Independence, and that's where we are headed now."

He turned red in the face at that bit of news.

"I'll just take those dispatches." He said.

"I don't reckon you will, Lieutenant. I have orders to give them to the CO at Independence, and no one else, and I intend to do just that. We also met Lieutenant Clay at the Cimarron crossing on the Arkansas, and he knows all that is going on, and has also sent dispatches to the CO at Independence by us."

The Lieutenant turns and stomps away, with a grinning private following him. Alex laughs, but I don't think it's funny. I have probably made an enemy, and we don't need that out here.

Tonight we have a fire going, and there are a number of folks visiting us. We are the experienced one's, especially with Alex being a true mountain man, and a pretty young Mexican girl with our group. It's a mile out to the Army camp, and I ride out there. The Lieutenant and a tough old Sargent are sitting by their fire, when I ride up, and I invite them to come visit us, have a cup of coffee, and ask us any questions they want to about our activities. They accept, and I wait till their mounts are brought up, and we ride back together. It's a good evening, the two soldiers leave in a better humor, and I sleep well tonight.

We are at the point on the trail where the settlers going to Oregon and California turn north. They will travel several miles to a village called Topeka, cross the Kansas River there and keep going north. We stop and look at the ruts made across the prairie north. There has been rain in the past few days and the mud is deep. A caravan of wagons pulled by oxen is just making the turn north. We wave and the Wagon Master rides back to us. He wants to know where we have come from, and we talk for awhile. He has been over the trail before, and figures they are the last caravan to leave for this summer. They plan on wintering on the North Platte River, in a little valley he knows of, and thinks they can handle it. They are a small group and have lots of grain in a couple of wagons. We wish them the best and ride on, watching rain clouds form ahead and behind us.

Since leaving Council Grove we have seen a few small farm houses, and they are now getting more frequent. We ride off the trail a ways to one which sits by itself, and I hail the young farmer who is busy building a barn.

"What's the chance of us putting our animals in your corral tonight and sleeping in your barn? We plan on getting into Independence tomorrow, and would like to stay dry tonight. We can pay you."

He walks over and stands looking at our horses.

"Are those by any chance Morgan's?" he asks.

That opens the gate for us. Soon we are telling him about raising Morgan's, and mules, and then his young wife joins us. The women start telling their own adventures, and then we are sitting around the only table in their small house, while the young wife fixes bacon, eggs and hot bread. The couple don't have any children, but plan on having them soon. I tell them of some of our plans, and some of the needs we will have, especially if the shining mountains south and west of the Arkansas are added to the US.

Their name is McConnell, and they came from over in the Virginia's. Wayne gets real excited about the prospects of being a part of our operation, and I advise him we will keep their place in mind as we start to map out our plans. We finally go to the barn and bed, but not before hobbling the animals and setting up our usual watch. Tim has the first watch, and Rosy stays up with him. They go off to the far corner of the corral, and as I go to sleep I can hear their low voices, and then I grin to myself, as I hear the soft patter of the rain starting.

I have the last watch, and there is a steady rain. At least our beds and the packs are dry, and it does not take long to get everything going, especially after hot coffee and hot bread from the McConnell kitchen. I pay them well for our lodging, and we wave goodbye as the animals line out.

CHAPTER 28

In a few hours we are in the outskirts of Independence. There sure isn't any grass around here, as the caravans camped here since early spring have trampled it, or their animals have eaten it. All the activity has slowed down, but we are one of the first groups of traders to come back from Santa Fe, and a crowd starts to follow us. We are sure a rough looking bunch, after about eighteen hundred miles of riding, fighting, walking and surviving. I'm leading, and look back at our outfit, and am proud of the condition the horses and mules are in. They sure show we have cared for them, and look better than we do. Only one has a scar from an arrow. Buck is trotting beside me as we start toward Danny Greenup's wagon barn. He hasn't paid any attention to the dogs barking and running alongside us, but he suddenly growls one of his terrible growls, and the hair on his neck stands straight up. We are right in front of Danny's barn, and there, standing with his feet wide apart, and a scowl on his dark face, is Mr. Quintara, Roberto's Pa.

"Where is Roberto?" he shouts.

I stop, and we all stop. I look at him, and say quietly:

"Why, last time I saw him, he was in a jail cell at Bent's Fort, being guarded by soldiers so he wouldn't get hurt any worse."

Quintara makes a motion, and before I can get my gun out, a braided leather whip comes at me from the side. It snaps around my neck, and next thing I know, I'm choking on the ground and Quintara is standing over me, with a long bladed knife in his hand. Then I hear a scream, and there is my pretty Samantha.

For the next couple of minutes I'm too stunned and trying to breath, to do anything, except watch what happens. Samantha turns into a wildcat, scratching and spitting in Quintara's face. A horse races up, and another, and Samantha is joined by two Mexican women, who are cursing Quintara in Spanish. They drive him to his knees, the knife is knocked to the ground, and a cocked pistol is held against his head. It's in the hands of Flor. Big Buck is also right in his face, and probably about all Quintara can see are those gleaming white fangs. Apparently a Mexican vaquero, or cowboy, had laid his whip around my neck, but within a few seconds has disappeared into the gathering crowd. Alex and Tim are still on their horses, rifles in hand, and offering to shoot anyone who wants to enter the fray. There is a shot.

Marshall Baer is standing behind me, pistol in hand, and right by him is Danny Greenup. The Marshall's deep voice rumbles as he speaks.

"Don't anybody move till I tell you to. Danny, get that whip off this young fellers neck." Danny moves over to me and unwinds the leather thong from my neck. What a relief.

"Now, Danny, pick up that knife, and keep it. You two with the rifles, just sit tight. If anyone pulls a gun besides me, shoot them. You, little lady, put that pistol away." Flor grins, and slowly puts the gun in its holster.

"Now, Danny, tie this gentleman's hands behind him, and I'll meet all of you in Danny's barn as soon as I get this feller safe behind bars." He looks closely at Quintara.

"I'm not joking you. You were about as close to death as you will be till it actually happens. Come on!"

He jerks Quintara to his feet and pushes him ahead as he goes through the crowd.

I'm on my feet, and Samantha has her arms around my neck, and is sobbing against me. I hold her close, and then we follow as Tim and Alex lead the way into Danny's barn.

Its half an hour till we have the horses and mules tied safely in the corral, and are gathered in the open space of the barn. The Marshall is there, and Danny, as well as Aaron Greenup, and our group. The Marshall holds up his hand for quiet, and just then there is a shout from outside the barn.

"Hey, Greenup!" I know that voice.

"Hey, Greenup!" I shout back.

A burly figure strides through the door, and Josh is standing there, grinning at us.

"Heard there was some fightin fun, and shore didn't want to miss it!"

The Marshall shook his head.

"Not another one!" he said, and shook hands with Josh.

We all rushed Josh, shaking his hand and pounding his back. Samantha gave him a quick hug, and then we introduced Alex, Flor and Rosy. Finally the Marshall got everyone's attention.

"Listen up, all of you. I have a surprise or two, and if you can hold your questions till I give you permission, I'd appreciate it. I'll be back in a couple of minutes." He looked around, and went out. We waited.

The Marshall returned in a few minutes, and with him was a husky young man wearing a star on his vest, who was holding the arm of a sullen Mr. Quintara. They seat him on a rough bench, and the Marshall stepped out again. This time he returned with two Army officers. He introduced them as Major Anderson and Captain James. Then he asked the Major to proceed. The Major took a sheaf of papers from an envelope, and cleared his throat. "I'll make this brief. Back in the winter, two criminals attempted to steal a horse and buggy from Mr. Tim Greenup, and a female cousin, Rachel. The attempt was thwarted by Mr. Ross Greenup, who shot and killed one of the thieves, and then the three cousins proceeded to disarm the other man, named Jenk. They took Jenk to the nearest village and turned him over to the village Marshall, who then retrieved the body of the deceased criminal." The Major paused and looked around. Nobody moved. He resumed.

"It was determined by the Marshall, that the man Jenk, and the dead man, were wanted by Federal authorities. A reward was offered, which was given to the Greenup's. Word of the killing and capture got out rapidly, and soon it was decided by certain individuals, the Greenup's had killed a courier of another country who was carrying a large amount of gold. This gold was to be used by these individuals to recruit mercenaries to fight with Mexico against the United States." The Major stopped again, and looked at Mr. Quintara.

"You caused a lot of trouble, Quintara, but you made a mistake.

The men the Greenup's captured and killed were not the couriers. They were common thieves, who had killed the courier, stolen and then buried the gold. The Pinkerton's and the Army have located the body of the courier, and have located the gold cache."

Mr. Quintara's face had gone pale, and now he slowly got to his feet. In a voice shaking with rage, he snarled at the Major.

"You are lying! The man named Jenk told people his companion was carrying gold when he was killed, and the killers, these despicable Greenup's, took the gold."

The Major turned and looked at me.

"Is that true?" he asked.

"Yes" I replied. "Something else you should know, Major. The dead man was carrying a money belt, with gold coins. We took the belt, and gave it to a trusted friend of ours in the village. The man Jenk did not mention it to the village Marshall when we took him in, which confirmed our suspicions he did not know about it, or it was stolen." I stopped and looked at the Marshall.

"Would you please go to the bank, right down the street, and ask the banker to come here."

He turned and started out, just as a small man, well dressed in a business suit and beaver hat, stepped into the barn. The Marshall stopped, shook hands with the man, and they both came back in. I looked at the banker, as that's who it was, and he smiled. I asked him,

"Sir, would you please tell the Major, the Marshall, and everyone else here, about the deposit I made with you about two months ago."

He did just that, explaining I had left a deposit of gold coins with him as surety on the trade goods we had purchased to take to Santa Fe. I asked him what kind of coins I had left, and he said they were French coins of the realm. Mr. Quintara gasped, and raised an arm, but was roughly grabbed by the stout young man standing by him. The Major actually laughed.

"So you have been chasing a sack of gold, which had probably been stolen from other travelers, thinking it was your precious Spanish gold, when it was just simply the work of a common thief."

Just then Samantha got right in front of Quintara. Her eyes were blazing, and she was clearly having a difficult time holding back from choking him.

235

"You stinking polecat. First, you let your skunk of a son come courting me, when I made it clear I wanted no part of him. Then he tries to steal the gold from the Greenup's, and failing that, tries to burn their barn. Then you hire people to trail them, and try to steal the gold, and kill them if they can."

She turned to the Marshall and Major, still spitting fire.

"The reason I'm here is because he and his scoundrel son, Roberto, told me they were going to kill Ross and Tim, get the gold, and then if I didn't marry Roberto, they would burn my folks out. I came here to warn Ross, but Roberto was too fast, and went after them!"

She drew back her arm as if to slap Quintara, and nobody made a move to stop her. Suddenly she turned, and cried out:

"Oh, Ross, I'm so glad you are alive." Bursting into tears, she grabbed me around the neck. I grabbed her back in a tight hug.

Its late evening, and we are all at Danny Greenup's house, except Mr. Quintara, who is in the Independence jail. He will be held there till the Army takes him back to St. Louis, to the Spanish Embassy. Then he will probably be deported to Spain, or even to Mexico. That's not my problem anymore. The Major made it clear he was not welcome in the U.S., and if he bothered any more citizens, he might get shot. I really feel sorry for him, and even more for Roberto, but the Major and the Marshall both tell me not to waste sympathy. The Quintara's made some poor decisions, and are paying the price.

The banker is here, and I have repaid all he loaned us on the deposit of gold. I ask him to keep the gold, since I have told the Major the total amount we took off the dead man, and the Major is going to see if there is any claim against it. He doubt's there is. I also told him there is still half the gold in the safe keeping of Uncle Jeremy in our village. If there is a legal claim against it, the gold is all available.

Tim and I have sold all our furs and buffalo hides, except a few special furs I'm keeping, and a buffalo robe for Pa and Ma. I have in mind a fur cape for Samantha, and I still haven't given her the beautiful doeskin dress I got for her in Taos. We sold all of Fierro's goods, except

MULE SHOES TO SANTA FE

the tools we are giving to Danny, for his share of Fierro's wagon. Fierro's money is with ours, and we split it all, leaving half here in the bank, and taking half with us. Combining the money we brought back from Santa Fe, with the money we got for our furs, we have had quite a trip.

Alex and Flor have sold their furs, and have decided to stay in Independence for a while, to see if there is any action for them. We have discussed having them represent the Greenup's in selling horses and mules, and helping traders plan their caravans. Alex will also be available as a Wagon Master, and he and Flor will do their own trading in Santa Fe.

Rosy and Tim have had some serious talks, and it appears to me Rosy has about decided to stay here with Alex and Flor. Danny raises his hand and shouts:

"Quiet everyone! Rosy has something to say."

Rosy is cute as she can be, with a red ribbon in her black hair, and not as much powder and red on her face as she had back in Santa Fe. She nods shyly, looks around the room, and begins to speak in broken English. Flor helps her with some of the words, but Rosy is understandable.

"First, I want to thank Alex and Tia Flor for all they have done for me, and the chance to get away from Santa Fe. Then I want to thank Tim and Ross for being so kind to me."

She stops and smiles at Tim, who turns red and looks down. Samantha is standing close to me and squeezes my hand.

"I have decided to stay here at Independence and work for Danny Greenup. He has a lot of Mexican and other Spanish speaking customers, and he needs someone who can understand them. Tia Flor and Alex have said I can stay with them." She pauses, then continues.

"I also want us to remember my good friend, Fierro. I miss him so much, and wish he could be here with us to celebrate."

She puts her hands over her face and turns away. It's very quiet for a few moments. Then I speak up.

"Thanks for your kind words, Rosy. We have all enjoyed your company, and I wish I had learned Spanish as well as you have learned English, and you have helped us out of some tight spots. You are a mighty good shot, and I've heard some Spanish words I sure don't want to know the meaning of. So everyone here will know Fierro really liked

Rosy, and wanted to help her, a portion of the money received from the sale of Fierro's trade goods has been set aside for her, and is on deposit here with our good friend, the banker."

Everyone clapped, then Flor held up her hand, and with a wicked little grin, looked first at me, then Tim.

"You forgot to mention, Rosy is also great with the back scrubs."

Now it's my face that gets beet red, and everyone laughs and claps again. Samantha grabs my arm and glares at me, but I see her then turn and wink at Rosy, and I know there are no secrets among these young women.

It's late, and finally Samantha and I have some time to ourselves. It's a warm, damp night. We walk down to a dock by the river. A three quarter moon is shining white on the dock, and shadows are deep. The steamboat Josh works on is tied up further along the dock, where it is undergoing some repairs. Black slaves are sitting around fires on the shore, talking and laughing. I hear one of them say.

"There goes one of dem Greenup boys."

Samantha squeezes my hand. Mist is rising from the water, insects and frogs are making a racket. Above those are the sounds of the water, rolling along on its way to the Mississippi and then the Gulf. We hold each other close. I marvel at how pretty she is, and tell her how much I have missed her. I pull the little buckskin bag out of my pocket, that she gave me many weeks ago, and she looks at the stains, and how worn it is. There is one dark blood stain, and she touches it, and touches my face, without saying anything. We stand awhile longer, just happy to be with each other. Then she speaks in a low, husky voice:

"I have missed you so much, but I am always praying for you, and for your safety." She paused. "Sweetheart, you have changed. When you told everyone about Rosy and Fierro, I could see a young man instead of a boy. I love the young man more than the boy, if that's possible."

She paused and looked up into my face.

"Not only that, but I know from the look in your eyes, you have seen the Shining Mountains."

Our embrace is long and passionate.

CHAPTER 29

This morning Josh, Tim, Samantha, Aaron and I meet for breakfast on the Big Mo steamboat. Josh is already the First Mate on this boat he started on when we left Paducah, Kentucky, about three months ago. We are talking about a letter that arrived on another steamboat last night, addressed to the "Greenup Boys". Sammie reads the letter aloud.

Greenup Boys. Dear Ross, Tim, Josh, and Samantha, if she is with you. We pray this finds you safe wherever you are. This is to let you know what is happening here in Kentucky, on the Clark and G double arrow G horse farm. Right now the partnership is Jim Greenup and his son, Ross; Rich Greenup and his son Tim; and Jeff Clark. It is agreed Josh Greenup and Caleb Greenup will be members of the partnership if they want to, and if there are no objections. Jim, Rich and Jeff have told me it is to be understood the wives are all part of this partnership. We have also been told this can never work among relatives, but we happen to disagree.

Jeff and Caleb brought our Morgan horses over from Tennessee, and Jim and Rich Greenup brought Morgan mares and a Morgan stallion to our farm right after you boys left. Later they brought cross bred mares and a jack. Right now there are eight new Morgan colts, and three more due any day. There are six new mule colts.

Ross, your Pa stayed on here about a week after they brought the horses over. He and Rich really like the farm, and Jim and Jeff had a great time planning on what they are going to do with the different pastures and fields. After he left here, Jim got to the Clinch River ferry just as two thugs had crossed the river on the ferry, had beaten Bob Greenup, who is still suffering from war injuries, and were holding him at gunpoint while they set the ferry afire, with him on it. When Jim got done straightening things out, one of the thugs was dead, and floating away down the river, and the other was severely wounded, tied hand and foot and begging for his life. The deck hand, who is a personal favorite of your Grandpa Greenup's, was found lying in the edge of the water, almost dead, but will live. It turns out they were two of the Allen boys, and were out for revenge. They are sure slow learners. So Caleb went back to help his Pa and Grandpa run the ferry till his Pa can get back on his feet.

Then just last week your folks drove up in a brand new buggy. Jim figured your Ma could not stand the trip on horseback from the mountains to here. Ross, your Ma has been real poorly since you left, and Jim thought she might feel better to visit here for a while. She sends her love, and is anxious for you and Josh to get back for a spell. They are going home in a few days, but I know she has really brightened up. Naomi just loves her, and Elizabeth and David pester her all the time to tell them stories, and go walking with them. She told me your friend Rachel has been courting with a village boy, and word has it they are getting married. Rachel told your Ma, when you rode away on your horse, she figured you would never come back.

Remember the man and his poor wife, who you gave tobacco to, and looked like she had been beaten? Well, he was found lying dead in their front yard, killed by a shotgun blast. She was found close to the road, where she had killed herself. I feel so sad about her. My heart went out to her that night by the campfire. Naomi has cried herself to sleep thinking about her.

Other than that, Naomi is doing fine. Young Stewart Campbell has taken her to a dance a couple of times, and his Ma seems to really take a shine to Naomi. Butch is working hard, and one of Jakes girls is always finding an excuse to walk over here and talk to him. It scares him to death.

Mr. Albright came home last week, and Jim and Jeff have spent two days with him, riding property lines and going over everything. He appears to be really interested in what we are doing, and Jim and Jeff think this is going to be a chance for a great business. I'm not sure what all is involved, but we sure need you boys to get home and let us know what you are doing.

Elizabeth and David are busy with chickens, the dog, and now some ducks. They miss you both.

We hear Ross and Samantha might be coming home together, and wonder if Tim is bringing someone home with him. If you see Josh, tell him his Pa, and especially his Ma, would sure like to see him.

Several people have passed through and told us about "dem Greenup boys". You seem to have built quite a reputation. We enjoy the stories, but want to hear them first hand. We don't know what has happened to the Quintara's, as there does not seem to be anyone at their place except a hired hand.

Your Uncle Will Bunch rode in here two days ago, and he is carrying this letter to get it on a steamboat, and maybe get to Josh. He said he wants to winter with some friends at Rocheport, on the Missouri River, and get an early start west next spring. Ross, your Ma thinks he has some other reason for going to Rocheport, but he isn't saying.

Ross and Tim and Josh, please get some word to us, or come back here as soon as you can. We need you. We have been praying always for your safety.

Your Friend, Ruth Clark

Samantha finished reading and looked around at us with a big smile.

"Well, Greenup Boys, what are we going to do?"

I smiled as I noticed she included herself. Josh was the first to speak.

"This boat will be repaired by tonight, and I'm responsible for everything to be ready to sail downriver tomorrow morning. We need to make plans this morning. The Captain told me the boat will probably be taken out of service for the winter sometime in December. Till that happens, about the most time I might have would be a week off this fall. I've already started finding farms along the Ohio and Missouri, both, where we can buy hay and pasture horses and mules when we start moving them next spring. This winter I'll probably be helping Big Jack build another barge."

Tim didn't say anything. He and Samantha waited for me.

"There are several things we need to do. First, we are going to be traveling, and I sure don't want to leave Sammie again till I have to. It's almost fall, so I think we should be married soon."

I know my face is getting red, and Sammie is laughing at me, but her eyes are sparkling.

"I want to get married too, but I sure would like to have a wedding at home, or anyway have my folks there." She said softly.

Right now I know it's time to change the subject.

"Sammie, We have a lot of planning to do, so think about it, and let's talk about it later. You came here with Aaron in his buggy, and I figured we would go back to Aarons with you, and then decide what to do from there. We have the mules and donkeys to get back to Kentucky for the winter, or work out something with Aaron."

The waiter is pouring coffee and serving a pastry, so I stop and take a few bites. We are not used to this kind of living. Tim is putting away food like he hasn't eaten for a month. He takes a long drink of coffee, then looks around.

"The way I see it, it's still early fall but we need to get the animals to pasture. I need to get back to all those new babies, that is, colts, because I just happen to be one of the best trainers in the mountains. However we have one other item of business."

"We do?"

"Yes. Fierro's granddaughter!"

Sammie stops eating and looks at me.

"That's right. It sounds like she has quite a bit of money coming her way. What's her name, and where is she supposed to be?"

I thought for a moment.

"Her name is Annabelle Margarita Diego Velasquez, and she evidently lives in St. Louis, or somewhere close."

Josh stops his coffee cup in mid-air.

"Did you say her last name was Velasquez?" I nod yes.

"Could she be related to Velasquez, a steamboat owner?"

"I'm not sure," I reply, "but there are two things which might give us an idea. In the letter Fierro gave me, he mentioned his son, Juan Velasquez, Annabelle's father, was a partner in a steamboat company. When Liz was still alive they said something about looking for the steamboat 'Prairie Queen.'"

"That's it!" exclaimed Josh. "The boat was built with one part of the hold made to convert to haul groups of people, like troops or slaves.

It is not well liked on the river, and that's the Prairie Queen tied up just ahead of us."

Again we are all quiet for a short time, thinking of the events of the last few months. Samantha spoke first.

"We don't know anything about her. I don't think we should tell anyone about Annabelle's money except Annabelle."

She is right. It's time to put everything in order. I take a drink of coffee.

"Josh, will you talk to the people on the Prairie Queen and try to find out the location of Annabelle. Sammie, Tim and me will get our packs ready to join Aaron and go to his home in Missouri. We can decide there what to do with the mules, and then go on home. If it's OK with Aaron we will leave tomorrow."

Aaron has been sitting quietly, enjoying the entire conversation, and now smiles and nods his approval.

"Ross and Sammie, why don't you go on the steamboat with Josh" said Tim, "and let me take the mules with Aaron. You can take your horses and saddlebags, and ride to Aaron's place from St. Louis in one day."

We had a busy day yesterday, and Tim left early this morning with the horses, mules, Buck and Aaron. Aaron was driving the buggy, lightly loaded with some of our gear. Buck did not want to leave Sammie, and she finally had to order him to go. Sammie and I have loaded our horses on the boat, and are standing together on the main deck. Danny is here to see us off. This is sure better than our last river trip together, on the barge. Departure time is just thirty minutes from now.

A burly Mate walks along the dock from the Prairie View and says something to Danny. Danny looks up at me and motions me to come to the gangplank. I leave Sammie and walk down to the dock.

"Are you one of the Greenup Boys inquiring about Miss Annabelle Velasquez?" the Mate asks.

When I nod he says.

"Why do you want to see her.?"

"Her Grandfather, Fierro, was a personal friend of ours, and when he was killed by Indians he gave me a message to personally give her."

The Mate thinks about this for a moment, then says.

"Miss Velasquez is presently at Rocheport, and you should be able to find her. She is with a personal servant and boarding with a relative. Since you boys are well known I'm giving you this information, but there better not be any problems." He turned and walked toward the Prairie View. Then he stopped and turned.

"Your brother Josh is well thought of on the river. Otherwise, you would get no information from me."

An hour later we are sitting comfortably in nice chairs on the upper deck, and the boat is moving rapidly down river. Since it's late in the summer the river is low, and the Captain is fairly sure of the channel. A warm breeze is blowing from the southwest, and it brings a strong and refreshing smell of trees and grass along the banks. Leaves are not turning color yet. The river water is almost clear where its shallow, and dark where its deep, not like the muddy brown we had in the spring. There are long legged blue herons, bald eagles, turkey buzzards, and numerous smaller birds on the gravel bars, and on snags along the banks. Sammie knows the names of most of them and gives us an education.

We seldom see Josh, as he is mighty busy about the boat's business. He is directing several deck hands securing lines, and is answering questions from other passengers about the boat and the river. We will travel at least forty miles today, even though it was a late start. This trip is giving us a good chance to get better acquainted away from the trail, and all the horses, mules, and dangers.

I hold hands with Sammie, and watch her face when she talks. It shows her feelings and her eyes may sparkle, or be grave, or tears may form. Compassion shows in her voice and words, and it amuses me to think of her actions when she thought I was in danger from Mr. Quintara, as compared to what she is saying and doing now. I'm definitely going to have a strong mate. We spend most of the day on the upper deck, talking about our hopes and dreams, and about our families. I tell her about some of the happenings on the trail, and about seeing the Shining Mountains.

I'm still dressed in buckskins, and other passengers often stop and

ask questions about what trails I've been on, and want to know how to
outfit, and when to start. The deck hands, both black and white, are
friendly, and attentive to us, especially to Sammie. They know we are
getting married, and they comment in low voices about her being tough
enough to be with "dem Greenup boys." This amuses Sammie, and I
think she is taking full advantage of her status. She knows all the other
passengers, and they each seem to think they are her special friend.

Supper is served in the main salon, where Sammie gets special
attention again, and we continue on down the river for another hour,
before tying up at a well-lighted landing, where we take on several cords
of wood for tomorrow's journey. Samantha has a first class cabin, and
I'm bunking in Josh's cabin. We stand on the top deck, in the light of the
moon, which is now almost full, and enjoy each other's nearness, with
the sounds of the river rising all around us. There is a moon path across
the water, leading straight to us. We ask questions, and make promises.

It's almost noon, of the third day on the river, and we are approaching
Rocheport. The trip is fast, and all day yesterday we watched the river
banks go sliding by, with two refueling stops, and three passenger stops.
We continue to talk, to touch, to smile, and the other passengers are
enjoying our pleasure with each other. They smile and go around us on
the deck. We will be at Rocheport for three hours, as it's a major port,
and there will be several passengers going ashore, and others coming
aboard, as well as a lot of cargo being moved. Josh will not be able to
help us because of his duties here. Sammie has on a dress I've not seen
before and sure catches the eyes of the other passengers. I marvel again
at how pretty she is, and tell her so. She tells me she is feeling there is
something important about to happen at this stop.

The sun is shining hot as we approach the dock, and there is quite a
crowd waiting to greet the boat. Dogs are barking, small boys running
around yelling in excitement, and dock workers waiting to catch lines
and make the big steamboat fast. I look for Uncle Will, since Ruth Clark
told us in her letter he was planning on wintering here. There are several
women in bright colored dresses, and a few buckskin clad figures in the

crowd. I soon spot him. Sammie and I walk ashore, and directly to him. He is taken by surprise, and grabs my hand and slaps me on the back.

"Ross, I sure didn't figure on seeing you here. I was watching for Josh, to ask him if he had any news of you." He drawled, and glanced at Sammie.

"Is this the young lady I've heard so much about from the Clarks?" I introduce Samantha and she immediately hugged him.

"I've sure heard a lot about you, Uncle Will, and all good!" she said. We are off to a good start. I lead the way out of the crowd.

"Uncle Will, we don't have much time. We are looking for someone, and figure you can help us."

I explain the situation, and when I give him the name of Annabelle Velasquez, he is surprised all over again, and laughs. As we walk he explains Annabelle Velasquez father was part owner in a steamboat company. He passed away several months ago, and his wife took over the position, but it was kept a secret he had died. This was done partially to protect her, as there were some rough competitors in the business, and there had been some questionable uses made of the boat, Prairie Queen. Widow Velasquez is now living here in Rocheport, with her fifteen year old daughter, Annabelle Velasquez.

"How do you know all this, Uncle Will" I ask.

"Because I am courting her, and we intend to get married!"

Now it's me that is surprised. Sammie giggles, and grabs my hand.

"What about the trips west, and the shining mountains?" I ask.

"Knew you'd ask that. The beaver are about played out. You could work hard all winter and maybe make enough to pay for your grub stake. It's easy to disappear during the winter and never be heard from again, unless someone finds your rotting carcass when the snow melts. Annabelle's Ma, Anna Marie, is willing for me to be gone to guide settlers, or to trade with Mexico. Course, I might throw in with the Greenup Boys, if they will have me. Don't know if I'm tough enough, but could try."

He laughed, slapped me on the back, and we walk up the steps of a small, modest cabin. Opening the door he announced to the woman standing in the room, that she had company.

She is medium height, slender, with hair as black as Sammie's, coiled in a bun on the back of her head. Her face is strong, too strong to be beautiful, but really attractive, with high cheekbones and a square chin, and dark eyes which look directly into mine. Then she looked at Sammie, and her face softened as she smiled.

"Will, based on what you have told me, this must be Ross Greenup and Samantha. I must say, if the rest of the Greenup's are like you and Ross, I sure want you on my side in a fight."

Her laugh was clear and not put on. I immediately like her, and from Sammie's smile, figure she does too. Uncle Will spoke up.

"Ross has a story to tell you, and it might be good for Annabelle to hear it. She has an interest in what you are about to hear."

About then a teenage girl walks into the room. I know I stared. She is a young image of her mother, with a softer face, long dark hair, even, white teeth, and definitely not afraid of strangers. She smiles at Uncle Will, and he introduces us. Annabelle, as that's who it is, glanced with admiration at Sammie, and all the while I'm thinking about what Tim and Josh are going to do when they see this girl. While Anna Marie fixes coffee, I tell what happened to her father-in-law, also Annabelle's grandfather, Fierro. I tell about Fierro and Liz joining us at Louisville, Kentucky, when we were on the barge, and about Liz passing away at the Inn in Missouri, and Fierro deciding to go on with us. It brings back deep emotions as I recount all the places we had shared with Fierro, and the pleasure of his cheerful company.

Neither Anna Marie nor her daughter ask any questions, till I stop and ask for more coffee. Then Anna Marie asked if Fierro had said anything about his son while we were on the river. I answer that my first clue to his son was the letter for Annabelle, which I have with me. Anna Marie then said.

"I knew there was some kind of trouble before Juan, my husband, died. A man came to see him in St. Louis, who wanted to charter the Prairie Queen. He was talking to Juan in private and I heard him mention soldiers. His name was Quintara, and another man with him was Jenk. Days later Quintara came back in a terrible anger, and I overheard him talking about a courier being killed, and Jenk disappearing. Soon after the last meeting Juan came down with malaria, and died." She paused and poured coffee. "I don't think my father-in-law knew about Quintara."

"That's it! That's the last piece of the puzzle. Jenk must have used what he knew about the courier and the gold, and teamed up with the man I killed, to kill the courier. That's another reason he did not say anything about the gold when we took him to the Marshall." I am excited.

I quickly tell Anna Marie and Annabelle what had happened, and also about Fierro's last wish and his death. Then I tell Uncle Will if they will accompany us to the steamboat I have a present for Annabelle.

"Make sure your weapons are loaded." I tell him.

Annabelle and her mother walk to the dock with us, and come aboard, where we manage to get them introduced to Josh. I notice Josh has enough time from his many duties to find deck chairs for them, while Uncle Will and I go to the Mate's cabin, and I retrieve the leather pouch with Fierro's gift to his granddaughter. Taking it back to the women, I hand it to Annabelle, and tell her:

"This is half of the money your grandfather, Fierro, entrusted to us. The other half is in Independence, at the bank, and you and your mother can get it from the banker. Your grandfather loved you a lot, and as he was dying on the side of the mountain made me promise to get it to you. I have now carried out the promise. Someday I'll tell you all the story."

CHAPTER 30

Stopping on the hilltop, I let my horse rest while I look across the Clark-Greenup horse farm. This is where we first saw it several months ago, and never dreamed of the things which were going to happen. The sun is shining on the red, bronze, yellow and brown hardwood leaves across the hills and valleys, and it's a beautiful sight, showing God's handiwork everywhere. Several pastures have horses and mules grazing, with colts bouncing around on their long, beautiful legs, or lying in the lush green grass. The barn shows a new roof over several new stalls, and there is a new room added to the small house.

When Sammie and I rode to Aaron's house from St. Louis, several weeks ago, we found Tim and Aaron already deep in plans to develop Aaron's farm as a staging station for horses and mules from Kentucky, Tennessee, and Missouri. We stayed several days, then, with a happy Buck along, Tim, Sammie and I boarded a steamboat back to Louisville. The First Mate, a friend of Josh, gave us a message from Josh, stating Mr. Quintara had escaped the Independence jail and disappeared. With that information we were immediately watchful and cautious as we traveled horseback here to the Clark farm, and Sammie's home. Her parents had not seen her since the terrible night she rode away from them, and were overjoyed.

One subject in our long talks over the past few weeks had been where we would live after we are married. The hills where I grew up are a long way from where our livestock is on the Clark farm. There is no room for another couple at the Clark's. We can probably stay at Sammie's folks for a while, but we need a place of our own, fairly close to the Clark's. I think we need to try to buy land, and let me build a house.

The first night after arriving back at her folks, she stays with them, and Tim, Buck and I go to the Clark's. The next night all of us, the Clark's, Corbitt's, Campbell's, and Allbright's get together for a big supper at the Allbright's farm. After eating Mr. Allbright makes quite a speech about how pleased he and his family are with the arrangements for our families, then makes a formal announcement of our plans to get married. There is hand clapping, cheering, hugs and handshakes. Then Mr. Corbitt, Sammie's father, makes another speech.

"All of you know most of what has happened over the past few months. We are so happy Samantha Ellen is safe, and we believe the Lord directed these fine young men, and this fine family here. We also believe the Lord is going to bless the marriage of Ross and Sammie. Since she is our only child, her mother and I are giving them, as a wedding present, half of our farm In Deed now, including the big blue spring, and they will get the rest of it when we are too old to work it."

I had grabbed Sammie and hugged her, and immediately began thinking of building her a new house.

Before I really understood what was happening, Ruth, Naomi, Sammie, Mrs. Duncan, and the two Allbright daughters-in-law had teamed up and were planning a fall wedding. It took me just a couple of hours the next day to figure out it was not my party, and I decided to go to the hills and see Pa and Ma. Tim stayed to help Butch carry and fetch for the women.

My first stop is at the ferry and Grandfather Greenup's. Caleb and his Pa and Ma were there and we have a good visit. I tell them all about the wedding, and the date, and to pass the word we want Rev. McClaren to perform the ceremony. I also tell them about Quintara's and the connection with the Allen's, and warn them to always be careful. Then I go on over the hills. Riding up the lane to the farm brought a smile of pleasure. The place where I was born and grew up looks the same. Brown corn stalks stand in the field, and there is a small haystack. There is one cow and one calf in the pasture, and of course I had only been gone about seven months, but it seemed like years.

Pa and Ma greet me like the Prodigal Son. Pa and I walk around the farm, looking at the pastures, and fences. There is just one team of mules, and two horses, since all the other animals are at the Clarks. Ma fixed a huge supper, and I sure don't disappoint her when it comes time to eat. After supper I give them the beautiful big buffalo robe I brought from Taos, and give Ma a turquoise necklace from the Taos Pueblo. I get out the account book and show them how well we did trading, and the money is in the bank. Afterward they listen while I describe the trip, and seeing the Shining Mountains. Pa's eyes glisten in the firelight, but he doesn't say anything, just puts a big strong hand on my knee and nods.

Now here I am back at the Clark farm, and about to see Sammie. I can smell the grass, and feel the mild fall breeze, and my horse nickers, and there is a response from one of the horses in the pasture. At once all the horses and mules heads come up, and look toward me. There is a great joy and longing in my heart, and then I see Buck, and hear him bark. Sammie appears in the door, shades her eyes, looks up and sees me. She starts running, out the gate and up the wagon trace, and I start my horse at a gallop. Before reaching her I stop the horse and swing to the ground, just for the sheer pleasure of watching her. Black curls flying, cheeks rosy, blue eyes shining, she runs into my outstretched arms.

THE WEDDING

I'm adrift, like a ship without a sail, or a boat without a rudder, or a horse without a bridle. I've never had as many orders given me in my entire life as in the week since getting back here. If I protest, anywhere from one to six women will glare at me. Two days ago Josh, Uncle Will Bunch, Anna Marie Velasquez Bunch, and Annabelle Velasquez drove up in a surrey, and are staying at the Allbrights. Pa and Ma, and Caleb are here, staying with the Clarks. The women have all been gathering at the Allbrights each day, with Tim and Butch there to help them. The Allbright's huge horse barn and show ring have been converted to a wedding chapel, like they have in New York City, according to the women. There are tables set up in a couple of big stalls, and last night food was beginning to appear from different places. The reason I know this is because last night, all taking part in the wedding were here for a practice run, and it did not take long to grab a few samples from the boxes and baskets.

Today is a perfect cool fall day, with a few fluffy clouds drifting around. I am bathed, shaved, in a new store bought broadcloth suit, and getting a lot of advice from Tim and Caleb, who don't know what they are talking about, and Jeff Clark, who does. The wedding is to start in two hours. Pa motions to me, and I walk with him out to the corral fence.

"Ross, I don't have much to say to you. You have always been a level headed feller, and from early on able to take care of yourself. It appears you have found a mate who is going to be right at your side, helping and supporting you, just as your Ma did for me."

He paused, and looked across the pasture, then directly at me.

"One thing that always bothered me, was that I was not more understanding with your Ma when our little gal died. So I'm telling you, be gentle and strong for your wife. Try to understand her needs and feelings, and support her. You are both believers, so keep your trust in the Lord. Your Ma and I will always be available if you need us, but we sure won't try to run your life, or interfere with you and Samantha."

It is clear he is done. Our two hands meet in a strong grip, and then a quick hug, and we walk back to the house.

The large entrance way of the barn has been turned into a bridal bower, with beautiful fall leaves decorating walls and doorways. A white latticework arch stands directly in front of a small table, and there are rows of chairs and benches filling the hall with an aisle down the middle. There is a sweet fragrance from numerous wax candles placed around the walls, and on a chandelier from the ceiling. It's sure clear these women have been waiting for a chance to show their skills.

Rev. McClain is standing behind the small table when Tim opens the door to the side room where I'm waiting, and motions me to come out. I walk to the front of the hall, with Tim behind me, then turn and face the crowd. Jake is standing at the back of the hall, and commences playing a tune on the violin. I hear another door open, and everyone stands, as my beautiful Samantha Ellen appears, holding the arm of her father. Her dress is a shining white, with a train held by sweet Naomi. Samantha's face is radiant, her blue eyes shine, and my heart feels like it will jump out of my chest with pride and joy.

My bride, Samantha, and I walk to the large tack room, which has been transformed. Beautiful red, brown, gold and russet fall leaves, festooned with red and blue berries, cover the walls and ever-green branches outline doorways. The large open hallway with the high ceiling is light and airy. Wooden benches and tables have been set up on the hard packed clay floor, which has been swept clean, then spread with sawdust. On a center table is a huge decorated cake. I've never seen a cake like it. The other tables are covered with food and drink. I don't seem to be as hungry as usual, but manage to put away some fried chicken and potato salad. Pa stands and shouts for attention.

"There are some gifts for the bride and groom. We know Mr. Corbitt has already given these young folks some land to build on. With my brother Richard's approval, I have picked out the best young Morgan mare from our herd, and it now belongs to our beautiful daughter-in-law, Samantha!"

We soon found we owned a new buggy, a new freight wagon built by Danny Greenup, and had lifetime free passage on the Prairie Queen steamboat, owned by Mr. and Mrs. Will Bunch. There are many other things, but a high point is when Sammie comes back into the room after being gone a few minutes. She has changed into her new, white doeskin dress, with a silver and turquoise concha belt, silver and turquoise necklace and earrings, beaded doeskin moccasins, and a beaded white headband over her shiny black curls.

Daylight is dimming to evening, and Sammie and I are on the way in a buggy to a country Inn close to Crab Orchard. We stop on a high ridge, and look west across the hills, at the setting sun, and the clouds shining gold, and pink, against a blue sky, and thank our Lord for bringing us together. A Whip-poor-will calls, and we sit quietly, close to each other, hearing the evening sounds, and savor this time of starting our new lives together. We talk of our plans to build a home here, and to start our family here. We mention the need to always be watchful, but even more so, as long as the Quintara's are unaccounted for. We agree we soon want to go west again. I want Sammie to see the immense prairies, feel the breeze, smell the grass and sunflowers, hear meadowlarks, and see the great herds of buffalo. I want her to watch the racing cloud shadows of the little white, fluffy clouds, and the huge, towering thunderstorms, and for us to climb the slopes of the Shining Mountains. Our hearts and minds are overflowing with joy. I cradle her small face in my hands, and together we say,

"By the Grace of God, this is just the beginning!"

CPSIA information can be obtained
at www.ICGtesting.com
Printed in the USA
LVOW03s0132160817
545157LV00001B/112/P